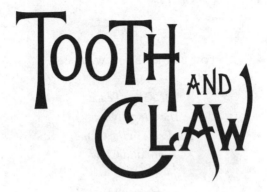

TOOTH AND CLAW

TOOTH AND CLAW

BY JO WALTON

TOR

A TOM DOHERTY ASSOCIATES BOOK

NEW YORK

TOOTH AND CLAW

Copyright © 2003 by Jo Walton

All rights reserved.

Edited by Patrick Nielsen Hayden

A Tor Book
Published by Tom Doherty Associates
120 Broadway
New York, NY 10271

www.tor-forge.com

Tor® is a registered trademark of Macmillan Publishing Group, LLC.

The Library of Congress has cataloged the Orb edition as follows:

Walton, Jo.
    Tooth and Claw / Jo Walton. —1st Orb ed.
        p. cm.
    "A Tom Doherty Associates Book."
    ISBN 978-0-7653-1951-7
    1. Dragons—Fiction.   2. Brothers and sisters—Fiction.   I. Title.
    PR6073.A448T66   2009
    823'.914—dc22   2008038433

ISBN 978-1-250-24272-3 (mini hardcover)

Our books may be purchased in bulk for promotional, educational, or business use. Please contact your local bookseller or the Macmillan Corporate and Premium Sales Department at 1-800-221-7945, extension 5442, or by email at MacmillanSpecialMarkets@macmillan.com.

First Mini Hardcover Edition: November 2019

Printed in the United States of America

0   9   8   7   6   5   4   3   2   1

DEDICATION, THANKS, AND NOTES

This is for my aunt, Mary Lace, for coming so far down the road toward fantasy for me, and for coming down so many other roads with me, plenty of them real as well as metaphorical.

This novel owes a lot to Anthony Trollope's *Framley Parsonage*.

I grew up reading Victorian novels. People since, from Joan Aiken to John Fowles and Margaret Forster, have done fascinating things with writing new Victorian novels from modern perspectives, putting in the things the Victorian novel leaves out. That gives you something very interesting, but it isn't a Victorian novel. It has to be admitted that a number of the core axioms of the Victorian novel are just wrong. People aren't like that. Women, especially, aren't like that. This novel is the result of wondering what a world would be like if they were, if the axioms of the sentimental Victorian novel were inescapable laws of biology.

I'd like to thank Patrick Nielsen Hayden for accepting a novel rather different from what he imagined he'd be getting; David Goldfarb, Mary Lace, and Emmet O'Brien for reading it in progress and making useful comments; Sasha Walton for drawing me a very helpful picture, making endless suggestions, some of them very good, and being forbearing (again) during the writing process; and Eleanor J. Evans, Janet Kegg, Katrina Lehto, Sarah Monette, Susan Ramirez, and Vicki Rosenzweig for beta reading for me.

I'd also like to thank Westmount and Atwater libraries for having excellent collections of Trollope, and the Trollope-l mailing list, especially Ellen Moody, for thought-provoking discussion. Thanks are also due to Elise Matthesen for my beautiful necklace The Crowded Minds of Dragons, and my partner, Emmet O'Brien, for love and delight during the writing process. Without all this, this novel would not have been written.

Man, her last work, who seem'd so fair,
    Such splendid purpose in his eyes,
    Who roll'd the psalm to wintry skies,
Who built him fanes of fruitless prayer,

Who trusted God was love indeed
    And love Creation's final law—
    Tho' Nature, red in tooth and claw
With ravine, shrieked against his creed—

Who loved, who suffer'd countless ills,
    Who battled for the True, the Just,
    Be blown about the desert dust,
Or seal'd within the iron hills?

No more? A monster then, a dream,
    A discord. Dragons of the prime,
    That tare each other in their slime,
Were mellow music match'd with him.

—Alfred, Lord Tennyson, from
"In Memoriam A.H.H.," 1850

She'd like me to bring a dragon home, I suppose. It would serve her right if I did, some creature that would make the house intolerable to her.

—Anthony Trollope, *Framley Parsonage*, 1859

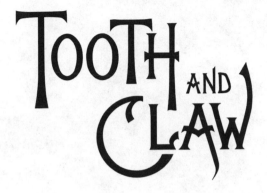

1
THE DEATH OF BON AGORNIN

1. A CONFESSION

Bon Agornin writhed on his deathbed, his wings beating as if he would fly to his new life in his old body. The doctors had shaken their heads and left, even his daughters had stopped telling him he was about to get well. He put his head down on the scant gold in his great draughty undercave, struggling to keep still and draw breath. He had only this little time left, to affect everything that was to come after. Perhaps it would be an hour, perhaps less. He would be glad to leave the pains of the flesh, but he wished he had not so much to regret.

He groaned and shifted on the gold, and tried to feel as positive as possible about the events of his life. The Church taught that it was neither wings nor flame that gave one a fortunate rebirth, but rather innocence and calmness of spirit. He strove for that fortunate calm. It was hard to achieve.

"What is wrong, Father?" asked his son Penn, approaching now that Bon was still and putting out a gentle claw to touch Bon's shoulder.

Penn Agornin, or rather the Blessed Penn Agornin, for young Penn was already a parson, imagined he understood what troubled his father. He had attended many deathbeds in his professional capacity, and was glad to be here to help ease his father into death and to spare him the presence of a stranger at such a time. The local parson, Blessed Frelt, was far from being his father's friend. They had been at quiet feud for years, of a kind Penn thought quite unbecoming to a parson.

"Calm yourself, Father," he said. "You have lived a good life. Indeed, it is hard to think of anyone who should have less to fret them on their deathbed." Penn admired his father greatly. "Beginning from very little more than a gentle name, you have grown to be seventy feet long, with wings and flame, a splendid establishment and the respect of all the district. Five of your children survive to this day. I am in the Church therefore safe." He raised a wing, bound with the red cord that, to the pious, symbolized the parson's dedication to gods and dragonkind, and to others meant mere immunity. "Berend is well married and has children, her husband is powerful and an Illustrious Lord. Avan is making his way in Irieth. His is perhaps the most perilous course, but he has strong friends and has done well thus far, as you did before him. As for the other two, Haner and Selendra, though they are young and vulnerable do not fear. Berend will take in Haner and see her well married under her husband's protection, while I will do the same for Selendra."

Bon drew a careful breath, then exhaled with a little puff of flame and smoke. Penn skipped nimbly aside. "You must all stick to my agreement," Bon said. "The younger ones who are not settled must have my gold, what there is of it. You and Berend have begun your hoards already, let you each take only one symbolic piece of mine, and let the other three share what little is left. I have not amassed a great store, but it will be enough to help them."

"We had already agreed that, Father," Penn said. "And of course they will likewise take the greater shares when we eat you. Berend and I are established, while our brother and sisters are still in need."

"You have always been just what brothers and sisters should be to each other," Bon said, and sighed more smoke. "I want to confess, Penn, before I die. Will you hear my confession?"

Penn drew back, folding his wings hard around him. "Father, you know the teaching of the Church. Not for three thousand years, six lifetimes of dragons, has confession been a sacrament. It reeks of the Time of Subjugation and the heathen ways of the Yarge."

Bon rolled his huge golden eyes. Sometimes his son, so careful of propriety, seemed a stranger to him. Penn could never have endured what he had endured, never have survived. "Six lifetimes you may have been taught, but when I was young there were priests who would still give absolution to those who wanted it. It is only in my lifetime and yours that it is forgiveness that has become a sin. What was wrong was paying for absolution, not forgiving the burdens of those who would lay them down. The rite of absolution is still in the book of prayers. Frelt would have refused me this, I know, out of spite, but I had thought you would have had spirit enough to do it."

"Yet it is a sin, Father, and one the Church preaches against as strongly as priest-flight." Penn flexed his bound wing again. "It is not an article of religion, true, but a difference in practice that has arisen over time. Confession is now abhorrent. I cannot possibly give you absolution. If anyone discovered it, I would lose my position. Besides, my own conscience would not allow it."

Bon shifted again, and felt loose scales falling from him down to the gold below. He did not have long left, and he was afraid. "I am not asking you for absolution, if you cannot give it. I merely think I will die more easily if I do not take this secret on with me." His voice sounded weak even to himself.

"You may tell me anything you wish, dear Father," Penn said, drawing closer again. "But you may not call it confession, or say that you are doing it because I am a parson. That could endanger my calling if it became known."

Bon looked at the red cords on his son's wings, remembering what he had paid to have him accepted into the Church and all the good fortune he had encountered there since. "Isn't it wonderful how so much came of your little friend Sher?" he said. Then he felt the pain spreading from his lungs, and wanted to cough, but did not dare. Penn had drawn breath to answer, but he subsided, letting it trickle out of his snout, watching his father's struggle in silence. Little Sher, once his schoolfellow, was the Exalted Sher Benandi now, lord of his own domain, and Penn was his parson, with his own house and wife and children.

"It is the way of the dragon to eat each other," Bon said at last.

"These days—" Penn began.

"You know I was the only survivor of my family, the only one of my brothers and sisters to grow wings," Bon went on, speaking over his son. "You thought that Eminent Telstie had eaten them, or perhaps his wife, Eminence Telstie? They did eat some of them, swooping down out of the sky to devour the weaklings, always leaving me alive, because I was the oldest and strongest. They held hard to the idea the Church teaches that they were improving dragonkind by eating the weaklings, they were even kind to me. I did not forgive them for eating my father and my siblings. Yet I pretended to be a friend to them, and to their children, for my mother had little power to protect me or prevent them eating us all if they chose. They had taken my father's gold and we had nothing but our name. When there were but three of us left, I had grown wings, but was only seven feet long, ready to leave home to seek my fortune but in great peril if I did. I needed length and strength I could not gain from beef. I ate my remaining brother and sister myself."

Penn lay frozen beside his dying father, shocked

far beyond anything he could have imagined the old dragon could have said.

"Will I die entire?" Bon asked. "Will my spirit fall like ash from smoke as the Church teaches? Or will I be reborn as a muttonwool to catch in the teeth of someone's hunger, or worse, a creeping worm or a loathsome wingless Yarge?" His eyes caught his son's, and still Penn stared dumbstruck at his father. "I have lived a good life since, as you said. I have regretted it bitterly many times, but I was young and hungry and had nobody to help me and a great need to fly away."

Bon's scales were falling with a steady pattering. His breath was more smoke than air. His eyes were beginning to dim. Penn was a parson and had attended many deaths. He knew there were only minutes left. He spread his wings and began the last prayer, "Fly now with Veld, go free to rebirth with Camran at your side—" but the smoke caught in his throat and he could not go on. He had read the old rite of absolution once, in horrified fascination; his father was right that it was still printed in the prayer-book. It was absolution his father needed, and a clear spirit to go on. Penn was a conventional young dragon, and a parson, but he loved his father. "It is a custom, there is no theology behind it," he muttered. He held his claws up before his father's eyes, where he could see them. "I have heard your—" He hesitated an instant, it was the word that seemed so bad. Could he call it something else? No, not to give his father the comfort and absolution he needed. "Your confession, Dignified Bon Agornin, and I absolve and forgive you in the name of Camran, in the name of Jurale, in the name of Veld."

He saw a smile deep in his father's fading eyes, which was replaced by peace, and then, last, as always, a profound surprise. However many times Penn saw this he never became accustomed to it. He often wondered what there was beyond the gate of death that, however prepared the dying dragon was, it should always astonish them. He waited the prescribed moment, repeating the last prayer three times, in case the eyes should begin to whirl again. As always, nothing happened, death was death. He delicately reached out a claw and ate both eyes, as was always the parson's part. Only then did he call his sibs, with the ritual cry, "The good dragon Bon Agornin has begun his journey towards the light, let the family be gathered to feast!"

He felt no grief, no shame at having gone against the teachings of the Church to give his father absolution, no horror at what his father had done. He felt nothing whatsoever, for he knew that he was in a state of shock and that once it wore off he would be quietly miserable for a long time.

2. THE SPEAKING ROOM

The whole family had gathered in the upper caves as soon as the doctors had shaken their heads and

Bon Agornin had crawled down to the undercave to die, accompanied only by Penn. In addition to Bon's four remaining children, the party consisted of the Illustrious Daverak, Berend's husband, the three dragonets that were the fruits of her first clutch, now four years past, and the local parson, Blessed Frelt. They were attended by four of Berend's servants, their wings tightly bound back. Also present in a serving capacity was the family's old retainer Amer, whose wings were fastened down, to be sure, but through long trust and casual habit of the family, scarcely tighter than those of a parson. None of them approached the full length of old Bon. Illustrious Daverak came closest at forty feet from head to tail-tip, but even so, eleven grown dragons and three dragonets can make anywhere but a ballroom seem crowded.

In consequence, after the first greetings and lamentations and exclamations as to who had come farthest to be there, they had divided themselves into two groups. The first, consisting of Berend and her party, accompanied by Blessed Frelt, went into the elegant speaking room to the right of the entrance, and the rest withdrew to the big dining room.

There was nothing whatsoever for any of them to do but wait and quarrel and they might just as well have remained in their own homes and waited for the cry to go up and then come circling down to swoop on the corpse. But some say this is what dragons did long ago, and this is why nowadays they know better and make themselves caves and undercaves so they can retreat into the undercaves to die in peace. This means that only those they choose can share the body. Still, it seems very hard to some that civilization and modern ethical beliefs should lead to such interminable waits as the one imposed on Bon Agornin's family.

The speaking room was carved from the same dark natural rock as the rest of the establishment. It was not embellished with lighter pebbles as was the fashion in Irieth, for the owners of the establishment had never heard of such a custom and thought it best to let the rock speak for itself. It had been carved here and there with fashionable landscapes, portrayed as seen from the air. These Bon Agornin had sanctioned, as they cost nothing. They had been done by the young ladies of the house, most especially Haner, who regarded herself as talented in that direction. Illustrious Daverak, who had a splendidly decorated home of his own in the country and another in Irieth for use in the two months of the year that the capital is in fashion, must have disagreed, for he gave the carvings one glance and then settled down by the door. His wife, Berend, or Illust' Daverak as her husband's rank now entitled her to be addressed, was less discriminating, for she exclaimed to her servants and children on the beauty of the newest of them, lamenting that they never had anything half so fine when she was a maiden, as if it had been three hundred years ago instead of a mere seven.

When the last flakes of interest had been scraped from the carvings, she settled herself in an alcove under the huge mantel on which were arranged a few pieces of stone sculpture, of no value, as one would expect in an upper cave, but of a certain charm nonetheless.

Blessed Frelt came and stood beside Berend as soon as she had stopped her restless wandering, which would have risked knocking over any companion. He arranged himself comfortably at her side. Berend turned her head to survey him. It was some time since she had last visited her father's home, and she had not seen Frelt since she left to marry Daverak.

The red priestly cords around his wings were long and trailing, his teeth were polished and filed almost flat. In contrast, his scales were burnished to a bright bronze glow, all of which reflected the rather conflicting views he held of his own position. On the one hand, a parson must be humble, on the other, he holds a high spiritual position, perhaps the highest in the community. Frelt explained it to himself as a strong belief in the sanctity of parsons, which encompassed both his humble teeth and his fine scales. He would never have flown, not even across a ravine, but he did not regard himself as beneath any dragon in the land, however well born. He held his head much higher than those immune were wont to do.

"What beautiful dragonets," he said now, cooing

over them. Long ago he had had aspirations to marry Berend, which was the heart of the trouble between him and her father. Because he had never spoken to her of the subject, she had no official knowledge of this, and they could thus be on civil terms in public. Unofficially, she had known it perfectly well, as well as any maiden who had heard her father fulminate against a suit and been sternly bidden to stay indoors to keep from being carried off. She had remained obediently within doors, but been much more flattered than offended. She had even hoped for a little while that the match would be made. Now that she was settled elsewhere and her scales shone the glorious red of a dragon both married and a mother, she thought him a safe and charming partner for conversation. On his side, he was inclined to see Berend's lofty marriage as proof of his own good taste, and he liked her more rather than less for it. He had found no other bride in the years between, though as a well-found parson with his own establishment there was no shortage of hopeful partners.

"Yes, all three at my first laying," she said, looking indulgently down at the dragonets playing under their nanny's feet. One was black, one was gold, and the third a pale green that would have caused it to be snapped up at once were it not the child of a powerful lord.

"How fortunate for you both," Frelt said, inclining his head towards Illustrious Daverak, whose posture spoke impatience and who was ignoring the conversation utterly.

"My mother never bore more than two at a time," Berend said. "I am hoping my next will be three also. The more children the better, under Veld."

"It is good to see you so obedient to the teachings of the Church," Frelt said, inclining his head to her this time. "Many of the farmers here seem reluctant to lay at all."

"It is exactly the same at Daverak," Berend lamented.

"What is?" Illustrious Daverak asked, looking interested for the first time when he heard his domain mentioned. He was almost as dark as his black dragonet, and very broad-shouldered, his eyes were so pale as to seem almost pink, not at all a good-looking dragon. If it were not for the binding of the wings, anyone would have thought Frelt a finer specimen, and Frelt rejoiced a little more than he should have to know it.

"The lack of dragonets among the farmers and lower classes, dear," replied Berend fondly.

"I don't know, there are plenty, plenty indeed," Illustrious Daverak replied. "Why, the Majes on the causeway farm had another clutch only six days ago. I meant to fly down and check them over today, if it hadn't been for this confounded summons."

Berend drew back a little. "My father is dying," she said, with dignity.

"Oh yes, my dear, we had to come, I know that. I

didn't mean that harshly," Daverak said, dipping his wings to his wife, who acknowledged this contrition with a tiny inclination of her own wings. "But the Majes have had four born, you know, and they can't possibly manage another four on that bad land, and I was thinking to bring something nourishing home for little Lamerak." He gestured with a wingtip at the green dragonet. "A bit off color, you may have noticed," he said to Frelt. "Temporary, strictly temporary. He needs fresh liver. He shall have it soon in any case. Our coming here made no difference to that, now that I think of it."

Frelt did not reply that his own little sister, who had been snapped up years ago by a lord for being too green, might have thrived on dragon liver, if she could have got it. "I am sure your own parson pays attention to such things, as you do," he said.

"I do my duty," Daverak said, drawing up his wings. "I would no more allow a weakling son of mine to grow wings than that of the meanest farmer. But that is no reason to be hasty. Lamerak will be fully recovered in a week or two."

"Veld gives us children and Jurale watches the order of the world," Frelt said, holding out his arms as if conducting a service.

Illustrious Daverak drew back, feeling rebuked, and Berend looked away, disappointed in Frelt and unwilling to speak. An uneasy silence fell in which the sounds of the dragonets playing seemed loud.

3. THE DINING ROOM

In the dining room, things were at first much happier. The room was much less elegant, being older. It had the most modern runnels in the floor for sanitary purposes, but otherwise it had remained unchanged since the cave had been hollowed, back in the Time of Subjugation. The inhabitants of the dining room knew it is not elegance that makes a pleasant gathering but the temperament of those gathered together. By selection of like to like, all the unpleasant members of the party had gathered in the speaking room, and all the pleasant in the dining room.

Haner and Selendra were hatched of the same clutch, had grown up together in their father's house, had comforted each other after their mother's death, and had endured their older sister and brothers leaving them with mingled fortitude and relief. They were old enough to marry, but because their father's treasure had been much depleted by the good marriage of their elder sister and the settlement of their two brothers they had been content to wait and kept house for their father until it should have replenished itself. They were therefore perfectly at home in his big dining room. They were used to complaining that it had no convenient alcoves so they were obliged to spread themselves out almost as if they were in a field, but it was their own field, and they were accustomed to such spreading out and might have missed it if alcoves had been carved.

The two sisters were delighted to welcome their brother Avan back into their company. Since he went to Irieth they had seen him only for a day or two, for his work in the Office for the Planning and Beautification of Irieth kept him fully occupied. For a time, Avan regaled them with stories of his life in the capital, emphasizing his triumphs and playing down his narrow escapes to such an extent that they each secretly felt they might have done as well if they had had claws and were able to make their way in the world.

"But you'll be coming home now, of course?" Haner asked at last, wiping the tears of laughter from her silver eyes.

"Home? You mean home here? I dare not. I can't think how you come to suggest it." All at once Avan became aware that the old servant Amer had stopped polishing Haner's tail and both his sisters were staring at him. "Did you really think I meant to do so?"

"Why, yes," Selendra said, after a quick glance at her sister and their attendant showed neither of them were about to speak. "We thought that after Father died you would come home and be Dignified as he was. Penn is a parson, and besides he has a house and a wife away at Benandi. You could have this establishment—"

"I see you have thought it all out," Avan said, pulling himself to his feet. "My dear maidens, have you not considered that in addition to being seventy feet long and fire-breathing, Father is, or rather was, nearly five hundred years old? I am barely one hundred, barely twenty feet long, and have no fire as yet, nor much prospect of gaining any soon. I am doing well enough in my career for one who began it when I did, but that was hardly ten years ago and I don't taste dragon meat twice in a year. Also I couldn't bring my career here with me. If I set up as Dignified, all the neighborhood Dignifieds and Illustriouses would eat away at our territory and eventually at us, sure as sunrise. There would be no way I could stop them, hardly more than you two could alone."

The two maidens looked at each other in dismay, and Amer gave a little cry of fear. "Then what will become of—of the establishment?" Selendra asked, not yet bold enough to ask about their persons.

"I don't know why you haven't asked Penn this, or Father," Avan said, shifting uncomfortably. "I am not the eldest. Nobody consults me about this sort of thing. But I dare say Daverak will take it on until one of his children is old enough to manage it for himself. That was part of the agreement when he married Berend, I believe, if Father should die before I was strong enough. Did nobody tell you any of this?"

"You may not be the eldest, but you are a dragon grown. We are just useless females," Selendra said, her violet eyes flashing. "Afterthoughts. Nobody tells us anything. We are doubtless to be the dinner for the rest of you, and I would have appreciated a little time to prepare myself for that."

"How?" Avan asked, amused and intrigued despite himself.

"By flying right away," Selendra answered, daringly.

"No, I was teasing," her brother said. "Your future is assured, both of you. Neither of you shall be dinner. Penn wrote to me that according to our father's wishes the gold was to be divided between me and you two, except for a symbolic piece each for the others. The establishment will go to Berend's children. One of you will go to live with Berend, and the other with Penn."

Amer and Haner gave little cries, and Sel flung her arms and wings around her sister.

"Anyone would think I had suggested you would be eaten immediately," said Avan. "You're the most ungrateful sisters a dragon ever had."

"Couldn't you take us?" Selendra asked. "We have never seen Irieth but we could keep house for you beautifully, just as we did here for Father."

Avan couldn't hide his shudder, it shook his wings. "I've no room for you," he said, truthfully enough, thinking of the comforts of his city establishment. "And Irieth is no place for maidens, unless they are chaperoned and have known names. I couldn't protect you there any more than I could here. You would be someone's dinner sooner or later, or worse. You'll be safe with Penn and Berend."

"Safe, but separate," said Haner, in tones that told her brother that this was tragedy indeed. "You know Selendra is so impulsive and I am so thoughtful that separated there is no knowing what she might do, while I will never do anything at all."

"And Berend doesn't like me," Selendra said.

"Well then, Sel, you should go to Penn," Avan said, as evenly as he could manage.

"Penn has a wife who is a stranger," Selendra said.

"And they have two dragonets already, she'll probably be very glad to have extra help with them. You're really much better off than most maidens in your position would be."

"How?" Selendra asked.

Avan knew so much more about this than he would have wanted his sisters ever to learn that he just shook his head slowly and let his gold eyes whirl warningly.

"I think I could bear anything if we were together," Haner said, and her voice broke on a sob in the middle of the sentence.

"You'll be married soon enough," Avan said. "I thought Daverak said something about Haner and some friend of his?"

Haner brightened a little at the thought of Londaver, her brother-in-law's friend. But she did not loosen her grip on her sister.

Just then, as both caves were silent, Penn called up from the undercave that Bon Agornin had gone down into the last darkness.

4. SOME UNSEEMLINESS IN THE UNDERCAVE

Bon Agornin and his son-in-law had not always understood each other perfectly. Illustrious Daverak had been informed, and even consulted, as to his father-in-law's distribution of his wealth. Nothing had been said to him about the distribution of his body. This was not from any fault either on the part of Daverak or old Bon, for each had thought the matter obvious—Bon that the body would be distributed along the same lines as the wealth, and Daverak that it would be divided equally among the family. It was thus that he had assumed the availability of liver for poor little Lamerak. To Bon, perhaps because he began its serious growth in the manner he had confessed to Penn, his body was a part of his wealth, part of what he passed on to help his children. To the Illustrious, a dragon's body was a matter altogether distinct from a dragon's gold, and this was so ingrained a belief with him as to hardly need stating.

When the cry came and the family gathered to go down, because of the geography of the caves, the group from the speaking room were ahead of those from the dining room. Illustrious Daverak, having been at the door of the speaking room, was to the fore. Immediately behind him was Blessed Frelt, then the dragonets, herded by Illust' Berend. Then came Avan and his sisters from the dining room. The servants, naturally, remained above, where Amer found plenty of work to do and Berend's attendants sat fanning each other and gossiping about their betters.

Penn waited in the door of the undercave, his head bowed so low in sorrow that he did not recognize Illustrious Daverak until he was almost upon him. There was no room for more than three in the undercave, so Illustrious Daverak came in, and the others perforce waited, most of them in polite silence, but the dragonets emitted impatient little hisses.

"Our father Bon is dead," Penn said. "We must now partake of his remains, that we might grow strong with his strength, remembering him always."

Illustrious Daverak bowed his head a little at the words, then with no further ado, snatched off his dead father-in-law's leg, shook off the few remaining scales, and took a huge bite. Thus far, Penn did not remonstrate, but when he took another bite, of no less size than the last, he put out a restraining claw.

"Surely, brother, you have taken what has been agreed," he said, quietly.

"Agreed?" Illustrious Daverak asked, for in his mind there had been no such agreement. He took another bite, blood dripping down his chin. "What are you talking about?"

"You and Berend and I were to take one bite each, and leave the rest for our less advanced brothers and sisters," Penn said, with the fraying patience of a dragon who has just lost his father in trying circumstances.

"No, Blessed Penn, that agreement was in reference

to his gold." Illustrious Daverak actually laughed as he took another bite, for he genuinely believed what he said and thought Penn absurd.

"Stop, stop now," Penn said, attempting to stand between his brother-in-law and his father's body. "You have already had more than we agreed. Put down that leg."

"Nonsense," Illustrious Daverak said. "If you have chosen not to take a portion, very well, but I shall take a son's and a lord's, and so shall Berend and my children."

Penn had very few options. If he could have considered fighting, Illustrious Daverak was a full ten feet longer than he was, even if neither of them had yet come to their flame. He was a lord, and fulfilled all of his duty when it came to consumption of excess dragonets and the weak and surplus population generally in his land. That would not have stopped Penn at that moment, had it not been for the fact that he was Blessed, an immune parson, his wings bound. He could neither fight nor call challenge unless he wished to leave his calling.

"Stop in the name of the Church, or face penalty," he said therefore.

Illustrious Daverak did stop, his mouth open. Then he turned to the doorway where Blessed Frelt was waiting, taking everything in. Illustrious Daverak did not have very high hopes of Frelt, after their conversation in the speaking room, but he appealed to him now as to a neutral witness. "Can he do this?" Illustrious Daverak demanded.

"Yes, tell him," Penn said, his silver eyes whirling so fast they almost made Frelt dizzy.

Frelt looked from the angry parson to the angry Illustrious, and preened his wings a little. He was no Illustrious's parson, but the parson for the parish of Undertor, a large area that took in six demesnes, of which Agornin was one. This was part of what had given him his independence, and his inflated sense of his own rights. He had eaten his parson's share of eyes from all the dead and unfit for all of Undertor for fifty years, and he had done it without angering any of the Dignifieds under whom he served, save Bon Agornin alone, when he aspired to marry his daughter. Now his enemy lay dead, and he was appealed to by both parties.

"Tradition would be with Illustrious Daverak," Frelt said.

Penn dipped his wings, acknowledging this. "But we are not talking about tradition but my father's desires," he said.

"Expressed how?" Frelt asked.

"In writing to me and in person, to me, to Avan, and to Illustrious Daverak when he first began to fail, and to me here today in the undercave. Berend and I, and Illustrious Daverak as Berend's husband, all being well established, should each take one bite only, and leave the rest for our brother and sisters, who need it more."

"He wrote and talked about his wealth only," Illustrious Daverak said, looking scornfully about the undercave where Bon Agornin's scant wealth lay under his body among the slime and the fallen scales. "His gold, such as it is, not his body."

"He may not have been clear in his writing," Penn said. "I understand now how you came to be mistaken. But he was very clear today."

"What did he say, exactly?" Frelt asked, enjoying himself hugely.

Penn turned his mind back and recalled his father's exact words. "It was I who mentioned it," he admitted. "My father was a little troubled and I thought he was worried about our sisters and brother who are not yet well established, and I sought to put his mind at rest by reminding him of the good provision he had made."

Frelt had resented his exclusion from the deathbed, and now that he learned Bon Agornin had been troubled he resented it more. He would have rejoiced in the occasion to torment Bon at the last, as Bon had insulted him badly over the affair of Berend. He did not especially like Illustrious Daverak, but all at once he felt he detested Penn, who had robbed him of his true place and of the eyes that he had looked forward to consuming. "If he did not say it himself in specific words, then I am afraid tradition must rule," he said.

"What he said amounted to an assent to what had been agreed before," Penn insisted.

"Exactly what did he say?" Frelt asked, smiling in a most unpleasant way that exposed his teeth. "If you can give me every word he said on his deathbed, then maybe I can judge. As it is . . ." He let the words trail off with a twitch of his wings.

Penn struggled with himself a moment, then let his wings fall. He could not repeat every word of his father's, not only because of Bon's disgrace, but because he had heard his confession, which by the old laws must never be revealed to anyone, and by the new understanding must never be done by any parson.

"Then tradition must rule," Frelt said.

Illustrious Daverak tossed the half-eaten leg in the direction of Frelt. He stepped around Penn, ignoring him completely. With both front claws he tore open Bon's side, exposing the liver. "Come here, children," he called, and the three dragonets ran through Frelt's legs in their eagerness to gain the treat their father was offering.

"No, stop, I insist," Penn said.

But they did not stop, and before Illustrious Daverak and the dragonets left, the liver had been entirely consumed. Frelt took the dropped leg and gnawed on it, smiling at Penn all the time. Penn's eyes were still whirling wildly, but he did not say a word.

Then Berend came in, walking delicately as always. She sighed at Penn, and he knew she must have heard the whole quarrel and wondered how she would act. She bent and took one bite, but one very large bite, from the breast. It was a bite that satisfied both what Penn had said and her husband's insistence. She could say to Penn that it was one bite, but she could also say to her husband that she had consumed the greater part of the breast. It was a most diplomatic bite, and Penn, despite himself, was awed at her grasp of such nuance.

Berend bent and took up a gold cup she had always admired, for she had now changed her mind about staying the night and wished to return to Daverak as rapidly as possible, to avoid as much further unpleasantness as she could.

She smiled and followed after her dragonets, making way for the others.

Penn almost wept as the three less established of Bon's children came into the undercave, for there was now less than half of their father's body left for them to share.

2

SOME FAR-REACHING DECISIONS

"We have been robbed," Avan stormed, "robbed of our inheritance, robbed of what our father fully intended us to have, and I will not stand for it."

"There is no way in the world of ripping it back out of Illustrious Daverak's belly," Selendra remarked.

"I would if I could, and that big bite from Berend's, too," Haner said. Her sister's bite, so diplomatically intended, angered Haner far more than her brother-in-law's indulgence. Illustrious Daverak was an Illustrious, after all, while Berend was by birth no better than she was. Such power there is, even in these days, in the title of Illustrious, at least to young maidens and the more impressionable farmers.

As can be seen, all three of the younger sibs had fed, if not gorged, upon their father's body, and were feeling the strength and courage such feeding brings. They were gathered on the High Ledge, as if they meant to plunge off and fly out into the void, though they had no such intention. They had come there to bid their sister farewell. Berend and her entourage had already departed for Daverak, the Illustrious and Illust' flying, and the others following below in a carriage. Haner, who had been intended to go with them that very night, had begged to delay her departure.

To this, Berend, in her urgent desire to be gone, had encouraged her husband to agree. Illustrious Daverak had made a show of reluctance, but all knew it was a show, as he would have to return to take formal possession of the establishment in any case and could easily escort Haner to Daverak at that time.

The thin skin of politeness over the deep wound of anger had held for the departure. As soon as the Illustrious Daveraks had left, Penn accompanied Frelt down to the Parson's Door, to bid him farewell and hasten him away. The other three remained where they were, anger breaking through calm, looking out at the view they knew so well and were so soon to leave behind them forever.

The sun was setting in a blaze of cloud away west down the valley, turning the curves and meanders of the river to flame, still bright enough for them to need to shield their eyes with their outer lids. It was the last day of the month of Highsummer. The crops were well grown in the square fields, spread out like a green and gold patchwork beneath them, outlined by the ragged hedgerows. Here and there they could see low buildings, tiled in mellow red, byres for the beeves and sties for the swine. They could see no abode of dragon, for the farmers of Agornin lived, by long custom, in their own section of the Dignified's establishment. Hidden birds were singing their sunset song, answered by the cry of the occasional muttonwool on the lower slopes of the hill. Berend and Daverak, flying south with the high winds, were almost out of sight already. Their carriage followed the road south towards the distant arch of the bridge.

"At least we shall have the gold," Haner went on after a moment.

"What there is of it," Avan said. The gold had been counted and divided and valued at about eight thousand crowns worth for each of them. "And gold is a great deal easier to come by than dragonflesh for someone in my position, or yours either. I dare say Father let you have a little occasionally, but that's not likely to continue."

"Penn won't have it to give," Selendra said, sadly, but fully intending to defend her priestly brother.

"And as for you, Haner, we've all just seen an example of Daverak's generosity," Avan said. "Why, I wish I could take the two of you to Irieth with me, but it's just impossible. If I ever become established I shall send for you at once."

The sisters gazed out at the countryside, eyes whirling slowly. "That's kind," Sel said at last. "But you won't change your mind about staying here?"

"It would be madness," Avan said. "If I were twice as long I might risk it, circumstances being what they are. That was what our father hoped for in the long term, bless his bones, but he did not live long enough. As it is, I have told you, it wouldn't work at all."

"But you would have the weaklings," Haner ventured. "You could grow."

"There aren't so many weaklings in a demesne this size. Would you have me be a Dignified like Mona-

gol, plunging down after every birth to take a dragonet whether there is a weakling or not, saying the
family can't manage so many? That's no way for an
honorable dragon to behave. There's no need for that.
Though when I think about what Daverak did I could
flame him to a crisp."

Both his sisters recognized this as an idle threat,
for they knew their brother would have no flame for
many years. Haner's silver eyes filled up with tears,
for it was an expression of which their father had
been very fond. Even with Bon Agornin it had been
words far more often than deeds, but, as she whirled
away the tears, Haner could just make out the scar
in the cornfield where her father had flared up at a
recalcitrant farmer five or six years before.

"I'll tell you what, though," said Avan, with a great
clap of his wings. "I could take him to law."

"To law?" Haner asked, astonished. "Wouldn't that
be terribly expensive?"

"You said yourself that we have the gold," Avan
said. "We have the right on our side. I have a letter
from my father clearly stating that we three were
to share what he left. Illustrious Daverak could be
made to—"

"To what?" interrupted Sel. "He cannot give us
back what he has taken, and how could he make restitution? Where is he to get the body of a full-grown
dragon to give us? It's hardly such a crime as they'd
execute him for it, even if we wanted to leave our sister a widow and her children fatherless."

"The courts do give the bodies of those who are executed and not owed to the victim, to restitution in such cases as ours," Avan explained, lifting off the ground a little in his excitement. "They wouldn't execute Daverak, of course not, but they'd make him pay gold through his snout and assign one of the spare criminals to us. If they found for us, that is. Daverak would pay. We could not fail."

"How much would it cost?" Selendra asked, bringing her brother back down to earth with a bump. "You said yourself that the gold is not much. Our shares may be barely enough to provide dowries for me and for Haner, though not if we wish to marry rich dragons. You have the means to make a living, and to prosper, we maidens do not. That gold and our own persons as we are are all we have. I would rather have the gold than the flesh if it came to it."

"Lawsuits are expensive, true, but it will not be above my share," Avan said, settling back to the ledge a little shamefacedly. He had amassed some gold already, which he could add to his inheritance. "I was not thinking of asking you to contribute." What he had said about gold being easier to come by in Irieth than dragonflesh was true, but this last statement was a polite fiction. He had calculated that the lawsuit would cost what the three of them had inherited. But sitting on the familiar ledge with his two beautiful sisters he knew he did not in the least wish to rob them of their prospects.

"Wouldn't it be better to ask him politely for some compensation first?" Haner asked.

"Penn tried politeness and it got him nowhere. No, a firm legal letter is what it will take, and if that isn't enough, then bring him before the courts to extract our due." Avan felt seventy feet long as he said this, the bold protector of his sisters, a dragon to watch out for.

6. FRELT'S INTENTIONS

Blessed Frelt's parsonage lay perhaps ten minutes' flight east of Agornin, over the mountain. Because of the geography of the underlying terrain this meant two or three hours' walk for a sturdy dragon. If Frelt had been offered a night's rest he would have refused it, but he felt it a little high-handed of the clan to throw him out with no more refreshment than the well-gnawed leg Daverak had tossed him in the undercave. In any well conducted funeral the parson was given fruit and beer in addition to his rightful consumption of the eyes of the deceased. As he bade a dry but polite farewell and eyed the upward road that was his way, without so much as a drink of water, he felt he was paying a high price for his earlier victory.

Penn kept his farewell to Frelt as brief and as formal as possible. He had observed Berend's haste to remove her household, and had a certain amount of sympathy for it. He was generally a peace-loving dragon himself, he hated rows and explosions. Even before he became a parson he had rarely initiated any combat. The last thing necessary now was a long lingering that would feed the flame of animosity. Penn knew himself well. After six months or a year in his own parish, with his own wife bringing him meals he liked to eat in his own snug dining room, he would be able to endure the sight of Blessed Frelt and even Illustrious Daverak with equanimity. At the moment, it was all he could do to bid Frelt go in the name of the gods without ripping him limb from limb.

"And you have a good journey back to Benandi," Frelt said, with heartiness Penn distrusted.

"I will be staying here for a day or two, then escorting my sister Selendra back with me," Penn said, curtly but unavoidably.

"Only Selendra?" Frelt asked. "What is to become of Haner?"

Penn's vision closed in on Frelt and he felt his claws flex involuntarily. The implication of Frelt's question, that the family might abandon Haner to her own devices, filled him with anger. Then he remembered his father's confession. A dragon whose father had eaten his siblings has little right to object to a suggestion that he might abandon his own. "Haner will be living under the protection of the Illustrious Daverak in future," Penn said, calmly and evenly as befit a parson.

"Then wish them both a pleasant journey from me

too. May Jurale see that none of you become weary and thirsty on the way."

"Thank you," Penn said, though he understood perfectly well that Frelt hoped to be provided with more refreshment for his own little journey. Let him drink from rainpuddles, Penn thought, as he smiled and raised an arm in polite parting ritual.

Fuming, Frelt set off along the rocky way. It would be quite dark before he reached home, and he had dismissed his servants for the day before he set off. How he wished he had a wife to wait up for him and prepare meat and refreshing fruit for his return. He could afford one. He had inherited only a very small store of gold from his parents, but his parish was a prosperous one and he had no expensive habits. He had gone into it all carefully seven years before when he had made suit for Berend. There was no doubt he could afford a wife, and dragonets, if they were not too many. A wife would be a great benefit to him. Yet when he had been disappointed he had not tried again. He had been too busy feuding with old Bon, and besides, there hadn't been anyone in the district pretty enough to catch his eye. He was too discriminating, he thought, walking on, his tastes were too refined. His first choice had become an Illust'. He could not be expected to settle after that for some farmer's daughter, or, worse, some Dignified's daughter twice his age and beginning to toughen under the chin. Yet since Berend's marriage those had been all the district had to offer. Maybe he should go to Irieth one spring and see the maiden dragons displayed by their mothers on the marriage market, pick out one for himself. They might all say they wanted an Exalted or an August or an Eminent and would settle for an Illustrious, but there were more maidens than Augusts to please them. He knew plenty of them would be glad of a wealthy parson, with a good living, thirty feet long, and already starting to accumulate something to pass on to his children.

He trudged onwards, uphill, the setting sun warm on his back. He did not resent the red cords that bound his wings. He was proud of them, proud of his own endurance of them. Some parsons, he knew, would have considered this circumstance enough to remove them to fly home. Frelt prided himself that he did not, that his inner piety was reflected in his outer obedience to every letter of the law. There were still a few parsons in Tiamath who flew every day, who wore cords only when they preached, and he condemned them as did every right-thinking dragon. They were few, but there were many who wore cords until circumstances were difficult, until the cords started to chafe, until they had a long uphill walk across mountains. Frelt condemned them equally. Parsons were immune and therefore they had their wings bound in red in sign of it, and therefore they walked. He did not hold with the extremists who said everyone should walk on Firstday, though he did think walking to church was good manners, unless the journey was too difficult. But parsons should walk, all the time, even when inconvenient, and this Frelt diligently did. He wished he had someone with him to be impressed, or someone waiting for him at home to bring him a drink and admire his fortitude and exclaim over the distance he had walked. A wife. Berend was lost to him, but he needed a wife.

For the first time he thought of Berend's sisters. He had never paid them much attention. When he had courted Berend they had been mere dragonets, and there had been little interaction between the parsonage and Agornin since they had grown up. He had hardly seen them except in church. Yet today he had noticed them, and they were both pretty and of marriageable age. He held his memory of them before his eyes as he walked on. Selendra had perhaps a touch brighter maidenly gold than her sister, and he thought her eyes were a little sharper, violet, like Berend's. Haner was definitely paler and dreamier, with silvery eyes. He hesitated for a moment, foot outstretched. Might not a quieter dragon suit him better as a wife? He would want home comfort and admiration, not drama and excitement. But liveliness often went with endurance. He wanted a wife who would give him dragonets and live on as his companion, not fade away and leave him widowed after her first clutch.

Selendra, then. He stepped on, carefully, for the sun was down and the road was darkening. Yet Selendra was the one who would go with Penn, while

Haner was to join Berend's establishment. Haner's connections would favor him, while Penn might oppose a match out of anger over today's decision. It was, in retrospect, a foolish decision, he realized. If he had thought of marrying one of the maidens ahead of time it would have been in his interest to decide with Penn and make sure they were given their fair share of flesh. As a parson he would have enough for his wife, but no abundance. He thought of little green Lamerak and shuddered. That dragonet should be culled, not indulged. His sister had been a pale gold, with only the faintest green blush. He should have decided against Daverak and let the younger ones eat, then Haner and Selendra would have been better nourished and grateful to him. Too late now. He would have to rely on the gratitude they would feel at being married and given their own establishment instead of living as poor relations.

He weighed the merits of the two maidens for the next hour's walk. Before he reached home he had decided, for reasons he called charitable, that he would offer for Selendra. Haner was going to the home of an Illustrious, to high society and fashionable life. She would have every opportunity to meet possible husbands. Selendra would be going to a country parsonage like his own, only as suppliant rather than mistress. (Surely he need not worry about her excessive liveliness if her brother Penn, who knew her so much better, thought such a life suitable for her.) He would be rescuing her from penury, or near-penury.

Her dowry would not be much, but it would nevertheless be a pleasant addition to the thin layer of gold that padded his undercave. If he acted soon, before Penn took her away, Penn's opposition would not count strongly. It might even be possible to persuade Selendra to agree to an immediate romantic elopement where he would sweep her off without waiting for formal consent and sort out the details later. Penn would not withhold the dowry in those circumstances. How convenient it would be to be married. A parson's wife can fly, except of course on Firstday, which would make bringing supplies up through the mountains very much easier.

By the time Frelt was quenching his thirst in his chilly parsonage he had the whole of the next ten years clear in his mind, beginning with trudging all the way back down the road again tomorrow to speak to Selendra before she left for Benandi with Penn.

7. AMER'S PLEA

Penn had passed on Frelt's good wishes for the journeys to his sisters in Avan's presence. Avan, waking early the next morning and flying down to the meadows to bring back a beef for breakfast, was therefore astonished to see Frelt making his slow way down the road over the mountain. A night's sleep had not changed Avan's feelings about the forthcoming lawsuit, nor had it made him feel better disposed to the parson who had decided for his brother-in-law against him. All the same, it is much easier to bear the weight of a grudge in the evening than on a fresh summer morning, so Avan flew over, the beef clutched between his claws, and greeted Frelt cheerfully enough.

"What a beautiful morning," he called.

Frelt had woken full of his new resolution, and had walked the footsore miles back over the mountain pondering his best approach. He had not noticed the sparkling dew, except as a damp inconvenience, nor the glorious sun, except as a source of too much light, nor the familiar beauty of the towering crags. He had to crane his neck to look up at Avan, gliding carelessly through the blue sky from which Frelt was barred. He did not envy the young dragon, or he told himself he did not, but he would have liked some acknowledgment of the sacrifice he was making, or at any rate the effort it entailed. "Veld made the world for our use, but Jurale in mercy added the beauty," he recited piously.

Avan was as religious as the next young dragon with his way to make in the world—which is to say that he held many traditional beliefs which he had never paused to examine, attended church because it would have seemed strange not to, rarely paid much attention when he was there, and found piety out of the pulpit thoroughly misplaced. If pressed, he would have been forced to stand with those who held that religion should be restricted to Firstday, though he would in all other ways have shunned such radi-

cal company. He was no free-thinker, but the place
religion held in his life could be described as traditional rather than spiritual. He enjoyed the familiar
Firstday service because it was familiar rather than
because it was a service, and he made sure to attend
a church in Irieth where the parson was famous for
keeping his sermons short. This sanctimonious
response to his greeting thus brought back all his
irritation with Frelt. He said no more, banked his
wings, and prepared to fly back up.

"Stay," Frelt called. Avan paused and circled, already much higher and drifting farther up on an
updraft. He looked down inquiringly. "I am coming
to pay a call on your family," Frelt said, of necessity
shouting to be heard.

"I can't stop you," Avan said, giving way to rudeness, but under his breath. "You know the way," he
said, more resonantly, and flew off to warn his sisters.

Selendra and Haner had been up late the night
before attempting to comfort each other for the loss
of their father. It was not the first loss their family had suffered, but the other losses had happened
when they were so young as to leave them almost
untouched. Their mother had died shortly after they
were hatched, they scarcely remembered her. They
were not yet truly aware how much they had missed
her guiding hand in their upbringing. Avan's clutch-
mate, Merinth, had been lost before they were of
the age of understanding. They had seen misfortune
come to other families, and thought they had come

to know through his long illness what their father's death meant. It was only now that they realized that there is nothing that can really be a preparation for death.

The beautiful morning that had lightened Avan's heart seemed almost mockery to Selendra, that the sun could shine when her father was dead and she was so soon to be separated from everything she loved. She left Haner asleep in the sleeping cave they had shared since they were hatched, and went sadly down to the kitchens to arrange breakfast. Amer was there, clucking over the depleted stores. "We've let it go badly, 'Spec Sel, over your father's illness. But if you're all to leave it's probably just as well, who would want to leave stores to Berend and that arrogant husband of hers."

It would have been appropriate for Selendra to have reproached her servant for speaking so freely, but Amer in her long service to the family had been allowed such privilege that it did not even occur to Selendra to do so. Though she could have recited maxims by the hour about keeping servants in their place, she had never thought to apply them to Amer, who had come to Agornin when Bon Agornin married and stayed to tend all the dragonets as they grew. "I dare say Illustrious Daverak would have turned up his snout at our preserves and smokes if we had made them," she said, colluding with Amer and encouraging her. "I hate to think of him having our beautiful home."

Amer shut the almost empty cupboard and turned to Selendra. "Will you take me with you to Benandi?" she asked.

Selendra hesitated. "Haner wanted you to go with her. I'll have Penn, you know, while she will have only Berend."

"I'm very sorry for 'Spec Haner, and I wish I could do something to help her, but I'm thinking about myself now," Amer said. "I'm an old dragon and I've served your family a long time and your mother's family before you. Please let me come to Benandi."

Faced with this determination, Selendra couldn't insist. "I don't know if Penn will allow it. I don't know if he could afford it for that matter. It's good of him to take me in, I don't know if he can manage you as well. He couldn't manage Haner. I'll certainly ask him as strongly as I can, but I can't promise."

"I'm a hard worker, you know I am, and one more servant is a different matter from a sister."

"He has a wife," Selendra said, remembering. "Her name is Felin. I met her only at the wedding, and briefly, I don't know her at all. She may have her own ideas about what servants she needs, and I'm sure they don't include my having my own attendant." She laughed at the thought. "Me with a personal attendant, like a very grand dragon. Like Berend."

"I'd be happy to be that, and you deserve to have your scales burnished as much as other maidens, but you know I'll turn my hands to whatever is necessary. I'll scrub the cave if they need that, and you know I make good preserves and medicines." Amer's hands were held out before her like a beggar pleading.

"She may have her own ideas about managing servants, about tying down wings very tightly," Selendra warned.

It has been told already that Amer's wings were hardly bound tighter than Penn's. It should further be admitted that on occasion during their father's illness, Selendra and Haner had allowed Amer's wings to be unbound entirely so that she could fly out to gather healing herbs. Let those who throw up their wings in horror at this consider that Amer had returned and was serving the family even now and had not taken the opportunity to fly off into the mountains and take up a new life.

"I can bear having my wings bound as tight as anything, it isn't that, and I'd be sure of that with Berend. What scares me is if they keep me at all. Those idle servants from Daverak were talking when you were in the undercave, and maybe they were just talking to try to frighten me, but they didn't sound that way, talking about how Daverak eats the servants when they get old."

"Eats them against their expressed intention?" Selendra asked, her dislike of Daverak making this easy enough to believe.

"Eats them before they've died," Amer said, and then caught up with herself when she saw Selendra's horrified expression. "Not quite as bad as that, no, not eating them alive but killing them to eat as if they were weakling dragonets."

"How terribly wasteful," Selendra said. "No, it can't be so, his parson wouldn't allow it." Selendra made her voice much more definite than she felt, to reassure the old servant as she quoted, "There must be no killing of dragons except after a challenge or in the presence of a parson, for the improvement of dragonkind—meaning the weakling dragonets, not a servant who isn't as fast as she used to be."

"Parsons don't see everything. There are corrupt parsons too, who might look away, and who's to say the Illustrious Daverak doesn't have one of those?" Amer looked imploringly at Selendra.

"I'll do whatever I can to persuade Penn to let you come with me," Selendra said.

Just then Avan came in, ducking his head to avoid the doorway. He had the beef slung across his arms. "I went out to bring back breakfast," he said, smiling.

"Oh bless you," Selendra exclaimed. "I've let supplies get very low."

"No use getting it in for Berend," Avan said.

"That's just what Amer was saying," Selendra said. Avan gave Amer a look that warned he was by no means as indulgent with servants as his sisters. She ducked her head obediently and took the beef from him.

"I met Blessed Frelt on my way," Avan said. "He's coming to pay a call on the family, he says. I have no

idea what he wants—I thought we'd seen the last of
him. I think father was right to quarrel with him, he's
such a prig."

"Well we can't quarrel with him before breakfast,"
Selendra said.

"More's the pity," Avan said.

Amer let a snort of laughter escape her at this. Avan
frowned, and even Selendra looked at her reproach-
fully, as if to ask if this was how she would behave in
the Blessed Penn's house. Amer heeded the warning
look and began jointing the beef neatly, saying nothing, keeping her place.

8. A PROPOSAL

Selendra felt it necessary to go down to welcome
Blessed Frelt. It so happened that this duty had
never fallen to her before. When her father and Frelt
were still upon good terms, before his ill-fated offer
for Berend, Selendra had been a mere dragonet and
Berend herself had always welcomed him. Since
then his visits had been few and formal, and he had
either been shown in to Bon Agornin by Amer, as if
he were a stranger, or even worse met with threats
upon the threshold. "Amer, keep on with the breakfast, and make sure it is suitable for a visiting parson,"
she said, sternly. "Avan, if you could inform Penn
and Haner of our visitor I would take it kindly." She
then checked herself rapidly for stray spots of blood,
brushed her front scales hastily, and hurried down

towards the lower gate. Such were the preparations of the maiden Selendra as she went to receive her first proposal of marriage.

Frelt was delighted to see Selendra bustling down to greet him. He had wondered a little, after Avan's abrupt departure, if he might be treated as badly by the children as by the father. He had remembered Penn's behavior to him the night before. Much as he hated it, he knew that if he wished to be on terms with the family he would have to admit that he was wrong. He had been unsure if he would be able to see Selendra at all. In the course of the night, he had convinced himself it was Selendra he wanted, and he now half-believed that he had been in love with her for some time. A farmer had shown him through the lower door, and he made his way slowly up through the narrow corridor, squeezing himself unpleasantly at times with some more concern for the burnish of his scales than might be thought appropriate for a parson. So when he saw Selendra coming down, the smile he gave her had much of genuine pleasure in it, along with a little of the pride that was his strongest quality.

"Blessed Frelt, how may we serve you?" Selendra asked. "Would you care to take breakfast with us?"

"Thank you, Respected Agornin. I should be delighted."

Selendra turned and the two of them made their way up towards the heights of the establishment. When the corridor broadened so they could walk abreast, Frelt immediately took advantage of this to come up to her side. He smiled at Selendra again, hoping she noticed the strength and evenness of his teeth. She did not smile back, but regarded him gravely. "Is there anything wrong?" she asked. "We were not expecting to see you today." The only thing she could imagine might have brought him was the irregularity over the funeral, which she knew her brothers would not want to discuss with any stranger, least of all Frelt.

"Respected Agornin, nothing is wrong, nothing at all. I just came once again to pay my respects to your family and to see if I might serve you in your time of grief." This speech was so bland it could have been made by any parson to any recently bereaved young maiden, but Frelt softened it with another smile, this one much less natural.

Selendra took him literally, and was confused. "We welcome you, of course, but my brother Penn is still here if we needed a parson, and the funeral is over and I don't see that there is anything you can do."

"I came to pay my respects to you, Selendra," Frelt said, whirling his dark eyes at her a little in a way that was quite unmistakable. "As you are going away soon and there is little time, I did not want to wait."

For all that Frelt was a country parson, he had spent some little time in society in Irieth, and he usually considered himself a more sophisticated dragon than those around him. He knew this was not behavior that would be condoned by society, and this was not at all how he had behaved when he had made an offer for Berend. But time was not on his side, and he wanted to seize his opportunity. They would soon be returning to the drier and more inhabited portion of the establishment and he did not know when he might have time alone with Selendra again. Also, he had been thinking so much and with such concentration on his plan that he had almost forgotten that Selendra had never thought of him in the light of a lover, indeed that she had seldom thought of him at all. He wanted to have matters arranged between them before he began to speak to her brothers.

Selendra stopped dead, unable to misunderstand him, and most especially the use of her personal name, but so completely astonished at his declaration that she could no longer control her legs. Frelt, not anticipating this, took another step and almost tripped over her tail.

"Do you think you might come to care for me?" Frelt asked, recovering himself, leaning close to her, looking into her eyes and putting his claw on her arm.

For Selendra this was close to a nightmare. No male dragon but her father and brothers had ever been so close. The corridor was dark and confining, and more than slightly damp. She had never known Frelt well, but she had always disliked him, thinking him nothing like good enough for Berend. He leaned closer still, leaning on her, well aware that she was a maiden dragon and could be awakened to love by such closeness. He had intended to use argument, but now that he felt her close, he was almost overpowered himself by the scent of her.

Selendra felt her wings rising, though there was no room for them. They brushed the cobwebs at the top of the passage. She clapped them back to her sides, and in so doing she regained the use of her senses and could back away from him a step or two.

"I am sensible of the honor you do me, but my answer is no," Selendra said, delivering the set speech all maiden dragons are taught to deliver, but in terrified tones. "Never speak to me of this again," she said, as firmly as she dared, backing slowly away from him.

"I have a fine parsonage in the mountains, and am parson of six demesnes," Frelt explained, ignoring her denial, knowing all females refused the first time. "If you married me you would be mistress of your own establishment, and you would not have to leave the countryside you love. Parsons' wives are not forbidden to fly."

"I said no," Selendra said, turning and scurrying away from him up the passage, letting her words drift back to him on the wind of her passage. "I hardly think you know what you are saying, sir. You do not know me and cannot mean to seek my person in marriage. You once loved my sister Berend, I know."

"Oh, that was long ago when you were but a dragonet. Before I saw your beauty I loved your sister as the shadow of what you would be." Frelt was rather proud of this speech, which he had prepared on the way over the mountain, in case she might refer to his earlier wooing. He wished he could deliver it in better circumstances—Selendra was scuttling away from him as fast as she could, and he had difficulty keeping up, so that he almost had to shout, and could not be sure she heard.

"My answer is no! Please do not bother me further," Selendra begged, all but crying, running with little leaps of flight whenever the ceiling was high enough. Frelt pursued her as fast as he could, but with bound wings he was at a disadvantage.

Selendra almost burst into the dining room where her family was gathered, with Frelt still in pursuit. Fortunately her good sense returned to her when she was far enough from him, so she could turn and face him in the broad hallway between the speaking and dining rooms.

"I am serious, sir, and I mean what I say," she said. "No, do not come closer, you are a parson and I know you were making me an honest offer and do not mean to ravish me."

Ravishing her was closer to Frelt's thoughts than he would have wished to admit, but he also was calmer after the chase and stopped as he was bidden. "Will you not take a little time to consider?" Frelt asked. "Must I consider my hopes dashed forever?"

"Yes, yes, forever," Selendra replied, still in some agitation. "Now go, please, if that was your purpose in coming here." Again she repeated the rote words of refusal, running them together in her haste to have them said. "I am sensible of the honor you do me but my answer is no. Please believe me, Blessed Frelt." She put her hand on the door to the dining room. "My brothers are here and I am under their protection."

Frelt found himself growling far back in his throat. She had not needed to say that. He was a respectable parson, not some bandit. He forgot for the moment that he had hoped to carry her off and go through formal arrangements later. He even forgot how close he had been to her, and that he might yet have succeeded in his object despite all her denials. He turned around huffily, and before him lay the long downward corridor, and beyond that the long walk home, and once more he was facing it without having partaken of any refreshment.

3
THE SISTERS' VOW

All three dragons looked up from their beef as Selendra pushed the dining room door open in its arch. It was a sturdy old-fashioned close-fitting wooden door, and it creaked beneath Selendra's hand. Some say wooden doors are Yargian and therefore abhorrent, lumping them with mantillas, confession, and cooked meat, others say they are simply out of the mode for the time being. Bon Agornin had yielded sufficiently to fashion to remove the door on his speaking room, but he had insisted that tradition must rule so far as concerned his dining room. The siblings therefore had the protection and warning a door affords, and prepared themselves to greet their sister and, as they still imagined, the Blessed Frelt.

Selendra came in in some confusion. At one moment she was flushed almost pink, at the next, she went pale, paler even than Haner's accustomed delicate gold. She closed the door behind her and stood a moment with her tail to her family.

"What is wrong?" Haner asked at once.

"Where is Frelt?" Penn inquired, only a moment later.

If Selendra had been given time to compose herself, she might have been able to give dissembling answers to these questions. She knew a dragon maid should not betray agitation after turning away a proposal of marriage. Yet the agitation was internal, she was given no time, and she could hardly feel that the proposal had been decorous. She turned to face them.

"Frelt has gone," she answered her brother. "And I am a little shaken," she informed her sister. She lowered herself to the ground, and Avan silently passed her a haunch of beef. She took it but did not begin to eat for a moment. The others stared at her.

"Gone?" Penn asked, collecting himself. "Without waiting for whatever business that brought him here?"

"He had no such business," Selendra said. "Or rather, I was his business. He came to propose to me, and he did, and I declined, and he has left. That's the whole of it." Seldom has a maiden been less gratified by an unwelcome proposal. She sank down on her haunches, again flushed pink and reduced to a condition of near-paralysis.

"Did he . . . approach you?" Haner asked.

"If he did I will have him torn out of the Church," Penn said, rising to his feet angrily.

"And I will tear him to shreds once he has lost his immunity," Avan said, his wings rising of themselves. "Selendra?"

"He has not hurt me," Selendra said quickly. "He did not assault me. But he approached closely enough to distress me and I seem to have lost my composure."

"You are pink!" Penn declared, though at that moment she was almost white. "If he has done that he will marry you in recompense."

"But that's what he wants!" Selendra said, pinkening again, and backing a step away from her brother without rising. "He came here hoping to claim me as a bride. I hate him, and I will never marry him."

"You should not have been alone with him," Avan said.

"A parson!" Haner said, stung into defending her sister. "Parsons are always greeted, you know that, because they cannot fly up to the usual entrances. You were there when Sel said she was going to greet him, you yourself told us she had gone with approval."

"He was abusing his position as a parson," Avan said.

"I am not hurt," Selendra insisted, the weakness of her voice belying her words. "Nothing has happened, except that he proposed and I rejected him."

"He should have asked me for permission to speak to you," Penn said, frowning. "Permission which I should certainly have denied. But if you are pink my dear, and I am afraid it seems you are, then it is too late to turn back and there must be a marriage. It is making the best of a bad situation, I know, but consider the alternative."

"I am not pink, I am merely agitated, I shall not be pink when I have eaten and rested a little," Selendra said, attempting to turn her head to examine her own scales. "I will never marry Frelt. He is a bully and a prig and a pompous swine."

Avan and Penn exchanged speaking glances. They were dragons who had seen more of the world than their sisters, and the thought of what could be done with a sister who was neither maiden nor wife hung heavily upon them. Avan was reduced to wondering if he had any acquaintance in Irieth who might consent to take his sister as a consort in such circumstances as this. It would not be a marriage such as he would desire, one which would give her an establishment of her own, but there were dragons rising in the capital who might find her dowry and connections sufficiently attractive for that, despite her blush, even if they might not want to share their names and status with her. It was not what any dragon would choose for his sister, but it might be better than a marriage with a parson she despised and who had deliberately ruined her.

Selendra took a few bites of her beef in silence. Then she looked up, her big violet eyes brimming with tears and whirling rapidly. "Why are you all looking at me without speaking?" she asked. "I have done nothing wrong, nothing. I am not in disgrace. I refuse to be."

"Of course you are not," Haner said, going to her sister at once and folding her wings around her.

"Come away to our own cave and rest, you'll soon be well again."

The sisters made their way out together. "Am I really pink?" Selendra asked Haner as soon as they were alone. "Pink so that everyone can see?"

"Just a little, sometimes," Haner answered. "It will soon pass off, I'm sure, if you didn't let him come up close to you."

"But I did," Selendra admitted. "I was so surprised that I couldn't move, and he came close and leaned on me."

"Whatever are we going to do?" Haner asked. "Penn really does mean it about making the best of a bad situation, he'll have you married off. But what else can you do?"

"Amer will know," Selendra said with decision. "Go to fetch Amer, and tell her what has happened. If there is anything we can do to get my color back, she will know."

Selendra made her way to the sleeping cave, and Haner hurried off to fetch Amer.

10. THE SISTERS' VOW

Amer tutted and blew out hot breath when Haner explained what had happened, and poured out scorn and expletives upon Frelt. Then she told Haner to bring Selendra to the kitchen, and put a kettle of water on the fire to heat.

"You are old enough to understand," she began,

when Selendra came in, pink and miserable. "I cannot treat you like a child to be given medicine without knowing."

"I'll take it whatever it is," Selendra pleaded.

"Most likely, this will restore you without danger," Amer said, as she ground her herbs. "But you should know there is a chance that it will not work, and another smaller chance that it will work too well. This is medicine, not magic, and medicine works by numbers and not by nature."

"By numbers?" Selendra was confused and still pink. "Let me have it, and I shall count as high as you like."

"That would be magic," Amer said, smiling and showing her teeth. "Besides, it has to brew, and you will have to wait. Haner said he touched you?"

"He leaned on me," Selendra admitted for the second time. She sank to the floor, couchant, her head bowed down on her upper arms and her wings half-furled over her, almost more affected by the memory than when it had happened.

Haner put out her own wings to help cover her sister, and there were tears in her eyes. "We have to do something," she said to Amer.

"I'm doing all I can," Amer said. "You will certainly need this tea to help you put it behind you. But what I mean by working by numbers is that for most dragons it works without harm, but there is no way of telling whether you are one of the few who will be harmed."

"I'll take it," Selendra said, so low as to be almost inaudible.

"You have to understand," Amer insisted. The water was boiling, and she poured it on to the mess in the pot. There were ground seeds and some green weeds and something red and dried that swelled in the water to look almost like a flower. Amer stirred it vigorously then set it aside. "If it doesn't work, you're no worse off than now. If it does, well and good. If it works too well, you'll be restored, but you'll not be able to blush when the right time comes. Now sit up and tell me you understand before I give it to you."

Slowly, Selendra rose from the floor. She stretched herself to her whole length, twenty feet without curling, and raised her crest and wings as much as was possible in the kitchen, crowding Haner and Amer into corners. "I understand, and I will take the risk," she said. "I have always wanted to marry and have dragonets with some dragon I love, despite the risk, but I will give all that up if only I may be restored to safety and not have to spend the rest of my short life with that repulsive Frelt."

"You don't have to give up hope unless you don't blush when you're close to a dragon who loves you," Amer said. "It's repeated doses of this that really do harm. Besides, don't overrate the risks of marriage. You speak of a short life as if that's the lot of every bride, but your mother didn't sicken until her third clutch, and they say such things go by blood. If you're careful, both of you, and if you marry a dragon who will be satisfied with two clutches, not too close together, you may live to be dowagers gloating over grandchildren yet."

"I think it's terrible that maidens must give up their gold and marry," Haner said. "Both their dowry gold and their own natural golden color. I don't wish to die as mother did, as so many dragons do."

"It's just as bad to be an old maid," said Amer. "You toughen under the chin, and then your gold turns gray." Amer herself was almost the same color of the rock of the caves. She picked up the pot of tea, sniffed at it, then strained it carefully into a cup.

"If I can't marry, I'll give you my dowry, Haner," Selendra said, as she took the cup. "With both of our shares, and your delicate beauty, you can make a splendid match to some very considerate August or Eminent, and I can come and live with you and be an aunt to your single clutch of dragonets." She sipped the tea, wrinkling her snout at the bitterness.

"Or if you find you can marry, I could do the same and come and live with you," Haner said. "Let's say that we will not agree to marry any dragon the other does not know and esteem, and that we will make our establishment together in that way."

Selendra drained the cup. "I can agree to that," she said. "But it seems as if you would have a much better chance of finding a good husband if it were known that you have sixteen thousand crowns worth of gold, instead of a mere eight."

"Most likely the tea won't have any bad effect,"

Amer said. "The more you fret about it the worse it will be."

"I'm feeling better already," Selendra said. Indeed, she seemed to be returning at once to her natural gold.

"Fretting about not being able to blush can stop you doing it just as much as my medicine," Amer said.

"I'm not fretting," Selendra said. "I'm just talking about Haner's marriage prospects. There's that friend of Daverak's, Dignified Londaver, he danced with you twice at Berend's ball."

"He's nothing to me," Haner insisted, but she smiled.

"I'd esteem him," Selendra went on.

"You'll like as not marry yourself and be happy," Amer said. She scraped the remaining herbs from the pot and threw them on the fire where they sizzled and shrivelled with an acrid smell.

"I'm feeling sleepy," Selendra said.

"That's the medicine working," Amer said, taking the cup from Selendra. "I'll just wash this for you. Go to your cave and sleep, when you wake you'll be as good as new."

Haner went through the passages behind her sister. As soon as they went into their sleeping cave, Selendra settled down on her gold.

"I mean it you know," she said to her sister. "Tell everyone you have sixteen thousand."

"Then you do the same," Haner said. "If it should

be that you can't marry, you'll find that out. If not, then whichever of us shall first find a husband will also give a home to the other. It would be so good to live together as we always have. I shall miss you so much when I am with Berend."

"I shall come and visit you there," Selendra said. "Berend invited me. I shall come for a few weeks or a month next spring. There will not be room in Penn's parsonage for you to visit me, but we shall not become strangers to each other."

"But then if you meet some dragon you wish to marry in Benandi he will be quite a stranger to me."

"I doubt I shall ever marry," Selendra said. "I thought I wanted to, but this was so unpleasant as to change my mind about it entirely. I shall remain a maiden, old and gray, and you shall be a ruby-red dowager, and we shall live together always." Selendra yawned in a way any mother, governess, or nanny would have said was unfitting for a dragon maid, showing the full expanse of her fangs and the great red cavern of the inside of her mouth.

"The first of us to find a dragon to love shall accept him only if the other knows and esteems him, and then we shall all live together," Haner said.

"I so swear," Selendra said, embracing her sister.

"I so swear," Haner repeated, embracing Selendra back.

Selendra settled back on her gold, yawned again, more befittingly with her wing before her mouth, and fell asleep. Haner watched her for a moment, feeling the first pang of what separation would really mean. For Haner, separation from Selendra seemed as great a sorrow as their father's death. She sat down across the mouth of the cave and prepared to guard her sister against any dangers that might come.

11. SURPRISES FOR PENN

Penn spent the whole day from breakfast onwards up on the heights, praying to all three gods. He prayed for mercy for Selendra, for wisdom for himself to do the right thing for her, and for the soul of his father, flying even now towards rebirth. He would have gone to the old church where he had first learned to know the gods, but for the possibility of meeting Frelt there. The more he thought of Frelt the more angry he became. He tried to forgive him, as a parson should, he tried to think better of him than he did, and he tried to find peace through meditation. He found no forgiveness, and could not but think worse of Frelt the more he considered matters, but at last he did find a kind of peace in sitting on the highest point of the crag, the winds and clouds around him, repeating the prayers for his father's soul over and over.

When he came down, he first encountered his brother. Avan had also spent the day fretting about Selendra. Frelt's proposal had eclipsed even the Illustrious Daverak's rudeness for both brothers. Penn's silver eyes were distant when he came in, whirling only once or twice in a minute, for he had kept them fixed on the depths. He almost stumbled over Avan where he lay couchant across the ledge blocking his brother's entrance.

"I have had a thought about Selendra," Avan said. Penn blinked, stepped back carefully, and tried to bring his mind up to the moment, losing all his hard-acquired calm in the process.

"What?" Penn asked. "I can't see that there's any choice but that she will have to marry him."

"I knew you would think so, but there may be another answer." Avan smiled and drew himself up sejant, legs under him, tail curled around his legs and his arms folded across his breast. "I have a good friend, the Exalt Rimalin. She has an establishment in Irieth, and one in the country, somewhere in the north. Her husband is a minister in government."

"I believe I have heard of him," Penn said, though his friends were not political. He was utterly puzzled as to where this could be leading.

"They have some gold, but are not rich, not as those of Exalted rank are considered to be rich. However, they own their establishments outright and owe nothing to anyone and are looked at on all sides as a respectable family. I believe the Exalted Rimalin might be induced to look favorably upon Selendra, with her dowry and being my sister, and yours of course."

"Look favorably on her?" Penn was even more confused. He even wondered for a moment if Avan could be suggesting some such position as governess to Rimalin's children. "Look favorably how?"

"As a consort, of course."

"But you said he had a wife, that his wife was your friend."

"Yes, that's just why this will work, don't you see?" Avan had been thinking this out all afternoon. "He wouldn't marry Selendra, even if he were free, nobody would marry a compromised maiden however attractive her dowry, and Selendra's will be only moderate even if you and I could add a little to it."

"I could not add anything," Penn said hastily. "I have a family of my own to think of."

"Well I might add a little, not being established yet," Avan said. "But that's neither here nor there, it would not be enough to make a difference. Nobody would take her as a wife, but through the good offices of Exalt Rimalin, Exalted Rimalin might take her as a consort. A second wife, you know," he added, after a moment in which Penn's countenance had become very forbidding. "The Church does allow such things," he ventured.

"I hardly know how you can consider suggesting such a thing for your own sister," Penn said. "No doubt such positions of concubinage are we'' ￢nough for some poor unfortunate females without any protection, but that you might think Selendra had come to that!"

"It would be better for Sel than marrying the

dragon who deliberately set out to ruin her, a dragon Father was at feud with for the last six years and whom she despises," Avan said. "Exalt Rimalin is a jolly, friendly dragon, and a political hostess. I could see Sel often and be sure her position in the establishment was what it should be, and not the drudgery such consorts often endure. And she would have provision made for her exactly as for a wife, I speak of a formal position as consort, not selling her into concubinage."

"She would most likely bear clutches without pause until she died, and her children would have no inheritance," Penn said. "The more formal the arrangement, the less power you would have to relieve whatever misery came of it. No, Avan. I would regard such an arrangement as a disgrace. I will not hear another word about it." Penn leapt over his brother, not quite a flight, yet his wings were spread rather more than some in the Church would like to see a parson's wings.

Penn landed neatly and walked away down the corridor without a backward glance, meaning to seek out Selendra to inform her immediately that he would consult with Frelt about their marriage. He found Haner first, sitting on her haunches at the door of the sleeping cave. "It's all right," she whispered. "She's asleep, but look!" Penn looked through the archway to where Selendra slept on the gold of her dowry. She lay curled up with her head under her wing, the picture of feminine grace. Her scales were clean and burnished, and shone a clear pale gold, with no trace whatsoever of any bridal pink.

"How have you managed it?" Penn asked. "What trickery is this? Paint?" But he looked again and knew no paint could ever be so perfect or even.

"She only needed to rest and become calm," Haner said. "Amer made her a tea and she has been well since."

Penn started in surprise. He knew only a little of the herbs to which desperate maidens might resort. He had been told in the seminary what a sin they were. "I will speak to Amer," Penn said, and stalked away, leaving Haner staring after him.

Amer was in the storeroom, arranging some fruit with the remains of the beef for supper. "How are you, Blessed Penn?" she asked. Amer had been his nanny, but since he had been a parson she had always behaved towards him most respectfully. He liked this, of course, and would have been most resentful of any undue familiarity, but it made him a little sad sometimes when he felt a constraint between them where once no constraint had been.

"I'm well," he said. "Amer, I'm here about Respected Selendra."

"'Spec Sel's sleeping. She'll do well enough now."

"What did you give her?"

Amer looked up guiltily. "'Spec Haner told you?"

"She said you'd made her a tea. Amer, I have to know. Respected Selendra is my sister, and she's coming into my establishment, to live with my wife and dragonets, mingle with my friends and patrons. Is she a maiden still, or have you given her color back by deceit? Should she marry Blessed Frelt?"

"She should certainly not marry any such blackguard who would do such a thing," Amer said, slapping the beef down hard and turning to Penn as if he were still five years old. "Deceit indeed. She's a maiden for sure, the same as if that dragon, who would better be called damned than blessed, had never crowded against her. Two minutes in the passage! It takes more than that to turn a maiden's scales for good, if she doesn't want them to be turned. I gave her some tea to help her body calm itself, the same as if I gave her sallow-bark for a fever, that's all, no tricks, no deceits, she's not been awakened to him. She'll make some good dragon a true mate one day, you need have no fear."

Penn was not entirely convinced by this, but he was nevertheless extremely comforted. He knew he had asked the name of the herb Selendra had taken, and that Amer had carefully not given it. Still he felt reluctant to inquire further. This assurance seemed enough. He remembered his wife, Felin, how her gold scales had blushed pink all at once when she accepted his proposal and his embrace. He wanted that for his sisters and no counterfeit. But neither did he want to force Selendra to marry a dragon they all despised. He had been trying all day to persuade himself that Frelt was not such a bad dragon, but the memory of his judgment in the undercave the day before had kept coming back to remind him that Frelt was not the kind of dragon he would seek as a brother-in-law. Now he could forget that, and forget too Avan's shocking suggestion, and put his mind at rest.

"Very well. Thank you, Amer," he said.

"One more thing," the old nanny said. "I spoke to 'Spec Sel but she won't have had time to say anything to you. I'd like to come with her to Benandi. I'll work hard and help your wife with the dragonets, or do whatever work you ask of me. I really want to stay near 'Spec Selendra now, in case she needs me at all, you know. And besides you were always my favorite when you were one of my young ones." She sank slowly down onto her back legs, her wings bound back, and her arms extended towards him. "Please, Blessed Penn. Let me stay with the Agornins."

Penn had by no means intended taking Amer with him. He knew Felin, his wife, would be astonished. He wasn't sure whether they could entirely afford another servant. But he also knew that he couldn't possibly refuse. The combination of the appeal with the hidden threat of what might happen to Selendra without Amer nearby to help was too much for him. He raised the old dragon back to her feet. "Of course we will take you with us," he said.

4
LEAVING AGORNIN

Among our great families such as the Telsties and the Benandis there is a tendency for dragons to act as if the world will go about its accustomed course forever, improving a little in each generation as best such improvement can be accomplished—the addition of a farm to an estate here, some marshland drained there, perhaps a new method of running beeves so that ten can graze where only eight grazed before. Change, to these dragons, is something slow and steady as the erosion of mountains. Proposals for improvement are examined very carefully, and a lord could say that this matter of improved grazing methods might be something his grandson could profitably begin—and this when the lord is himself scarcely married. Yet somehow, despite the great demesnes these families hold, and the great influence they control in the Assemblies, progress in a different sense has swooped down on them at the speed of wings and not the slow considered creeping steps they would prefer.

Bon Agornin's gold, not that which he had passed on to his three younger children, but that which he had used three hundred years before to purchase the estate of Agornin and the title of Dignified, had been made in ways those dignified, illustrious, exalted, august, and eminent personages we have chosen to make lords among us lump together and dismiss in a word as "trade." True, Bon had shaken off these associations as soon as he could. He had used them to climb and achieve position in the world and, once he had achieved the position he desired, had dabbled in them no more. He had purchased his establishment, married his ill-dowried but indubitably gently born bride, and proceeded thenceforth to amass wealth and improve his estate through honest farming. All the same, through the succeeding centuries the stench of trade had clung around him a little. Much though he might speak of his youth on the Telstie estate with his widowed mother, and of his estate of Agornin, never mentioning the intervening period, there remained something of the city about him. The cities, as hardly needs to be mentioned, are anathema to all right-thinking dragons, except only for Irieth, and Irieth only when the Noble Assembly is sitting, or in the months of Budding and Flowering in those years, very rare of late, when the Noble Assembly shall hold no session.

This shadow of the city was but rarely apparent in his Dignified years, and it had cast but little reflection upon his children. Illustrious Daverak had considered it for a moment while courting Berend, but had soothed his conscience with the memory of her mother, who had been a Fidrak, which, though the family was now sadly impoverished, meant that her ancestors had held their acres since before the Conquest. Penn, in the Church, had prospered on his own accomplishments and the patronage of his friends, in particular the Exalted Sher Benandi and his mother the Exalt Zile Benandi. The younger maidens had as yet not made their way in the world at all, but had hitherto not anticipated much difficulty following Berend into good marriages. As for Avan, how he presented himself at home and what he did at Irieth were rather different, as we shall see.

At Undertor, the only visible sign of old Bon's earlier ventures into trade was the railway, which cut across a corner of Agornin land. It was a corner distant from the establishment, and in no way blocked or spoiled any prospects which any dragon would especially wish to view. Indeed, the land where it now ran had always been marshy and good for nothing. The railway engineers had, in putting it in, drained the land and freed up a field or two next to the line for farming, of which Bon made good use by running drafters. These drafters would become slowly accustomed to the noise of the passing trains and could then be sold into the cities as bustle-hardened, raising their value greatly.

There had been a great commotion in the district when the railway had been proposed, and some of the neighboring Dignifieds had quarrelled, or tried to quarrel, with Bon Agornin for allowing it to blight the countryside. Bon's commercial past was remembered when he took the gold from the railway company. If Bon had not agreed, the railway must have taken a very different course and stayed far away from Undertor altogether. By allowing it to run through this neglected corner of his land Bon made freight flow through directly from the mines of Tolga to Irieth, not to mention speeding the mails considerably and incidentally providing transportation for any dragons who, through heavy burdens, through age or infirmity, or because they were traveling with dragonets or parsons or servants, might not wish to fly where they were going.

Bon Agornin had insisted, when he leased the land to the railway, on having a station put on it. "It will be useful for Penn," he said. Penn then had already been in training for that most respectable of professions, the Church. In general the station was mostly used by the local farmers to send fresh russets and pippins up to the city, where fruit always obtained high prices. This had slowly come to reconcile the neighbors, who also grew fruit and used the station for shipping it, so much that now Bon was almost accounted a benefactor to the district for having allowed it to be provided. Penn had several times made use of it in coming home, and it was his intention to make use of it again. The railway did not run all the way to Benandi. The previous Exalted Benandi, Sher's father, had refused indignantly to have anything to do with it. It ran at its closest to within twelve miles of the establishment, where there was a little halt to which a carriage could easily be sent when there was a parson or a visitor to be collected. Naturally carts could also go to this halt to load their produce, in Benandi's case usually sweetberries in summer and russets in autumn. In Benandi the railway was still far more deprecated than in Undertor, where the blessing was easier to see, as it ran so much closer.

Penn had intended to take the railway as far as the Benandi Halt with his sister, and then have her fly the last few miles while he traveled by the carriage which he could cause to be sent for him. Now that Amer was added to the party, he reconsidered this and wrote to his wife, Felin, accordingly.

Most dragons regard writing as a feminine accomplishment, and letter writing doubly so. In ordinary circumstances, even Penn would have asked one of his sisters to write a note to his wife for him. Yet he was a parson, and had mastered the difficult art of holding a pen between his claws, and he felt that what he wanted to say to Felin was of a sufficiently private nature to make it necessary to write it out himself.

"My dear," he wrote carefully. "I hope you and the children are well. My father is dead, as we expected, may his soul fly free. Selendra and I will depart for Benandi the day after tomorrow, and should be with you by the afternoon train. I find that it is necessary to bring with me my father's servant Amer, who was my nanny when I was a dragonet. She is anxious to accompany us rather than go to Daverak's establishment, for reasons which I am afraid are largely sentimental, and of which I am very much afraid the Exalt" (here he meant Exalt Benandi) "will disapprove. Amer will doubtless prove useful to us with the children, and a help in the kitchen, she is very skilled in making preserves and potions."

After a moment's thought he struck out the last two words, considered recopying the letter, gnashed his teeth, and let the matter stand as it was. Penn had already decided not to take Felin into his confidence on the matter of Frelt's attempted seduction of Selendra. He told himself that it would distress Felin to no purpose, but in his heart he knew that it would cause his wife to distrust his sister, which would lead to an unhappy family situation for himself. "I know you will welcome her, and consider the extravagance of another servant one which we can endure," he wrote, thinking that this was the best way of approaching the matter with his wife. "However, Exalt Benandi, who takes such an interest in the affairs of her domain, may not see likewise, and may interfere in a way which I would find intolerable. Therefore, hire an extra eight drafters to pull the three of us home from the Halt in the carriage. This is an extravagance, but it is one for which we can endure Exalt Benandi's reproaches, while if Selendra flew and Amer walked behind, she should be sure to begin at once to believe that we could not afford another servant." Penn knew, or believed he knew, how to manage his patroness. He had learned of such little deceptions or, as he preferred to consider them, misdirections from her son.

"Let her know you have hired the drafters, and if you wish to, complain with her of my extravagance." Thus Penn ordered his wife to be lectured, and permitted her, if she chose, to side with his patroness against him. He may have understood the Exalt Benandi, but as yet he knew very little of Felin. This seemed to him all it was necessary to say, and he was nearing the end of the page, so he reminded her again that he hoped to be with her for dinner in two days' time, that is the fourth day of the first week of the month of Leafturn. He added his best wishes to her and to the children. Then, feeling quite pleased with himself, he sealed the letter, directed it, and had Amer take it down to add to the mail that would be collected from Agornin Station that evening.

13. PENN AND SELENDRA LEAVE

Illustrious Daverak flew to Agornin the next morning, as had been arranged. His intention was to take formal possession of the demesne and to escort Haner home with him to Daverak. He arrived not long after the family had breakfasted, a melancholy affair, for now that parting was so close the two sisters were inclined to weep whenever they caught sight of one another. They all gathered on the ledge when they had finished eating, and although the clouds were low, they soon caught sight of Daverak beating steadily towards them.

"I wonder that he has not brought Berend with him," Selendra said. "It would give more of an air of legitimacy to this whole affair."

Penn turned on her angrily.

"Unlike the division of his body, this is what our father wished," Avan interposed before his brother could speak.

"I know," Selendra said, bowing her head submissively. "I won't be rude to him, and didn't mean to be now, it's just everything's so different and I feel like crying all the time." Haner put a wing around her sister and the brothers left the pair to weep together until Daverak landed.

"Good day, brother," Penn greeted him. "Did you have a good flight?"

"The winds were quite strong, but they will be with us going back," Daverak said. It was a flight of a little more than an hour to Daverak, perhaps twenty miles if distances might be measured in the air.

"Did Berend not want to struggle with the winds both ways?" Haner asked.

"No, she didn't." Daverak smiled and looked away in the direction of his distant demesne. "She has just discovered that she is in a delicate condition, and did not want to leave home at this time."

"With egg already?" burst out Selendra, unable to hide her astonishment.

"Yes, thanks be to Veld," Daverak said, nodding politely towards Penn as he mentioned the god, as if acknowledging that he was infringing a little upon the other dragon's territory and graciously asking permission.

Barely four years had passed since Berend's first clutch of three. Even Penn who, as a parson, had to preach that increase was Veld's blessing, felt a little taken aback at this news and the evident satisfaction which Daverak took in it.

"You will have your caves full of dragonets," Haner said, brightly, feeling the pause in the conversation grow too long.

"We certainly hope so." Daverak inclined his head. He had never paid much attention to his wife's sisters, but he was glad now that it was Haner he was taking into his establishment. Though he had not shown it, he had not liked Selendra's outburst at all.

"Is Berend well?" Avan asked.

"Thriving so far," Daverak said. "Making sure to eat all the right things, of course, as you would expect. She feels quite experienced now, of course, not nervous like last time."

Although she was their sister, none of them liked to ask if she had already laid the first egg, nor did Daverak volunteer the information. It was also impossible for any of them to accuse him of risking the life of their sister by forcing her to produce another clutch so soon after the first, though this was in all their thoughts.

"Well, we should be going if we are to catch our train," Penn said, breaking another awkward pause. It was as yet far too early for the train, but it provided an excuse for Selendra to depart to gather her belongings, and Haner to accompany her. The three male dragons sat a while and looked at the view in silence. It was raining.

"I must speak to the farmers about the crops for this year and next year," Daverak said, looking at the fields. It was his duty and old Bon's wish, but both of Bon's sons felt that it was insensitive of Daverak to be thinking about this already.

"Will you have a bailiff live here to supervise the Agornin farmers?" Penn asked.

"Yes, we thought that would answer for the time being," Daverak said. "I have a cousin who would do well. We considered asking you, Avan, but Berend thought you were doing well enough in your career in Irieth that being bailiff of your father's estate would be a step down for you."

"Yes," Avan said, mechanically. While it was true that his career was prospering, as far as gold and prospects went, he had no security whatever and could be snapped up at any time. A secure job as a bailiff under his brother-in-law's protection would prevent him continuing his career, but he could still hope to rise by making judicious investments with his friends in Irieth. It would enable him to give his sisters a home together. He would need to bring his clerk to join him, but that could be managed somehow, he thought, glossing over the difficulties such a thing would cause. It would have been better if Daverak had suggested this before, he would have to give up his intention of a lawsuit. At once a whole edifice of complicated interlocking plans set itself in motion in Avan's nimble brain. "I think on the whole that it would suit me very well, all the same. Thank you, Daverak."

Daverak blinked slowly. "I am sorry you feel like that, we were sure you would not want it. I have offered it already to my cousin Vrimid, who will arrive at Daverak today." He made a wing motion of slight regret, and put down his foot as if that closed the matter entirely.

Selendra came back to find Avan sitting drawn up sejant, and glowering, Daverak sprawled out, indifferent, and Penn, uneasily couchant, between them. "I am ready," she said.

"Let us go then," Penn said. "There's no need for any of you to come down with us. Good-bye, Daverak, blessings on your increase, and give my best wishes to Berend. Good-bye, Avan, and good luck in Irieth, write and tell us how things are for you."

Selendra embraced Avan.

"Take care of yourself," he said.

"You be careful in Irieth," she replied. Then she bowed to Daverak, which he returned coldly. Haner accompanied them to the station, fussing over the boxes that contained Selendra's dowry and the boxes Amer had brought from the kitchens until the train came. Then she and Selendra clung together as if they would refuse to be parted. Penn and the porters saw to the stowing of the boxes, then Penn hopped up onto the flat bed of the train. Amer followed him up. The whistle blew, warning the tardy that the train was about to depart, and at last Selendra let go of her sister and flew up to her own place beside her brother. She watched until Haner was quite out of sight on the platform behind her, until she could not make out the gold of her sister's scales from the gray of the stone, then she set her head resolutely towards the engine and the new life she would find in Benandi.

14. HANER LEAVES

After even the plume of steam from the train was quite out of sight, Haner turned and flew back up to Agornin. She tried to console herself that she was not, like Selendra, going quite away to a part of Tiamath she had never seen before and where she had no friends. She would only be at Daverak, hardly an hour's flight from home any time she might find someone willing to escort her on such a flight. She had visited Berend at Daverak on several occasions, sometimes for as much as ten days at a time, and she knew Daverak well, while Penn's wife was a stranger. They were not very consoling reflections. She might know the Illustrious Daverak, but she did not like him. She had spent time in his establishment, but she had never felt at home—the greatest pleasure in visiting Berend was returning home afterwards. Now there would be no home, and if she visited Agornin it would be as a guest, and everything in the establishment would be changed.

Those of her family who loved her and cared about her seemed to believe that she would soon leave Berend's establishment for one of her own with Dignified Londaver, a friend of Daverak's. Haner herself doubted it strongly. She liked Londaver, but their association thus far was limited to two dances at Daverak last Year's End, since which time he had not even come to call at Agornin, though she had asked her father to invite him. She did not think his preference for her was sufficiently strong that he would take her with only eight thousand crowns, nor even the sixteen she would have if she and Selendra considered themselves to have pooled their resources. Londaver was not a Dignified by rank, as Bon Agornin had been, but was Dignified by nature of being heir to his father's Illustrious status. Berend had taken forty thousand crowns with her when she married, and Haner had no reason to imagine that Londaver would accept less than Daverak had. While her father was alive and there was plenty of time for him to accumulate more gold, this was no obstacle. Now it seemed that in addition to her other sorrows it had loomed up to divide Haner forever from a dragon she felt she could have been happy to marry.

Small wonder then if her wing-beats were half-hearted as she rose up from the station and back around the mountain to the place she must learn not to call home!

Only Avan awaited her. "Daverak has gone off to see the farmers and make sure they understand him," he said, imitating Daverak's tones cruelly. "As if our farmers need that kind of telling."

"Oh dear," Haner said, alighting gently beside her brother and settling herself comfortably sejant beside him. "I do hope he doesn't introduce too many new ways of doing things and change everything."

Now Avan, as a rising young dragon in Irieth, was in general in favor of new ways of doing things and change, but in this instance he agreed with his sister absolutely. "He says he thought of installing me as bailiff here, but as soon as he said it he snatched it away from me again, saying he had offered it already to some cousin of his."

"But you said you couldn't live here," Haner said, timidly.

"I couldn't live here and take a place as Dignified in the neighborhood. But with Daverak's backing and as his bailiff I could have overseen the place and made a home here for the two of you."

"Oh Avan, you'd have sacrificed yourself and your career for us," Haner said, much moved.

Avan preened himself a little, seeming to grow longer in the sunlight. Now she mentioned it, he would have been sacrificing himself for his sisters, although he did not forget that he need not have quite given up his hopes and that the safety of the position had also been a factor in his considerations. He allowed those to recede into the back of his mind and enjoyed his sister's admiration as she made much of him. They remained on the ledge and talked of Avan's nobility, and old times, and idly watched a cart creeping towards them along the river road.

"That will have come from Daverak to take back your dowry," Avan said at last, indicating the cart.

"How I wish I did not have to go there," Haner said.

"It might be awkward for you when I am taking Daverak to court on all our behalfs," Avan admitted.

"Awkward? It will be impossible. I cannot put my name to any such paper while I am living under Daverak's protection," Haner said. "Selendra will no doubt join with you, and I do see that you are quite in the right to seek reparation, but please don't ask me to help you."

"He might make himself unpleasant, but he wouldn't throw you out," Avan urged.

"He wouldn't need to throw me out to make himself so unpleasant, as you put it, that I couldn't live in his establishment. I don't think you realize how different it is for me than for you. You can make your way by your own wits and claws, while I must always be dependent upon some male to protect me. Wits I may have, but claws I am without, and while hands are useful for writing and fine work they are no use in a battle. Without them I am completely dependent, and may not turn on those upon whom I am dependent, at least, not without some other protection in prospect. If I had a husband, or if you, my brother, could receive me into your establishment, then I could turn on Daverak with pleasure. As it is I must bend to his whims, whatever my own wishes are, and dare not join you."

Avan bowed his head very low, considering some sacrifices it would be very difficult for him to make. "It would not be an easy life," he said, after a moment. "It would also be difficult for me, and could not happen quite at once, not at any rate today. But if you truly do not wish to go to Daverak I will take you to Irieth with me. You could not live as the Respected Agornin should, for I could not afford to support you in that way. You would need to work in place of my clerk, or possibly beside my clerk. Nor can I say it would be truly safe, for you would only be as safe as I am, which varies from day to day as affairs in the city and the office change. It would mean some hardship for both of us, but I am prepared to endure that if necessary." He hardly knew what Penn would think of him, suggesting on one day that Selendra might become a consort and on the next that Haner might become a clerk.

"Bless you, brother, but it isn't necessary," Haner said, kissing Avan on the side of his muzzle. "I can endure to live with Berend and Daverak, as long as you do not ask me to join with you in attacking Daverak in the courts."

"Of course I shall not ask it," Avan replied. "It is

only that my case will seem a lot weaker if the three of us do not stand together. But I shall not ask it if that is how things stand."

They sat together sadly for a little while more, until Daverak came back, full of his own importance. The boxes of Haner's dowry were loaded onto the cart, and brother and sister bade each other farewell.

"Do come and see us at Daverak any time you can get away from Irieth," Illustrious Daverak said generously as they made ready to depart.

Avan assented pleasantly, but he and Haner knew that once the court case began the offer would be withdrawn and never repeated. He wondered for a moment if it was worth the cost of dividing him from his sister, even if it could succeed without Haner's help. Yet Avan was so set upon getting revenge in this way that nothing could turn his purpose. He smiled and wished them a pleasant journey. Then he rose up and flew against the wind for Irieth, intending to break his journey that night at Mosswindle. Haner and Daverak went with the wind, west towards Daverak. Haner looked back only once, to see her brother dwindling south and the peak that had been her home already almost lost among the clouds.

15. SEBETH

When Avan returned at last to his lodgings in the capital, late on the evening of Firstday, tired, but not as weary as he would have been if he had flown through the night, he found a great many cards and notes awaiting him. Many were from his acquaintance in the city—Exalt Rimalin had sent a very friendly note—expressing their sorrow at his loss. Some of these were genuine enough, for though few of them knew Bon Agornin, they were sympathetic in their friend's loss. Others were more speculative, as if they rather intended to reassess Avan's worth now that he had inherited, or now that Agornin no longer stood behind him. Some of these made him uneasy, and these he laid to one side to consider when he woke. The rest, and this included most of the cards, were invitations to entertainments. Irieth was not crowded at the beginning of Leafturn, but those who lived there all year enjoyed a little burst of jollification at that time, which was the anniversary of the founding of the city, many thousand years before, by the ancient and possibly mythical Tomalin the Great. (Some said he had named Irieth after his bride, others argued that it had first had a different name which had been changed during the Yarge Conquest, others said that Tomalin had named it for the rainbows, sometimes called riths, that could be seen in the city in the spring months.) Such exotic offerings as unison flamings, water parties, and circuit walking thus joined the usual delights of dinners, balls, dice-evenings, rout-parties, and picnics, and to many of these Avan was bidden.

When he had dealt with this weight of correspondence, he had four piles and three notes left over. The first two piles consisted of notes of sympathy divided by sincerity. The second two were cards of invitation, divided into those to which he would return polite but negative thanks, owing to his bereavement, and the much smaller pile which he would certainly attend. He kept the remaining three notes in his hand for a moment. The first was from his attorney, Hathor, offering any help that might be needed with storing or investing Avan's inheritance. "I'd bet a farm that he knows the amount to the last crown," Avan said to himself, setting the note on top of the pile of invitations which he would accept. The second was from Liralen, his immediate superior in the Planning Office, offering condolences and wondering when Avan would be back at his desk.

The third was from the Exalted Rimalin, and said nothing whatsoever of Bon Agornin but merely hinted, rather cryptically, that if Avan had any money to invest, he knew of an opportunity. Avan looked at this note for a long time, then sought the note of sympathy from Exalt Rimalin. There was no doubt that they were written in the same hand. When a dragon uses his wife as his clerk, it means one of two things. Either he is economizing, which, as Avan had explained to Penn, would not have been how he would have read his friend's situation at all, or he is dealing in very confidential information. Avan would have listened to Rimalin's proposition in any case, but now he would listen to it very much more carefully.

He left the piles where they were. His lodging was a comfortable double-domed building, made of stone that at least gave the appearance of solidity. Underneath, there was only one sleeping cave, which, however, had an exit of its own to the street. Avan did not consider the place secure, but it did manage to combine respectability and inexpensiveness, so he kept his valuables with his attorney and continued to lodge there.

He whistled as he went down towards the sleeping cave, not from any lightness of heart but to wake his clerk, Sebeth, and give her a little warning, if such might be necessary, that he was returning and would expect to find her alone. Avan called Sebeth his clerk, but it would have been hard to say what her status really was. Certainly she performed the functions of a clerk, she wrote Avan's notes and carried his messages, she was educated enough to act as a respected maiden clerk. But she was of no Respected status and was for that matter no maiden, she was head to toe an even eggshell pink. She shared Avan's quarters, and often enough his bed, though she was not his wife. She cared for his clothes and his food, but she was not his servant—her wings showed some sign of having been bound at some time, but they flexed now as freely as those of any Exalt in Tiamath. The truth of her history and condition only she and Avan knew.

She was alone in the sleeping cave when Avan reached it, stretching and yawning. "I didn't expect you until tomorrow," she said, smiling at him. Avan knew better than to inquire if there had been some friend visiting who had left at his arrival. The whistle was sufficient. He did not know whether her other lovers were real or part of her imaginative life, and as long as he was not forced to meet them he was happy that way.

Sebeth welcomed him into the sleeping cave. She had arranged the gold already, he noticed. "This won't be staying here," he warned. He had not enough gold to spare for comfort or display, and they generally slept on rocks.

"I know, it'll all be invested and taken away." Sebeth pouted, then laughed. "But we can enjoy it while we can. See how delicious it is to stretch out on?" She suited the action to the words, smiling enticingly.

Sebeth was, or claimed to be, the daughter of an Eminent Lord—not even Avan knew which one. Counting up the nobility and their ages, he sometimes suspected it may have been an Exalted or an Illustrious rather than an Eminent, but he did not challenge her illusions. She had little enough to comfort her. At an early age, scarcely thirty years, with her wings barely grown, she had been kidnapped when on her way from her tutor's to her father's demesne. The kidnapper held her for ransom. He tormented her with his presence, causing her to blush, but he did not dare actually assault her until the ransom demand was scornfully refused. Thereafter he made her something which it pleased him to call his consort. Later, he forced her to walk the streets of

Irieth with bound wings, a streetwalker who could refuse no stranger who offered her gold. This gold she was forced to hand over to her captor. The worst of it was, she had told Avan, that he had made her believe that she owed it to him, because the ransom had not been paid. The betrayal of her father was almost worse to her than the subsequent servitude to which her family had left her to be subjected. "He said he had dragonets enough and that they were welcome to keep me," she said when she first told Avan the story. For once there was no artifice in her voice, no teasing, her sapphire eyes were almost still. "I stayed with my captor until I had paid him back, by my calculations, the ransom he had expected. Then I killed him while he slept."

Whether she had in truth waited until she had repaid the ransom or until she had a more acceptable protector, Avan was not sure. Sebeth's life was full of daring escapes, murders, doomed lovers, and drama. He never knew what to believe, and sometimes the stories changed. He was quite sure she was gently born and kidnapped into servitude, but the details shifted with her moods. He had met her in his first year in Irieth, when she had been employed as a dealer at a gambling club. He had at first been fascinated, and been one of the many lovers she took now for her own choice, not for gold. From this they had progressed to friendship and an alliance, in which Avan gave her employment and his protection, such as it was. He did not call her his consort or wife, and he paid her for the clerkly services she performed. He paid her something more than that from time to time as it suited them both. Avan could not have married her. He was quite aware that she was no longer someone who could be considered respectable, and that however much of that had initially been by no fault of her own, the way she had chosen to continue to live was not one that could have been condoned by the respectable world. All the same, he was very fond of her, and it would have been a great sacrifice for him to put her aside had he brought Haner to Irieth as he had offered.

"Do you miss your father?" she asked, after a little while.

Avan had not had time to think about it. "Yes," he said, after a little consideration. "But almost worse than his death was the manner of his funeral, and the way my sister's husband Daverak went against all my father's wishes. I am going to take him to law and make him wish he had behaved as a gently born dragon should."

"Is he not a great dragon, and an Illustrious?" Sebeth asked. She laughed. "You'll get scant justice in the courts against one like him. You'd do better to save your gold and your animosity until you see a good opportunity to do him harm elsewhere."

Avan considered for a moment. "The courts are just," he said, hesitantly. He had never had much to do with them, but his father had always told him so. "I want revenge on Daverak this way. Besides, his rank is not so much more than mine, and he is married to my sister."

"If family feeling didn't restrain him in his offense, what way will it restrain him now?" Sebeth asked.

"The law will make him pay," Avan said.

"Well, if you believe that," Sebeth replied, and put her head down upon her arms and was, in any case to all appearances, immediately asleep.

16. THE PERILS OF CONSUMPTION

Haner's first shock on arrival at Daverak was to discover that little Lamerak had been devoured. "He was ailing all this year," Berend said, a single tear in her eye.

"The liver did him no good, the poor little chap couldn't hope to survive," Daverak said, shaking his head portentously. "Come in to dinner."

Haner found it hard to understand why, if Lamerak had managed to survive so long, he should have been allowed to be consumed now. True, it was a duty of a lord to cull even his own dragonet for the general improvement of dragonkind, but this case of consumption seemed terribly abrupt. It was during one of Berend's long rambling complaints later that evening about the strains of increasing that she thought she caught a glimmer of understanding. Berend needed additional sustenance, and Daverak had nursed the feeble hatchling along until it was clear he could be replaced. Haner prayed to Jurale to be forgiven for thinking such wicked thoughts of her own sister and brother-in-law, but what they said on the subject as the evening went on seemed to confirm rather than deny her suspicions.

After an uneasy night's sleep in the comfortable chamber her sister had provided, she breakfasted with the family. The dragonets were subdued and kept looking over their shoulders for their missing clutch-mate. Haner's heart softened towards them, especially as their parents seemed to care so little about their loss and tore at their breakfasts with enthusiasm. She made an attempt to divert and entertain the children, with some success. By the end of the meal they were smiling and had eaten almost half a muttonwool between them.

"How do you feel this morning?" Daverak asked Berend. "I'm going to fly to the Causeway Farm and see how the Maje hatchlings are coming on. Would you care to accompany me?"

"It's very near," Berend said, with an apologetic glance to Haner, as if to excuse herself for not flying to Agornin on the previous day.

"Hardly more than a glide," Daverak confirmed. "Maybe you'd like to come with us, Haner? Get to know some of our farmers a little? See the countryside?"

"The Majes are a very old family," Berend said, glancing at her husband for confirmation. "They've lived in the Causeway Farm almost as long as the Daveraks have held Daverak."

Daverak inclined his head in confirmation of his wife's statements.

"I'd be delighted to accompany you," Haner said, politely.

Nannies came in and took the dragonets away. Daverak also went out. Haner sponged her face and chest in the dining room with Berend. This was the first time she had been entirely alone with her sister since her arrival. "Have you laid the first egg?" Haner asked, quietly, as she could not have asked in front of Daverak and the children.

"Yesterday morning," Berend said, with a smug little smile. "No difficulty at all, though I have been ravenous ever since. That's normal, as you'll see when you have a clutch for yourself."

"That might not be for some time," Haner said, wondering if she would ever be able to marry.

"It's lovely to have you here, of course, and I want you to feel perfectly at home and have a long stay with us. But all the same, before very long we must find you a nice husband and see you settled comfortably. It's much better to have the security. How much did Father leave you for a dowry in the end?"

"Sixteen thousand crowns," Haner said, as she had agreed, feeling tears coming to her eyes as the remembrance of her vow made her think of Selendra, so far away. Berend, kind as she was being, was a very poor substitute for her beloved clutch-mate.

"That's more than I feared, but not as much as I hoped," Berend said, briskly, drawing herself to her feet. "I'm well aware that it was my good fortune to be well dowered, and do not mean to see you marry beneath yourself because of that. Now hush, Daverak is coming back. We'll talk about this later."

Daverak led them to the ledge, and from there out into the cool fresh air of a sunny morning in Leaf-turn. The russets were ripe and the scent of them drifted up as they flew over the orchards. They flew towards the lake that was the center of the Daverak demesnes. It seemed almost the shape of a dragon's eye, though of a deeper blue and more still than any eye she had seen. As they drew near the shore Haner spotted a little island in the water, connected to the land by a causeway of heaped stone. There was a little farm on it, also of piled stone. As they circled lower to land she caught sight of a herd of beeves, with a bronze dragon among them.

"There's Maje," Daverak said. "I expect the family are inside."

They came boiling out as their lord and lady landed, even the youngest flattening their claws and tails to the ground in an old-fashioned gesture of respect. Haner counted three half-grown dragonets, well on their way to having wings, and two small hatchlings. "Well, well," Daverak said, smiling benignly.

A dark red dragon, clearly the mother of the family, was the first to straighten. "Welcome to the Causeway, Illust', Illustrious," she said.

"This is my sister, Respected Haner Agornin,"

Berend said. "She's come to stay with us for a little while."

"Very nice, I'm sure," said the farmer. One of the older dragonets, whose gold scales showed that she was a maiden, looked up at Haner. She smiled reassuringly, but the maiden did not smile back as any farmer at Agornin would have. Strangers everywhere, Haner thought.

Just then, the father, the bronze dragon who had been among the beeves, came running up, keeping himself low to the ground as if he were in a cave.

"How is everything here?" Daverak asked him.

"Very well, very well indeed, thank you for asking," he said. "The russets are half harvested already, and the beeves are doing nicely."

"And your hatchlings?"

He looked at his wife uncomfortably. "Safely hatched," he said, but the set of his wings betrayed his discomfort.

"And the other two?" Daverak asked sternly. "The two I don't see out here?"

The mother rushed forward and threw herself down at the ground at Daverak's feet. "Spare my hatchlings!" she cried, rubbing her head on the ground. "Have mercy, Illustrious."

"It is not I who will have mercy but Jurale," Daverak said, stepping away from her. "I will see all four hatchlings, or I will see the unhatched eggs. Maje, take care of your wife."

Maje, the farmer, looked at Daverak for a moment. His gray eyes whirled with emotion. He put his tail back straight, and for a moment looked almost as if he would attack Daverak, though that would be suicidal. He was twelve feet long and Daverak forty. His stance subsided to subservience.

"I told you it would do no good, not after last time," said Maje, putting his arm around his wife and drawing her aside. She began to howl and cry loudly.

Daverak stalked over to the smaller hatchlings on the ground and began to examine them.

Berend stepped closer to Haner. "The lower classes always make this unseemly fuss," she said. "It can be quite heart-rending. They've hidden the weaklings, even though they know it won't achieve anything. The two out here will be the stronger ones, and the others will be hidden somewhere in there."

Daverak entered the house. The two dragonets he had inspected clung together in silence.

"Shouldn't the priest be here?" Haner asked. She was shaken by the experience, especially by the wretched howling of the mother, which showed no signs of ceasing.

"The demesne's too big for him to go everywhere. Daverak will send him the eyes," Berend explained.

Daverak came out with a hatchling under each arm. They were small and green and clearly not fit to survive. Their mother set up a renewed wail at the sight of them, louder than ever. They were still moving, and responded to this with piping wails of their own, with which their healthier siblings joined.

Haner shivered. "I'm sorry to subject you to all this," Berend said, politely.

"It is for the good of dragonkind, as the Church teaches," Haner said, repeating the words by rote. "And they're very clearly the kind of dragonets who really do need to be culled," she added, looking at them.

"Nobody enjoys it, but it is necessary, and well-bred dragons endure it without this terrible racket," Berend said, shouting to be heard.

The howling and wailing almost drowned out Daverak's recitation of the prayers. Haner heard an occasional phrase drifting through, "Veld's blessings," and "Jurale's mercy," and "that the rest might grow stronger." Daverak then dismembered the dragonets neatly. Once they were dead, the family fell silent. He dropped the eyes into a pouch, doubtless for the priest. Then he looked at the collected dragons.

"These unfit hatchlings died for the good of dragonkind and according to the teachings of the Church," he said, sternly. Maje touched his claws to the ground in submission. His wife bowed her head. Daverak dropped two of the tiny limbs on the grass in front of the family. He handed another to Haner, who took it in surprise, and divided the remainder between himself and Berend, giving Berend almost all of one of the dragonets.

Haner looked at the leg hesitantly, aware of the eyes of the family on her as she put it to her mouth. They had not yet touched their portion. She took a bite, and at once felt the strong magical taste of dragonflesh burning through her, making her feel immediately longer and braver. She met the eyes of the mother, and saw in their whirling purple depths resentment, grief, and fear.

5
EXALT BENANDI'S DEMESNE

Felin Agornin stepped out of her home, arched her neck, leaned forwards, spread her wings to the wind, and soared upwards. It was a beautiful day. The sun shone, the trees were still green, but there was a chill in the early morning air that said that the month was Leafturn and that winter would soon be upon them.

It was the morning before Penn and Selendra left Agornin, the morning on which Felin had received her husband's letter informing her of the addition to their household he had arranged. She had received the letter at breakfast and her emotions had chased each other over her countenance swiftly as she read it. She had been pleased and surprised to hear from Penn, then increasingly distressed by the news of the letter as it continued. Another servant! Another servant who had been Penn's old nanny and would be full of herself and her importance to him and to his sister! Felin was ready to do her best to welcome Selendra into her establishment, but she wanted it to be quite clear it was her establishment into which Selendra was entering. Selendra was Penn's sister whom they were choosing to feed and shelter and protect. She did not want abject gratitude, but she did want the facts to be recognized. If Selendra was bringing her own servant it quite changed the position in which she would be regarded. Felin was not deceived by Penn's words about Amer being useful with the dragonets and in the kitchens. An old family retainer arriving with Selendra would be seen as Selendra's servant, whatever other work she did. Worst of all, her husband expected her to break the news to Exalt Benandi.

In the invisible court in her head Felin arraigned, tried, and convicted her absent husband of cowardice, extravagance, and folly. But even as she set the letter down she knew she would never reveal this judgment to anyone, least of all to Penn himself. Nor, as he had suggested she should, would she side with Exalt Benandi against him. Had she wanted to do so, she would not have waited for his permission, but she would never do anything of the kind. She knew what a wife owed to a husband, even if he did not. She sent a servant at once to order the drafters for the next day, checked that the nanny had the children well in hand, and, not putting off the unpleasant task for a moment longer than was necessary, stepped out to visit Exalt Benandi.

Benandi was a great place, much bigger than all of Undertor, and it was all the demesne of the Exalted Benandi. The name of Benandi was used for the whole demesne, stretching for several hours flight in all directions. In the center of the domain lay the mountain establishment that was the chief home of the Exalt, and of her son when he was home, which generally meant only those months of spring and autumn when the hunting was good. This establishment was known as Benandi Place.

Benandi Place was a complicated honeycomb of caves at the top of a cliff. Benandi Parsonage lay almost at the foot of this cliff. The parson (whoever he might be, for the parsonage, as usual, went with the position), had easy access to the ground, and a passage up within the rock connecting his dwelling with that of his patrons. There was a splendid chapel a little in the old style within Benandi Place, where the Exalt generally heard a Firstday evening service. In the morning she preferred to attend the church (which was dedicated to Sainted Gerin, but known to all as Benandi Church) conveniently located downwind in the valley. With many of our gentry who have chapels of their own but who prefer to attend divine service in public, the impulse springs from a desire to be seen, or to be seen to do one's duty, or sometimes simply from a dislike of the early rising required to have a service in the chapel, which must necessarily occur before the one in the church. With the Exalt, however, everyone knew it was rather that she desired to see everyone else doing their duty in church. If she did not see any of her farmers, or indeed her neighbors, in church on a Firstday morning, she regarded it as part of her duty to visit them within a day or two and inquire into the matter. The dragons in the neighborhood of Benandi Place were thus much given to admirably regular and punctual churchgoing.

Felin could have used this Parson's Passage and walked up through half a mile of tunnels, past the chapel, and into the upper caves of Benandi Place. As she was not a parson, she could choose to fly instead. She never walked up except on Firstdays, and on the rare occasions, generally when the Exalted Sher Benandi was in residence, when she was taking her dragonets to visit the Place. Sher liked children. The Exalt did not care for the disorder they could cause. On almost all other occasions when Felin visited the Place, even when Penn was walking up, she caught an updraught from the parsonage ledge and simply glided up the cliff. Felin loved to fly, loved it, that is, when she had the excuse for it. She never neglected any of her duties in favor of flying. But there was no joy to her like that of feeling the wind in her wings. She banked gently and rose in a lazy spiral, hardly moving out from the cliff at all, for she knew the winds very well, and landed on the ledge of the Place with hardly a jolt.

"Well flown," said an unexpected voice.

"Sher!" said Felin, turning in astonishment. The Exalted Sher Benandi was lying couchant along the ledge, the burnished bronze scales of his sixty-foot length shining in the morning sunlight. "I mean Exalted Benandi," Felin corrected herself in a little confusion. "I had not known you were home."

"Oh, good hunting to you, Blest Agornin, if we must be on such terms, which I say we should not. I have called you Felin and you me Sher since we were little wingless dragonets crawling around together. As for not knowing I was here, do not you say you are here to see my mother and will have none of me," Sher said, dropping his jaw in an absurdly exaggerated leer.

Felin laughed, a spontaneous chuckle that seemed to rise from her toes. She did not think it appropriate in a parson's wife to laugh like that, but she had, as he said, known Sher since they were dragonets. "I am delighted to see you, just surprised, that's all. I saw your mother only yesterday and she didn't tell me you were expected."

"Does she keep you dancing attendance every day?" Sher asked, disapprovingly, then went on without waiting for an answer. "Well the truth is I came on the flick of a wing. My visit was proving damnably dull, and I thought a little rest at home would be pleasant."

"Would prove restorative after a debauch, you mean," Felin countered, though as she spoke she wished she could catch it back. Sher did look tired, not just weary after his long flight but worn as if from troubles.

Sher laughed, dutifully. "My mother was pestering me," he said.

Felin smiled, disbelieving, knowing how well Sher had learned to ignore and bamboozle his mother. "She must be very pleased to see you now," she said.

"She would have been happier if she'd had a month to prepare," Sher said, ruefully. "I've come out here to escape from all the preparation being done at once now I am here, even if it is to result in the most comfortable gold in my bed and all my favorite dishes for dinner. No doubt you'll be invited."

"Not today, for Penn is still away."

"Away? When it was Firstday but three days ago and will be Firstday again in another two? What was my mother thinking to allow that?"

Bon's death had loomed so large in Felin's life she had forgotten there could be anyone who did not know it, and was taken aback for a moment by Sher's teasing. "The Exalt did have to manage without Penn for one Firstday, though he arranged for Blessed Hape to come out to take the service in the church. But his father was dying, and has died, so she had to agree."

"Old Bon has died? I'm very sorry to hear that," Sher said, his big dark eyes suddenly remorseful. "I don't suppose you knew him well, but he was a wonderful old dragon, rock of the mountains. I visited Agornin several times when I was in school. What's to become of the place? Penn can't take it, of course, can his little brother?"

"No, though old Bon hoped to live long enough that he could," Felin explained. "Avan, the brother, isn't up to it, so it'll be managed by the Illustrious Daverak who is married to Penn's hatch-mate Berend, and at last go to one of their children."

"I remember Berend," Sher said, smiling. "I see her from time to time up in Irieth, where she acts the haughty Illust' with me as if I'd never chased her down a mountain when she was learning to fly. All the same, that's sad about Agornin. Penn should have said, I might have been able to help his brother. Too late now."

This offer of help when once it was too late to be of use seemed to Felin so characteristic of Sher that she could not answer it. "I must see your mother," she said.

18. THE EXALT

If the inside of Benandi Place was not in quite the disorder Sher had represented, this was because his mother was a remarkable housekeeper. Felin, accompanied by Sher, made her way with accustomed ease through the maze of the upper caverns to find Exalt Benandi in her own office, near the kitchens.

On most mornings, the Exalt would have been delighted to see Felin. Felin was a favorite of hers, insofar as the Exalt allowed herself favorites. The Exalt certainly took a fond interest in Felin and approved of her as much as she approved of anyone. She herself had helped to bring Felin up, and had arranged her marriage to Penn. Felin was no relation to the Benandis. Her father, a dragon of gentle birth but small means, had been a comrade-in-arms of the Exalt's late husband, Exalted Marshal Benandi. At

about the time of Felin's hatching they had been together in a skirmish on the Yarge frontier, and both
been wounded. Felin's father had died of his wounds
almost immediately. The Marshal had recovered to
some extent, but retired home, leaving the border
to be defended by younger dragons. In bringing the
news of his friend's demise to his grieving widow and
dragonets (the news was all he could bring, for the
body had already been consumed by his comrades,
as remains the immemorial custom of armies) he
discovered them living in some distress. The kind-
hearted old Marshal brought them home to Benandi
and provided them with a small establishment of
their own. Felin's brother unfortunately fell sick and
was consumed shortly afterwards, but the mother
and daughter continued to live under Exalted Marshal Benandi's protection until his death.

Exalt Benandi had begun by resenting her husband's kindness to these strangers, had little by little
come to manage it for him, and had at last become as
genuinely fond of Felin as she was of anyone beyond
her only son, Sher. There had been times, especially
in the years after Felin's mother's death, when the
Exalt had treated Felin almost like a daughter. A little coolness had grown between them when Sher was
at the Circle, for it appeared on his return visits to
Benandi that Sher might be developing an unfortunate tenderness towards his companion. This coldness had been dispelled and replaced with a greater
warmth than before when Exalt Benandi realized

that her ward was doing the best she could to gently discourage her son. The Exalt had then made plans to find a suitable marriage for her ward—in what the Exalt considered to be her own station in life. Penn, Sher's schoolfriend and companion at the Circle, was taking vows of priesthood and, to the Exalt, looked eminently suitable. Benandi was bound to support a parson of its own, and by good fortune the position had fallen vacant. The Exalt persuaded her son to invite Penn down for a long visit. Once he was there, she made sure to give him plenty of chance to fall in love with Felin. Unsurprisingly, for Penn was a serious-minded dragon and already of an age to settle down, Felin and Penn became attached. Once a betrothal was accomplished, Exalt Benandi offered him the living, permitting them to marry at once. She would have reacted with horror if anyone had suggested that she had acted so improperly as to dower Felin, but the effect was much the same nonetheless.

This morning, however, the Exalt was busily engaged on organizing the establishment for her son's comfort, and she did not want to be interrupted by anyone, least of all the son whose comfort she was considering and who had by this unexpected arrival considered hers so little. "Sher, I thought you were settled outside for a time? Good morning my dear," she added to Felin.

"Good morning, Exalt, I won't disturb you long," Felin said, kissing the Exalt's proffered cheek. Exalt

Benandi was the dark red of a damask rose, while
Felin was the color of an evening sky that betokens
fine weather. The sight of their cheeks together made
Sher feel an unwonted pang. He remembered the
brief time in which he, though hardly considered
adult, had not treated Felin like a sister. For a moment he wished, or he almost wished, that he had a
pink-scaled wife of his own to salute his mother like
that and perhaps to greet him in the same way. For
years, ever since he had left the Circle, he had been
content to fritter away both his time and his gold.
Now he was reaching an age where this contented
him less than it had. He wanted to be building up
gold in his sleeping chamber and not scattering it in
idle amusements, making a home and guarding his
demesne and enlarging it if he could. His mother had
always warned him that one day he would want to
settle down, yet he was amazed, as all dragons who
are fortunate enough to live so long are amazed, that
the impulse had come upon him at last.

"Bless you, Felin, for I have a thousand things to do
today," the Exalt said, pushing away a letter she was
writing.

"I wanted to come up to tell you that Penn will be
home tomorrow by the afternoon train."

"I will have them send the carriage," said Exalt
Benandi, making a note at once.

"He wrote telling me to hire extra drafters to bring
him from the station, for in addition to his sister he is
bringing home one of the servants."

"She is bringing her own attendant?" the Exalt asked, rolling her eyes a little. "That sort of pretension is not at all what I would have expected of one of Bon Agornin's daughters."

"Selendra is a good quiet maiden from all Penn says of her," Felin said, pushing away her real thoughts on the subject of Amer and Selendra and speaking the part Penn had set her. "The servant is for all of us, for the household. It will be useful to have more help around the place now the dragonets are not hatchlings anymore. It will be so much more convenient having this servant that Penn knows and trusts than training one up, or hiring one who is a stranger to us all."

"There is never any cause to hire a strange servant at Benandi," the Exalt said, jumping at this bait as Felin had known she would. "I would have provided you with a farmer's daughter who only needs training in your ways, whose parents would have been glad to see her going to such a situation. I could have done that in an instant if you had only let me know you were thinking about taking another servant." The Exalt believed Felin really had been considering taking another servant, as she would never have believed Penn had he told her the same story.

"I had hardly got beyond thinking of it when I found the difficulty settled in this way," Felin said, spreading her hands deprecatingly.

"Well, I hope she is a well-trained and obedient servant," the Exalt said. "I shall examine her when

I have the chance. I'm quite astonished that Blessed Agornin thought it worthwhile to hire drafters to bring them from the station. It's no distance. Twelve miles, no more. The servant could have walked and his sister could have flown. The extravagance of it."

"No doubt old Penn can afford a drafter or two," Sher said, smiling at Felin in a way that let her know that he recognized all her, or rather Penn's, stratagems for dealing with his mother.

"No doubt he can, but is it prudent?" the Exalt asked. "Is it something he would have done if he had considered? Gold saved today may be the salvation for the family tomorrow. If Felin's poor father had saved his army pay his family would not have needed to have lived on our charity all those years."

"Surely the hire of a few drafters won't mean Penn's dragonets starving in the road," Sher objected.

"It is not one thing, but many things taken together," his mother replied, icily, for this was a lesson she wished she had taught him better when he was a dragonet.

"Penn is never extravagant in the general way," Felin said, loyalty to her husband again overriding the voice of her private judgment. "I have ordered the drafters as he asked me."

"A parson should set an example," the Exalt said.

"I'm sure taking in an old servant is setting a good example," Sher said.

"Old? Not too old to work, I hope?" the Exalt pounced on the statement.

Felin frowned at Sher, who gave her an apologetic smile. "I don't know her precise age, but she can't be a young dragon as she was Penn's nanny. He says she is very experienced with dragonets," Felin added, hoping this might help deflect the Exalt.

"Sentimentality," the Exalt sniffed. "I hope she doesn't turn out a burden to you, Felin."

"I'm sure she'll be a great help," Felin said, though privately she agreed with the Exalt entirely.

"You must all three come to dinner tomorrow," the Exalt said. "Bring the servant up for me to meet beforehand, then we can send her back and Blessed Agornin can introduce me to the Respected Agornin in the dining room. We do want to make her feel at home among us. Poor maiden, it will be hard for her to go away from everything she knows. We must be kind and make her feel welcome."

"They will be arriving by the afternoon train," Felin said. "That might be a little late for dinner tomorrow, as you won't want to see them covered in dust from the railway. Might it be better to postpone it until the day after, and then I can bring Selendra up to meet you in the morning, which will be more comfortable than Penn presenting her at dinner?"

Exalt Benandi put her head on its side and stared at the wall for a moment. "Very well," she said, as if making a great concession. "But in that case you yourself must dine here this evening. I have seen nothing of you since Penn has been away, and to-night will be just family."

"Yes, do come, Blest Agornin, and save us from sitting down alone to dinner and doubtless murdering each other over the body of the swine," Sher added.

Felin choked, but attempted to contrive to look shocked rather than amused.

"None of us need your crude jokes here, Sher," the Exalt said. "They don't amuse us in the least."

"I'll leave you now and see you this evening, then," Felin said. She had achieved what her husband wanted, which had been her intention, and she did not wish to trespass on her patroness's time. Without the slightest idea of the effect it had on Sher, she kissed the Exalt's cheek again in leaving.

19. SHER'S PROSPECTS

The Exalt Benandi was not much given to thinking of those ancient days, much beloved by poets and songsters, in which dragons lived in caves on hilltops distant from each other and knew nothing of civilization. If anyone ever did mention anything to her from before the Yarge Conquest, she would generally lift her wings in a tiny indication of disdain. Yet she had heard, as who has not, many splendid, romantic and no doubt inaccurate songs about them, and one thing from them kept coming into her mind whenever she considered her son. In those days, young dragons who had grown into their wings would go off and have adventures, as young dragons still wish to do, but in those days the adventures would include amassing gold, not dissipating it.

In the eight or nine years since Sher had left the Circle, his constant extravagance had been a torment to her. Dragons customarily think in terms of hundreds of years, and when planning families and demesnes, often in thousands. It caused Exalt Benandi almost physical pain to see gold that had taken ten years to accumulate slip through her son's claws in one night at the gaming table. Young dragons will seek adventure, whether that is to be found by discovering princesses to carry off and knights to battle, or by hunting dangerous game all day and playing dice half the night. There are some, like Bon Agornin, and like, had she but known it, his younger son Avan, who even now manage to accumulate a fortune by taking risks in their wild years. There are rather more like Sher who part with one, scarcely knowing where the accumulation of centuries has gone.

Some parents attempt to harness the wildness of their sons by sending them into the army, which works well enough in time of war, but can be ruinous in peacetime in a fashionable regiment. Others organize tours of distant lands—but the romance and adventure that was once found in distant lands is today, alas, often the same rattle of the dicebox that can be found at home, but wielded by skillful Yargish fingers. Exalt Benandi had done neither but rather trusted to her son's good sense, and was beginning to come to the end of her trust in it when he returned home so unexpectedly that late summer morning.

She recognized his return as what it was. In the days of song, after fighting his battles and amassing his treasure, a strong young dragonlord would return to his demesne when he was ready to settle, generally bringing a bride with him. Even now this was often the pattern, it would be the prospect of some particular maiden that would tempt a dragon to settle down. Every mother of daughters dreamed that theirs would be the maiden to catch the eye of some eligible titled dragon who had reached this point in his life. Exalt Benandi gave thanks that she had never been the mother of daughters, and that she had reared just one son to disturb her peace. She had hoped that Sher's eye would be caught by no particular maiden, which it never had except for that childish passage with Felin, years ago. She had dreamed through all his wild years that when the urge came to settle down she would be able to pick out a pleasant, congenial daughter-in-law, with wealth and rank appropriate to her son's station.

What she wanted to do was something that would have been quite unthinkable in prehistoric times, not because the dragons then were less amenable to persuasion by their elders but because a mother surviving that long after the birth of a son would then have been something almost unknown. For years she had been visiting neighboring demesnes to meet the maidens of the families, and even going up to Irieth in the season and looking over each year's crop of daughters as they were presented. Sher had shown a supreme indifference to all this, and she had thus far let him go his way. Now, when he was showing indications of wanting to settle, was clearly the time to present him with the results of her work.

Exalt Benandi's favored maiden at the present moment was the Respected Gelener Telstie. This maiden was the niece of the present Eminent Telstie, so though she bore no high title of her own she came of excellent family. Her father was a parson, high in the hierarchy of the Church, very wealthy, and expected to be made a Holiness at the next opportunity. He had two sons to provide for in addition to Gelener, but as their Eminent uncle had no surviving children, one of them was expected to be adopted into the main branch of the family, leaving the other to go into the Church where their father had excellent influence. Gelener, the only daughter, was said to have a dowry of seventy thousand crowns. Besides that she was a prettily behaved maiden, and her mother, who was still alive, was one of Exalt Benandi's particular friends. Blest Telstie, the mother, was anxious to have Gelener well married, for her daughter had been seeking marriage for two years now and was proving hard to please. Above all things Blest Telstie wished for an alliance with Exalt Benandi and a title for her daughter.

Therefore the Exalt had that morning written to her old friend encouraging her to come and visit, bringing Gelener, and either stay herself or leave her daughter at Benandi for a long visit. It was this letter which Felin's visit had interrupted. Exalt Benandi took it up again as soon as her friend and her son had left her. If she had known that Sher was planning to come home she would have arranged the visit far in advance, so that it might seem like a chance meeting. That might have made things seem easier. Sher did not like to feel herded. Still, she was sure he was feeling broody and wishing to settle down. At this stage it seemed likely any beautiful young maiden— and Gelener was beautiful, with a cold perfection of beauty that was much admired in Irieth—would do to entice him.

Exalt Benandi finished the letter and sealed it. She had been much afraid that her son would bring home a stranger who would wish to turn her out of the house. At different times she had dreaded an August's daughter who would despise her, and an entertainer from the clubs whom she must despise. Seeing either being installed as Exalt would have blighted her old age. Gelener Telstie, with her beauty and her seventy thousand crowns, was someone she could share her home with, and therefore exactly what she wanted. And should Gelener not suit Sher for some sentimental reason—young dragons, she knew, were often sentimental, look at Penn bringing his old nanny home—then she had another half a dozen appropriate maidens on her short list.

20. THE TRAVELERS ARRIVE

It was the first time Selendra had traveled by train, and she found much in the first hour or so of the journey to interest and amuse her. After that, when the billowing steam of the engine and the drawing together of the tracks into the distance ceased to charm, the journey passed in a pall of tedium. Rail tracks, by the needs of their kind, must pass through the flattest and least picturesque parts of any landscape. While there are few parts of the Tiamath that are entirely flat, the route the train takes between Undertor and Benandi seemed to Selendra to pass through most of them. Conversation was not possible, because of the noise of the engine and the rattling of the carriages. Penn engaged himself with his books. Amer curled up on top of the chests of gold and slept, her head tucked under her wing. Selendra wished she had room to curl up beside her nanny. She read for part of the journey, but once she finished the novel she had chosen she soon tired of the improving book of essays Penn pressed on her.

She found it all painfully slow and wished she could soar above the train and settle back to it again as she saw some other passengers doing. This, of course, was impossible for a well-brought-up maiden, unless she had someone to accompany her, and for this purpose Penn and Amer with their bound wings were both perfectly useless.

She was delighted to reach Benandi Halt, but

disappointed to discover the carriage and the drafters waiting. Penn had said nothing to her about this arrangement. "I thought I could fly the rest of the way," she said. "It isn't far, and my wings are so stiff. I won't get lost, I can circle the carriage along the road."

"There's room for us all in the carriage," Penn said, helping Amer up. Amer looked stiff and weary, her legs could hardly bend.

"I see that there is, but I'd rather stretch my wings a little," Selendra said. "Oh please, Penn."

"I'd rather not begin our lives together with a quarrel," Penn said, and pressed his lips together. Selendra dutifully climbed into the carriage and perched herself as best she could between her brother and the chests. Amer again climbed on top of the boxes containing the dowry and immediately closed her eyes.

Felin had known the time the train was due. She had been waiting, and as soon as the smoke of its passage came in sight she took off from her doorstep and soared up high above to watch for the coming of the travelers. After a few moments of idly circling, leaning into the wind and letting it carry her around, scanning the ground for the carriage, she was joined by Sher.

"I was sitting out and I saw you up here," he said. "Are you neglecting your hatchlings for the joy of flight, or is there some exciting purpose bringing you up here? Ah, yes, there is the carriage crawling towards us. You have come up to welcome your husband, and I shall join you."

"Are you so bored already?" Felin asked.

Sher laughed. "I'll greet Penn before you do," he said, and folded back his wings in a dive. Felin did not hesitate an instant but swooped over him, catching the wind from his wings, and plummeted towards the carriage. She was less than half Sher's length, not thirty feet, but that was no disadvantage now as she hurtled downwards. Although he had started first they were neck and neck when they finally pulled up, just above the ground wind, and landed, with no breath for laughing, beside the carriage.

Selendra had met her sister-in-law only once, at Penn's wedding, when the only impression Felin had made on her had been as a delicate rose-pink maiden, half-buried in the lacy folds of her veil. She did not at first recognize her in this neat flame-colored vision swooping down to them. She had been looking up, and when she caught sight of two such beautiful dragons cavorting across the open sky as if it belonged to them, her heart filled with delight. Penn unfortunately recognized his wife immediately, and his old friend too. He clicked his tongue in disapproval. Flying out to meet them was all very well, racing down the wind with Sher was something else. The Exalt would not like it when she heard.

"Welcome home, Penn," Sher said, while Felin was still trying to catch her breath. "And my deepest condolences on the loss of your father."

"Thank you. I did not know you were here," Penn said, quite taken aback. He wanted to scold Felin, especially since he had prevented Selendra from flying, but felt he could not in front of so many dragons. Penn was tired and would have liked to rest before finding himself in society. Although Sher was his closest friend, he had never been able to forget the social chasm between them that yawned wider every year.

"I came yesterday. I didn't give my mother any warning, and yes, I know it's shockingly unfilial of me. And while we are speaking of my sins, let me apologize for tempting Felin into that dive. But by Veld it's good to see you again."

Penn spluttered for a moment, but could say nothing. Felin was smiling. The drafters plodded onwards and Felin and Sher walked beside the carriage. "Exalted Sher Benandi, allow me to introduce my sister, the Respected Selendra Agornin," Penn said, taking refuge in formality.

"Respected Agornin," Sher said, bowing to Selendra in full Cupola fashion. She only nodded back, having no idea how to react. "We have met," Sher went on. "But you were a wingless little grub when last I was in Agornin, showing no sign that you were about to transform into such a very lovely maiden."

Selendra could say nothing. She had been looking at Sher, and now she saw genuine admiration behind the stock compliment, which in itself was enough to unsettle her. To most young dragons it would have been very little, but for Selendra it was quite un-wonted. She had lived very quietly in Agornin and entered very little into what small society the place had to offer. She looked down in confusion. "It must have been a long time ago," she murmured, at last.

"Felin, my dear, you remember my sister Selendra?" Penn asked, passing on quickly.

"Of course," Felin said, smiling at Selendra. "We only met for a moment before, but I'm sure we're going to be very good friends."

"I hadn't realized you could fly so well," Selendra said, her admiration clear in her voice. "Especially considering the mountain and the crosswinds here. That was magnificent. I'm sure I could never do that."

"Oh, I've lived here since I was barely more than a hatchling," Felin said, flattered. "I know all the winds. But I'll take you up and introduce you to them, you'll soon get used to flying here."

"There are only a few places where there's anything challenging," Sher said. "Don't worry about Penn's bindings, Repected Agornin, Felin and I will show you where to fly. Do you hunt?"

"I never have. There isn't much hunting around Undertor. But I have always wanted to," Selendra admitted.

"I should have remembered that about Undertor. Penn was longing to hunt too, when he came here first, before he was a parson. Felin and I will have to take you up with us."

"You know I don't approve of female hunting,"

Penn said. "If Veld had meant them to hunt, he would have given them claws."

"Do you think they starved in the days before the Conquest?" Sher asked, heatedly, for this was a matter on which he had decided opinions. "Some of the best hunters in Tiamath are female, why last year I hunted beside Grevesa herself! It was weapons that drove off the Yarge after the Conquest, after our bare claws proved insufficient. And you surely don't mean to keep Felin in? She's been hunting since she could fly. No, she didn't hunt last year, and the last time I was here for the hunting before that she was increasing, but surely—"

"I have no wish to hunt now that I am married and a mother," Felin said, smoothly. Penn looked at her with gratitude. Sher stopped, she had taken the wind out of his wings for the second time that day.

Selendra bowed her head. She had always wanted to hunt, but she could see she was not going to be given the chance. She hoped her new life would not be too terribly restrictive. She consoled herself with the thought of poor Haner, bound for Daverak. Things could be much worse.

"I think I shall fly back to the parsonage and prepare a hot drink for your arrival," Felin said, into the little silence that had grown since she had disavowed any wish to hunt. "Will you come with me, Selendra?"

"Oh, gladly," Selendra said. She wriggled her way free of the carriage, past the still torpid form of

Amer, and rose up on the wind. Penn said nothing, having already learned the lesson of the give and take of managing his family.

Sher stayed with Penn and the carriage so Felin and Selendra were alone in the air. "I do love to fly," Selendra said, when they were away from the others. "I wanted to fly from the station, but Penn insisted I stay in the carriage."

"The winds can be tricky sometimes," Felin said, flying sedately as if she wished to make up for her earlier spectacular dive. "You'll be safe with me, but you might have had trouble alone. I'm sure dear Penn had your safety at heart, as he did about the hunting."

Selendra looked at her sister-in-law, ready to protest Penn's injustice, if she saw any slightest sign of alliance against him. She found none, for Felin had early in her marriage decided to hold with her promise to obey her husband, and also to support him. She hated to quarrel, and she genuinely liked Penn and did not find him excessively tyrannical. She liked to hunt, but would glory in doing without it rather than have strife in the house.

"Penn's old nanny was asleep," Felin said, wanting to establish Amer's status with Selendra as soon as she could. "I was hoping to speak to her about what she can do, but no doubt there will be time enough."

"Amer? She's been asleep almost all the way from home. From Agornin," Selendra corrected herself quickly. "You'll find she's very handy with dragonets, and also in the kitchen."

"We have a nanny, but she may well come in handy there," Felin said, glad that Selendra had not claimed Amer as her own assistant. She was cautious generally, but she thought she already liked her sister-in-law, for which she thanked merciful Jurale, as life would be so difficult if they disliked each other. "Speaking of the dragonets, mine are longing to see you," Felin said. "They've never had an aunt before, and they're on fire to know what you're like."

"I am greatly looking forward to meeting them," Selendra replied. But her heart sank a little at Felin's cheerful claiming of Amer and acceptance of restriction, and she felt a great wave of homesickness for Agornin. She was already terribly lonely for Haner.

6
AFFAIRS IN IRIETH

21. THE IMPORTANCE OF HATS

Avan woke with the sense of having slept soundly, as one does on gold. Beside him, Sebeth yawned delicately, her ladylike wing in front of her mouth. She settled back onto the gold and looked at Avan through half-lidded eyes.

Though he found her as alluring as always, Avan laughed and rose. "There's too much to do today," he said. "Later."

"But I'll be out this evening," Sebeth said, continuing to loll, her bright blue eyes revolving languorously. "Besides, part of what there is to do will doubtless be disposing of this delightful gold."

Avan didn't rise to the bait and ask her where she was going. He leaned over and kissed her. "You're adorable, and you're right, the gold isn't safe here. Besides, hired out it will grow."

"Frittered away on lawsuits it won't do anything," she said, sighing and getting up at last. "Shall I find you a hat?"

Now it was Avan's turn to sigh. He did not like hats. In the country, in summer, it is permissible to go about with any hat or none. Blessed parsons may be seen in battered old toppers, Respectable young ladies fly around bareheaded, and August ladies take to the skies in caps of tattered lace. Avan had been in Agornin for two weeks and hardly found occasion to put on any hat at all except to go to church. In Irieth, however, at any time of year, hats were obligatory for any dragon who wished to be thought gently born.

Sebeth opened the wardrobe, selected a hat, and offered it to Avan with a bow, like a personal attendant.

"Not that one," Avan said, frowning at the hat Sebeth held as if it were a rival he was about to devour.

"What's wrong with it?" Sebeth asked, turning the rejected hat in her hands to examine it. It was black leather, with a wide brim, narrow crown, and a black ribbon, appropriate for mourning and almost new. Sebeth had chosen it for Avan for an end of season promenade and he had worn it only twice.

"I need to fly, and that thing will come off in the first breeze and then where will I be?"

"To fly?" Sebeth echoed, and put her wing up to cover another yawn. "Fly where? Will I need to fly?" She picked up her own chosen hat, a confection of silken fruit with cream and lavender ribbons that looked as if it would fall off if she shook her head too vigorously.

"No, you can wear that pretty piece of froth," Avan said, indulgently, looking at it with his head on one side. He was sure he had not seen it before, but he felt no urge to inquire where she had acquired it or how she had financed the purchase. If the bill came to him he would pay it without saying anything.

Hats were a necessary extravagance. Since she was his clerk it was his responsibility to see that she was well dressed. If no bill came, he would know some-one else had paid for it. In such matters, as in so many others, he had learned that it was better for domestic harmony for him not to know. "You won't need to fly," he went on. "You should stroll in to the office and deal with anything you can. There are four piles of letters upstairs, sorted as usual. You can make a start on the polite regrets and thank you kindlys." Avan reached over Sebeth's shoulder to select a dark green end-of-summer cap which he thought combined fashion and practicality.

Sebeth blinked. "You're not going to the office?"

"I'll look in later," Avan said, settling the cap firmly between his ears.

"But what about Liralen and Kest? They'll be ex-pecting you."

"Tell Liralen I'll be in towards noon," Avan said, adjusting the strap. "It's none of Kest's business where I am, so let him wonder."

"Don't you think it would be wise to go in first?" Sebeth asked, her eyes beginning to turn more rapidly.

"No," Avan said. "I need to arrange for the gold, right away."

"Hathor?" Sebeth asked, turning to the bronze mirror and pinning her hat carefully at a jaunty angle.

"Of course," Avan answered. He didn't say anything

further about the lawsuit. She had already expressed her disapproval, and it wasn't her business.

She turned from the mirror to look straight at him. "There are those in the office who will seek to take advantage of your father's death," she said.

"Meaning Kest?"

"Not meaning anyone in particular, just that everyone will be reassessing where everyone else is standing now. It's a change, and a change that makes a real difference to your position." She looked away, closed the wardrobe, and picked up her office bag.

"I know," Avan said. "And that is a good reason for coming in nonchalantly late, a dragon with business to settle. If I scurried in the moment I was back in town, eager to catch up with whatever they've piled up for me to scratch through, they would see that as weakness." Avan smiled.

"You're right," Sebeth said. "You have the touch for making your way, you know how to behave. If I were to try it, I should be eaten up on the first day."

Avan laughed. "You know your way and I know mine. That's why we get on so well together."

Sebeth laughed, and rubbed her snout caressingly against his. "I'll see you in the office when you can make it in, o busy one."

"Don't forget the letters," he reminded her. She rolled her eyes once deliberately, mocking his cautions and reminders, as always.

He opened the back door and left. Sebeth stood still for a moment after he had gone, waiting and listening. Then she opened the wardrobe again and took out another quite different hat. This one was made of black lace, folded and pinned with a comb, so that it would have been difficult for even the most charitably inclined to call it anything other than a mantilla. This hat she slipped into her bag, then she made her way up the slope to collect the piles of letters.

22. EXTENDED CLAWS

Hathor's offices were in the Migantine quarter. This was convenient for most of his clients, and for the City, but it meant that Avan, who lived within walking distance of his office near the Cupola, had to cover almost the whole length of Irieth to reach him. There were other attorneys nearer at hand, many of them more fashionable, but Hathor's father and then Hathor himself had served old Bon, and Avan felt he could rely on him as he could never have counted on a stranger. Accordingly, as soon as he was safely out of the house he blinked his middle lids over his eyes to protect himself from the morning sunlight, made sure his hat was seated safely on his head, and rose straight up on the early morning winds.

Flying in Irieth could never be the joy it was in the country. Many dragons refused to fly at all in the capital, saying it was dangerous as well as unpleasant, because of the unpredictable winds caused by the buildings and the heat of so many dragons living together. They walked the streets, or hired drafters and carriages. Avan thought of them as soft. He had flown from Agornin back to Irieth, and he would fly to see Hathor. In his secret soul he liked to think that if he had found himself one of the solitary dragons of the heroic age, relying on his wings and his claws for his life, he would have made a good showing.

He rose rapidly, not stopping until he had gained enough height to be safe from the worst of the unpredictable low winds. From up here, the city looked beautiful. He could see the patterns made of the tiles on the rooftops, and the accidental patterns made by so many rooftops together. He swept by the six towers of the Cupola, taking care not to fly directly above them, and glimpsed children playing down in the courtyard. The houses were silent, but the streets were full of early commerce—here a market selling fruit, fresh from the country, there beeves and swine being driven from the railway to their final market. The silver shining lines of the railway led from the grand arches of the Cupola station across the city. Avan followed them, swooping along, with the sky almost to himself. He descended at last only when he had come to the region of squat stone hemispherical buildings that marked out the Migantine quarter.

Hathor's outer office was spacious. It had a typically Migantine barrel-vault ceiling, making it seem pleasantly cavernous. On the walls were old-fashioned two-color ground-level views of Migantil. Several clerks, all respectable maiden dragons of various shades of gold and beige, sat busily writing at desks around the room. There was space for three or even four waiting clients to seat themselves, if they were careful. There was only one client waiting when Avan arrived, though he was probably as large as two of Hathor's usual clients. Avan was surprised to see such a very prosperous dragon there, and even more surprised when he recognized him as his acquaintance the Exalted Rimalin. He had not known, and was a little surprised to discover that the other dragon did business with Hathor. All the while, as he gave his name to Hathor's clerk, he felt Rimalin's gaze on his back.

"Well, Respectable Agornin," Rimalin said, as Avan came to sit beside him, curling around so that his head rested on his tail. "Or should I say Dignified now?"

"Not yet," Avan said, and smiled so that his teeth showed. He thought Rimalin meant it kindly, but he had not needed Sebeth's reminder that others would be reassessing his position.

Rimalin laughed, putting his head back to expose his throat and thus demonstrate his complete confidence in Avan's friendship. Then he sobered rapidly and looked Avan in the eyes. "I believe Ketinar wrote to express our condolences on your loss," he said.

"I am very grateful to the Exalt and to you for your thoughts of me," Avan said, politely. "I received her note last night, as soon as I was back in Irieth."

"Then you're only just back?" Rimalin leaned back a little to see more of Avan.

"I flew in last night, very late," Avan confirmed.

"And you've come here first? I hadn't known you were one of Hathor's clients," Rimalin said.

"I hadn't known you were," Avan replied warily. "Or is this a new venture?"

"We politicians like to spread our business about," Rimalin said, with a flick of his wing. "But I've been dealing with Hathor for years."

"He was my father's attorney, and I've been using him all this time," Avan said. "I find him very reliable."

"I have found the same, but confirmation is always good," Rimalin said.

"You can't judge an attorney by the decor of his outer office," Avan said, one of the terrible Migantine pictures catching his eye.

Rimalin laughed again. "Ketinar outright asked Hathor about them once. He said that his father bought them in Migantil, when he was a young dragon."

Avan looked at the one in front of him again. The sky was pink and the outline of the buildings blue. "You mean that they were actually painted by Yargish hands?"

"I can't vouch for it, but that's what Hathor told Ketinar."

"I don't know if that makes them better or worse," Avan said, in horrified fascination.

"Oh, worse, old chap, definitely worse. But one does see why it is that Hathor doesn't replace them.

It's always the same with old family things, you have to hang on to them whether they're ugly or beautiful, valuable or valueless, they don't really belong to any one person, they exist to be passed along to the next generation. We have a lot of things like that out at Rimalin, lot of nonsense really, but I wouldn't touch them all the same."

"No, how could you?" Avan murmured, thinking that it could be little hardship when he spent so much time in the city, where his house was furnished completely in the most fashionable modern style.

"I wonder if you might like to come and stay with us in Rimalin some time? This winter, perhaps, if they can do without you in the Planning Office for a little while?"

Avan was so astonished he could not speak for a moment. He had many friends in Irieth, especially since his job required him to move on the fringes of political circles, but had never before been asked out of the capital. He had counted Ketinar, the Exalt Rimalin, as his friend, but her husband had never before been quite so forthcoming. His father's death had clearly changed his status in ways he had not yet been able to assess. "I'd love to," he stammered. "If I can get away."

"I'll have Ketinar send you a proper invitation, good for any time you can spare us a few days," Rimalin said.

Just then the door to the inner office opened and a young, very beautiful dragon maiden came out, followed by her very large, very formidable ruby red mother. "Isn't she gorgeous? Dowry arrangements do you think?" Avan ventured very quietly.

Rimalin said nothing until the outer doors had closed behind the pair. "That is the charming Respected Gelener Telstie, and her no less charming mother Blest Telstie," he said. "Gelener is one of the most marriageable maidens on the market this year, and for the last two years, but if a marriage has been arranged, it hasn't yet been announced."

One of the clerks rose and gestured to Rimalin to go in to see Hathor. The door was open, and Avan could just get a glimpse of the inner office where Hathor crouched on papers and books as most dragons would on gold. "I have to go. But come and see me soon. And if you have any capital to venture, don't tie it all up before you've spoken to me. I have something to suggest."

"I read your note, but—" Avan began, but Rimalin was already on his feet.

"There's no terrible hurry about it," Rimalin said, and walked into Hathor's inner office, closing the door carefully behind him.

23. OFFICE POLITICS

Avan reached the Planning Office a little before noon. The gold had been placed on deposit for the time being, and Hathor had made arrangements for collecting it. After hearing all the facts, Hathor had agreed Avan had a case, though not as good a case as he would have if Haner and Selendra would join with him. The writ against Daverak had nevertheless been issued, and would be sent out the next morning. As he flew back, happy with his morning, Avan had considered making himself even later by visiting a public bathhouse. He thought better of it. He could not afford to lose his position. He wished to appear confident, not insolent. Besides, he had sluiced himself only three mornings before in the chilly river Nia that flowed through the Agornin demesne. Too frequent bathing was supposed to be bad for the scales. He smiled, showing his teeth a little, then straightened his cap, pushed away hesitation, and walked confidently in through the archway.

Kest was leaning over Sebeth where she was attempting to write letters. Kest was a fine bronze-scaled dragon, much the same size as Avan, a little over twenty feet long, and therefore almost twice the size of Sebeth. "You have time to do this copying," Kest said, caressingly, leaning closer. Avan paused where he was.

"Have your own clerk do it," Sebeth said, icily, withdrawing as far as she could behind the block of granite that was Avan's desk.

"I don't have a clerk, as you well know, little Eminence, and the drudge who does all the copying won't get to mine until tomorrow now."

"I fail to see why this is my problem," Sebeth said, squaring some papers and looking up at Kest.

"Oh, you fail to see why it's your problem," Kest echoed, mimicking her voice. "Well, it's about time you did see, and stopped giving yourself airs, little Eminence v—. It's your problem because when Avan gets back, if he does, he won't have a position here and I'll be taking over his responsibilities, and that includes your pretty—"

Avan had heard enough. On the word "v—" he had entered the room, and before Kest could speak the obscenity Avan's claw had taken him under the armpit and tipped him sideways. Before Kest could recover himself, Avan leaped forward, his whole weight falling onto Kest's thorax, his teeth at his throat. Avan had the advantage of surprise, and perhaps a little that of size also. He had grown since eating his father's body. Kest owned himself defeated immediately, denying Avan the pleasures of the fight and the hope of eventually killing and eating his opponent. Kest laid his claws and tail flat and closed his eyes. For a moment Avan regretted that he was a civilized dragon, then he was reminded of the tussling he had done with his sibs long ago. Poor Merinth had signalled surrender just like that.

He lifted his head a little, ready to bite again if necessary. "Do you yield?" he asked.

"I do," Kest said, faintly. Avan was still lying on him, almost choking him.

"And do you yield position in the office?"

"I do," said Kest, opening his eyes a crack.

"And do you apologize to my clerk and promise

never to so insult her again?" Avan asked, keeping his weight where it was.

"I do," Kest echoed, and when Avan did not move, added, "I apologize, 'Spec Sebeth, for insulting you and swear I will not do so again."

Somewhat reluctantly, Avan backed off and allowed Kest to breathe freely. "Tell anyone else you may know who thinks to intrigue for my position that I am back, and not reluctant for a struggle, if that is necessary," Avan said.

"Yes, no, I'm sure nobody will bother you now, Dignified," Kest said, backing away, coughing a little. Still backing, he went through the arch that led to the other offices.

Avan picked up his cap, which had fallen off at some point in the struggle. He smiled wryly at Sebeth, who looked flushed and excited. "You did warn me," he said. "Is he always that obnoxious when I'm not around?"

"Little Eminence is his usual name for me," she said, and spread one hand in incomprehension. "Trying to impose on me to do his copying because he thinks it's important is something he's done before. He's always been more familiar than he should, he clearly thinks my status is ambiguous and wants to take advantage of that." She looked down at her exquisitely pink shoulder and sighed. "The rest was new."

"I should have killed him," Avan said, staring at the doorway where Kest had disappeared.

"With all that envy and covetousness and scheming coursing 'round his blood, he probably tastes disgusting," Sebeth said.

Avan laughed. "If he says anything to you again, anything beyond ordinary chilly politeness, anything you don't want to hear, tell me," he said. "I'm prepared to take the risk on how he tastes."

Sebeth opened her mouth to answer, but before she could speak, Liralen came bustling in. Liralen was an elderly dragon, black scaled, almost fifty feet long. He carried a file under his arm, not just at that moment but almost all the time.

"Oh Avan, Kest told me you were back," he said. "My condolences on the death of your father."

"Thank you. And thank you for your note of condolence. I was held up with some urgent family business first thing this morning," Avan said.

"Oh, that's of no consideration, as you're here now," Liralen said. Trust Liralen to care about nothing but work. "'Spec Sebeth informed me. But while you were away rather a difficult situation has come up concerning building rights in the Skamble." The Skamble was one of the very rough areas of Irieth, across the river. Sebeth moved some papers on the desk, making both the others suddenly aware of her presence.

"Is this confidential?" Avan asked.

"Tolerably, but not from your clerk," Liralen said, with a wintry smile that was all in his pale eyes. "I'll leave the folder with you. I didn't have time for it my-self, but I couldn't trust anyone else to deal with this properly, so it has been waiting for your return."

Avan felt the implicit reproach, but as he had been to his own father's deathbed and stayed away less than two weeks, a scant nine days, he did not feel the slightest guilt.

"I'll become conversant with the details and deal with it as soon as I can," he said, taking the folder. This particular folder was pale lavender colored. Liralen handed it over reluctantly and looked almost naked without it.

"It's a delicate matter," Liralen said. "You'll see when you read it. Let me know what action you de-cide on."

Avan blinked, startled. Generally he investigated, then thought out possible actions and then put the possibilities before Liralen, he did not decide for himself. This responsibility was something new.

"Is this promotion?" he asked, daring to say it out-right.

Liralen hesitated. Sebeth lowered her head over her papers and tried to look inconspicuous. Avan waited calmly.

"It may be," Liralen said. "It may be indeed." He paused, looking at Sebeth with clear disapproval. "I am getting older, and in a year or two I can take my pension and go home. At that time, somebody will be wanted to take my place here, and I would prefer it to be someone who gets the work done and not someone with no idea of propriety."

This was the first time Liralen had ever mentioned retirement to Avan. Avan tried to still the frantic whirling of his eyes. What did Liralen mean about propriety? He knew his superior disapproved of Sebeth on principle—she was pink, but unmarried, and therefore by definition not a respectable dragon. There was no appeal, and though Avan had staunchly represented his employing her as redeeming the unfortunate, he knew Liralen had only grudgingly become reconciled to her when he saw how good her work was.

"Propriety?" he ventured to ask.

"It is not so long since dragons have been dismissed from this office for partiality," Liralen said. "There are others still with us who appear to believe they are living in the days before the Conquest when promotion could best be achieved through violence. You, I am glad to note, are not one of those."

Avan, still full of the exhilaration of beating Kest, tried to look peaceable.

"I'll look forward to seeing how you deal with this case, and so will the Board," Liralen said. The Board were shining figures to whom Liralen answered. Avan bowed his head at the mention of their name. "Well, there is work to be done," Liralen finished.

"I'll do what I can to make up for lost time," Avan agreed, and opened the folder at once.

24. A SECOND CONFESSION

Just before sunset, Sebeth left the Planning Office. Avan was still working, engrossed in the contents of the folder Liralen had brought him earlier. He had spent some time catching up on what she had done in his name in his absence, but always he returned to the lavender folder. He barely grunted a farewell as she left. She walked from the Cupola in the direction of the river. Nobody had asked her where she was going, and nobody seemed to pay any attention to her. She walked through the park, ignoring the fashionable strollers and the mill workers alike. Occasionally she saw a clerk she knew, and they exchanged a nod or a word. Though they were generally polite, none of them were her friends, most of them found her suspicious. She knew they thought she should not be in respectable employment. She preferred strangers, who had no way of knowing she was not a bride.

When she came to the promenade by the river she hesitated, and turned around, scanning the walks to make sure nobody was watching her. She paused, as if hesitating as to left or right on the river walk. Right would have taken her towards the shops and entertainments and grand Houses of the fashionable Southwest and Marshalling quarters, while left would have brought her back towards the mills and offices of the Cupola and Toris districts, and at length home.

Once she was sure she was unobserved, she took

off her hat, the marker of her status and respectability, and folded it into her bag. Then she ignored the promenade and walked with rapid and assured steps across the high-arched stone bridge that crossed the river Toris. Once on the other side she continued to walk with confidence, tracing her steps without hesitation through the twists and turns of the narrow streets. She was soon in the quarter lying between the river and the railway tracks which was known as the Skamble. She wondered as she went about the contents of that lavender folder. Building rights, in the Skamble? Every claw's width that could be built on was built on already, though much of it was covered with wretched shacks where poor mill workers scratched out what comfort they could between thin patched walls. The roads were narrow and the buildings huddled together as if for warmth. There were few open spaces, and those there were had clearly been caused by recent fires.

At last, when the sun was almost down, she came to a church, larger but hardly better built than the houses around it. She paused for a moment, again looked both ways, though nobody at all was in sight, then pulled her mantilla from her bag and set it on her head. She could not help feeling a thrill of excitement at doing something illicit. Going to a church of the Old Believers was no longer illegal, except for a parson, but it was certainly frowned upon. Many things fall in the shadows between the bright light of illegality and the comforting darkness of approval.

Avan could certainly not have continued to employ her as a clerk had her religious affiliation become known. She pushed away the excitement, murmuring a prayer to Veld for clarity of mind. Then she put a claw to the wooden door, which swung open, and went straight in.

The room Sebeth entered was much like any church in a poor quarter. It was a dim vault, barely half underground, half-filled with dragons, many of them with the bound wings of servitude, all of them small, hardly one of them longer than seven feet except the priest, who stood at the center of the narthex, about to begin his service. Such a sight could be seen in any church on any Firstday morning or the evening of any day. Only the nodding mantillas and the carved wooden side-doors that led to the confession room marked it out as in any way different. A visitor seeing those might have been surprised as Sebeth gestured and joined the prayers, but surprised because nobody was feasting on cooked meat or howling out grotesque and titillating confessions, merely behaving as any dragon might have in any congregation. Even the prayers were the same.

The one theological difference could be seen on the doors. As in most churches, the walls were covered with the carved intertwined and writhing forms of the gods. Jurale's great dark eyes whirled sympathetic understanding from all the walls, Veld's pictured face was wise and stern, the world lay clutched safely between his claws. They were immediately recognizable as themselves. There were no pictures of Camran, except those on the doors. These representations would have made most dragons blink, and some run screaming heresy. Camran was pictured on the left bringing the Book of the Law, and on the right as walking up to the Cave of Azashan, as he might be anywhere, but the artist in this church had depicted him as a Yarge, soft, wingless, and unarmed.

A parson, if any had dared enter this church, might not have been so surprised. There were old books that showed Camran this way. Penn, for instance, had been taught at the Circle that this was an old symbolic way of showing Camran's peaceful nature and humility, much like the way Avenging Veld could be shown as the harsh noon-day sun and Jurale as a sheltering mountain. But the Old Believers, and Sebeth with them, did not see it as a symbol, like the red cords that bound the wings of priest or parson, they really did believe that Camran had been a Yarge.

After the service, Sebeth waited before the doors, praying patiently, until it was her turn to confess. The priest, who called himself Blessed Calien, absolved her, as always, of living with Avan without the sacrament of marriage, and on this occasion of coveting Avan's gold and reproaching him for starting his lawsuit, all the details of which she told Calien when he inquired. Then, with a little more hesitation, he forgave her for having enjoyed seeing the two dragons fighting over her that afternoon. "It may be our nature, but Camran taught us that we can overcome our nature and surpass it. May you with Veld's grace do better if such temptation comes your way again. Is that all?"

"There is one more thing, Blessed One," she said. "It isn't a sin of mine, and indeed telling you may be a sin, for Liralen said it was tolerably confidential. But Avan has been given a certain folder concerning building rights in the Skamble, and I wondered if it was best to warn you about it."

"You did right, little sister," Calien said. "Tell me all that you discover of this affair as it passes through your hands. The lesser sin of betraying your employers will be offset by the great help you do to the nurturing egg of the Church."

"Yes, Blessed One," Sebeth said, obediently.

Then the priest set his claws against her eyes as she sat perfectly still. "I have heard your confession, Sister Sebeth, and I absolve and forgive you in the name of Camran, in the name of Jurale, and in the name of Veld."

7
THE DINNER PARTY

It was the fifth day of the month of Leafturn, the day Exalt Benandi had fixed for her little dinner party to welcome back Penn to Benandi and inspect his sister and his nanny. According to her arrangements, Penn brought Amer up the Parson's Passage for inspection in Exalt Benandi's office, a little while before the time appointed for the dinner. The Exalt was in a good mood. She had heard from her friend Blest Telstie that her daughter Gelener would arrive in the afternoon of the seventh, in two days time. Accordingly she smiled at Penn when he went in first alone, leaving Amer to wait in the corridor, and while she reproached him for his extravagance in the matter of the carriage, she did so benignly. "A parson has a position in the world, but you are entirely dependent on your living, you have a comfortable establishment and a sufficiency, not enough for frivolity," she finished.

"You are right, Exalt, I shall be more careful another time," Penn said. He was rested now, and being at home, having had Felin's undivided attention and seeing Selendra behaving very well for the whole span of a night and day, had conspired to make him much more relaxed.

"My condolences on the loss of your good father, too," the Exalt said, a little aware that she had been tardy in saying so.

"He died in the arms of Camran," Penn said, and the conventional words stung him a little as he spoke them, reminding him of his father's confession.

"Then let me be introduced to your old nanny," the Exalt said. "You need not stay, go and find the youngsters. They will doubtless be amusing themselves on the ledge or in the Little Talking Room."

Penn beckoned Amer to come inside. Amer had asked Selendra to bind her wings back severely for this interview. She had not wanted to ask Felin lest her new mistress should decide not to loosen them later. Amer did not fear having her wings tied, but she preferred her accustomed measure of freedom and comfort. Nevertheless, she knew that for this interview her bindings must be as tight as they could be. She was not at all afraid of Felin, not when she had Penn and Selendra to defend her, but she knew Penn was afraid of the Exalt, who was the real mistress here. When Penn beckoned she bowed her head, drew in her breath, and went in.

What Exalt Benandi saw seemed in all ways satisfactory. Amer was clearly an elderly dragon, set in her ways, not at all what she would have chosen for Felin's household. But they had inherited her, and must make the best of her. At least she was small, her wings were well bound, and she seemed properly subservient. She bowed so that her head touched the floor while Penn introduced her, and even when she looked up she kept her eyes lowered.

"How long did you serve at Agornin?" the Exalt asked, waving Penn away impatiently. He bowed and left, not without a little trepidation. He had told Amer to be careful to behave herself, but he knew how she had been accustomed to speak her mind to her betters.

"Since the Dignified Agornin married my mistress, who was then the Respected Fidrak, Exalt," Amer said.

Exalt Benandi had discovered the Fidrak connection when she had researched Penn's heritage before deciding to offer him the living as her parson. It had helped incline her towards him. She smiled now, as graciously as she could. "And how long had you served the Fidraks before that?"

"All my life, Exalt, my mother was stillroom attendant to old Exalt Fidrak and my father was a dooropener in the establishment. His parents and their parents back since before the Conquest had been servants on the Fidrak estate."

"A commendable ancestry," Exalt Benandi said, genuinely pleased. "And how old are you?"

"Old enough to have years of hard work left to me, Exalt," Amer said.

This was a good answer, as Amer did not look feeble, but the Exalt frowned at the levity of it. "How old exactly?" she demanded.

"Four hundred and seven years, Exalt," Amer said,

deciding the Exalt would not notice if she were to forget fifty years.

This seemed to satisfy her, at least she did not probe further in that direction. "In what capacity have you served the Fidraks and the Agornins?"

"First as a kitchen attendant, then as Respected Fidrak's attendant, and then when she married and became Dignity Agornin, still as her attendant but mostly as nanny to her hatchlings. As they grew, after my mistress's death, and as Dignified Agornin grew older, I came to be more in the kitchens again."

"You understand that Benandi Parsonage is a small establishment?" the Exalt asked, looking at her closely. "They have no room for luxuries and extravagances, though they live the lives of gently born dragons. Why did you wish to come here?"

"I have served the Agornins for so long, I did not wish to go into a different family," Amer said, keeping her eyes lowered as best she could so that the Exalt could see no spark of resentment or defiance.

"So it was your choice? Not that of your betters?" The Exalt leaped on the admission as if it were a wild swine whose neck she wanted to break.

"I could have stayed with the Daveraks," Amer admitted.

"The Daveraks were taking over Agornin, you could have stayed with them and been with the family you have served so long, yet you chose not to."

"That's a different family, for all that Exalt Daverak married the Respected Berend Agornin," Amer said, thinking she was on safe ground. "I knew that Blessed Penn had true Agornin hatchlings, and I wished to serve them if I could."

"It has always been my belief that hatchlings are best served by young nannies," the Exalt said, severely.

"Why?" Amer asked, although she could have bitten her tongue the moment the word was out.

Exalt Benandi sat in silence contemplating her for a moment. She never allowed familiarity in servants, and this looked very much like insubordination. Fortunately, the Exalt was in a mellow mood, and Amer had made a fairly good impression until now. She had not questioned an order, merely asked for clarification, the Exalt decided. "Because it is better for the young to be served by the young," she said.

Amer made no reply, though she longed to denounce this view as the nonsense it was. "In that case I shall help in the kitchens as best I can, or serve 'Spec Selendra," she said.

The Exalt looked on Amer now with dislike. "As I said, Benandi Parsonage is a small establishment. The Respected Agornin can expect to keep no personal attendant."

"No, Exalt," Amer said, woodenly.

"Surely she does not expect that?" the Exalt asked.

"No, Exalt," Amer repeated, remembering how Selendra had laughed at the idea and wishing they were all back in Agornin in the last happy years.

"I do hope she isn't a foolish maiden with her heart set on high fashion?"

"No, Exalt," Amer said again, lowering herself as if she would sink through the hard stone of the floor.

The Exalt sighed. "Go back to your duties. I will keep inquiring if they have been done to Felin's satisfaction, and if they are not I shall make my displeasure known."

"Yes, Exalt," Amer said, and backed carefully out of the room. As soon as she was far enough down the passage that she was sure the Exalt would not hear her, she gave a sigh of relief and eased her wings as far as she could in their tight bindings. She wondered if Daverak, even with the threat of being eaten against her will, might not have been better after all.

26. FIRSTDAY AT BENANDI

Selendra felt altogether overawed at the splendor of Benandi Place. That first evening she did nothing but sit quietly and eat as politely as she could. She answered questions in a murmur almost too quiet to be heard. Sher was forgiving when he did not hear her, recognizing shyness and unhappiness, but his mother often asked her to repeat what she had said. Despite this, Exalt Benandi was more pleased than she had expected to be with Penn's sister. She had been afraid Selendra would put on airs and expect more than her position would naturally provide. Instead she found her almost too retiring.

The next morning, which was Firstday, the whole Benandi household attended church together. Exalt

Benandi and Sher took the whole right side of the church, Felin and Selendra stood on the left, and though there was plenty of room beside them the servants were left to mingle with the villagers in the front and back of the church. Penn stood in the narthex and conducted the service. He preached a good sermon, which he had largely composed in the train, about Jurale's nurturing mother qualities, in which he managed to compliment the Exalt twice and Felin once. On the way out of the church, while the Exalt was catechizing one of the farmers about the absence of his daughter and Felin was helping Penn out of his ceremonial headgear, Sher took the opportunity to linger by Selendra for a word.

"I just realized I hadn't said to you how sorry I was to hear about your father's death. You may not remember me at all from when I visited Agornin, but I was there long enough to grow to thoroughly like your father. Bon was a wonderful dragon, such a marvellous storyteller, real rock of the mountains. I wish I knew more dragons like him. The world seems smaller without him."

To her embarrassment, Selendra felt her eyes filling with tears when she heard this. Nobody had spoken to her about Bon beyond conventional pieties since she had left Haner, and now hearing him recalled brought him back almost too vividly. "Thank you," she said, and knew she had revealed her tears in her voice.

"I didn't mean to hurt you," Sher said, very gently.

"I know," she said, and managed to look at him. "You'll think I am very foolish, only I do miss my father very much, and you recalled him to me so clearly."

"Then I am not sorry at all, for it is right that we remember Bon as much as we can."

Selendra managed to smile at that, an approved ladylike smile with her mouth closed.

"Are you finding everything very strange here?" Sher asked.

"Yes," Selendra admitted. "But it's also very beautiful country, what I've seen of it."

"I haven't forgotten Felin and I promised to take you flying. Not today, perhaps, but soon."

"I think better not today, all things considered," she said, and smiled. The party had walked to the church, and would walk back. Firstday flight was not something the Exalt approved. "It's good to have such a beautiful church," she went on.

"It's very old, I believe," Sher said, glancing back at the church building which was almost too familiar for him to be able to see it clearly. "It's one of the oldest in the whole northwest of Tiamath. I've been coming here since I was a dragonet."

"Such lovely carvings," Selendra said.

"When I was a dragonet I used to imagine climbing into the walls and going to help Camran against Azashan, in that panel up there," Sher said, remembering, and pointing it out.

"Oh yes," Selendra said, seeing at once. "You could have climbed up those sun-rays there!"

"Yes, that's exactly how I used to think I'd do it," Sher said, smiling at the memory.

"Azashan's carved as such a fright there," Selendra said. "I'm sure he'd have given me nightmares if I'd come here as a child. But no, I suppose not, because Camran's so strong against him."

As the Exalt and Penn joined them they were harmlessly discussing the beauty of the representation of Veld on the left wall.

Later that afternoon, Felin came up to bring the Exalt a few pots of the preserved looseberries she and Amer had been preparing. As it was Firstday, she had walked up instead of flying.

"How are you finding her?" the Exalt asked, when they had made their greetings and this had been explained.

"She's definitely very deft in the kitchen. I'm quite happy with the nanny you found me, but I think I can use Amer to get more preserving done. You know how one tires of nothing but meat in the winter months. Last year I barely put up any looseberries because I had to watch the servants every minute when they were doing it. I believe Amer knows the work well enough to trust her with it." Felin was already beginning to be glad Penn had insisted on bringing Amer back with him.

"She hasn't shown any sign of wanting to fuss over Selendra?" the Exalt asked, suspiciously.

"Not so far," Felin said.

"Then you just haven't caught her at it," the Exalt said.

"She as good as admitted that she chose to come, and that's why. You keep her in the kitchen and keep a firm grip on her."

"I certainly shall," Felin said. "But I don't think Selendra would want her to be a personal attendant. I think Selendra's very sweet. The children adore her already."

"Dragonets will give their affection to any young person who spends time with them," the Exalt replied.

"She's a pretty thing, too," Felin went on.

"Too quiet and shy to be a beauty, and a little pale for it as well," the Exalt dismissed her. "Harmless enough. We'll have to watch out for eligible male dragons of her rank who won't mind her being so retiring. What's her dowry, Felin?"

"Sixteen thousand, I believe," Felin said, for so Selendra had told her, in accordance with her agreement with Haner.

"Better than I would have expected," the Exalt sniffed. "I thought old Bon had all but bankrupted himself selling the elder daughter to Daverak. Still, all to the good. A pale quiet thing like Selendra will go over well enough with sixteen thousand, to some parson or even some Dignified's son."

"It's too soon to be thinking of that yet," Felin said. "She's hardly over the shock of her father's death yet."

"Is the maiden in deep mourning?"

"Well, as it's only a week since her father's death, I wouldn't suggest taking her to any balls," Felin said, a little more sharply than she usually answered the Exalt.

"I was just intending to give a formal dinner party tomorrow night. Some friends of mine will be here." The Exalt smiled in a very self-satisfied way. "The Blest Telstie, who you have met, and her daughter the Respected Gelener Telstie, who I don't believe you know. She left school two years ago and I only met her when we were in Irieth for the season."

"I'll be delighted to make her acquaintance," said Felin, who immediately saw through her friend's scheme. Poor Sher, she thought, caught like a swine between rocks and served up to the maiden on a dish with a jar of looseberry preserve poured over him.

"But is Selendra to be considered in too deep mourning for a formal evening party? She is certainly old enough, and I have no complaint about her behavior, having seen her in our family dinner last night, except that she will need to speak up a bit if she is ever to make a mark in society."

Felin thought about it. Selendra had been generally quiet with her, too, though she had seemed to enjoy playing with the dragonets. "I think it would do her good to do more things and leave the parsonage a little more," she said. "She shouldn't brood on her grief."

"I'm not thinking about doing her good," the Exalt said, drawing back a little. "I'm wondering about the propriety of the thing."

"Well, were you intending to ask Penn?" Felin asked.

"Oh certainly, I can't manage without Penn, he's the only other male I have, and we're thin enough on males in any case. Besides, they're an ecclesiastical family. They would think it very odd if Penn were not there." It was an accepted part of Penn's duties as parson of Benandi that he would dine with the Exalt whenever she needed an extra dragon in her dining room.

"Well as Bon was Penn's father as well, mourning should be the same for them both, and if Penn, as a parson, can be there, Selendra should be able to attend as well," Felin said.

"Good," the Exalt said, dismissing the question of whether it was proper for Penn to attend a formal dinner party a week after his father's death. "The Telsties will arrive tomorrow afternoon. I shall see you all up here for dinner."

27. SELENDRA AND SHER

When Selendra heard that she was invited to a formal dinner party at the Place she was horrified.

"I'd much rather stay here and read," she said. "Must I go?"

Felin was irritated. "It's very kind of the Exalt to invite you," she said. "You should be grateful, and make the most of what social opportunities come your way."

Selendra settled back a little on her gold and gulped back tears. She didn't know if it was delayed grief or missing Haner or just the strangeness of being in such different surroundings but she kept wanting to dissolve into weeping. "Of course it is very kind," she said, mechanically. "But I have never been to such a dinner party and I don't want to let you and Penn down."

"Just do as you did last night," Felin said. "Nobody will be looking at you. The party is for some friends who are coming to visit, they'll be the center of attention. There's a daughter, Gelener, who is supposed to be very beautiful. She's been brought down here for Sher."

"For Sher?" Selendra echoed stupidly.

"To marry him," Felin explained sharply. "I think all this reading in the dark is tiring your brain, you should go out for a little walk."

"If it wasn't Firstday I'd fly," Selendra said.

"If it wasn't Firstday we all would," Felin snapped, then repented of it. "I'm sorry, Selendra, I'm a little tired myself. I'll take you out flying tomorrow after breakfast unless Penn wants me to go with him."

"Thank you," Selendra said, getting up and slipping a wing over Felin in a sisterly way. "Can I help you with anything? I don't need a walk. Can I look after the children?"

This offer was gratefully accepted and they parted on good terms.

The next morning they breakfasted abstemiously on half a side of beef, divided between the three of them and the two hatchlings. Selendra found eating with the children a little strange, as they had no table manners at all and were inclined to scatter gobbets of bloody meat everywhere as they ate. "Amer can dry the rest of this beef this morning," Felin said. "Do you need me today, dear?"

Penn looked up from his beef. "What? Yes, I thought you could come with me to see the Southgates. One of their children was ailing, and should either have recovered by now or be in need of helping out of this world."

"Yes, dear," said Felin, and grimaced at Selendra to indicate that their flight would have to wait for another day. Selendra accepted this with a little sigh, but after her brother and his wife had left, and she was trying to control the little ones, she was surprised when Amer showed in Sher.

"The Exalted Benandi," she announced.

As little Gerin was on Selendra's back at that moment, Selendra could not move for fear of dislodging him. But the moment the children saw Sher they ran to him, demanding preserves and treats and stories. "It's not you little monsters I've come to see today but your aunt," Sher said, fending them off in a way that was clearly an accustomed game which he let them win, so that when he turned to Selendra apologetically he had a dragonet perched on each shoulder, in a way that could not help but make her laugh. He was so much larger than they were that they looked like ornaments.

"Good morning, Exalted Benandi," she said, and bowed.

Sher laughed. "Call me Sher, if you would, for Penn and Felin do, so it's absurd for you not to."

With the children perched on top of him, and Wontas waving a triumphant claw, Selendra could not be afraid of Sher. Besides, she liked him. He had a terrible mother to contend with, but he himself was gentle and thoughtful. He had liked her father. She also believed, from what Felin had said, that he was about to be married. "Very well," she said. "Then good morning, Exalted Sher. I am sorry to inform you that Felin has gone with my brother to visit an ailing farmer's family."

"My mother would say it was my duty to go with them," Sher said. "But bother that, for I promised to take you out flying this morning, and it is a beautiful morning, crisp and clear." He reached out a careful claw and tickled Gerin's underbelly. Gerin collapsed into giggles and stopped digging his claws into Sher.

Selendra had already noticed that it was a beautiful morning, before she had had her hopes dashed at the breakfast table. Now her heart rose again. "Are you sure it would be all right?" she asked.

"Certainly," Sher said, deciding at that moment not to mention to his mother that Felin had not accompanied them. "Find the nanny to take these little terrors, and come on."

"Take us with you!" the dragonets piped.

"When you have wings we will," Sher promised. "How could you fly now?"

Selendra called the nanny, still not entirely convinced, but ready to be tempted. The dragonets were taken away, screaming loudly for Uncle Sher and Aunt Sel as they went.

"They call you uncle?" she asked as they stepped onto the ledge and blinked their lids across in the brightness.

"You see, I am like family," he said. "I was in school with Penn, and then at the Circle, and my mother brought up Felin, so we're all very close. You'll just have to join in as best you can."

Selendra had no idea that Sher spent most of his time away from the Place, so this all seemed quite reasonable. She smiled at him shyly, glad to have acquired another and such an amenable brother. They took off and rose, spiralling slowly outwards.

"Now, do you want to see the farms and the railway track, or would you rather see the wild places and the mountains?" Sher asked.

"Oh, the wild places, please," Selendra said, promptly. When Sher's laugh came back to her, she added, "It's only that all farms are much alike everywhere, and all wild places have their own beauty."

"You're right," Sher said. "We'll make a hunter of you yet, whatever your brother says. And in that case we want to go up higher if we want to cover some ground. There's too much to see in one day, but I can show you more another time."

Until that moment, Sher had been being kind to her as he might to Felin's dragonets, whom he enjoyed when he was home and forgot when he was away. He had wanted to coax a smile from her, and been disappointed when Felin was not there to accompany them. Now, as he looked down at Selendra's trim golden form as she followed him up the wind, he thought that she was, if not exactly beautiful in the style of Irieth, certainly a good-looking maiden. He had admired her since he had first seen her. And she had such an amusing way of looking at things. Imagine liking the carvings in the church, and thinking about them, and seeing how he could have climbed up into them. How nice that she preferred the wild to the dreary old farms. Sher always had, whatever his duty was. That was why he spent so little time at home. If he was going to settle down, Selendra might be as good as anyone to settle down with. She was right here, and she was his old friend's sister, and she liked dragonets. Some of the maidens in Irieth looked as if they'd faint if a dragonet climbed on them, but she'd had Gerin on her back when he came in. He'd have to think about it, he thought, and the prospect of thinking about it seemed most pleasant to him.

Selendra, following him, was merely thinking what a joy it was to soar upwards on the clean sharp winds of morning.

28. A DINNER PARTY

Selendra was disappointed in Gelener. She had expected better for a future wife of Sher's. At first sight, she was most impressed. Gelener was beautiful as only a maiden dragon fresh from the milliners and polishers of the capital can be. She had been burnished until her golden scales almost shone. She was wearing a headdress of great elaboration, covered in sequins and beads and jewels and bows, with tiny mirrors on stalks. Selendra, who had been given a quick rub by Amer when she came in to tie on her headpiece, a twist of gray and black ribbons Haner had made her, felt positively dowdy in comparison. Even the Exalt, resplendent in a dark green velvet bow decorated with one huge emerald that perfectly complemented her ruby skin, looked dull beside Gelener. Gelener's mother looked as if she could have been the Exalt's sister. Her bow was gold cloth, and the outsized jewel was a diamond.

The speaking room at Benandi was large, amply big enough for the party of seven who waited in it, and with charming alcoves. The walls were decorated with light stones set in the dark rock of the mountain out of which the room was hewn. These had been arranged tastefully only the year before by an artist specially imported from Irieth for the occasion. They were still very fashionable, although in some houses in the capital dragons who wished to be thought in the forefront of the mode were ignoring the age-old prohibition on bringing precious objects into public parts of an establishment and decorating their speaking rooms with tiny fragments of gems. This was so far a fashion of Irieth only, it would have been quite excessive in the country, and the Exalt's speaking room was exactly what it should have been.

The dining room, which could be seen through a large arch, was even larger. Twenty full-size lords could have dined there, and had. The gutters on the floor were swabbed to perfection before the meal began. There were no modern decorations here, the purpose of the room spoke for itself. Servants were moving in and out with great dishes of freshly slaughtered beef, swine, and muttonwool, at least two animals for each guest. The carcasses were all skinned and dripping with blood. Many of them were decorated with fruit, fresh or preserved.

Selendra's disappointment began when she was introduced to Gelener as "The Respected Telstie." Felin had not given Selendra the other maiden's formal name when she had mentioned her the day before, so this familiar family name came as a surprise.

"My father knew yours, long ago, or perhaps it would have been your grandfather," Selendra blurted when she heard the name. Gelener inclined her head an infinitesimal fraction to the right, making her mirrors and sequins dance and catch, and waited. After too long a pause, Selendra realized that this was intended as a head quirk of polite inquiry. "My father began life as a tenant on the Telstie estate," Selendra explained. "I have often heard him speak well of the Eminent and the Eminence Telstie."

"That would most likely have been my grandparents. Or it may have been my uncle, who is the present Eminent Telstie, but though he is an elderly dragon your father's rise to respectability was probably before his time." Gelener simpered.

"My father, the Dignified Bon Agornin," Selendra said, allowing her voice to stress her father's title, of which she was justly proud, "died only recently, having attained his full five hundred years. His childhood on the Telstie estate was long ago."

"It would have been my grandparents that he knew, then, no doubt," Gelener said, and moved on a little.

The Exalt had been hovering nearby. Seeing Gelener move to speak to Sher, she turned to Selendra.

"My dear," she said. "I know you will not mind a word from someone so much older and more experienced in the ways of the world." Selendra inclined her head, attempting to copy Gelener's elegance with the gesture, but aware she came nowhere near succeeding. "Well then, it'll do you no harm with Gelener, she's a lovely maiden, very well brought up. Her mother and I are close friends, she won't think less of you whatever you say. But generally, as you go about in society, I would not mention your father's low origins. I do not mean you should lie about them—after all they are easily discoverable. But do not bring them gratuitously into conversation. After all, your mother was a Fidrak, and there is no higher blood than the Fidraks. They rank in the first ten families of the land. You have an uncle, or at any rate a cousin of some degree, who is an August lord. If you must mention family ties, mention your cousin the August Fidrak."

Selendra stared at the Exalt, barely capable of understanding what was meant. "But I do not know my cousin, so I would have nothing to say of him," she said. "Besides, my mother's branch of the Fidraks is fairly remote from the present holder of the title."

"You may not know him, but he is a connection of yours of whom you may be justly proud," said the Exalt.

"I am not ashamed of my father!" she replied, much too loudly. Everyone turned to look at them. Penn, who had been talking to Blest Telstie on the other side of the room, took a step towards them.

"I was not suggesting that you should be," said the Exalt, soothingly.

"Merely that I should not mention him in polite society!" Selendra retorted, her violet eyes blazing and whirling rapidly. "I loved my father, and I am proud of him."

"Selendra—" Penn said, warningly. Blest Telstie looked confused. Felin's teeth were bared in distress. In the other room the servants had stopped arrang-

ing the feast and were openly watching the unexpected drama.

Gelener tried to exchange a pitying look with Sher,
only to see that his eyes were blazing. "She's quite
right, mother," he said.

Selendra turned to him, grateful for help from such
an unexpected quarter.

"Bon was a splendid dragon," Sher went on.

"Nobody is saying he was not," the Exalt said, icily.
"Selendra misunderstood the intent of my words."

Selendra knew that everyone was looking at her.
She was quite aware that she needed to apologize
to the Exalt if she was to salvage the evening, but
she could not quite control her voice. She hated to
lie in such a position, and she knew that she had not
misunderstood. She wanted to run out of the room
to cry in peace. "I am sorry if I misunderstood your
intent," she said stiffly after a pause that was much
too long.

"That's all right, my dear," the Exalt said, and
pressed her arm before moving across the room to
speak to Blest Telstie.

Sher abandoned Gelener and took the two strides
necessary to bring him to Selendra's side. Penn and
Felin exchanged a glance, after which Penn moved
towards the abandoned Gelener and Felin headed
towards Sher and Selendra.

"Don't cry," Sher said quietly. "I don't know what
my mother said, but I know what a ridiculous snob

she can be. Don't take any notice. Anyone who knew Bon Agornin appreciated that he had the true qualities of a gently born dragon, which count for so much more than empty titles won by distant ancestors."

Felin joined them in time to hear the latter part of what Sher was saying. "I'm sure the Exalt meant to speak no harm of Bon," she added. "Do calm down, Selendra, unless you would rather I took you back home to rest."

Selendra could hardly speak. "My father earned his own title," she said, gulping between words.

"He did, and there was none better for him unless the Majestics of old should return and begin again naming dragons Honorable," Sher said solemnly.

Felin's eyes whirled faster at that. She knew Sher from long experience to be carelessly kind to the broken-winged, unless it gave him inconvenience. She did not want Selendra to become one of his cases. Everything caused him some inconvenience in the end, and he would not persist through it. Felin had taken over the work of caring for a baby muttonwool who had lost her mother, a cat with a broken leg, and a farming family whose lease Sher had promised to investigate. More recently, she had had to deal with the distress of her children every time he went away without saying good-bye. "Would you like to leave now, Selendra?" Felin asked again. "I told the Exalt you were perhaps too soon bereaved for company. She'll understand."

"Perhaps I should," Selendra acquiesced gratefully.

"No," Sher said, putting out a claw to Felin. His dark eyes were grave, turning slowly in the depths. "If she runs away now, she hands my mother the victory claw, and besides it will allow everyone to feel sorry for her and discuss her in her absence. If she stays, it will soon be forgotten."

"I had no idea you were so experienced in social gaffes," Felin said.

Sher laughed. "You have no idea," he agreed cheerfully. "Well, Selendra?"

Felin's own gray eyes speeded up a little in surprise. She had not known they were on personal name terms.

"I will stay," Selendra said, in control of her voice now. "I am not a coward, and I am not ashamed of my father, nothing could make me be."

"Stay, let it pass over, that makes it nothing," Sher said.

Felin looked at the Exalt's magnificent back as she spoke to Blest Telstie. Penn was engaging Gelener in conversation. She thought the incident was more likely to be forgiven if the Exalt were allowed to get away with it for now and then Felin did her best to smooth things over later. There was no arguing with Sher in this mood however, nor, clearly, with Selendra. Felin spread an inward hand and gave up the affair. The Exalt would be furious if Gelener was scared away, but she herself would be happier to see

Sher with a partner who might bring a smaller dowry but who had a sense of humor. All the same, as they went through at last into the dining room, Felin felt her wings tremble a little on the winds of the storms ahead.

8
THE WRIT IS RECEIVED

29. THE COMFORTS OF DAVERAK

Haner's life in Daverak Place was in many ways delightful. She had her own attendant, a graying maiden called Lamith, who had no other duties than to obey Haner's wishes, burnish Haner's scales, and make up becoming headgear to Haner's satisfaction. The family breakfasted in their rooms, enjoyed the afternoon as they chose, and came together for dinner, for which there were often guests. Afterwards there was frequently dancing and jollity until late into the night.

Haner might have settled into enjoying it, had the company been more congenial.

After a day or two, Haner noticed that her attendant was moving very stiffly. "Come here, Lamith," she said. Haner ran her fingers over Lamith's back and soon found that the bindings on her wings were so tight they had caused a sore, which was rubbing raw as she moved.

"Let me loosen that and dress it with a salve," Haner suggested.

"Thank you, 'Spec, but I don't think I could do that," the attendant said, ducking her head nervously. "Master doesn't like us to have our wings untied."

"Just for a minute, while I treat it, and then they

should be bound back more loosely," Haner said. "I'd be happy to tell Berend and Illustrious Daverak myself and explain that it's not insubordination on your part but concern for your welfare on mine."

"Please don't tell him I'm ailing, 'Spec!" Lamith seemed desperate. She cowered away from Haner. Haner was not a large dragon, a mere twenty feet, but Lamith was barely six, and seemed hardly more than a dragonet as she shrank away. "It's just a little sore. I've had them before."

"I won't tell them if you don't want me to," Haner said, astonished. "But if it is left like that it will hurt you, and it might make part of your wing weak so that you could never fly again."

"Fly?" Lamith said. "I'll never fly again no matter what. I'll work here until I weaken, and that'll be the end of it."

"Many things might happen," Haner said, encouragingly. "There are servants who fly, even if you never leave the condition. Some establishments employ servants to fly to the station to collect the mail. Amer, our servant at Agornin, who has gone now to Benandi, used to fly out regularly to gather herbs for medicine."

"Yes, and doubtless you trusted her to come back," Lamith said. "That isn't the way of things here, 'Spec, there's no trust on either side and we know we're bound for good."

Haner's gentle silver eyes were sad. "It's not what I'm used to," she said.

"Never mind, 'Spec, things could be worse. We're well fed here, and we know our families get the good of it."

"The bond payment, you mean?" Haner asked.

"That isn't much, in Daverak. But any family who has a member in service at the Place knows their other hatchlings have more of a chance of growing up. And we're not dead and eaten, after all."

"Are you saying Daverak eats dragonets that are not weaklings?" Haner asked, in horror.

"He will if he says the family can't manage so many," Lamith said. "Please don't say I said anything about it. They eat us if we're ailing, and it doesn't take much to make them think so these days, not with Illust' Berend increasing and hungry all the time. I'm only saying this to you to stop you saying things out of kindness that would make matters worse."

"I can't believe Berend would condone any such thing," Haner said, decisively. "Daverak, maybe, but Berend is my sister and knows how things were done in Agornin."

"When she first came and she was shocked at anything, the Illustrious told her not to be provincial," Lamith said. "That's how I know how much trouble saying things kindly can cause. Now she keeps her eyes on the roof and acts more Illustrious than he is. I'm sorry to say these things, 'Spec, but it's nothing but the truth and you need to know it."

"I am going to put salve on your wing," Haner said, taking the salve out of the box Amer had made up for her before she left home. "I'll bind it up very tightly again afterwards, if you insist, but I am not going to be served by a dragon with an unsightly sore like that. It's stopping you doing your duties, and easily curable. That's what I shall say, if anyone says anything, which they won't. They won't notice."

"Likely not," Lamith said, and sat still to submit to Haner's ministrations. "That feels a deal better," she said, when Haner had bound her up again. "Now let me arrange your hat for tonight, 'Spec."

Haner lay awake for a long time that night, turning on her comfortable bed of gold as if it had been slate. She had known all her life that the conditions of servitude were harsh. Yet she had never truly understood it until Lamith cringed away from the offer of salve. She had thought of Amer and the other servants at Agornin, whose service was hereditary and seemed almost as comfortable to them as to their masters. She wondered how much of that was mere seeming. But Lamith's sore was real, and so was her fear. She had read of the conditions of factory workers with bound wings. She flexed her own wings nervously. She wanted to do something about it, and had not the least idea where she could possibly start or what she could possibly achieve. She could not even think of anyone she could talk to about the subject, except Selendra, who was so far away. She would write. She would write in the morning. So resolved, she was able to find uneasy sleep at last.

30. THE WRIT ARRIVES

The next evening, unusually, the family were dining alone. It had been raining all day and not even Daverak had been far from home. Haner had not been out at all. Berend was due to produce another egg at any moment, making her snappish and disinclined for company. The three of them and the two surviving dragonets gathered in the speaking room, where the native rock was inlaid with marble and limestone pebbles according to the fashion. Berend could not settle at all but kept pacing.

The two dragonets, one gold and one black, both had the same huge pinkish eyes as their father. They sat silently beside Haner, shoulders together. They had been very quiet since Lamerak was taken from them. Perhaps they missed him, or perhaps they feared that they might join him at any moment. Haner spread her wing over them caressingly for a moment. They looked up at her but barely smiled.

"It seems so dreary to be alone this way," Berend said, pausing in her pacing.

"It was your decision," Daverak replied, waving a claw in front of a great yawn that showed his huge strong teeth.

"I know, and it seemed like a good one this morning, because I didn't want to see anyone. But it seems terribly dreary now," Berend said.

"It's cozy, being just family for once," Haner said, peaceably.

Berend snapped her teeth as if to bite her sister's remark. "Cozy is one way of putting it. Dreary is my way, and much more accurate. Don't you wish Londaver were here, Han?"

The Dignified Londaver, living so close, was a frequent guest, as were his parents. He did not seem to single Haner out for any attentions now, which Berend had noticed, so it was cruel of her to mention him.

"I should think she'd welcome any company but yours tonight," Daverak remarked.

Before Berend could retort, or Haner think of any calming reply, a servant came in with a packet of papers in his claws.

"The mail has arrived," Daverak remarked. He had a bad habit of pointing out things that were perfectly obvious.

"Anything for me?" Berend asked.

"Almost all of it, doubtless," Daverak said, sorting through it idly and handing a large pile to Berend. "Two for me, one from my broker, and one from my attorney. And here's one for you, Haner," he said, passing over a folded and sealed letter.

"It's from Selendra," she said, smiling, looking at the seal.

"Aren't you going to open it?" Berend asked.

"I thought I'd save it for after dinner," Haner said, meekly. "Are yours interesting?"

"Just invitation cards, hardly any of which I'll be able to manage until I'm through with the clutch,"

Berend said, leafing through her pile of mail desul-
torily. Then Daverak gave a snarl which caused the
children to huddle together in fear and both the
adults to turn their attention to him. Berend even
dropped some of her cards.

"What is it, dear?" Berend asked, sounding really
concerned. Daverak was at all times black, now he
seemed almost purple.

"I cannot believe he has the audacity," Daverak
snarled.

"Who?" Berend asked.

Haner knew immediately. She had been hoping
Avan would change his mind, and she had not imagined a writ could have been obtained so quickly.

"Your wretched brother and sister are taking me to
court over the issue of your father's body."

"Haner?" Berend asked, turning to her.

"No, no," Haner said, feeling that she might well
have been devoured on the spot had she joined her
name to Avan's in his venture.

"No, Haner knows which beef to leave for breakfast," Daverak said, flinging down the paper savagely.
"You have two sisters, in case you've forgotten. Did
you know about this, Haner?"

"What?" Haner asked, genuinely frightened.

"This attempt to take me to court to recover the
flesh I ate from your father's body, as was judged correct and in accordance with your father's wishes by
Blessed Frelt at the time, if you remember."

Daverak's jaws were scant claw-widths from Haner's

throat, she shrank back in fear. She had never seen Daverak so incensed. "Avan said something about it in anger at the time," she said. "I had no idea he had actually done anything about it." This was the truth, though she had known he would.

"I'll sue him back, reclaim your share of the gold the two of them took, and Berend's too," Daverak raged, moving away across the room. The dragonets crawled closer to Haner and sheltered under her wing.

"We don't need gold, darling," Berend said, very calmly.

"Then it can all go to Haner's dowry. You were saying the other day you wanted us to add to it so she could make a good match." Haner had known nothing of this and gasped a little now it was mentioned. "Very well," Daverak said savagely. "Let's add that to it. Twenty-four thousand crowns and whatever your brother Avan has saved up from the bribes of his office will make her more attractive, wouldn't you say? As she has thrown in her lot with us, and not with those scheming adventurers I was stupid enough to treat as family. You have thrown your lot in with us, haven't you, Haner?"

"Yes," Haner whispered, feeling the bodies of her niece and nephew tight against her, and knowing she had no other choices at that moment.

"I've never seen you so angry, darling," Berend said, putting a hand caressingly on Daverak's arm.

"Shouldn't you calm down a little? You look as if you might explode."

"I'll go up to Irieth tomorrow and see my attorney," Daverak raged, shaking her off. "I won't let them get away with this. The impertinence of it. I'll take every crown they have, I'll fight it all the way. And I'll make Penn come into court and admit Bon didn't say anything about it on his deathbed. He as good as said that at the time. I'll teach them to think they can get anything out of me this way. I'm good to my family, and I was prepared to be good to yours, Berend, see how I agreed to take Haner in!"

"I know, darling, I know, and I'd never have imagined they could all be so terribly ungrateful. I always knew you were right and they were wrong," Berend crooned.

"This piece of brazen effrontery is even worse than I expected," Daverak said, holding up the writ and scowling at it. As he did, all of a sudden, smoke came out of his nostrils, and a jet of fire streamed out of his mouth and set the writ blazing. He dropped it abruptly and set sejant for a moment, his claws held out in front of him.

"You have fire, darling," Berend said, smothering the burning writ with her tail. "Just let me put this out before it makes a stink."

"Fire," Daverak said, sounding quite pleased with himself. "I had no idea it was so close." He breathed out another experimental gout of fire.

"Maybe you should practice outside until you can control it well," Berend suggested, practically.

"I shall do that tomorrow," Daverak said. "Fire, and I'm not three hundred yet."

"They are signalling that dinner is ready at last," Berend said.

Daverak frowned at his wife.

"They say early fire is a sign of greatness," Haner ventured, not adding the frequent corollary that early fire was a sign of early death. Flame was certainly a strain to a dragon's system. Her father had used his seldom but judiciously.

Daverak smiled at her, exposing teeth that had been blackened by his blasts of fire. "Thank you for the confidence," he said, attempting his usual languid tone, but far too excited to achieve it. "Now, by all means let us eat before some of us starve to death amid the excitement."

31. A SECOND DINNER PARTY

As the family were alone, dinner consisted of six muttons, their skin and wool removed before they reached the table by farmers expert in that craft. Wool, and whole muttonwool fleeces, were much prized in millinery. The fleeces would be sent to the cities and reappear in the form of cunningly contrived headcoverings. Daverak immediately took hold of the largest and began to rend and tear at it. Berend took up another. Haner, with the dragonets still close to her, began on a third. The dragonets soon crept out and began to eat, only to cower again when Daverak's flame erupted again, engulfing the haunch of mutton he had in his claw, filling the whole room with the scent of seared meat.

"I do think it would be a better idea to practice outside," Haner said, when the gout of flame came a little close to her tail.

"Nonsense, it's perfectly safe," Daverak said, selecting a second mutton and doing it again.

"I wonder why it is that there is a prohibition on cooking meat?" Berend said, conversationally, swallowing a great bite of the fatty underbelly of her mutton. "It smells rather pleasant."

"Flaming at it isn't cooking it," Daverak said, looking a little guilty.

"Oh, I see, how foolish of me," Berend said, and gave a little snort that might have been laughter at her foolishness or might just have been part of her digestion. She was gulping down her meat rapidly.

"The prohibition is because the filthy Yarge do it," Daverak said, turning his seared haunch in his claw a little as if wondering if it would make him a social pariah to eat it. "That's what they told me in school anyway. Apparently they tried to make us do it during the Conquest, and it was one of the reasons we revolted. Disgusting cooked meat sticks in the craw. That's what they said, anyway. I've never tried it myself."

"Is the haunch you flamed disgusting?" Berend asked.

"I already said that was different from cooking," Daverak said, frowning.

"But how does it taste?" Berend asked. "As cooked meat is illegal, that's probably the closest I'll ever come to seeing any, and it does smell pleasant, or at least interesting. How does it taste?"

"The same as always, only a little warmer," Daverak said, taking a tentative taste. "Besides, if you really want to try cooked meat there are places in Irieth you can get it. It's one of those thrills some dragons go in for. I never fancied it myself, but a few years before I married you there was a fad for going off to the Migantine quarter to try it. I don't think anyone went more than once."

The conversation then turned to reminiscing about fads of past Irieth seasons. Haner, naturally, could have little part in this, but she ate and made occasional remarks to keep the conversation on this neutral topic. She also made sure the dragonets ate their share, or more than their share. She was not hungry. When the servants returned to remove the bones and sponge down everyone's scales to remove drops of blood, all the mutton had been eaten. Daverak had taken three, Berend two, and Haner and the dragonets between them only one.

After dinner, Daverak announced that he would be going out to taste the wind, by which everyone understood that he intended to practice using his fire. The nanny returned to take charge of the dragonets. Berend settled down couchant in front of the mantel, beckoning Haner to sit beside her. Haner would much have preferred to withdraw to her room, but felt sorry for poor Berend, abandoned by her husband when she was in such a delicate condition. She accordingly took her place beside her sister and sat back on her own haunches. "I can't think what possessed Avan to be so idiotic," Berend said.

"You know he was counting on that flesh," Haner said. "You know he needs to make his own way in the world. He's working in the Planning and Beautification Office, that's very competitive. There are dragons there who would eat him first and face an inquiry cheerfully afterwards when he wasn't there to stop their bribing the judges. He needs his position, and that means he needed father's flesh far more than Daverak possibly could."

"Oh yes, I understand all that. I only took one bite myself, you know."

"One big bite," Haner said, for she still resented Berend's one bite.

"And you took your share, did you not? You are a foot or two longer than you were." Berend measured Haner with her eyes. "Don't worry, we'll find you a husband yet," she said, more kindly.

"Not by ruining Avan!" Haner objected.

"Daverak's very angry," Berend said. "You saw that. Usually I can make him do what I want, eventually, but that one might be hard to get him to relent. That's what I meant about Avan being an idiot. If he'd just left it, after a while I'd have had Daverak invite him here after this clutch was all finished, at a time when there was a cull and he could have made it up. I had him halfway around to agreeing to add a little gold to your share as well. He likes you."

"He has a strange way of showing it, shouting at me that way," Haner said.

"If he didn't like you it wouldn't just have been shouting," Berend said, placidly.

Haner stared at her, but she just shook her head a little. "What do you mean?" Haner asked.

"I mean he likes you, and you should be glad he does. But now Avan has got on his bad side, and he'll hound him. He really will ruin him if he can, and I don't think there'll be anything you or I can do to help him, and I'm warning you not to try."

"Avan was quite confident he could win," Haner said.

"Avan with father's attorney up against all that Daverak can hire? You were the one who mentioned that there are judges for sale, and if necessary I doubt Daverak would hesitate. We just have to think of Avan as lost, because of his own foolishness in pushing this. I'm sorry, I've lost a father and a son this month, now I have to face losing a brother too."

This was the first time Berend had mentioned Lamerak, and Haner unfurled a wing and laid it in comfort across her sister's shoulder. "What about Selendra?" she asked, quietly.

"I think I can persuade Daverak that Avan bullied her into putting her name to it, if I'm allowed to work on him in my own way in my own time. I can manage him, but not if he's kept constantly stirred up. He's quite pleased with me for starting this clutch now. And that, by the way, isn't accidental but quite deliberate timing on my part."

"But the risk to your health?" Haner ventured.

"There's no risk as long as I eat well enough," Berend said. "And that means dragon as well, of course, spiritual as well as physical sustenance."

"Daverak is killing more than the weaklings," Haner said, lowering her voice.

"I have enough to worry about with myself and my family, I can't concern myself with all the farmers and servants, Haner, really, it's too bad to ask me to. That's his business, and we shouldn't meddle." Berend shrugged off Haner's wing and turned to her sister crossly. "Don't interfere. Leave Daverak alone, and let me try to salvage you and Selendra and the dragonets as best I can."

"I'll do my best," Haner said.

32. LETTERS

When she was safely alone in her own room with the door closed and Lamith sent to bed for the night, Haner opened the letter she had received earlier. She found much to comfort her in Selendra's letter. Although it was clear her sister missed her greatly, she also seemed to be settling down happily in Benandi.

"Everyone here is very kind," she wrote, "especially

Felin, who is really good to me. I don't think Penn could have found a better wife if he'd spent a hundred years looking. She's very beautiful, more now than she seemed at the wedding. Her scales have come to be the kind of red of clouds at sunset, very unusual, and very striking. I'd think she spent hours burnishing them, except that I know she doesn't have time to give them more than a wipe over after dinner most days. She spends a lot of time with her dragonets, and she often goes out with Penn to see the parishioners, helping them out with food and medicine. I go too, sometimes, I'm learning my way around the place."

Selendra went on to write about flying in the mountains with Sher, "Who is, if you please, the Exalted Sher Benandi, but he's not the slightest bit stuck up or pleased with himself, though his mother, the old Exalt, really is. Now I know you'll tease me because I mention the name of a gently born male, but you need have no fear, he's betrothed, or as good as, to a very elegant young maiden, the Respected Gelener Telstie, who is also here, so you see we have much company. (She is apparently the granddaughter of Father's old patrons, but Exalt Benandi thinks I should not mention such things.)"

Selendra had tried her hardest to make the letter as cheerful as it could be, and Haner was almost entirely taken in by the tone. She took comfort as best she might from the thought that at least her sister was quite happy. The letter ended with professions of effusive sisterly love, and then beneath her sister's name she had written "Amer especially wishes to be remembered to you." Dear Amer. How well Haner now understood her desire not to come to live in Daverak! Still, she could not say that, or she would distress Selendra. She did not want to distress Selendra, which was why she had not written before. Telling her sister how unhappy she was would do no good, and to write that she was happy would be a lie.

She took up pen and paper at once to reply, then hesitated, not quite sure what she should say. She wrote the direction carefully: "The Respected Selendra Agornin, Benandi Parsonage, Benandi." Then she stared over the paper for a moment, her silver eyes whirling, missing Selendra so much that her wings ached.

"My dearest Selendra," she wrote, "writing your name makes me feel a little closer to you. I am glad to hear you are well and largely enjoying your days. I'm sure you'll be cutting out this Telstie female with the Exalted Lord, now I see that you are on first name terms with him—or is that only on paper? I am well, and well cared for. Berend seems to be increasing without undue trouble, she is thriving so far and hopes for another clutch of three." After this she sketched out the trouble with Daverak and Avan, along with a little drawing of the look on Daverak's face as he discovered his fire, which she was sure would make her sister laugh. "Berend says she will try to intercede for you, but that we should think of Avan as lost now that Daverak has set himself so firmly against him," she wrote. "I will never give up Avan, but I will not be able to hope to see him while this case continues. It might be as well for you to remove your name from the Writ in case, for while it remains there and I live here we cannot visit each other, and I would dearly like to see you should there be any occasion."

This, with the drawing, almost filled the sheet, there was room only for another two lines.

"Have you ever considered, dearest sister, that the situation of servitude is morally indefensible, and bad for master and servants alike? It is surely wrong for any dragon to give up their whole life to the whims of another," she wrote, and had no room for more. There was also no room for the avowals of love and promises to hold her sister in her thoughts that Selendra had made her. She signed it simply "H" and folded the letter up. Under the seal she drew a tiny dragon with her wings spread wide to embrace another. She then sealed it carefully. The sight of her own seal, which she had brought with her from Agornin, made her a little sad. It was very splendid, gold set with pyrites, and it matched Selendra's, which was set with amethysts. They had been Hatch-day gifts from Bon the year before. She sighed, set it down on her pile of gold, and went out to lay her letter on the ledge where the servants would collect it and take it to the mails.

When she was back in her room, she realized that she should have flown herself to deliver it to the mails at the station the next morning. She could no longer rely on the servants to take it. She would never have thought Daverak would read her mail before, but then she would never have thought he would be inches from eating her alive before, nor that he so mistreated his servants. Now she had seen him angry and suspicious she thought it more than likely he might intercept a letter to Selendra. He would not find she had said anything she should not, but he would not find the picture very flattering. She crept back out and retrieved her letter, thoughtfully.

9
THE PICNIC

Exalt Benandi looked at her son in surprise. "My dear, Leafturn is advancing. There has been one snowfall already. It's no time for picnics."

"Yes it is, Mother, it's exactly the time," he said. "You're right, the leaves are turning and beginning to fall, summer has gone, it's the last opportunity to picnic before we are all frozen into place for winter."

"You know you spend half the winter hunting," the Exalt said, but her voice was fond. She knew he would go away as abruptly as he had arrived if she did not make his visit pleasant. If he really wanted a picnic in Leafturn, she would have to arrange one. She wished every day that Sher were not free of her control, not realizing that it was because he was that she loved him.

"You remember the wonderful picnics we used to have when I was home from school?" Sher asked, coaxingly.

"I do," his mother admitted. "But they were in Greensummer, not on the edge of Freshwinter."

"It would be very nice to go out for a whole day, up into the mountains, before the snow comes for good, don't you think? Show them to those who haven't seen them before?"

"Gelener has probably seen plenty of mountains," the Exalt said, a slight edge of bitterness apparent in her voice. It wasn't working out the way she had wanted. Blest Telstie had returned to Irieth, leaving Gelener with her for what they all described as "a nice long visit." Sher was polite and amiable enough to her, but he showed no sign of being attracted. Gelener, seeing this perfectly well, became colder and colder to them all as her visit progressed. Although the Exalt had rarely invited the Agornins up to the Place since that first night of Gelener's visit, Sher spent a lot of time down at the Parsonage.

"She won't have seen ours, though, Mother," Sher suggested. "And Penn told me his dragonets haven't either. We used to have a contraption for carrying children about, a basket? Do we still have it?"

"We do, but Sher—"

Sher ignored her in his enthusiasm. "We could all go up to the Calani Falls, and maybe even explore the cavern a little. I used to love that as a child. We used to go when Father was feeling a little better, do you remember?"

"Sher, you are not going to head me off like this. I need to ask you a question." He spread his claws, and waited, the picture of innocent readiness. If any sixty-foot-long bronze-scaled dragon could look like a dragonet, Sher did his best to do so. "Are you—" She hesitated. She had to be careful with Sher. "Are you growing fond of little Selendra Agornin?"

Sher's immediate reaction was to prevaricate. Easy

denials were on his tongue, but he bit them back. He would have to fight this battle with his mother, he knew, he just hadn't been expecting it yet. He knew he would have to work her around slowly, and it might be as well to know how much opposition he had to expect and from what quarter. "I think I may be," he said, slowly, keeping eye contact with his mother, trying to sound as sincere as he could. "I'm not quite sure yet. I have said nothing to her, you know I would want to talk to you about anybody I was considering seriously. But I do like Selendra, yes. She's charming and interesting to talk to."

"Oh dear," the Exalt said, wincing a little. "She's almost penniless, you know."

"She has sixteen thousand crowns," Sher said. "Not much by our standards, perhaps, but that's hardly penniless. And our standards mean, or ought to mean, that we don't need to look for an heiress. Benandi is rich. I am rich. A bride of mine doesn't need to be."

"No, not necessarily, though it does help," said the Exalt, thinking of the bills Sher had run up in Irieth and elsewhere in the last few years. "But Selendra isn't of our kind. She's pretty, in her way, but her father rose to his rank, and his rank was only Dignified. That might not matter, and her mother had very good blood. But she has no discretion. Penn doesn't mention his father's beginnings, Selendra blurted them out in her first dinner party. Would you want your wife to do that? She doesn't have the poise a wife of yours needs. Think of your position. You came to it very early, but you have to act in accordance with your rank. I'm telling you what your father would if he were alive. Your wife will be Exalt Benandi. Selendra has never been to Irieth, never managed a great estate, never even lived in one. She should marry someone of her own kind, and so should you. Marriages too far apart in rank may seem exciting, but marriage is a day-to-day affair, you have to rub along together, and differences of that nature become like grit in the gold of the comfort of daily life."

Throughout this speech Sher had been shifting restlessly. "I have thought about what you're saying," he said when his mother had finished. "But there isn't such a huge difference as that. Bon died Dignified, that's only two steps down from Exalted, and besides the Fidraks thought him good enough for their daughter."

"She was the daughter of a minor branch," the Exalt put in.

"There are only two ranks that matter," Sher went on, ignoring this. "The gently born, and the others. There's no doubt that Selendra is gently born, and I'm sure you'd not dispute that."

"No, certainly not," the Exalt said. "But darling—"

"In that case, we are of the same rank," Sher said. "You wouldn't worry if I wanted to marry the daughter of an Eminent, would you?"

"Do wait until you have known her a little longer," the Exalt counselled.

"I intend to. I have by no means made up my mind to marry her," Sher lied. He did not want to make his mother angry now, he wanted to bring her around slowly. "This conversation has made me feel more inclined rather than less, but marrying her to prove I do not subscribe to an outdated convention of class would be just as foolish as refusing to marry her because I did." He shook his head. "You asked me if I was growing fond of her, and I think I have answered you. I think I may be."

"Yes, you have answered me," the Exalt said, and sighed. "Was it to show her the waterfall that you wanted to arrange a picnic?"

"Partly," Sher admitted, with a disarming smile. "But the dragonets have never been up there, and they'd love the cavern. I started thinking about it and I do want to take this chance before the water freezes. We could invite a big party if you like, all the pretty maidens for miles around, one last frolic before winter."

"Oh very well," the Exalt said. "But I really do advise you that I feel she'd be a terrible choice. Do look around a little before you set yourself on Selendra."

"I will," Sher said. "Thank you about the picnic. It's just the sort of thing I enjoy. Invite as many dragons as you like."

"I certainly will be inviting some other maidens. Do pay a little attention to them please, and don't spend all your time with Selendra."

"I'll be polite to every one of them, and look at

them closely, and you'll be the first to know if I give my heart away forever," Sher said, smiling again. "But do try to find some that aren't entirely icicles. I don't know what made you pick Gelener Telstie, but I get a chill every time I go near her."

"Oh Sher, you're impossible," the Exalt said, laughing and waving him away.

34. THE WATERFALL

The Exalt had fulfilled her promise to make up a big party. Sixteen cheerful laughing young dragons set off from Benandi Place in the morning sunshine. There were a few clouds over the high peaks and the air was cold. Nevertheless the sky was a wonderful blue. If not for the chill it could almost have been Highsummer. Sher carried the basket with Gerin and Wontas dangling beneath him. The basket was old, dating from before the days when the railway was so extensive. Felin had worried that it might not still be strong enough. She remembered being carried in it herself when she had first come to Benandi. They tested it carefully. Sher reared up rampant, dangling the basket so the children could bounce about in it no more than three feet from the ground. At last Felin was satisfied and strapped them down carefully for the flight.

Other dragons carried baskets of fruit. Sher had promised that there would be a little hunt for something to supplement them, males only, all claws and no weapons. (Penn, out with the Exalt to wave the others off, felt this was directed at him, and frowned.) General spirits were very high. Sher was right, it seemed, everyone did want some last excitement before the snows came. Everyone's headgear was bright and summery; several of the maidens even wore hats with trailing streamers. Gelener made some little concession to the wind with her choice of hats and put away her sequins and dancing mirrors for the occasion.

It was a two-hour flight to the Calani Falls. It was for this reason that Selendra had refused to go so far on an ordinary day, prompting Sher to develop the whole picnic idea. The countryside all the way consisted of limestone uplands, cut and dissolved here and there by vanished rivers. Everywhere the bones of the land poked out through the thin soil. Rowans clung where they could, higher up there were stands of pines. Heather and gorse, dying back now, covered the ground between them. Selendra found it bleak but beautiful; she knew Haner would long to draw it.

When they reached the falls the sun was still shining, though the clouds seemed much nearer and the chill much sharper. They approached the falls from the south, flying towards the falling water and the cliff face, then angling down towards the pool and the meadow below. The pool was deep. Only one end was churned by the waterfall; the other was smooth enough to reflect the sky, and the flying dragons as they circled down to land.

"You're right, it's very beautiful," Selendra said to Felin as they landed, first down after Sher. "But don't you find flying with a large party is less fun than with a small one?"

"Less chance to talk, certainly. This is where we've always come for picnics," Felin said, frowning at Sher, who was carefully unloading the dragonets a little way away. "I didn't imagine we'd come all the way here again this year."

"Sher seems ready to twist himself in a knot for the dragonets," Selendra said, following her sister-in-law's gaze.

"When it isn't too much trouble to himself," Felin said. "Selendra—" she stopped, as Gerin and Wontas were freed from the basket and came hurtling over to their mother and aunt. Sher strolled over behind them, leaving the basket empty on the grass.

"We flew," Gerin said. "Did you see us, Mother? Did you see us, Aunt Sel?"

"We could see everything spread out down underneath, like in a picture," Wontas said.

The other dragons landed in a whirr of wings and stretched themselves after the flight. Gelener gave a little shiver as she looked around. "It's very empty," she said.

"The beauty lies in the absence as much as in what's here," Sher said. "You haven't seen the cavern yet. It's behind the fall. Come and see."

"Cavern?" asked Wontas.

"A natural cave, not someone's home. It's a splendid

place, primitive and wild, going on for miles under the rock, with hidden pools deep down there," Sher said. "It's from the days when male dragons scratched out caverns with their claws and their wives waited at home to polish the gold and jewels they brought them."

Gelener looked down her snout at him.

"I think Respected Telstie might like some fruit first," Felin suggested tactfully. "And didn't you say something about some meat to go with it?"

Sher smiled. "I'll find you some immediately," he said. He bounded off, the dragonets watching him enviously, and soon all the male members of the party were high in the air above them.

"What do you think they'll find?" Selendra asked, staring up. Sher was the largest of them, and the brightest burnished. His scales caught the sun as he flew.

"Maybe a wild swine, or if we're really lucky a venison or two," Felin said.

"Most likely nothing," Gelener said. "I didn't see anything as we flew here, though even lower down the trees are almost bare enough for real hunting."

"Do you hunt?" Selendra asked.

"I have hunted since I could fly, with a spear of course. Though after I marry I think I'll take up a rifle and do some fire-hunting. My father doesn't think it right for a maiden, but I'm longing to try it." Selendra was relieved to see that Gelener did have something in common with Sher after all. "I think

I'll go up to my uncle's estate at High Telstie for the hunting this year. He's having a party of friends for the season. Will you hunt here, Felin, or go into the real mountains?"

"I'm too old for all that now," Felin said, beginning to unpack the fruit.

Gelener's eyes sped up in mild surprise. Selendra was suddenly tired of the conversation.

"I'll take the dragonets and walk by the pool," she said.

Felin waved her away. "No swimming today," she warned the dragonets.

"We'd freeze," Wontas said solemnly.

There were tracks of venison at the edge of the water. The grass was trampled and there were hoof-prints in the mud at one shallow point. Selendra pointed these out to the children, who immediately wanted to track them and drag them back for dinner. "They might have been here days ago," Selendra said. "Uncle Sher will find some up in the crags." The crags above were mostly pinewood, with gullies, perfect hunting territory as the gorse thinned, if there were any venison there at all. Now she had seen tracks, and knowing it was too early in the year for formal hunting, it seemed very likely to Selendra that they would find something.

There were cries from the others at that moment, and Selendra, looking up, saw the hunting party returning, bearing triumphant carcasses. "There, see," Gerin said, craning his neck upwards.

She walked back towards the party. They were maidens for the most part, so the general impression in the sunshine was of golden scales, with here and there the pink of a bride. Felin's deeper pink in the center of the group as she handed out fruit, was very conspicuous. This had not been so obvious when they set out, with the bronzes and blacks of their husbands and brothers mixed among them. Selendra wondered about it a little. Was the Exalt offering Sher some alternatives to the fashionable but frosty Gelener? Or was he seeking an escape for himself?

Sher landed, a venison clutched in his claws. "We were there, under his claws like that," Wontas said, poking Gerin.

"We flew," Gerin informed Gelener.

"I know, I flew too," she said. "Soon enough you'll have wings of your own and be flying everywhere."

"I want to see the cavern now," Wontas said.

"After dinner," Selendra assured them.

The hunting party had managed two venison and a full-grown wild boar. This seemed barely a taste for a party of sixteen who had flown so far, but everyone agreed that food tasted better under the open sky, and it was so inventive of Sher to think of having a picnic at the end of Leafturn. Some thought, and Gelener said, that there should have been four beasts, to allow them each a quarter. They made do with what they had, and found hunger a very pleasant spice.

As they ate, the clouds drew over them. "I'm afraid it's going to snow," Felin said, regretfully.

Some of the party who had long flights home from Benandi, or who could reach home more quickly from the falls without making a detour back, decided to leave immediately after the meal was finished. More and more of the others joined them, until at last only the Benandi party, Sher, Felin, Gelener, Selendra, and the dragonets, were left.

"I think we should go home too," Felin said. "Those clouds are getting heavier. The dragonets might get very cold in the basket if we leave it too long."

"You're right," Sher said, regretfully. "What a pity we didn't have time for a peek at the cavern. Next time. We'll bring you up here in Greensummer, Selendra, you'll see it all that way."

"I'm sorry to miss it," Gelener said, her tone expressing rather the opposite. "Well, if we are to return, shouldn't we start?"

It was at that point that they discovered that Wontas was missing. "He must have gone to see the cavern," Gerin said, wide-eyed.

"Did you see him go?" Felin asked.

"No," Gerin said, his eyes shifting pools of deceit.

"When did he go?" Sher asked. But Gerin refused to be pressed, saying he thought Wontas had been right beside them, like everyone else.

There was clearly nothing for it but to go into the cavern and find him. Felin apologized to Gelener for the bad behavior of her dragonet. "I should have been watching him," Selendra said.

"It's terribly cold, but of course we must find him,"

Gelener said, giving every sign of putting up with terrible hardship for the sake of the children. Selendra had never liked her, but now she began to detest her.

They made their way to the mouth of the cavern. As Felin and Sher already knew, the entrance was a large room, with several tunnels branching off it. The light came in through the fall outside, and it did look very primitive, but not very exciting in the circumstances. There was no sign of Wontas, nor did he come when they called.

"What a terribly unfortunate way to lose a dragonet," Gelener said, preparing to turn away again.

Gerin howled and clung to Felin's leg. Felin put her head down and nuzzled him and slowly sank down until she was entirely supine on the floor of the cavern.

"We will make a proper search for Wontas," Sher said, impatiently. "Feel free to go home if you'd prefer, Gelener."

"I don't know the way," Gelener complained. "You'll have to come with me."

"I need to stay, because I need to carry the dragonets when I find them," Sher said, with commendable patience.

"Then maybe Respected Agornin could show me the way?"

Sher looked at Selendra, who had been trying to comfort Felin. "Do you remember the way?" he asked.

"I think so," Selendra said, hesitantly, looking up from her prostrate sister-in-law.

"I'm not going with anyone who doesn't know it properly," Gelener said, her voice rising and her eyes whirling dangerously. "You'll have to take me and come back, Exalted Benandi."

"Can't you see it's too far?" Sher snapped. "You'll just have to wait." He turned and called Wontas again.

"Then Blest Agornin?" Gelener asked.

"I think that might be a good idea," Selendra said, cutting off Sher before he could snap. "Felin, you're very upset, and you should go home. Gelener needs somebody to take her. Sher knows the caves and will find Wontas."

"But he'd have to manage Gerin as well," Felin said, getting control of herself and looking up at Selendra. "And there are places where he's too large to go now, where Wontas could easily have gone. And when he finds him, he'll need me to help fasten the carrying basket to go home."

"I'm smaller than you, I'll stay and help. I can look after Gerin. I can do anything you could do, Felin, and while it's you the children would most want to have with them, I can't take Respected Telstie back."

"But you shouldn't be alone with an unmarried male," Felin said.

"I won't be alone, the dragonets will be with us, and anyway, it's only Sher, you know he won't crowd me. Don't be silly Felin, this is an emergency, and Respected Telstie insists on going home."

Felin looked at Gelener with her eyes completely hidden by her outer lids, as if they were in bright sunlight instead of the dimness of a cave. She pulled herself slowly to her feet then lowered her head again to her one remaining dragonet. "Gerin, you stay with Aunt Selendra and do everything she or Uncle Sher tells you, and help them find Wontas."

"Yes, mother," Gerin said, entirely cowed now.

35. THE CAVE

As soon as Gelener and Felin were gone, Sher turned to Gerin. "Now, your mother isn't here, and you understand how bad things are. Wontas could get lost in here and never be found. I was a child myself not too long ago, and I understand you don't tell your clutchmate's secrets, but this is more important than that. When did Wontas leave?"

"When Mother said we had to go home because of snow, without seeing the cavern. He couldn't bear to miss it. He just scuttled off quietly," Gerin said, his head bowed, struggling to keep from tears. "He wanted to find Majestic Tomalin's treasure. I would have gone too, only I was right in front of her so Mother would have seen me."

"Majestic Tomalin's treasure? Whatever gave him the idea it was here?" Sher asked surprised.

"You said the cavern was from those days," Gerin said accusingly. "And our nanny has told us stories."

"We're wasting time," Selendra said, deciding to take charge to stop them bickering as if they were both dragonets. "If he left when Felin said it was time to go, that wasn't long ago."

"Not long before we came to start looking for him, anyway," Sher said. "Good. Any idea which way he would have gone first?"

"Down?" said Gerin, uncertainly.

"Well, let's try it," Sher said. "He can hardly be out of earshot yet, even if he's running. You try calling, Gerin."

Gerin called, and Selendra called, but they had no more effect than Felin and Sher had had.

"Don't worry," Sher said, looking very worried. "I know all the paths down here, or I did when I was smaller. We'll find him."

Sher turned and plunged off down the first downhill passage. Though he was so large, he could sprint along as fast as anyone in caves and passages. Selendra and Gerin had to scurry to keep up with him.

The search was at first fruitless. They saw a number of caverns with pools and limestone teeth reaching up and down that would have delighted them in other times, but they saw no sign of Wontas.

"Why does nobody live here?" Selendra asked as they returned to the entrance cavern to try the second downhill passage.

"Too damp, and too far from anywhere," Sher said. "It's Benandi land. Some of my ancestors used to live up here once, probably giving rise to the rumors the dragonets have heard, but you can see that was long ago, maybe, yes Gerin, in the fabled days of Honorable Ketar and Majestic Tomalin, before the Conquest. I'm sure they weren't driven out by the invading Yarge though. They probably left because it was damp and draughty. I entirely understand why they preferred the comforts of Benandi Place, even if this is terribly romantic."

The passage led through three interconnected rooms, one of them with a seam of marble like a dragon's eyelid in the roof. "Felin and I used to pretend that would open and look at us," Sher said. Gerin looked up in awe, whether at the thought of the eye behind the lid or of his mother having been a child Selendra did not inquire.

In the next room, another with huge limestone teeth, she stopped abruptly. "What was that?" she asked.

They all stopped and listened. There was a broad passage leading off into another cavern, and a thin passage, much narrower, more like a crack in the rock than a proper passage, through which a draft came.

"It was probably the wind," Sher said, and then they all distinctly heard the sound of a dragonet crying.

"Wontas must have hurt himself," Gerin said.

"I was afraid of that," Sher said. "I'm not sure I can get down there. I haven't been for years. There are pits down that way, the whole section is dissolving. He must have fallen in one of them."

"Wontas?" Selendra called. There came a distant answering cry.

Sher went to the crack and began to squeeze himself along.

"I think I can fit, if you can't," Selendra said.

"I'm long, but I've never been broad-shouldered, and I'm not grown gross yet, I don't think," Sher said, his wings folded tight to his back, moving more like a snake than a dragon. Selendra folded her own wings tightly and followed him into the crack. Gerin brought up the rear. He was the only one of them who could move easily. Selendra felt the walls uncomfortably close, and though he did not stop she could hear Sher scraping his scales against them.

At each pit, Sher stopped and called. He and Selendra could step over them, Gerin had to leap. It was at the fourth, the widest yet, that Wontas could be heard shouting from below. "I'm on a ledge," he called.

"I have never been down there," Sher said, peering from the edge. "He's too far down to reach from here. There's no room to fly properly. Maybe I should go back and get the basket. I could get down, but I might knock any loose stones down onto him and push him off the ledge."

"If there's room for you, then there's probably room for me with less risk of knocking anything loose," Selendra said.

"But—no, you try it if you think you can," Sher said.

Sher crossed the pit and sat sejant on the farther lip, looking down. Selendra moved up to where he had been. The pit was about thirty feet wide at the top, it seemed to narrow below. She could not see the bottom, making it seem uncomfortably endless. It would be impossible for Sher to do anything but slither down the side, but she was small enough to try a proper descent.

"Hold tight, Wontas, I'm going to try it," she said.

She would have had plenty of room to dive, if there had been clear air below for her to pull up and land. As it was she was going to have to descend feet first, as if standing, so she could land on whatever was there. It was not a flight, more a controlled fall, using her wings for balance and to slow herself. Selendra tried not to let herself think about how she was going to come up again. The pit narrowed as she descended until it was only about twenty feet wide. Selendra drew in her hands and back claws carefully to avoid scraping the sides. Soon enough she saw Wontas clinging to a ledge. His eyes were shut, and he was using three claws to cling with. The fourth, one of his front legs, was clearly broken.

It was a very narrow ledge. She could not use it. She braced herself, hind claws and hands across the pit, just above Wontas. "I'm here," she said.

"I've hurt my claw," Wontas said, gulping back tears.

"You'll mend," she said, as Amer had said to Avan years before when he had broken a leg.

"Oh Aunt Sel, Aunt Sel," Wontas said. "Have you looked down?"

She hadn't, since she had begun her descent. She had been concentrating too much on the sides. "I need to get hold of you somehow and go back up," she said.

"Look down," Wontas pleaded. "We have to go down."

She risked a quick glance. Not far below, the pit widened into a huge cavern, and the floor of the cavern seemed to sparkle with gold. Selendra gasped.

"Did you see the treasure? We need to go down!" Wontas insisted.

"We may have to, but we're going to try up first," Selendra said.

"But it's treasure," Wontas said.

"Most likely some rock crystals, or something like that," Selendra said. "There isn't enough light to see properly."

"There isn't any light at all," Wontas said. "This is the darkest cave I've ever seen. But it's treasure, I'm sure it is. That's why I was going down."

"Well, you need to go back up if you can," Selendra said, feeling almost relieved that she would never have dragonets of her own to tug at her heart like this. "Now let go of the wall." She took hold of Wontas in one hand and clutched him tightly to her thorax. She tried to rise, unsuccessfully, and wedged herself again. She tried again, but there just wasn't enough room for her to spread her wings and gain lift.

"Sher," she called. "We're going to try going down. I have Wontas safe, but we can't come up this way."

"I don't know what's down there," Sher said. It was very reassuring to Selendra to hear his voice.

"I think I can see the bottom and there's room to land," she said. She let herself sink slowly again. The walls widened as she went down, making a funnel shape. She came to rest at last, a remarkably comfortable landing. There was no mistaking the feel of gold beneath her.

"Treasure," Wontas called up.

"Treasure?" Sher asked in surprise, and Gerin squeaked from high above.

"Gold and cut amethysts and diamonds," Selendra said, astonished, turning it in her hands. "Some old hoard, I'd imagine, which must be yours by inheritance, Sher."

"It's Majestic Tomalin's treasure, and it's mine, I found it!" Wontas shouted.

"You're welcome to your share," Sher called. "Not that it does any of us any good down there. Can you come up again, Selendra?"

Selendra stared up. If she could take off upright she might be able to manage it, even clutching Wontas. But there was no way to get off the ground and go straight up into the funnel, it began to narrow too soon, and what little air came down this far was damp, and dead against her. She looked around. "No.

But there's a broad passage out of here westward we could try."

"But it could go anywhere," Sher said. "West is away from everywhere. This is no good. I can't let you go off into the middle of the mountain and never be seen again."

"It'll come out somewhere, and then I'll just have to go up to find my way back," Selendra said, with more courage than she felt. She was used to granite, not this untrustworthy limestone, and she didn't feel sure of her way even on the outside of the mountains.

"I'm coming down," Sher said.

"What good will that do?" Selendra asked. "You'll just get four of us lost instead of two." Killed, she thought, but did not say, for the sake of the dragonets. The Exalt would be furious if she got Sher killed, she thought.

"But if I am there I'll recognize when we find where that sinkhole connects up to places I have been before," Sher said, sounding confident. "You wouldn't know. Besides, I want to see the Majestic's treasure you've found, you can't keep it all to yourselves. Go into the passage, out of the way of falling stones. Gerin and I are coming down now."

36. TREASURE

From inside the passage it sounded as if Sher was pulling half the mountain down after him.

"Are you hurt?" she asked cautiously, when the crashing had stopped.

"My scales may be a little scraped," Sher replied, casually. "But we are armored for a reason, and no landing on gold can be called a bad landing."

Selendra laughed and poked her head into the cavern. Sher set Gerin down carefully, and the dragonet scampered over to where Selendra held the injured Wontas.

"This gold looks to me like Yargish work," Sher said, examining a linked chain set with stones.

"Not from before the Conquest then?" Selendra asked, a little disappointed.

"Oh, it could well be. More likely, in fact. You remember the knights and princesses in the stories and the Yarge towns the dragons of old were always sacking, before the Yarge turned the tables and attacked back? I'd think this might well be the plunder from such a sack. It's much too delicate to be dragonsmith work, not to mention too small." It barely fitted over Sher's claw.

"Is it very valuable?" Gerin asked, turning over a golden casket with his claw.

"Just as gold, I should imagine it's worth quite a few thousand crowns," Sher said. "But as romantic antiquities it'll be worth even more. I'd say you two dragonets can think of yourselves as rich, if you can find a way of getting the gold out."

"Which means we need to get ourselves out first," Selendra said. "Starving to death here and leaving our bones with the treasure might be romantic—"

"I had no idea you had read so many old stories," Sher interrupted, smiling.

"I have a weakness for them," Selendra confessed.

"Aunt Sel tells them to us," Wontas said, smugly.

"Well, let's do what dragons always do in the circumstances and take one piece each. Can you walk, Wontas?"

"I think so," Wontas said.

"It's a front leg you've broken. If you were a maiden you'd hardly ever use them to walk," Selendra said encouragingly, setting him down. He limped into the treasure cave.

"You use yours," he said, turning around accusingly.

"Only underground and on Firstday," Selendra said, showing him how thin the pad of callus was across her knuckles. He touched a gentle claw to it. "And some fine ladies don't touch them to the ground even then. I'm sure if you look at the Exalt's hands she'll have no callus there at all, or Respected Telstie. You can manage to walk for a little while. Amer will set your leg when we get home."

"My mother has callus, and so does any dragon who lives the life Veld gave them," Sher said. "Gelener Telstie is one of those fine ladies who prides herself on the softness of her hands and the uselessness of her accomplishments."

Selendra looked at him in surprise. "I thought she was your promised bride?"

"Even my mother has given up trying to make me marry an icicle," he said. "She'll leave here as pristine a gold as she came. She's not at all the type of maiden who moves me."

"She's pretty," said Gerin, looking up from the treasure.

"Not as pretty as your Aunt Selendra," Sher said.

Selendra felt her eyes whirl in confusion, and she could not reply. He was not betrothed to Gelener. He always complimented everyone, she knew that.

"I'll try to walk, and I want some treasure," Wontas said.

"One small piece then," Sher said. "How about this chain?" He held up the chain he had picked first and dangled it by his claw. Although there was no light, the jewels seemed to glow red and purple and lilac and evening-water.

"Rubbish," Wontas said, dismissing it with a glance and starting to rummage. "I want a real crown, or a sword."

Gerin had picked up a cup and was turning it in his claws. "To think Majestic Tomalin might have drunk out of this," he said, awe in his voice.

"Selendra?" Sher asked, taking a step towards her and offering the chain.

Still wordless, she took it and ran it through her fingers. The stones all had tiny holes drilled through them and the gold ran through the holes and then made a loop which connected to the next link. It was knotted, and she teased the knot out. The work brought her back to a proper state of calmness, in which she knew she was being a fool to let herself become agitated, because Sher was almost like a brother and his compliments were a form of teasing.

"You're right that it must be Yargish work," she said, offering it back. "It's the most beautiful thing I've ever seen."

"Take it then," Sher said, smiling. "Beautiful maidens should have beautiful things."

She looked up, and her eyes met his. Her heart seemed to be beating faster than usual, and she couldn't quite draw enough breath. She almost wondered if she was blushing, though Sher was not touching her and had done nothing more than pay her one of his compliments. It was just his way of talking. She should have been used to them by now, she told herself sternly. "Whatever could I do with a chain?" she asked. "It isn't a hat or a gorget so I couldn't wear it."

"That's fashion, not a law," Sher said. "It looks wonderful against your scales. Selendra—" He took a step closer.

"Besides, it's yours, all of this is, it's on your land and therefore yours by right," Selendra said, taking a step away and almost backing into the wall.

"If it's mine I can give it away as it pleases me," Sher said.

"But it's mine, I found it!" Wontas protested.

"We'll divide it evenly," Sher said. "Have you found anything to take? One thing, easy to carry."

"I've found Majestic Tomalin's crown," Wontas said, settling a golden circlet awkwardly on his head.

"It fits you, fruit-chewer," Gerin said.

"So?" Wontas asked.

"So Majestic Tomalin was a grown dragon, and a crown that fits you would have been too small for him," Gerin said.

"Maybe it belonged to his dragonet then. What do you call a Majestic's dragonets, Aunt Sel?"

"Respected," Selendra said, firmly, making Sher chortle.

"No, come on," Wontas persisted. "An Exalted's dragonets are Dignified, aren't they, so a Majestic's must be something better than Respected. We're Respected."

"An Exalted's heir is Illustrious, and an Illustrious's heir is Dignified," said Sher, who had been Illustrious before his father's death. "A Majestic's heir would be Highness, and the others would be Eminent."

"Eminent Wontas," Wontas said, consideringly. "We still have Eminents."

"Are we staying in this cave until spring?" Gerin asked loftily. He had a golden casket in one claw.

"Wrap the chain around your arm," Sher advised Selendra, taking up a gold stick thickly encrusted with diamonds. "I don't know what this was for, but I'll take it. We'll talk later."

Selendra wrapped the chain carefully. She couldn't wear it like that, though it looked splendid. Maybe she could have it incorporated into an evening hat, like Gelener's sequins. Or maybe she'd just sleep on it, like the rest of her gold. She tried not to think what Sher wanted to talk to her about. First, get out of the cave, afterwards worry whether it might be possible that she'd misinterpreted the whole situation.

Sher led the way along the passage, warning them of pits. With Wontas limping and Gerin burdened by his heavy casket, the easiest way of crossing pits in this new lofty hallway, was for Selendra to lift the dragonets under her arms and fly the few steps across.

"Do you recognize anywhere yet?" Selendra asked, while the children were lagging a little behind and Sher confidently took the lower fork at a junction.

"Not a thing, though I will if I come back," he said. "I'm sure we're going to make it out, though. I'm following the moving air."

There were no more surprises for a long time. The hallways were a maze of passages with occasional rooms wide enough for two or three dragons. One of them had shallow grooves in the floor, as if it had once been a dining room with primitive channels to carry away blood. Another had signs of ancient scorching on one wall. None of them held any further treasure. After a period of time that was hard to measure they came into another treasure cave, only in this one limestone teeth had caught up the treasure fast in their unbreakable embrace. "The rock is taking it back," Selendra whispered, putting a hand to her chain. They tiptoed through the cave without discussion, all subdued by it.

"How long do those take to grow?" Gerin asked, several hallways later, but everyone knew what he meant.

"Years," Sher said. "Decades. Centuries. You were talking about Majestic Tomalin, didn't you think how long ago he lived?"

"Thousands of years," Wontas said. "Thousands and thousands. Aunt Sel, is magic real?"

"Of course it is," Selendra answered, surprised. "If not for magic, how could we fly, big as we are? If not for magic, how would we grow larger from eating other dragons but not from eating beef and venison?"

"Not that kind of magic," Wontas groaned. "The other kind, the story kind. Spells, and wizards, and mountains eating dragon gold, and rocks coming to life and dancing?"

"I have never seen any of that," Selendra said. "The Church teaches that Camran cast out the wizards, so there must have been wizards at some time."

"Were they Yarge or dragons?" Gerin asked.

"This is a ridiculous conversation to be having lost under the mountains," Selendra complained.

"We're not lost," Sher said. "Look!"

Far ahead, and from somewhere below them they could see a dimness in the dark that must signal an opening to the outer world.

10
THE CHOICE OF ASSOCIATES

Avan's friends, like Avan himself, could be found in Irieth in season and out of season. Avan had been enjoying himself since his return to town. Having beaten Kest in a fair fight, his position in the Planning Office was for the moment unassailable. His work—the affair of the rebuilding of the Skamble which Liralen had handed to him on his return—required a great deal of research before he could make a decision or take any action. As Liralen knew this, Avan was freed of many of the usual chores of his office. He often had the satisfaction of asking Kest to take care of some tedious routine business, and seeing Kest accept his superiority in doing it. As for his social life, it was just as full and interesting as would excite no reproach in a dragon whose father had died not two months since. He declined some invitations and accepted others, and made sure those he declined were the prominent but tedious affairs which were attended mostly to be seen, and those he accepted were the more amusing smaller parties. He did not dance, save with the most beautiful maidens. His life, in short, would have been as happy as possible but for two things.

The lawsuit, begun in such bravado, was proving

slow and expensive in execution. Hathor shook his head over every fresh deposition. Selendra had written asking to have her name removed from the writ, because she could not endure to be separated from Haner. Penn had written in a passion which Avan could not at all understand, refusing to give any evidence at all. "Our best hope was for you all to stand together," Hathor said, wrinkling his snout. Avan had, naturally, told Penn he need not make a deposition if he did not wish to, but he could not understand what "religious scruples" might prevent him.

The second piece of grit in Avan's golden bed that winter was Sebeth. She remained as beautiful and captivating as ever. She continued to share Avan's desk every day and his bed most nights. But there was a sadness about her since the day Kest had insulted her that nothing seemed to ease. She worked with more than her usual enthusiasm, but she did not tease Avan as she had done. When he asked she said that she was happy and nothing was wrong. Bonnets in the latest style did not cheer her, nor did parties out on the frozen river with a group of friends, none of whom could have put the word Respectable before their names. Avan wondered if some other lover for whom she had really cared had left her, but did not ask. He tried to be gentle and caring towards her and hoped at least to provide some support.

Exalt and Exalted Rimalin had been out of town for a little while in Leafturn and Freshwinter. Avan had received an invitation to join them at Rimalin.

He had been far too busy even to consider it, he had sent them polite and genuine regrets. Then he received a note saying they were in Irieth and asking him to dine that evening. He had Sebeth dash off an immediate acceptance and set off for their town house with a light heart. He had been looking forward to discovering what investment opportunity the Exalted Rimalin had discovered, and he always enjoyed meeting Ketinar, Exalt Rimalin.

Servants showed him in, through the fashionable front hall, inlaid with pebbles and semiprecious stones, into the speaking room, where Ketinar came forward to greet him. She was a dark red, having survived three well-spaced clutches, and though her headdress bore sparkling citrines and garnets, proving her a lady in the forefront of fashion, nobody would have called her beautiful. Her face had an animation that made beauty irrelevant. Her eyes may have been too close to her snout, but they sparkled more than the jewels nodding among the lace on her forehead.

"I haven't seen you in an age," she said to Avan in welcome.

"I haven't been here since before my father's death," Avan said, and hastened on before she could speak. "And thank you so much for the letter of condolence you sent me, it was a comfort in a dark time."

"It's good you could come tonight. Rimalin especially wanted to see you. We're very thin of company in Irieth at present. Everyone is out of town, most of them off drearily chasing down venison with their bare claws, or with bare steel if they are female."

"So what brought you away from that delightful pursuit?" Avan asked.

Ketinar laughed. "I truly don't find it delightful, after the first day or two it's about as exciting as picking blackberries. But we came up to town because Rimalin has some business, which concerns you as well."

She clearly wanted him to ask about it, but he resisted for the time being. "I find I am the first to join you," Avan said, looking into the empty room, which was usually crowded in all seasons.

"You are our only guest tonight," Ketinar said. "When Rimalin finally comes up, we'll be able to eat. We do have some fairly fresh venison, brought up from the country. Be sure to admire it, for Rimalin caught it all himself."

Rimalin joined them presently, and the venison was duly eaten and admired. After dinner, in place of the usual sponging, Rimalin suggested that Avan might like to join them in their bathhouse.

"I didn't know you had your own bathhouse," Avan said. "I'd be delighted."

"It's only big enough for three, so we don't usually use it for company," Ketinar said.

She led the way down into the family part of the establishment. A servant with a pike clutched in his claws stood barring the way down, but he stepped aside with a smile as Ketinar waved him away. The lower parts of the cavern were gorgeously appointed in marble with statues and ornaments in gold and silver. The water in the great bath was steaming slightly and was lightly scented with cedar and sage.

"What a delightful scent," Avan said, wondering what it cost. Sebeth would like it. If he could buy her some it might bring the sparkle back to her eyes.

"It's one of Ketinar's extravagances," Rimalin said, fondly. The three of them took off their hats and slipped into the water.

"It seems a shame to talk business in such comfort," Rimalin said after a moment of basking.

Avan stared up at the ceiling, marble inlaid with jasper and amethyst in scale patterns. This was luxury at a level he could only envy. "It is very comfortable, but I am listening," he said. He was in fact consumed with curiosity.

"Old Eminent Telstie is dying," Rimalin said. Avan raised his head in surprise. This was not at all what he had expected. "Oh yes, he's not so very old, for an Eminent, but his fire came early and it's burning him out. He's not expected to last until summer. He has no surviving children. His heir was expected to be his elder nephew, but I heard they'd quarrelled. It can't be his younger nephew, he's a parson. The elder nephew won't hold it unless the will is nailed down. He's young. You know how it is with Eminents. The father is a parson, too. The nephew hasn't been brought up as the heir to an Eminent should be—old Telstie wasn't expecting him to need to be, he had plenty of children, but they all perished one way or another. But there's also a niece—the one we saw in Hathor's that day. Pretty thing, remember? She has just as good a claim on the Telstie estate as her brothers, or would if she were married to a rising dragon like yourself."

"But why would she be?" Avan asked, his expectations entirely confounded by the turn the conversation was taking. "I can't afford to marry. And I'd have to fight her brother."

"He's no bigger than you are," Ketinar put in. "And if you were married to Gelener Telstie and the Eminent's choice, her brother probably wouldn't even challenge."

"She has seventy thousand crowns of her own, even if the other affair didn't come off," Rimalin said.

Lulled by the warm water and the rich scents Avan almost began to consider it. To be an Eminent was like something out of a dream. His father had been born on the Telstie estate, and from what he had heard it was a wide demesne, in which he could soon grow large enough to defend his position. Then, like cold water down his scales, he remembered Kest's insulting name for Sebeth: "Little Eminence." A dream indeed, and not something in his reach, and to reach it he would have to marry a stranger and give up Sebeth. He might have given her up to save someone very dear to him, Haner, or Selendra, but not for this insubstantiality. "I don't even know the maiden," he protested. "She wouldn't consider me for an instant."

"We could introduce you," Ketinar said. "We've always wanted the best for you, Avan. We could also talk to her mother and father and tell them how much we esteem you and how suitable you are."

"What's the catch?" Avan asked bluntly.

"Somebody has to marry her, and somebody has to become Eminent Telstie. Why not a friend of ours?" Rimalin asked.

"And what would you want in return?" Avan asked.

"Your political influence, when you are Eminent and sit in the Noble Assembly in the Cupola. That wouldn't be difficult, considering that we agree on most things. Besides that, to manage some of your money. You know how well I manage my own. There are affairs that need lots of capital but bring a huge return. We could help each other. And immediately, for we would introduce her to you immediately, and she is about to return to Irieth immediately, there is one small thing you could do for me." Rimalin was sunk entirely below the water, only his eyes and nostrils showed. "I believe you are investigating property rights in the Skamble?"

"I am . . ." Avan said, and waited.

"Well, my friends and I might find it quite useful to know what you are going to decide. If the whole area is to come down, which seems the most likely thing, there will be fortunes to be made in demolition and rebuilding. It's a slum at present, but if it could be reclassified so warehouses could be built there, it could become a goldlode. That's where I'd advise you to invest your patrimony, if you want it to rival the wealth Gelener will bring you."

Avan could not speak. "Is it confidential?" he had asked Liralen, and the old clerk had replied "Tolerably." In his first week in the Planning Office four dragons had tried to bribe him in the street. His contempt for them had been small in comparison to his contempt for any dragon who would accept such a bribe. The work of the government offices was done by such dragons as would not. Even Kest, whom Avan detested, even Kest, he knew, would not even consider accepting a bribe for an instant.

The moment had stretched and stretched. He could not walk away, he was soaking in hot water and deep in Rimalin's hospitality. There was even a guard with a pike to stop him getting out. And was it a bribe? They had offered him a great deal, but what it amounted to was an introduction to a maiden with possibilities, no more. Besides, Rimalin had not asked him to change his decision, merely to let him know what his decision would be. Avan's decision was not yet made, but it already seemed more than likely that it would be the decision Rimalin wanted, to pull down the slum and have the Skamble made into warehousing to serve factories, river, and rail. It was only Sebeth's protests about the welfare of the working dragons who made the Skamble their home that had been causing him to hesitate and consider some well-built but affordable housing as part of his plan. He could tell Rimalin all this and accept the introduction and the chances that came with it, and lose nothing. Sebeth was not truly his and never could be. If he were a rich Eminent he could give her a small fortune of her own and she could move to another city and pose as a widow.

He opened his mouth, and he was almost ready to tell Rimalin all he knew about the Skamble. Then he remembered Liralen again, the first day he had gone to the Office for the Planning and Beautification of Irieth, directly after he had made his oath of service. "If ever you do accept a bribe, don't think that will be the end of it. Even if nobody finds out, which isn't likely, the person who has given it to you will know, and will accept more, and be able to blackmail you into giving more because of the existence of the bribe. And you will know, and you will have to wake up on your bribe every morning and live with yourself knowing how you got it."

"I can't tell you," Avan said, his teeth jarring together as he spoke. "I have sworn an oath that I will not do such things. Besides, I have little desire to marry a stranger for position."

"That's exactly what you need to do," Ketinar said. "You can't afford to have that sort of scruples, in your position."

"Scruples are for parsons, who are immune," Rimalin growled.

Avan stood, dripping. To his relief, Ketinar called a servant to dry his scales. "I think I'd better go," he said.

Ketinar walked to the door with him. Rimalin remained in the water. "What a pity," she said, when she had made her farewells. "I expect there's some maiden somewhere you're in love with, and though it doesn't show for men as it does for us, sometimes it's just as permanent a change."

Avan was grateful she took it so well. Nevertheless, as he flew home he did not expect to receive any more invitations from the Rimalins, nor ever to see Ketinar again.

38. DAVERAK CONSULTS HIS ATTORNEY

The Illustrious Daverak had occasionally chanced to come to Irieth out of season before this, but had never before been forced to spend several days there when he would have preferred to be in the country. Now, on a chill Freshwinter morning that would have been perfect for hunting, he had to knot his tail waiting in an overheated attorney's office, and then deal with irritating detail. The affair of the writ was more troublesome and time consuming than he had imagined. His attorney, Mustan, believed it would be possible to defeat it, but not as easily as Daverak would prefer. It seemed it would be necessary to go to court and have a judgment. The attorney wrote at once to all Bon's children, demanding statements and evidence.

"It isn't as clear-cut as you seem to think," Mustan said, pushing his eyeglasses closer to his eyes as he read his own notes. He was a young dragon, barely twenty feet long, but rising in position. Daverak had once been served by the long-established firm of Talerin and Fidrak, as had his father and grandfather before him. He had met Mustan at a party in Irieth, in season, several years before, and been completely won over by his energy and knowledge of the world. Slowly, over the next few years he had come to entrust all his business to him, first his investments and then almost everything, until Talerin and Fidrak did no more than the most routine parts of the management of the estate of Daverak. It was barely thirty years since Daverak had begun working with Mustan, but he had come to trust him completely. Even now he had no doubt of Mustan's competence, nor of his honesty. But for the first time, as Mustan questioned him closely on the affair, he did not experience complete confidence in his attorney's abilities. He wasn't sure Mustan saw things as he did. He wondered if he might have been better with an old established firm like Talerin and Fidrak after all, in such a delicate family matter as this. Yet he had entrusted Mustan with the affair of his marriage settlement and never twitched a claw.

"It would be a clearer case if the parson at his deathbed hadn't been his son," Mustan said, glancing up.

"There was another parson, one Freld or Frelt. My wife will know the name, she knew him. He judged the case at the time."

When Daverak had explained everything about

the matter, Mustan sighed, and threw a little more coal on the fire, although Daverak found the little room already intolerably hot and close. "That will help show you had right on your side when you acted. If Freld or whatever his name is will come to court, it will help. Speak to him about it when you get the chance, perhaps even invite him to dinner if that wouldn't be too onerous. We'll need his goodwill."

"I'll speak to him," Daverak said, though he regarded Frelt as a social inferior.

"But he's useful as a witness, not a parson. The parson who was with Bon is the only one who can help show his intention, and that is Penn, and he will speak against you from what you say."

"He as good as admitted at the time that Bon didn't mention it. And he won't go back on that now if he knows what's good for him," Daverak said, allowing a little flame to show in his throat.

"He is a parson, and immune," Mustan said, looking a little shocked.

"I didn't mean anything improper," Daverak said. "Just that he knows his preferment is dependent on family influence."

"I thought it was rather dependent upon this—" Mustan looked at his notes. "This Benandi family, to whom he has allied himself?"

"They will not like to hear of him speaking against his own family," Daverak said, irritated by this quibbling.

"Well, whatever he says, I'll make sure we have a

very experienced Pleader in court to question him about it. I was thinking of retaining Dignified Jamaney."

Daverak looked at him blankly, and the attorney sighed again.

"Dignified Jamaney is one of the best Pleaders in Irieth," he explained. "He can make eighty-foot Marshal Augusts weep like dragonets and proud Exalts admit their faults. He's expensive, but with him on our side, we have a much better chance of overcoming."

"But surely we don't need to resort to such tactics," Daverak said, repelled. "We have a good case. The will speaks of treasure, not of his body. They are being totally unreasonable."

"It depends entirely on how the jury see it," Mustan said, sitting back and resting both claws on his stomach. "Not the judges, in this case, the jury. The question is old Bon's intention. How you see matters isn't important if they can show that Bon saw them the way his sons seem to, do you see? Bon was a Dignified, and he held land, and he was your father-in-law, but he seems to have been a vulgar old fellow for all that. If it can be shown that he meant treasure in the vulgar sense, including his body, the judgment could go against you."

"That's absurd," Daverak said, half-decided to take this business back to the old established firm.

"Absurd or not, that's what we have to avoid. Splitting the family unity will help. If your wife and her sister who is your ward—" he picked up his notes again.

"Haner," Daverak said. "The Respected Haner Agornin. She'll be sensible about it."

"Yes. Good. If they, and especially if the other sister, the one who is at Benandi, speak for your side, then Avan will have very little case. But if all the children agree as to Bon's intention, then I don't know. There is a strong feeling among the common dragons that the bodies of their parents are the one bit of dragonflesh they will reliably come to consume, that this is what makes them different from the servant class, who never get any at all and never grow more than seven foot long in their lives. Now in a trial in Daverak this wouldn't be a problem, the jurors would all be your own farmers. But the writ was issued here in Irieth, so it definitely will. The jury are selected from the free population of the city. Considering the free population of Irieth, that means you may get a clerk, but to get someone Respectable would be a wonder. The majority of the seven will be common workers. They will be against you on principle."

Daverak sat back, almost knocking his shoulders on the wall. He hated the cramped office where he had to sit curled around, he hated the law for being so inconsiderate of the feelings of the Illustrious, he hated Mustan for knowing more about the business than he did, and he hated Avan for making the whole thing necessary. "Engage Dignified Jamaney then," he said. "Do whatever you think best. You have a free claw. Spend what you need. But Avan must be utterly defeated, he must learn that you cannot treat the Illustrious Daverak this way."

Mustan knew that blows to pride were as stinging as any other blows, so he merely made another note. "I'll have to talk to the Blessed Penn Agornin," he said. "I'll ask him to come and see me. I'll talk to Hathor too, Avan's attorney, and see if I can gather anything about what he really wants."

"Do that," Daverak said, feeling almost faint from the close air in the room.

"Will you be in town for another few days? I'd like to talk to you again when I have some more information."

"No, I have to go back to Daverak," Daverak said, knowing he couldn't stand any more of the city. "My wife is in a delicate condition."

"I'll write to you then," Mustan said, standing and opening the door. "I'll let you know as soon as there's a date for the hearing. There will probably be two hearings, a few weeks apart."

"And I want you to bring a case against Avan," Daverak said.

"What for?" Mustan asked, taking off his glasses.

"Harassment. Distressing my wife when she is expectant. Willfully annoying me."

"Better to win this case first, and then go forward with a case like that," Mustan said. "Besides, if he loses this case he'll lose all he has, without need for a countersuit. We'll be able to claim our costs, and they're likely to be high. He'll likely lose his position in his office as well—what is it, the Land Office? The Planning Office? They don't like scandal in those sorts of places. In which case he'll be out on the streets and not worth pursuing in court."

"Good," said Daverak. "We'll leave that for now. But get on with the other, and write to tell me how it's going. I'll come up to Irieth again if I must."

"You'll probably not need to come up before the case," Mustan said, nodding to Daverak as he squeezed out of the door. When his patron had gone, Mustan sat down with his papers before him and shook his head over them. "No telling how this one will go," he murmured to himself.

Out in the street, Daverak could breathe more freely. Mustan's office was in the fashionable Toris quarter, not far from Avan's workplace, had he known it. He strolled down the Promenade towards his club. He would tell them he was leaving and set off for home tonight. He wondered again about going back to Talerin and Fidrak. He wasn't sure that Mustan sympathized with him. He gave Mustan his business precisely because they had always been in agreement about the way to do things. Now, when it was most important, Mustan didn't seem to feel that Avan had done anything so terrible in taking him to law. Still, he had put the matter in Mustan's claws, and taking it out might be difficult, if Mustan wanted to make difficulties. Certainly it would take time, and it was certain that he would have to explain the whole wretched business again. No, he would let Mustan get on with it. He would have a reviving dinner alone in his club—none of his friends would be in Irieth now—spend the night there comfortably and then when morning came get out of the city as fast as his wings would bear him.

39. A SECOND PROPOSAL

In Daverak's absence, Berend had continued to entertain, if anything with more enthusiasm than when her lord was by her. Haner's warnings that she should conserve her energy for her clutch were overruled or even scoffed at. This was Berend's second clutch, she felt she knew all about it by now. She had produced two eggs, which sat in splendor in the gold-lined hatchery, wrapped in fleeces. She was, however, still in a delicate condition in expectation of a third. Since the loss of Lamerak she had stopped boasting of her ability to produce clutches of three, and indeed confessed one night to Haner that she would have been as glad to stop at two this time.

One evening when Haner slipped into the speaking room before dinner, she found Berend deep in conversation with the Dignified Londaver. His parents were also present, as were a few others of their neighbors. Many of those Berend liked best were away, making up hunting parties in remote locations. As Haner made herself attentive to the elderly Exalt Londaver, she could not help noticing that Berend and young Londaver kept turning their heads to look at her.

After dinner, and after sponging, Dignified Londaver suggested to Haner that as it was such a fine night they should go out and look at the stars. The elder members of the party smiled at the thought, and, Haner suspected, at the predictable nature of it. She herself could not for the moment tell what she felt. She had once been excited by Londaver's attention, but then when once it had been withdrawn she could not feel the same excitement again. Nevertheless she followed him out to the topmost ledge and opened her eyes to the winter sky, which was magnificent. The stars hung against the blackness in their multicolored profusion, like a spilt box of gems. Haner picked out the familiar constellations. The Great Beef was rising, with the Little Veal at her tail. The Winter Princess held out her hand in blessing.

"Aren't they glorious?" Londaver asked.

"Oh yes," Haner agreed.

"And think of our ancestors seeing them just the same and finding all those shapes in them. I've thought of that since you told me about that, that time, you remember, when you were staying here before?" Londaver spoke as if he had not seen her since her visit to Daverak when they had danced and looked at the stars, as if the polite but formal intercourse they had shared in the last months had never happened. She did not feel at all romantic, she felt angry.

"So what brings you out under them tonight, Dignified?" she asked, as coldly as she could.

"The beauty of your eyes to outshine them," he said, awkwardly.

Haner wanted to bite him. "Don't you think this is ridiculous, when you've been ignoring me all this time?" she asked.

"Ignoring you?" He was confused. "I wasn't. I always liked you."

"I'd respect you a great deal more if you spoke the truth," Haner said. "Now I believe I shall return to the speaking room, there's a chill in the air."

"Only on your side," Londaver said. "Honestly, I've always liked you. But you know I'm a poor dragon, living on what my parents allow me, and they're not really rich. I couldn't afford to marry where there wasn't a little dowry to ease things along. After your father died I kept my distance because I hadn't made any promises and I didn't want to make any I couldn't keep. I tried to put you out of my mind, but I always cared for you. Now Berend tells me things have changed again. She says Daverak will treat you as a daughter and dig out some extra gold to pad out what your father left you, to make it the same as hers was. That's uncommonly good of Daverak, and it means I'm free to think of you again."

He was a Dignified, and he would be an Illustrious. Selendra had given him her approval. If she married him she would be away from Daverak and the terrible practices condoned there. Yet her heart did not beat faster, her breath did not catch in her throat, and though he took a step closer to her on the shelf she did not feel the tide of pink rush through her scales the way it did to maidens in stories.

"How do you treat your servants?" she asked abruptly.

Londaver stopped where he was, frowning. "My servants?" he asked. "How do you mean? I keep their wings strapped down and make sure they know when I like dinner, that sort of thing."

"And what happens when they grow old?"

"Oh, usually we unbind their wings and let them live on farms nearby," Londaver said, relief at having a question he understood plain in his voice. "Mother usually sees to it. She sends them beef and preserves now and again."

"That's what we did at Agornin," Haner said. "Here the servants are all afraid. It's making me think the whole institution is wrong. No dragon should be unable to use their wings."

"Parsons," Londaver countered quickly.

"That's free choice," Haner said. "That's different. It just seems wrong."

"Are you a free-thinker?" Londaver asked, taken aback. "A radical?"

"I don't know, what do they believe?" Haner asked.

"Well, that servants should be freed, that religion should be kept to Firstday, and the Old Religion tolerated, that everyone should be equal before the law, that kind of thing."

"I think I may be," Haner said, consideringly, surprised at herself.

"You'd better keep that to yourself," Londaver advised.

"Are you still making me an offer?" Haner asked.

"Yes, certainly, why would that change anything?" Londaver asked, sounding honestly puzzled. "You're not going to unbind all the servants at Londaver or anything are you?"

"Not immediately," Haner said. She wasn't sure that this indulgence of her beliefs as if they were an eccentricity was what she wanted, but it was much better than what she might have had. She shuddered to imagine Daverak's response to her declaration of free-thinking, or even her father's.

"Then how would you like to come over here and embrace me?" Londaver asked, uncertainly.

Haner hesitated. If she did, she would blush, and then she would be committed. "Don't you think you ought to check with Illustrious Daverak about the dowry first?" she asked. "Before you're entirely committed?"

"You're so practical, Haner," Londaver said. "So clever and so practical, and so pretty in that delicate way. I really do like you the best of all the maidens I ever met. Do you think Daverak would try to cheat us? I suppose I would be in a better position to negotiate with him if you're not looking all bridal. Very well, let's just keep it a verbal agreement until I speak to Daverak. But I shall consider that we are to be married, whatever color your scales are, and I dearly look forward to seeing them pink, and then redder and redder."

He was no dragon out of legend, bold, wild, and firm of resolve. But he was considerate and not cruel and he could give her a home where Selendra could also live. "I'll marry you as soon as you like, once you have the dowry all arranged," she said, thinking that she must write to Selendra at once.

40. A SECOND DEATHBED

Haner and Londaver returned to find the establishment in uproar. "The Illust' Daverak has been taken unwell," Exalt Londaver said gently to Haner. "We'll be going now, I only waited for you to come in. You'll want to be with your sister, Haner dear." She smiled at Haner in a way that showed she guessed what had passed under the stars. Haner was almost too concerned to notice.

"How serious is it?" she asked the older dragon. "Should I send for a doctor?"

"One has already been sent for," Exalt Londaver said gently. "My husband has gone to fetch one for her. I'd go to your sister at once, that's where you can do most good."

Without hesitating to bid good-bye even to her newly affianced husband, Haner hurried down to Berend's sleeping cave, only to find it empty. She stopped a hurrying servant and asked where Berend was.

"Hatching room, 'Spec," the servant said, and hurried on, head bowed.

Haner went to the hatching room with a heavy heart.

She heard her before she saw her. Berend was groaning horribly, catching her breath and groaning again. Haner hurried in. Berend was sitting curled around her two safely delivered eggs. She was more green than red, and some of her scales were falling. Next to the nacreous swirling iridescence of the eggs she looked like spoiled meat. She looked up as Haner came in, and Haner saw that her eyes were whirling wildly.

"Illustrious Londaver has gone for a doctor," she said, her voice losing confidence in the middle of the sentence.

"A parson would be better," Berend said, between groans. "The egg is broken, I can feel it. It's killing me, the same way Mother died. You were only an egg, but I remember."

"The doctor might be able to help," Haner said, without much hope. "I wish Amer were here. She'd know what to do."

"Daverak would have eaten her by now, for being old and slow and ugly," Berend said, tossing her head and groaning again.

Haner could say nothing.

"And just the worst time," Berend went on, quite conversationally. "I have no idea what Daverak will do, but it won't be anything good. I was hoping you'd have thoroughly secured young Londaver, but I see you didn't."

"Don't worry, we're to be married," Haner said, soothingly.

"Then why aren't you pink?" Berend asked. "No, he'll slip away now, because unless he felt really committed he won't marry you when Daverak won't stand by my promises."

"I'll be all right," Haner said. "Don't worry about me."

Berend's eyes rolled and she let out another very loud groan. "Look after my children," she said. "All four of them."

"I'll do what I can for them," Haner promised.

"They like you," Berend assured her.

Haner knew that already. "I like them," she said, feebly.

"Do you think you could shift this egg?" Berend asked, abruptly, panting a little. "It's definitely broken, no doubt of it. It's hurting me."

"I can try, but I'm no doctor," Haner said. She walked around her sister and lifted her tail. She almost dropped it again. She had never seen so much blood. More was oozing from beneath her sister's tail. The flesh of Berend's private parts looked stretched and torn. Haner could not see an egg. As she moved her hand, a scale fell from the tail where she had been touching it. "Should you be in here?" Haner asked. "If you start to thrash around you'll break those two eggs."

"That would be the last beef to break the bridge as far as Daverak's concerned," Berend said, and slowly dragged herself to her feet. "I came here because I thought I might manage to deliver the egg, and here is where it would need to be. I started to bleed in the dining room. It was almost funny. Our guests didn't know whether to help me or eat me."

"Oh Berend," Haner said, torn between laughter and tears. "Can I help you to your sleeping room?"

"I don't think you can help, unless you can free the fragments of the shell."

"I can't see them," Haner admitted.

"That's bad," Berend said, and groaned again as she began to drag herself along up the corridor, one step at a time, towards her sleeping cave. Her scales were falling as she moved.

Haner's attendant, Lamith, met them part way. "The doctor's not here yet, 'Spec," she said, to Haner. "Shall I send for the parson?"

"Yes," Berend said. "Send somebody who can fly, because I need him soon." There was a great smear of blood stretching down the corridor from the door of the hatching room.

"There's nobody here with wings unbound," Lamith said, not harshly but stating a fact.

"I could go," Haner suggested, tentatively. "Or Exalted Londaver may come back with the doctor, and he could go."

"I don't know how much g——ing time this will take," Berend said, and the frank obscenity shocked her sister. "I think you'd better go, Haner, I don't want him to come too late."

"Good-bye then, Berend, beloved sister, in case we don't meet again."

"Come back with him, come in with him," Berend said. "I want someone of my own with me while I die."

"Should Lamith fetch the children?" Haner asked.

"For Jurale's sake no, have pity on them," Berend said, explosively. "I had to watch my mother die this way, no need to inflict it on them."

Haner made for the nearest open ledge and flew off towards the church and the parsonage. The night was still clear and full of beautiful stars, the air was chill but clean, bearing a taste of distant fir trees, and she could not help feeling a deep relief to be outside and away from the blood and the pain.

The parsonage was dark, and she had to wake both the parson and his wife to explain who she was and what she wanted. "If the Illust' is dying, it is an emergency, I will fly," the parson declared at last, looping the red cords around his claw so that he could bind his wings again after he had reached Daverak. Haner wanted to ask if he would have walked to a farmer's deathbed, or perhaps not gone until morning. "Has the Illustrious been told?" he asked, as they flew. "Somebody should send to him at once, in Irieth."

"There's nobody to fly," Haner said, only then realizing how ridiculous this was, when there were so many farmers on the estate. "I'll find somebody to send," she said.

"She may not last until his return," the parson warned. "If she's as bad as you say. Irieth is far away. But Jurale has mercy, and she may."

They landed on the ledge. It was now well on into the night. The establishment seemed unnaturally quiet. Haner could smell the blood at once, though it had been cleaned from the floor. The doctor was coming out of Haner's sleeping cave when they got there.

"Dead," he said, briefly.

"That isn't her room," Haner said. "It's mine. Hers is up the corridor."

"Perhaps this was nearer," the doctor said, looking at her strangely. It would have been, Haner realized, much nearer. But she did not want Berend to have died in her room, on her gold, and with nobody with her.

The parson went in, alone. He put up a restraining claw to stop Haner in the doorway. She waited, numb.

"Where is the Illustrious Daverak?" the doctor asked.

"In Irieth on business," Haner answered.

"So unfortunate that this should have happened when he was away," he said.

"She took every care of herself," Haner said. "She wanted this clutch. She was looking forward to the third egg. She was eating well."

"It's a terrible thing," the doctor said. "She wasn't herself at the last."

Haner wondered what Berend had said to him, but dared not ask.

The parson came out, licking his lips. Haner could not even indulge her grief by beginning to eat her sister, she knew she must wait for Daverak. It was only then that she realized how alone she was here now. Daverak had taken her in as Berend's sister. With Berend dead, would he even be prepared to keep her? Berend had said that he liked her, but she had also said that he would no longer make up the dowry so that she could marry Londaver. Useless to curse Daverak for being arrogant and selfish, or Londaver for being poor and weak, or her hands for not being claws. Whatever they were, she was in their power in her own despite. At last she wept, outside the room where Berend lay, and the parson and doctor thought it most appropriate, for they were not to know that her tears were far more for her own situation than for her dead sister.

11
A MAIDEN'S LOVE

To turn our minds and our attention back two weeks in time and sixty hours flight west, the attentive reader will not have forgotten, even amid the excitement of Irieth and the dramatic developments in Daverak, that the last we saw of Selendra, Sher, and Penn's two dragonets they were lost in a cave deep beneath the Benandi mountains and the falls of Calani.

There we shall rejoin them, in the drear dampness of the chilly limestone, hurrying towards the daylight Sher had glimpsed, hurrying indeed so much that they almost, in their haste, fell down another pit. Sher saved himself on the brink, drawing to a halt so sudden that the two dragonets, immediately behind, stepped on his tail.

Sher peered down into the pit. "The light's coming from down here," he said. "It seems to be a substantial cavern. I think we'll have to go down."

"Is it a good idea going deeper and deeper like this?" Selendra asked, anxiously.

"This is where the moving air seems to be coming from," Sher said, without answering her directly. "I'll go first, and I'll take Wontas. There's a terrible glare of light down there, we can't be far from the outside.

It makes it harder to see, though. Wait there until I call."

With no more hesitation, Sher took Wontas and plunged down over the edge. Selendra moved forward into the space he had freed. Gerin cowered down beside her, looking over the edge. She immediately realized what Sher meant about the light. From behind she had been in the familiar homely darkness of any cavern. Now, leaning down on the slippery edge it was too bright to see without blinking her inner lids over her eyes, but that made it much dimmer than it would be without any light at all.

She waited, unable to see much, for what felt like a long time. She felt an uncomfortable drip on her neck, water heavy with lime, ready to grow a limestone tooth on her scales if she waited here much longer. She thought of the half-eaten treasure and imagined the teeth growing through her fallen scales and bones. Gerin began to speak, but she shushed him, not wanting to miss anything Sher might say. She had almost become convinced that he had managed to kill himself in the depths before she heard his voice, thin and echoing.

"It's a bit tricky, but we're out. Can you hear me, Selendra?"

"Yes," Selendra called, deeply relieved.

"It's a big cavern, and there's a slot halfway down the wall which leads to the outside. There's no ledge or cave, just a slot. The difficult bit is managing to fly straight out and then down to where you can land,

below. I've left Wontas down there, by a little stream.
I know roughly where we are, though I'll need to go
up high to check. One thing is for sure, we're facing
due west into the setting sun, which makes it hard to
see."

"Where are you now?" Selendra asked, fighting
down panic.

"Outside, circling in the air. It's too steep to perch.
It's not a cliff, but it's sheer."

"And where is the slot, relative to me?"

"It's due west, and you're facing it, below you."

"Then make sure you're not in the way, we're coming now," Selendra called, then waited for a moment,
drawing breath and tensing her muscles for the dive
into the uncertain light.

She never knew how Sher had made it. Even knowing the slot was there, and knowing there was nowhere to alight immediately outside, it was all she
could do to clutch Gerin tightly and let her wings
carry her down and forward, aiming for the center of
the space. She was almost blind as she came directly
into the light. The gap, or slot as Sher had called it,
was not large. She flew for it, struggling against the
damp air and the sensation that the cave wanted to
suck her down and swallow her.

Once outside, she could see. An undistinguished
hillside of tumbled rocks and grass lay below her,
with a few muttonwools grazing unconcernedly
among the boulders. At the bottom of the slope
ran a small, fast-moving stream, then another slope

rose up, not as high nor as steep as their own ridge, and beyond that other ridges. She flew down to the stream, delighting in the warmth and movement of the clean outdoor air. As she went down, she lost the direct rays of the sun, and it was suddenly cold, colder than the cave had been. She caught sight of Wontas, drinking awkwardly from the water, his broken leg caught up against his chest.

She landed as close to him as she could, then looked around for Sher. He was high overhead, circling.

"Sher said he'd go up until he saw which way to go to fetch the basket," Wontas said, looking up, water dripping from his mouth.

Selendra spread out her wings, feeling a great urge to stretch them after so long in such cramped conditions. She folded them, then opened them out again completely and arched her back. Only then did she bend her neck to drink. The water was icy, making her teeth ache when it touched them.

"Did that stone move?" Gerin asked, suddenly. Selendra looked up where Gerin was looking, at the opposite slope. It was strewn with boulders, ranging in size from the size of a hatchling's head to almost as big as she was. None of them were moving. She looked back to Gerin, puzzled.

"It seems as if they move when I'm not looking at them," he said. Selendra looked back at the rocks. They were still, very still, with a stillness that seemed more like waiting than the natural stillness of rocks that lie where they have fallen.

Sher came swooping down. "It's cold here in the shade," he said, closing his wings with a great clap. "I know the way back to the falls, but it's an hour's flight. We have come a tremendous distance under the mountains."

"The sun is almost down, we must have been underground for hours," Selendra said. "You go as quickly as you can and fetch the basket."

Sher drew her upslope a little, away from the dragonets, who were both drinking in the stream. "You couldn't carry one of them?"

"Not for an hour, and not safely at all," she replied, quietly. "Why?"

"Nothing you don't know. Just the cold, and Wontas being hurt." Sher frowned. "Try to keep them warm if you can."

"I'll do my best," Selendra said. She had never before seen Sher when he was so serious.

"And Selendra," he said, taking a step closer. She trembled, but did not retreat. "I wanted to say I think you've coped with all this marvellously."

"So have you," she said, meaning it. "I don't know how you did that flight, not knowing what was there."

"Luck," he said, smiled, and took another step towards her. He was now so close as to be almost touching her. She did not move. She knew what he intended, but her mind flashed back to Frelt, to Amer's potion, to the talk of numbers. "You were wonderful, keeping the children's spirits up, and doing it all without complaining. I can't think of a better dragon to be lost in a cave with, and indeed, I can't think of a better dragon to spend my life with. What do you say?"

Selendra looked down along the length of her scales. They remained plainly and uncompromisingly gold. Her protestations that she did not wish to marry seemed thin in her own eyes, looking at Sher, so strong and handsome and certain beside her. She could almost feel the warmth of his body. Her heart was beating strongly enough to make her feel faint, but she cast another despairing look down and still she was gold, stubbornly maiden pale.

"Selendra?" Sher said, questioningly, for she had not spoken.

"Your position, mine, your mother, my brother," she said, in more than a little agitation. "I do not think you would find that we suit each other."

"But I can deal with my mother, soon she will love you as a daughter. As for the rest it is nonsense, you are gently born and your nephews have just found you a fortune," Sher said, gently, putting his claw out towards her. "I love you. If you—"

"You have your answer," she said, roughly, stepping away deliberately. "Now I know you would not make my life difficult by pressing me on the mountainside when we are still dependent on each other to return to the protection of our families."

"Of course not," he said. "But Selendra—" It had hardly occurred to Sher, who had been pursued by maidens and their mothers ever since he grew wings, that the one maiden he wanted could reject him.

"Please don't press me," she said, taking refuge in coldness though her heart was breaking and her eyes were full of tears. "Go and get the basket. Please, Sher."

He rose into the air and caught the wind, turning as he rose. She watched him out of sight, but still she could not cry, because now the children were there and their questions had to be answered. She looked once more at her traitorous scales which, if they had followed her heart, would have been as pink as the wing of cloud that rose above the ridge ahead, where still the stones kept as unnaturally still as if they had no power of movement. She stared hard at the stones while she dealt with the children, hoping to catch just one of them moving. Her eyes whirled faster and faster, but still she was gold, and still the rocks kept their places for all of the small eternity until Sher came back with the basket.

42. CONVERSATION IN THE PLACE

Three days after the dramatic rescue of Wontas, Exalt Benandi sent down a note by a servant, summoning Felin to come alone for an audience. Felin was always in and out of the Place, hardly a day went by when she did not make some call, formal or informal, on the Exalt. It was rare, however, for the

Exalt to demand that she call without providing a reason. Felin received the note at breakfast without remark, merely telling Penn that the Exalt needed her. This was so common an occurrence that Penn scarcely looked up from his own letters to note it. Felin looked at him, consideringly, and then turned her gaze on Selendra, who was reading a letter and eating mutton with an air of being about to dissolve into tears. It was far more likely Selendra than Penn whose behavior had caused this summons. "Alone" was certainly meant to ensure the absence of one or the other of them. She could think of nothing Penn might have done recently to earn the disapprobation of his patroness. Selendra, however, might well have. Felin had spent the time since the disaster of the picnic largely concerned with the well-being of Wontas, who seemed to be recovering, though he still talked of nothing but treasure. Now she considered Selendra. She had come back shaken by her ordeal, far more tremulous and tearful than Felin would have imagined such a trial would have made her.

"I will see to the dragonets before I go up," she said. "Will you be going out today, Penn?"

"I need to reply to this letter," he said, frowning over it. "I'll be in my study."

"Shall I need to write for you?" she asked.

"No, I'll do it myself, or if it's too much, Selendra shall do it," Penn said, managing a half smile, though his eyes still whirled too quickly for his wife to believe that he was calm. Felin decided to leave him alone with his trouble, he would bring it to her if he thought she could help.

"Then will you help Amer with the dragonets unless Penn needs you, Selendra?" Felin asked. Selendra looked up dreamily. She had clearly not been paying any attention at all to the conversation. Felin patiently repeated everything and waited until Selendra gave her assent. Then she set her little green topper on her head and flew up the cliff to the Place.

Sher was not sitting on the ledge that morning. Indeed, the snow on the ledge was largely uncleared, indicating that he had not sat there for a day or two. Felin frowned as she picked her way over it, leaving clear tracks behind her. She wondered very much what it was the Exalt wanted.

The Exalt was waiting for her in the lesser speaking room, not in her office. She was sitting comfortably couchant along the wall. "Felin, my dear," she said in greeting. "How lovely to see you."

"What can I do for you, Exalt?" Felin asked.

"I just wanted to have a few words," the Exalt said, gesturing. Felin obediently sat. "Can I offer you a bite?"

"We just had breakfast," Felin said, waiting for the Exalt to begin on whatever was troubling her.

"I've decided to go to Irieth early this year," she said.

Felin's eyes sped up a little. The Exalt hated Irieth, and rarely went there a day before the fashionable time. "In Thaw?" she suggested.

"No, earlier than that," the Exalt said, looking away from Felin. "In Icewinter, or maybe even before the end of Freshwinter."

"So you are planning to spend almost the whole winter in the city?" Felin asked, knowing she wasn't hiding her astonishment.

"Yes, I know," the Exalt said, spreading her hands in helplessness, and answering Felin's thoughts rather than her words. "I do hate Irieth, and I never leave home in the winter. It's Sher."

"Sher?" Felin echoed, puzzled. Sher rarely spent much of the winter in Benandi anyway, but why did it concern his mother? "Does he want to go to Irieth?"

"No, he wants to stay here." The elderly dragon put her great ruby-red head down between her hands for a moment, as if the weight of it was too much to support, then she looked up at Felin again. "That's why I need to go to Irieth, for he can hardly stay here without me."

"I don't understand," Felin said, though she was beginning to wonder if she did.

"This is very difficult," Exalt Benandi said. "My dear, without meaning the slightest disparagement of yourself, or your husband, or indeed of his sister, I have to ask you to keep Selendra away from the establishment until I get Sher away from here. He has taken it into his head to fall in love with her, and I know you haven't done anything to encourage it, nor Penn. I'm inclined to lay at least half the blame with Sher."

"Half?" Felin said, drawing herself up sejant. "I don't think Selendra would have done much to encourage him."

"Well it's natural for any young maiden, with an unmarried Exalted Lord, I'm sure," the Exalt said. "But I'm sure you can see why it won't do."

"I don't see at all," Felin said, feeling a little hurt on Selendra's behalf. "She comes of good family, she's Penn's sister, she has an adequate dowry—"

"You can't call sixteen thousand crowns adequate for Sher," said the Exalt, though Felin knew there was no real reason why Sher needed to marry for money.

"Adequate, if not spectacular," Felin said. "It might not be what you'd have chosen, but I don't see why it would be such a disaster, if she is the one Sher has chosen to love. If they care for each other, why shouldn't they marry?"

"Sher is young and easily swayed. You know that." The Exalt's blue eyes whirled in a deeply agitated manner, but her hand gesture dismissed Sher's choices.

Felin did know he was easily swayed. She remembered when Sher's fancy had lighted briefly on her. After the first giddy moment she had known that he was a brother to her, and not a husband. Besides, she knew his mother would never countenance it, and that Sher would not, could not, fight his mother. She had been gently discouraging, and Sher had given way at the first opposition and his mother's offer of a month hunting the high mountains. If Selendra was enough to make him offer battle to his mother then he must love her more than lightly.

"Besides," the Exalt said, uneasily, going on although Felin had not spoken. "Sher will soon forget her if he is in Irieth seeing other maidens."

"Not Gelener, I don't think," Felin said.

"Don't be cruel, Felin. I already know that. But if he's put in the way of a number of pretty maidens with well-formed tails and shining scales he'll forget Selendra."

"And Selendra?"

"She will forget him too. She must. She must turn her eyes to those of her own rank. It's the way of the world. You know it and I know it."

"What I know—" Felin broke off. She had remembered that she must on no account quarrel with the Exalt. She began again more gently. "Sher is old enough that you cannot make him do your bidding."

"No, but I can distract him," the Exalt said. "It seems that we have been lucky so far. He made advances to Selendra on the mountain, which she did not reciprocate."

"Jurale's mercy!" Felin said, astonished.

"Yes, I have been sending up thankofferings to Jurale myself," the Exalt said, her eyes sharper now, mercifully deciding to regard Felin's ejaculation as a prayer rather than a profanity. "She did not reciprocate it?" the Exalt said again, as a question this time.

"No, she is as pure a maiden gold as the day she arrived," Felin said. "There's no question of that."

"Then we have no difficulties, except keeping them apart to thwart their affection at this stage," the Exalt said. "Which means that when I invite you and Penn to the Place, while Sher is here and before we go away, please leave Selendra at home with the children."

"I can't," Felin said, not knowing she intended to until the words were out. "It's grossly unfair, Exalt, surely you see that. She has done nothing wrong, and you're punishing her, and asking us to punish her, as though she had transgressed terribly."

"I am merely asking you to leave her at home, and also to deny your door to Sher for the time being, though I doubt he would seek her out at the parsonage."

"He will if he doesn't find her here when he expects her," Felin said. "I won't encourage him to call, but I can hardly keep him out, have you forgotten he has every right to enter anywhere he wishes, as the Exalted Benandi?"

"He's unlikely to go to those lengths," the Exalt said, dryly. "Do you think he would come to consume the dragonet he risked his life to save?"

"That's another reason I can't refuse him entry," Felin said. "I owe him so much gratitude for rescuing poor Wontas. It is for you to control your son's movements, if you feel you have that right, but you cannot impose that on me in the circumstances."

"I will tell Sher I think it unwise for him to see her," the Exalt said, her snout wrinkled as if she could smell decaying venison. It had been years since she had been able to control Sher.

"Then I will promise you that I won't leave him alone with Selendra in the parsonage, should he choose to visit," Felin conceded.

"That will do," the Exalt said, looking as if she had bitten into a spoiled preserve. "And leave her at home when you come to dinner."

"I can't do that either," Felin said. "I can't leave her at home as if she's in disgrace."

"I cannot have her here dangling under Sher's snout like a tender morsel he longs to snap up," the Exalt said.

"Then for the time being, until you choose to invite all of us, the three of us will remain at home," Felin said.

The Exalt looked darkly at her, but Felin refused to shift her ground. The two stared into each other's eyes, and though Felin was fond of her old guardian she felt she owed it to Selendra, and to Sher as well, the saviors of her hatchling, to stand firm. She held the Exalt's gaze until the Exalt shook her head. "Very well," she said. "I'm disappointed, Felin, but that will do. The sooner we go to Irieth the better."

"I hope you have a very pleasant time there," Felin said, dipping her head slightly. She turned and made her way out, leaving the Exalt alone and brooding over her son as she had done since he was in the egg.

Sher was waiting outside. "Has she forbidden you

to bring Selendra here?" he asked, looking so miserable that Felin melted towards him completely and did not even call him a fool.

"I have said we'll accept no invitations that are not for the three of us," Felin said. "I've also said I'll never close my establishment to you, but that I'll not leave you alone with Selendra there."

"I hadn't thought she'd make it so difficult," Sher muttered.

"Give it a little time. Give yourself a little time. You know how changeable you are," Felin said.

"I'm not," Sher growled. Felin just looked at him, memory in the depths of her gray eyes. "Oh Felin, I suppose I am. I didn't mean to be cruel to you, and you gave me no encouragement."

"I am very happily married to Penn," she said. "But it might do you good to consider how long you mean this for, considering how opposed your mother seems to be."

"You mean not see Selendra?"

"Stay here. Wait. If you still feel the same in two months, which would make it at Deepwinter Night, then I'll take you seriously, and arrange for you to have some time alone with Selendra—outside. I didn't promise anything about that. You can go flying together. But make sure you're ready for the battle it'll take with the Exalt."

"I'll wait," Sher said, smiling. "I know I can. Thank you, Felin."

Felin shook her head as she went out to the ledge. She had been giving way to him for years, as they had both been giving way to his mother for years. Habits could be very difficult to break.

43. CONVERSATION IN THE PARSONAGE

As soon as Felin left for the Place, Penn put down his letter and looked at Selendra.

"What possessed Avan to try to take Daverak to law? And what possessed you to join your name with him?" He sounded thoroughly irritated, and even a little worried.

"You agreed that Daverak had no right to eat as much of Father's body as he did," Selendra said, startled. "You were furious."

"That's different. That's a family disagreement. Personally, yes, I agree, Daverak had no right. I argued as much at the time. But Selendra, taking him to law, taking the matter out of the family, exposes us in a way that is potentially most uncomfortable." Penn looked at her helplessly. "Can he be persuaded to withdraw?"

"You can ask him, of course, but he seemed adamant that he would go ahead with it," Selendra said. "It is Avan who was most harmed by Daverak."

"I shall write straight away, refusing my cooperation," Penn said. "You must do the same, withdrawing your name."

Selendra bowed her head. "Haner urges the same," she said, touching her fingers to the letter she had just received. "She says we will not be able to maintain our friendly intercourse unless I do."

"Well, of course not," Penn said.

Selendra felt the tears spilling out of her eyes and down her snout. "I couldn't bear not to see Haner," she said, the words catching in her throat.

"Then write and withdraw your name," Penn urged.

"I suppose so. But poor Avan."

"Poor Avan! Avan has started all this. He doesn't understand what trouble he can cause. They want me to tell them everything Father said on his deathbed," Penn said, tapping the letter on his knee. "Preposterous. Outrageous. Impossible."

"Why?" Selendra asked.

"Why?" Penn's eyes shifted from side to side uncomfortably. "His privacy, my position. It's unthinkable."

"I see," Selendra said, although not knowing the circumstances of the confession, she did not see in the slightest why Penn could not simply tell them what they needed to know.

"I shall write to them myself, immediately," Penn said, bustling out, flexing his claws in anticipation of the pen.

Selendra turned her attention back to the half-eaten mutton before her. She did not want it. She had barely been able to eat since Sher—since the rescue of Wontas. She had not seen Sher since their return. She had not been out of the parsonage. Penn and Felin had treated her extremely well, thinking the ordeal in the cave had exhausted her. They had both expressed their gratitude, and Felin had made Wontas thank her too. Nobody had pressed her to do anything she did not want to. She had even been able to escape the Firstday church service the previous day, though Penn had come and prayed with her in her bedroom. She had not minded that. She did not wish to neglect the gods, indeed she especially wanted to implore Jurale's mercy. She had not wanted to go to church because she hadn't wanted to see Sher.

One of the servants was peering around the doorway, to see if it was time to take the bones away. "I've finished," Selendra said. The servant made a pleased bob, glad of the leftovers no doubt. Selendra drew herself to her feet, took up Haner's letter, and went to look in on the dragonets.

The nanny was rebinding Wontas's claw, and Gerin was helping to keep Wontas entertained through the process. After checking that the smell of the break was still clean, Selendra left them to it.

Amer was alone in the kitchen, making a foul-smelling potion. The other servants were still clearing the dining room.

"Is that for Wontas?" Selendra asked.

"It's to keep the break clean," Amer explained. Then she stopped, frowning. "What's wrong, Selendra?"

"Nothing," Selendra said, trying to keep her violet eyes from spilling tears. "I have a letter from Haner."

"What's happened to her?"

"She doesn't sound happy. Avan is taking Daverak to law and it's disturbing her. Daverak has taken flame, look." Amer could not read, so Selendra could safely show her the drawing.

Amer laughed, and pushed the paper back. "Read it to me," she said.

Selendra read it, leaving out the teasing about Sher, which she knew her sister had meant kindly but which now felt like a spear against her tender breast. When she finished, Amer shook her head. "She didn't say a word of greeting to me? And where you had put in your letter that I sent my regards, she put that comment about the institution of servitude being wrong?"

"That's right," Selendra said. "I suppose she's right, it is unfair, but it's the way the world is. So many things are unfair." She sighed.

Amer flexed her wings a little in their bindings. "So what unfairness has life brought you?" she asked, with a great deal of generosity. She was fond of Selendra.

Selendra looked behind her to make sure no other servants had come into the room unnoticed. "It seems the numbers were against me with the potion," she said, lowering her voice.

"Are you sure?" Amer asked.

Selendra gestured to her relentlessly golden flank.

"Who was it? Did he touch you?"

"Sher," she admitted, in a whisper.

"The Exalted Benandi?" Amer asked. "You're aiming to do well for yourself, my dragonet!"

"It wasn't like that at all!" Selendra protested. "I never thought of him that way until he made it plain. I thought he was betrothed to Gelener Telstie."

"So did his mother, no doubt," Amer said, and chuckled. "So you didn't think it in advance? He took you by surprise? That might be reason enough for not coloring."

"I didn't expect Frelt either!" Selendra whispered angrily.

"No, but Frelt leaned against you, and he was expecting it. Did Sher lean?"

"No. He came quite close, almost touching, but he didn't exactly lean." Selendra's eyes whirled dreamily as she remembered.

"Did he touch you at all?"

"He put his claw out, but he didn't touch me. He was much closer than dragons are supposed to come, Amer! He was right next to me, less than a foot away."

"Get him to come closer next time," Amer advised. "It might be the potion, but it might not. Cuddle up to him as you might to your sister and see if that makes you blush."

"I don't expect there'll be another chance," Selendra said. "I told him to go away. And as you just said, he's an Exalted Lord and I am merely the parson's sister, he'll think about that and be glad I pushed him away." The tears spilled down now.

"Well, if you're not crying to be gold, you're crying to be pink," Amer said.

Selendra choked. "It isn't funny," she said, laughing despite herself.

"If he cares, he'll try again," Amer said, comfortingly. "Give him a chance, and get close to him. Touch him. You can't lose anything even if you don't color up."

"Only my dignity," Selendra said.

"And what's that worth in the marketplace?" Amer asked.

"But if I can't color, then I can't give him children. It would be very wrong to marry if I can't."

"Nobody ever heard of anyone marrying and staying a maiden," Amer said, quite loudly, as the servant who had been clearing the dining room came back into the kitchen with a pile of bare bones. "Take this potion to 'Spect Wontas, if you would, 'Spec Selendra, it's done now. And if you're writing to 'Spec Haner, tell her I'd be interested to hear more of what she was saying."

Selendra took the pot of potion and left.

44. CONVERSATION IN THE MILLINER'S ESTABLISHMENT

Felin considered as she flew home what she would tell her husband and her sister-in-law with respect to her conversation with the Exalt. Though she had defended Selendra as strongly as she dared, she was not sure how to begin the subject with her. As for Penn, Felin did not know how he would react. He was dependent on the Exalt for his position as Parson of Benandi, which provided the family with both home and income. He might be angry with his sister for causing trouble, and with Felin for not having acquiesced to everything the Exalt wanted. It would be easier not to open the subject with either of them. Yet both of them would notice that no invitations were forthcoming from the Place, and some explanation would have to be given.

On her return home she found Selendra playing with the dragonets. She did not venture any information, and Selendra also kept her own counsel.

When Penn came out of his study, wiping the ink from his claws, she had had time to think of her strategy. She took him aside to the speaking room. "The Exalt wishes to keep Sher and Selendra apart," she said.

"What? Why?" Penn's mind was still with Avan's scheme and the risk it posed to his profession.

"It seems she thinks Sher will grow too fond of her," Felin said.

"Sher? Nonsense. With all the maidens in Tiamath throwing themselves at his head why would he look at a pale little thing like Selendra?" Penn asked, unkindly.

Felin, who had guessed that this would be his reaction, merely spread her hands. "Who knows what makes the Exalt take ideas into her head?" she asked. "But for a little while we're not going to go to the

Place socially. You will, naturally, go up alone for everything you normally would, and so will I, but we won't visit them as a family for dinner or anything like that, until Sher goes away again."

"If that's what the Exalt wants," Penn said, frowning. "But does she really imagine that of Selendra?"

"Do you think she's not old enough?" Felin asked.

Penn did not want to discuss the Frelt incident with Felin, so he simply grunted. Husband and wife then joined Selendra for dinner, united in that perfect confidence which the enduring state of marriage inspires in so many dragons.

Several weeks passed in this way. The parsonage family and the Place family met only at Firstday services. The Exalt made sure that Sher stayed by her side on those occasions. Selendra missed no more church, but she sat with her head bowed, aware that Sher was looking at her but not daring to return his gaze. Sher did not attempt to visit the parsonage, and Selendra did not inquire as to her good fortune in not being forced to visit the Place. Freshwinter became Icewinter, and still Sher and the Exalt lingered in Benandi. Icewinter lived up to its name, showering them with snow. In the second week of Icewinter the news of Berend's death was brought to Benandi, casting Penn and Selendra into gloom, though neither of them had been especially close to their sister since her marriage.

Firstday came two days later, in the regular five-spoked turning wheel of the week. For the first time since the picnic, Selendra raised her head in church and met Sher's gaze. She did no more, but she allowed herself to look at him. Life was short and death was everywhere. If, by Jurale's mercy, Sher was there across the church, she would no longer forbid herself from the sight.

The morning after that, Felin announced at breakfast that she would take Selendra to visit the milliner.

"But we are still in mourning for our father, she does not need a change of headgear," Penn said.

"Not to change into mourning, no, but the few hats she has are sadly shabby. It will be Deepwinter in two weeks, and she should have something better to wear on Deepwinter Night than a hat she has been wearing almost daily since Highsummer! It is not so cold today, and it is hardly two hours flight."

"There is no need, Felin," Selendra murmured. Her sister-in-law overbore all protests and they soon set off.

It did Selendra good to be on her wings again. She had hardly been out since the picnic, except to church, which was a walk, of course. She had almost forgotten the feeling of the wind in her wings and the way the world looks in sunlight. The world was a whirl of white from above, broken only by the darkness of firs and the straight dark lines of the rails when they passed over them.

"It's cold, but it's glorious to fly," Felin said after a while, and Selendra was pleased to agree wholeheartedly. She felt better than she had for weeks.

"How far are we going?" she asked.

"Not far, unfortunately," Felin said. "I don't know why, but I love flying in the cold. My mother hated it. She used to say that before the Conquest her family came from warmer climates, which are all Yarge countries now, and her blood was too thin for up here."

Selendra laughed. "You must take after your father," she said. She had heard tales of Felin's brave father already, most often from Wontas, who bore his name.

The milliner's establishment was in the little town of Three Firs. Hepsie, the milliner, was neither so fashionable nor so elegant as those in Irieth. She was the widow of a dragon whose ambitions had not been as great as his prowess. She had taken up the profession out of desperation after his fall, hoping to feed her children without needing to take service with a great family. To her own surprise, she had prospered mildly as all the dragons in the region took advantage of her cunning fingers and reasonable prices. Felin had been buying hats from Hepsie for years, and even the Exalt would deign to buy the occasional country cap from her.

Selendra's hats had all been made at home, or occasionally bought ready-made by her brothers. She had never visited a milliner's establishment. She could not have imagined the range of hats available, nor the way they were fitted. The establishment was a wonder to her. They had to wait while a maiden was being fitted for a charming red-and-gold Deepwinter cap. The maiden was one of those who had been to the picnic, and greeted them as if they were long lost friends. Felin chatted to her while Selendra just gazed at the hats displayed in the nooks carved into every space in the walls of the little cavern. She had never imagined hats in such a profusion of shapes, colors, and textures. There were berets, tricorns, toques, cloches, sunbonnets, and other styles whose names Selendra did not know.

When their turn came, Hepsie bustled forward. "Blest Agornin! How lovely to see you. What can I do for you today?"

"More black, I'm afraid," Felin said. "You know what I like. And I'm also looking for something, black fleece, becoming, for 'Spec Agornin here, my husband's sister."

Selendra barely acknowledged the introduction, so caught up was she in all the hats. "It's almost like treasure," she said, remembering the cave under the mountain. Her chain was safe in her bed at home.

Hepsie and Felin laughed indulgently, then Hepsie scurried off to find materials and patterns. At last she fashioned a cap in several layers or flounces of fleece. "There, that'll look fine while you're in mourning, and if you want to put some sequins or jewels in it later, they'd go here," Hepsie said, indicating by poking bright blue sequins in along the inner flounce.

"It looks lovely," Felin assured her. Hepsie held up a bronze mirror, and Selendra admired her reflection.

"Thank you," she said, and gave Felin a shy hug.

Felin arranged payment with Hepsie. "Will you send them to the parsonage?" she asked.

"If you don't mind waiting half an hour, 'Spec Agornin's is almost made up, now I've done the fitting. You could take it with you."

Hepsie busied herself about her construction in an inner cave, leaving them alone among the hats. Selendra and Felin sat down comfortably. This was the opportunity Felin had been waiting for. "You look beautiful in that hat," she said.

"I really like it," Selendra said.

"I'm sure Sher will be most taken with it," Felin went on. Selendra looked at her guiltily. "Yes, I know. The Exalt told me something about it."

"The Exalt? What does she know about it?"

"What Sher has told her. He told her he loves you."

Selendra's eyes were whirling so fast they felt as if they could fall out of her head, but she could find nothing to say.

"Don't you love him?" Felin asked. "Couldn't you try?"

"I quite clearly don't," Selendra said, looking at the

smooth golden scales of her curving flank with distaste.

"How could you not?" Felin asked.

Selendra could not argue with that, for she knew she had indeed grown to love him imperceptibly. She hung her head.

"Do you love someone else?" Felin persisted.

"No," Selendra said.

"Then why not? If Sher loves you enough to brave his mother for you, which he has never done for anyone else—" Which he wouldn't do for me, Felin thought, sighing inwardly, though she was devoted now to Penn, "—then I think it is your duty to try to love him."

"Surely the Exalt doesn't want me to?" Selendra asked, her eyes now wide with horror.

"No, she doesn't, quite the opposite." Felin smiled, showing a glimpse of her sharp white teeth. "But if this was one of Sher's usual shallow infatuations he would have gone away by now to some other distraction. He's still here, and still looking at you in church. My dear, can't you see it's cruel to do this to him? Don't you love him at all?"

Selendra thought of what Amer had said. Perhaps if he touched her. Yet he had been so close. Her heart had been touched, but her coloring had not. Surely if he was close enough to touch her heart then her scales would have turned if they could? "I like him a great deal, but it's impossible," she murmured, almost inaudibly. "I'm sorry, Felin, I would if I could, but I can't."

"Most maidens in your position would be only too glad to have any Exalted running after them, let alone one as handsome and amusing as Sher," Felin said, deeply disappointed.

"There is so little power we have, as females," Selendra said. "Only to be able to choose to accept or reject a lover. We have to wait for them to ask, even then. You're telling me to think about wealth and position and disregard what I feel."

"No. Nothing of the kind. A competence is sufficient for happiness, as I know well. That's all extraneous to what I'm really telling you, which is that if you could love Sher it's your duty to marry him and make him happy," Felin said.

"If I could have loved him I'd have come back from the picnic with blushing scales," Selendra said, harshly.

"Will you at least talk to him?" Felin asked.

"He hasn't tried to talk to me," Selendra said.

"He wants to go flying with you on Deepwinter morning," Felin said. "Will you go?"

Selendra looked up, tears glimmering in her lavender eyes. "Of course I will," she said.

Felin wanted to embrace her, but wasn't quite sure. There was something reserved in Selendra, she thought, something that made her difficult to love as sisters should love one another. Maybe that was what prevented her from loving Sher as anyone sensible would.

Selendra sat blinking back tears and trying to think of her new hat, not of Deepwinter morning, and Sher, and Amer's numbers, and her obstinately golden scales.

12
HIGH SOCIETY

45. A THIRD CONFESSION

In the third week of Icewinter, Sebeth was again in the confession room of the little old church in the Skamble. It was again evening, after the service. Sebeth had made her confession and been absolved.

"Is there news?" Blessed Calien asked, as he took his claws from her eyes.

"Good news, Blessed One," she said. "Avan has completely changed his mind. One day he would hardly listen to my suggestion of keeping a few houses, now he is definitely going to keep half the Skamble, including this street."

The priest blinked in astonishment. "What changed his mind?" he asked.

"I don't know, Blessed One. It happened overnight, the day after I saw you last. I had been so worried about it, and he wasn't interested in what I was saying about it. Then suddenly, he would listen to everything you told me to suggest, and he liked it, and most of it is going onto the new plan."

"Are you sure?" Calien's dark eyes whirled faster.

"I have copied it twice," Sebeth said, unconsciously flexing her fingers at the memory. "The upper part, near the railway tracks, by the goods yards, will all be destroyed and turned into warehouses."

"I could hardly hope to save that, it's no more than slums," the priest said. "Besides, though it provides homes to some of the poorest in the city, nobody should have to live to the sound of shunting engines. That is according to my plan."

"Avan says the houses there scarcely have excavations, the dragons are just sitting on top of the topsoil and loam," Sebeth said, shuddering a little at the thought.

"Do not despise the poor for what they must endure," Calien said, sanctimoniously. "Do not despise the servants, for they did not bind their own wings."

"No, Blessed One," Sebeth said, subdued.

"What about the rest of the Skamble?"

"It's saved!" Sebeth said, her eyes lighting up like twin blue stars. "The Office is Planning and Beautification, you know, and Avan's going to keep some of the money raised from the warehouses and use it to beautify what's left. Only the worst houses will be razed, and in their place will be better houses, and little orchards near the river. He hopes to bring the area up. There will be grants for those who are prepared to work on their houses."

"And the church building?"

"This street is safe," Sebeth said, proudly. "I persuaded him to draw the warehouse line just a little north of here."

"Well done," the priest said. "It must be a miracle of blessed Camran that changed his mind so abruptly when I had almost given up hope of so much as keeping the darkness over our heads. Bless you, little sister, you did very well." He frowned, and Sebeth wondered why.

"Thanks be to Camran," she said, bowing her head.

"You are sure that Avan has the right to make this decision? That the Planning Office cannot be overruled by some other office?" Calien asked, anxiously.

"I have copied and recopied the documents controlling that, some of them dating back to the Conquest and the original foundation of Irieth. He's sure, and so am I."

"Did you learn anything of the foundation of Irieth?" he asked.

"Only what we already know, that it was founded after the Conquest, when the Yarge had most thoroughly defeated us, and they wished to herd us all together within borders, as a farmer might pen swine away from muttonwools." There was a little bitterness in Sebeth's tone.

"Some say Irieth was a city before that," Calien said, the slightest rebuke apparent in his tone.

"Majestic Tomalin was named in one old charter," Sebeth admitted.

"Who can tell, about time so long ago?" the priest said. "It was the mercy of Jurale that the Yarges knew the gods and brought them to us, instead of killing us all when they might have."

"Yes, Blessed One," Sebeth said.

They sat for a moment in silence, contemplating this fact, of the Yargish conversion of dragonkind, which was, for them, the truth, and which was considered by most right-thinking dragons the most rank heresy. Then Calien began to worry again. "Can Avan be overruled within the Planning Office?" he asked.

"Why, yes, but I do not think that will happen in this case," Sebeth answered.

"Why not?"

"He was entrusted with this project alone by Liralen, and it will be to Liralen's credit that he carry it out well. Liralen will present the project to the Board, and the Board always do what Liralen suggests to them. Normally, there might be rivalry within the Office, but in this case as Avan so recently bested Kest, he is standing rampant over them all."

"Good . . ." Calien hesitated, his eyes still troubled. "Kest is no longer causing trouble?"

"Kest causes trouble the way normal dragons fly, but at present it is all insinuation. You know, Blessed One?" Sebeth made her voice into a whine to imitate Kest. "Though Avan attacked me from behind and without warning I did swear to support him so I will not allow the words peculation or simony to pass my lips with respect to him."

The priest laughed. "Does that win him friends?"

"The opposite," Sebeth confirmed.

"Then tell me when the matter has passed the Board, and we will all gather to give thanks to the gods for our escape," he said.

"Thank you, Blessed One, I will," Sebeth said, gathering herself up sejant preparatory to leaving.

"Wait," Calien said. "I do have some other news for you."

Sebeth waited obediently, bowing her head.

"Your father is very ill," he said.

Sebeth's head came up and her eyes flashed blue fire. "I have no father, you know that," she said. "You know how he rejected me when most I needed him, you know what happened to me and what a life I led. You and the other Blessed Ones helped me then. I have no father but Veld, who is father to us all. You know that."

"You have an earthly father, whether you acknowledge him or not, and he is very ill," Calien said, calmly. "The Church teaches forgiveness for any sins."

"For any sins repented and confessed," Sebeth said. "He will never do that. I need not forgive him."

"Are you Veld to know what he keeps hidden in his heart?"

"No, Blessed One," Sebeth said, but she did not lower her head in submission. "He may have repented, but he did great harm to me and I cannot forgive him."

"That is a sin you should have brought to confession," he said, sternly.

"Yes, Blessed One, but when I was in most need he said he had dragonets enough and abandoned me." Sebeth did not sound penitential. "Camran might forgive him, and Jurale, who are so wise, but I think even they would have trouble if he had done that to them."

"However that is, he is sick, and word is that he is looking for you."

"For me?" Sebeth blinked. "He said—"

"And I said he may have repented of saying so," the priest interrupted gently.

"How do you know?"

"I hear many things. I heard that he is near the end of his life, and he is looking for you. I am telling you this. You must do as you think best. If you cannot forgive him for his sins against you, maybe you should consider whether you could bring him to a true confession at the last."

"You mean I should take you with me to see him?" Sebeth asked.

"If you go, you should go alone, but ask him to see me, or some other priest. He might be prepared to listen. Camran has given us one miracle. He may be about to offer another. Any soul saved is a blessing, and one in such a high place is an example to others."

"He would never convert in public," Sebeth said, sure of that. "Oh Blessed One, I do not want to see him. I should forgive him, but I cannot, and seeing him when I feel that way would just distress us both. If he wants me it must be for me to forgive him, and I am not ready."

"You may not have very long to prepare yourself,"

Calien said. "But go now, and think about what you want to do."

Sebeth gathered herself together, took off her mantilla, and went out into the streets of the Skamble. She had come to the church almost dancing with delight for the joy of having saved it, she left with dragging feet and a frown so hard it pulled her ears forward.

46. A FOURTH PROPOSAL

Daverak neither fulfilled Haner's worst fears nor her best hopes. He did not blame her for Berend's death, nor did he usher her politely to the nearest ledge and tell her to take herself off. He did not devour her on a slight pretext, nor demand that she marry him in her sister's place, as had been the case in a nightmare she had the first night after Berend's death. Nor did he insist that she continue to sleep in the room where Berend had died, providing her with another sleeping cave immediately after she mentioned her uneasiness with her old one. On the other hand, he would not augment her dowry as Berend had told Dignified Londaver he would. The most he would say on the subject was that he'd see about it after he had subdued her brother.

She was given her fair share of Berend's body, and Lamith measured her later at twenty-five feet. Daverak, who, with the children, naturally took the greatest part, grew to an even greater length, reaching almost fifty feet.

She remained in Daverak, helping to run the household, helping to look after the dragonets, caring for Berend's eggs, and trying to improve the lot of the servants and dragons of the demesne, quietly, without attracting Daverak's attention. The dragonets found the loss of their mother hard to understand, and were inclined to cling to her as a substitute. Dignified Londaver visited the day after Daverak's return and spent a little time closeted with her brother-in-law, but did not speak to her. She was surprised, a week later, on the first clear day after several days of snow, when he paid another call and asked for her.

She went to him in the elegantly appointed speaking room, where Lamith had shown him. He was standing uneasily before the mantel, at least appearing to admire the agate inlay. He was a full thirty-five feet long, with dark scales well burnished to a good shine. He was holding a book under his arm. He should have looked magnificent in the speaking room, but instead he looked uneasy.

Haner stopped in the doorway, as if she meant to stay only a moment. "Illustrious Daverak is gone to Agornin on business," she said.

"It's you I've come to see, Haner," he said.

Haner didn't want to make it easy for him. "Did you have something you wanted to say to me, Dignified Londaver?"

His green eyes met hers, and for the first time since his first wavering she felt a stirring excitement.

"Haner, you know I love you," he said. "I told you so on the mountain last time. I consider myself bound to you, whatever you said then. But Daverak—"

"I know. He refuses to make up the dowry now Berend is dead," Haner said, taking a step into the room. "He told me."

"I want to marry you, but I just can't afford it. I explained it to you before," he said, his voice strained with desperation. "We'll have to wait."

"Wait? For what?" Haner asked.

"For one of my uncles to die and leave me some gold, or for some relation of yours to do the same." He did not sound very confident of this plan. "Or I could go to Irieth or one of the other cities and seek my fortune—except that it's a bit awkward doing that when I'm a Dignified, you know?" Londaver shifted his weight uneasily.

"I can't imagine you going into trade, or into a government office like my brother Avan. The only fortune you could seek would be a rich bride," Haner said.

"I've never met anyone I liked as much as you," Londaver said, his sincerity plain. "And you're so clever. I'm not terribly clever myself. But you're what I need. You could be clever for both of us. I think about what you say, about the stars, and about treating servants well. I agree with you about that, the more I think about it. I'd like to hear more of what you think about things. I don't want to marry anyone else."

"Oh Londaver," Haner said, her heart softening immediately. She took another, involuntary, step towards him.

"Only we have to wait," he said, putting out a claw to stop her.

"I'll wait," she said, staying where she was. "But waiting indefinitely without any fixed thing to wait for is very difficult."

"You're completely free to change your mind at any time," he said quickly. "If someone else makes you an offer. I was thinking I'd tell you that in that case I'd never marry another, which is what heroes say in stories, and really how I feel, but of course you know, I'd have to, because of the family. There's an obligation, if you're the heir, whatever you privately feel. But I'd always be sorry."

"So, shall we tell everyone we're waiting?" Haner asked.

Londaver thought for a moment, his eyes whirling. "I don't think so. It complicates everything so." He sighed. "It's such a pity I can't just go off and take the gold of some Yargish town and come back to marry you. Life was so much simpler in those days. I hate the very thought of gold sometimes. But if we married now, we'd soon be spending our beds. Londaver isn't a rich place, you know, and we do like to be fair to the farmers and the servants."

"I admire that," Haner said, truthfully.

"You're so wonderful," Londaver said. "I brought you a book." He held it out shyly towards her, and she took it, tentatively.

"*The Subjugation of Servants,* by Calien Afelan," she read.

"It's a book of my mother's," Londaver said. "I thought you'd like to read it, to do with what you were saying."

"Thank you," Haner said, deeply touched.

"It's going to be very hard to wait," Londaver said, sighing.

He left her feeling much more fond of him than she had been when he first proposed, but also much less betrothed to be married.

"What did he say, 'Spec?" Lamith asked, when she went back to her new room. Several months of being Haner's attendant, and a week of being without Berend in the establishment, had helped Lamith relax into something approaching familiarity when alone with Haner.

"He said he loves me and we should wait until we can afford to marry," Haner said, flinging herself down on her gold with a sigh.

Lamith's familiarity did not extend to saying what she thought of such statements as that, so she contented herself with clucking and taking up a fleece to burnish her mistress's scales to as bright a gold as she could manage.

47. THE FIRST HEARING

Hathor and Avan were strolling together through the Toris quarter of Irieth towards the Courts of Justice. Hathor, with a presence larger than his measurements, was striding confidently along. Avan walked like a dragon who could only just keep his tail from whipping about uncontrollably.

"There's no need to be nervous," Hathor said. "This is only a preliminary hearing, to decide whether there is a case to answer."

Avan tried to smile, but was aware that his eyes were betraying his agitation. "You told me that six times already," he said.

"Why are you so worried?" Hathor asked, encouragingly. "I don't understand it. It's Daverak and his expensive attorneys who ought to be nervous. We have everything on our side."

"It's actually going there," Avan admitted, trying to keep his tone light. "You have been to the courts so many times. I am a provincial dragon and this is all new to me. The real power."

"Power, yes, but it's all contained in ritual. You're in more danger with your colleagues who want your position at the Planning Office. Illustrious Daverak probably won't even show himself today," Hathor said.

"I'm not afraid of Daverak," Avan snorted. "This is a case of nerves from the stories my nanny used to tell me."

"You'll soon get over it when we get there," Hathor said, attempting to be reassuring but with his complete incomprehension showing in his voice.

Their walk took them past the famous Malnasimen Brewhouse, which was that day belching out a smell of yeast thick enough that they almost needed to cleave the air with their claws.

"I hear there's a movement afoot to make the brewers move out of town," Hathor said, in quite another tone.

"What a wonderful plan," Avan said, almost choking. "Beer is a blessing of Jurale, but brewing is a disgusting process."

"You haven't heard anything at the Planning Office then?"

"A petition was circulating about it last year, but if anyone in Planning is taking action I have heard nothing of it." Avan's confidence grew as he spoke, the whirling of his eyes slowed, his tail steadied, and he sped up his walk, making the attorney scurry on his shorter legs to keep up with him. "It isn't my department, but I believe the Malnasimens have an ancient Charter Grant allowing them to brew from the River Toris. They also say beer is heavy and doesn't travel well, so unless we want Irieth to drink worse beer at higher cost, we should leave them alone. The other brewers say the same, only without waving their Charter Grants because they don't have any."

The lawyer said nothing for a moment, looking at his client speculatively. "So they'll stay?" he asked.

"My guess is that they'll still be brewing here, and dragons will still be raising petitions about it regularly, when our grandchildren are fathers," Avan said. "But that's a guess, not official word from the Planning Office."

"Your guesses are as good as gold to some dragons," Hathor said.

"I wish I didn't know any of those dragons," Avan said, bitterly.

Hathor eyed him again, but said no more. Just then, they rounded a corner, and all at once the entrance to the Great Chamber of Justice was before them. It was a huge cavernous entrance, carved all around with hearts, flowers, and other abstract representations of justice. Avan checked his stride.

"Now take a piece of advice from me," Hathor said, clicking his teeth for attention. Avan swung around to face him, staring into his attorney's eyes. "Stay calm. Stay confident. You're so confident talking about your own business, I don't know why mine should give you pause . . ."

"Lack of familiarity, as I said," Avan blinked, keeping his tail still only by effort of will. "I know the judges won't order me eaten, but they have the power to do so. The law stands to allow dragons like me redress against dragons who are stronger, but the judges can order anyone to fight anyone at any time."

"Is this about Daverak's letter? Because I can assure you that it helps our case to be able to prove his intimidating tactics. He may have threatened to strip you of everything down to the bones, but it demonstrates that he'd have threatened your sisters similarly, and thus coerced their withdrawal from the writ. Don't worry." Despite himself, Hathor allowed a shade of impatience to show in his voice.

"It's not that, truly," Avan said. "But look at that." He gestured towards the gateway. "It's designed to be intimidating, and it intimidates me."

"It's designed to intimidate wrongdoers and dragons bringing suit lightly," Hathor said. "You're neither. But it's important that you make a good impression on the judges. Be calm. Above all, don't look guilty or worried. Keep your mind on the streets of Irieth and the importance of brewers. When you were talking about that, anyone could have seen you were in the right."

Avan laughed. Hathor nodded to the guard at the gate, who recognized him and raised the bar deferentially. The two dragons entered and descended.

The court lay deep underground in an enlarged natural cavern, rare in Irieth. Hathor led Avan past carved depictions of the execution of Justice. Here, a judge held up a still bleeding heart, there a Yarge and two magnificent dragons conferred over a flower. Avan knew it was ridiculous to twitch at the sight of them. He had been so steadfast throughout the whole process, it was ridiculous to want to turn tail now.

Hathor left Avan to sit in an alcove just outside the great circular justice chamber while he bustled forward to consult with the court scribe and the other attorneys. Avan tried to think about his work as Hathor had suggested, but found his eyes straying to the imposing might of the chamber. Liralen had approved the plan for the Skamble enthusiastically, soon it would pass the Board. Was that one of the judges coming in? No, only another scribe. He sat restlessly and in time came to be more at ease with the place through sheer boredom.

Hathor came to fetch him after a small eternity of time, and led him past more guards to a slab about a quarter of the way around the room. "You don't have to do anything but answer that you're here," Hathor reminded him quietly. "If you do address the judges, the term is Honorable, just as if they were ancient heroes."

They were facing a flight of granite steps topped by three huge steps, with another threatening carving of hearts surrounded by flowers and coils of fleece set over it. Equidistant from them across the chamber was another stone slab, where three attorneys stood, all strangers to Avan. A scribe in a long fleecy wig waited patiently in front of the steps. There was an entrance behind the steps, as well as the guarded passage behind them. The roof was very high up, high enough that Avan wondered if it was a natural cavern after all. Hathor nudged him and he hastily returned his eyes to the chamber.

The three judges were filing in at last. They took their places on the top three of the great steps. One judge was black-scaled, one was bronze, and one was a rusty bronze that was almost green. They wore huge piled rolls of white on their heads, the famous justicewigs. Avan trembled before them for a moment, seeing the naked power of the law that could order him dismembered and eaten. It was all very well for Hathor to say that he was in more danger in the office, there his own teeth and claws counted for something, here they were nothing before those of the judges, and the guards who would carry out their wishes.

Hathor set out three wigs of his own on the slab before them. The other attorneys bustled their wigs onto their heads. All the wigs seemed to be different styles. Avan, who had never had much to do with the law, didn't recognize any of them.

"The Respectable Avan Agornin in civil suit against the Illustrious Daverak of Daverak, concerning the intentions of the deceased Dignified Bon Agornin," the scribe intoned suddenly, a paper clutched between his claws.

"Are they here?" the central, bronze, judge asked.

Hathor settled the smallest and most tightly rolled wig on his head and rose. "The Respectable Avan Agornin is here," he said, indicating Avan, then sat again.

"Are you the Respectable Avan Agornin?" the central judge asked Avan.

Avan rose and bowed. "Yes, Honorables," he said, his voice coming out much more faintly than he had intended. Hathor put out a claw to pull him down again.

Across the echoing chamber a young dragon in an identical small wig to Hathor's rose. "The Illustrious Daverak of Daverak is not here, but contests the case and is ready to appear at another hearing if there is found to be a case to answer."

Hathor rapidly replaced his wig with the central fleecy wig and rose again. "Query, Honorables," he said.

"What is it?" the black-scaled judge on the left asked, his voice bored.

"If the Illustrious Daverak cares so little for the case, maybe it should be settled immediately in favor of my principal," he said. Avan looked at him in amazement.

A dragon on the opposite side of the chamber rose, his wig as fleecy as Hathor's. "Objection, Honorables," he said.

"Your objection?" the judge asked. There was something strange about the way he said it.

"It has been established, Salak against Cletsim, that those accused in civil suits need not attend until it has been established that there is a case to answer, lest important dragons find all their time eaten up by frivolous lawsuits."

"And lest those bringing such lawsuits find they are themselves eaten up," the black-scaled judge said. Everyone laughed in a dutiful way, except Avan. He had worked out what was so strange. They were speaking like dragons making the ritual responses in a church service. "Objection upheld. Shall we continue?"

Hathor bobbed to his feet, bowed, then sat again.

"Do you have papers to present?" the bronze-scaled judge asked.

Hathor put his first small wig back on, and walked up to the steps with a packet of papers. The young dragon on the other side of the chamber did likewise. Hathor returned and sat down at Avan's side.

"What's going on?" Avan whispered.

"This is the important part. They've seen the papers already, they'll check them together, then they'll say there's a case and set a date for it."

"And what was going on before, with you objecting to Daverak not being here? I thought you said he probably wouldn't?"

"Ritual. We had to do that, but I knew what would happen. Don't worry," Hathor said.

Avan wasn't worried anymore, he was curious. "Why do you have three wigs?"

"Attorneywig, for when I'm establishing plain matters of fact to the court, like your identity, or handing in papers," Hathor said, gesturing at the small wig he still wore. "Querywig, for making queries and objections. Then this one," he indicated the third and largest, almost as elaborate as the ones the judges wore, which must have taken the fleece of a whole mutton-wool. "This is the pleadingwig, for use when talking to witnesses and summing up my case."

"Why are there three dragons on the other side, in one of these wigs each?" Avan asked.

"I told you he hired expensive legal talent," Hathor said. "That just proves he's worried. He has an attorney, a querier, and a Pleader, and the Pleader is Dignified Jamaney, one of the best known Pleaders in Irieth. The attorney in the querywig is Mustan, a good enough dragon, though young and impetuous. The third, in the attorneywig, I don't know, probably one of Mustan's associates or assistants."

"Does that give him an advantage?" Avan stared over at the three lawyers on the other side. "Because they don't have to change their wigs? Should we hire some help?"

"No. Definitely not. I thought about it, but we're a lot better without. It doesn't give him anything like as much advantage as he thinks it does. In some trials it would, but not this one. I told you, it means he, or at least his attorney, is worried. He knows we have all the claws on our side, so he's trying to impress them with wigs. In the second hearing, what matters most is what the jury think. We'll have a city jury that start off half on your side. We want to establish certain things, firstly that this is about your father's intent, secondly that Daverak is a rich bully and you're a hardworking rising dragon cheated of your inheritance. See how that will look, with me changing wigs and grinding away for you, and him with three attorneys sitting at their ease?"

"You make it sound more like theater than justice," Avan said, half-disappointed.

"It is," Hathor said, in a passionate whisper. "It is theater. You watch me with the wigs. When it doesn't matter, I'll change them so smoothly you won't notice, but when I fumble with them it'll be to show how you have one attorney working for you and they have three, or because we want a little pause for the jury to think about what's just been said. You'll see. It'll be to our advantage."

"I start to see why you thought I was being a muttonwool to be afraid of all this," Avan said.

Hathor frowned. "No, it's right that dragons who aren't familiar with all of this have a certain reverence for it. That's part of the theater too. Now, hush, the judge is going to pronounce."

The old rusty-bronze judge, who had sat like a statue of a dragon on a pedestal ever since he had come in, put a claw to his wig and rose to his feet.

"We find there is a case to answer," he said, his voice a quavering whisper, and sank down again.

"Query." Daverak's querywigged attorney was on his feet immediately.

"What is it?" the black-scaled judge asked again.

"We wish a compulsion order for the witness Blessed Penn Agornin."

"Why?" the judge asked, a faint thread of curiosity spicing the accustomed boredom of his tone.

"He has refused to make a statement and give

evidence, and my principal feels that his evidence is vital."

"Any objections?" the judge asked, looking at Hathor and Avan.

Hathor rose, his querywig firmly in place on his head. "No objections, but we would like similar compulsion orders for the Respected Haner and Selendra Agornin, who we fear have been intimidated into withdrawing from my client's writ and from testifying."

The black judge blinked, visibly. The bronze one leaned forward a little. The rusty one did not move. "Intimidated by whom?" the black one asked at last.

"That will be established in the case," Hathor said, confidently. "To answer that now would be to make an unfounded allegation and to prejudice the evidence we wish to bring."

The black-scaled judge exchanged glances with the other two. "Very well," he said, after a moment. "Petition granted. All three petitions granted. The four surviving children of Bon Agornin will all be gathered here to give evidence or be found to have despised the usage of this court and be subject to extreme penalty. See the scribe for the necessary documents."

"The case will be heard on the twelfth of Deepwinter," the bronze-scaled judge said.

He looked from Hathor to Daverak's attorneys, neither of whom objected to the date, then nodded to the scribe.

"First Hearing dismissed," the scribe said loudly. The judges left through their door. Hathor and the other attorneys hurried to the scribe for the papers. Avan waited, bored now, no longer even slightly intimidated by the glories of justice.

13
DEEPWINTER AT BENANDI

On the last day of the month of Icewinter, the mail was delivered as usual to Benandi Parsonage at breakfast. That day there were two gilt-edged envelopes, the Compulsion Orders for Penn and Selendra, bidding them attend the Court of Justice at Irieth on the twelfth day of Deepwinter.

Penn could barely prevent his claws from trembling as he read his Order. The majesty of the language had its full impact on him, as the thought of the ceremonial of the courts had upon his brother. "Where you will speak the truth as it shall be asked of you," he read, and "shall be found to have despised this court and be subject to extreme penalty" and "face the full consequences of the law."

He stared at it for some time, trying to calm himself, but before he felt he had his eyes under control Selendra spoke.

"I have to go to Irieth!" she said.

Penn looked at his sister over his Order. Her violet eyes were shining. She looked happier than she had for days.

"Irieth!" Felin said. She had never been to Irieth. "Why?"

"I would not have thought Daverak would have demanded your presence," Penn said, putting his paper down carefully.

"Daverak? It's Avan who demands me," Selendra said.

"What are you talking about?" Felin asked, plaintively.

Penn tried to speak but found he could not.

"My brother Avan is taking Daverak, who was married to Berend, to court over what happened with my father's body," Selendra burbled, still full of innocent excitement.

Felin looked inquiringly at Penn. The terrible thing about that look was that there was no reproach in it, though she must have guessed that he had known before. "That's right," he said.

"When do you have to be in Irieth?" Felin asked, in a tone of bright inquiry. "Will you need to be away over a Firstday?"

"The twelfth of Deepwinter," Penn managed to say. "So I'll miss one Firstday at least."

"That's very soon," Felin said, neutrally. "I'll write to Blessed Hape and see if he can take the services."

"I need to talk to you about this," he said, realizing as he said it that it was true, he could keep Felin sunblind on the matter no longer.

"You'll need to leave on the tenth," Felin said, still calmly. "Where will you stay in Irieth?"

"We could stay with Avan," Selendra suggested.

"I've always wanted to see the capital, and he'd be able to show us everything, the Cupola, the Theater, do you think we'd have time to see a play?"

"I don't think we'd better stay with Avan," Penn said. "He doesn't have much room." He only just stopped himself from adding something about the floozy Avan kept there.

"Then where?" Selendra asked. "Apart from Avan I don't think we have any acquaintance in Irieth."

This cast the problem back to him. On his own, he would have stayed at his club, but that was impossible with Selendra. "We'll stay at a respectable hotel," Penn said after a moment's thought.

Felin winced at the thought of the expense of two nights in a hotel in Irieth. "Must you go?" she asked.

"I'd give anything to avoid going," Penn said, passing the Order to his wife.

"The full consequences of the law," Selendra quoted, rather as if she relished the thought. Females, Penn thought, not for the first time, did not properly understand what it was to live in constant fear of needing to fight for your life. It was not cowardice that had driven him to the priesthood, rather the need to provide for himself, but he had been surprised what a change the red cords of Immunity had made to his habits of thought. He had preached several popular sermons on the uncertainty of life.

"I shall ask Sher to recommend a hotel," Felin said.

"Not the Exalt?" Penn asked.

"Sher is likely to have more current recommendations," Felin said.

"I'll wear my new hat," Selendra said.

"Oh really Selendra, must you be so worldly?" Penn asked in exasperation. To his amazement, his sister dissolved into tears, and Felin cast him a look in which there definitely was reproach. He would never understand females, not if he lived with them for a thousand years. Felin hustled Selendra out saying things about resting.

Penn waited, with no more appetite for breakfast. Felin came back shortly, a coil of efficient dark pink in the doorway.

"Is Selendra all right?" he asked.

"She's a little high-strung, she'll be fine," Felin said, coming into the room and settling herself. "Do try not to snap at her like that when she's trying hard."

Penn frowned. "I don't know what I said that was wrong."

"Never mind now," Felin said. "Tell me what's upset you so much about the thought of giving evidence in this case?"

Penn, unworthily, thought of prevaricating, of saying how much it distressed him to see his family at odds with itself. But Felin was his wife, his helpmeet, whatever he brought upon himself he brought upon her also, and on the dragonets. "Forgive me," he said. "I did something terrible. I did it with good intentions, and thinking it would remain between me and the gods. All the same, I should have told you, because it puts everything into doubt."

"Everything?" Felin asked, her gray eyes a whirl of confusion. "What do you mean?"

"When my father was dying he made confession to me, confession, the rite of the Church."

He saw understanding dawn on Felin after a moment. "You'll have to tell them in court?"

"They're bound to ask what he said, exactly what he said. They'll accept that the confessional is sacred, of course, but it will come out that I heard his confession and gave him absolution."

"Can the court impose penalty on you for that?" Felin asked.

"The court? No. But it will all be public, and the Church will know, and then they will cast me out, and the Exalt will do the same, and we will lose the parsonage and all we have."

"But why did you do it?" she asked.

"My father was dying, and he wished it," Penn said, stiffly. Then he groaned. "I've asked myself over and over why I was such a fool. I wanted to give him comfort, and the rite is in the book, it is only a custom that we don't use it. I thought it would remain secret. The gods are punishing me with this trial."

"Maybe they won't ask you about it," Felin said.

Penn smiled grimly, showing his teeth. "That is all the hope we have, and it's a slim one. Why are they summoning me, if not to ask me what my father said on his deathbed?"

"If you lose your cords I will stand by you," Felin said. She rose to her feet. "Maybe your brother Avan will find you a position in an office. Maybe Sher will be able to recommend you."

"Sher won't want to know a parson stripped of his cords. Nobody will. You haven't thought of the disgrace," Penn said. "You and the dragonets would be better off if I were dead. At least the Exalt would look after you then."

"We have a little store of gold," Felin said, moving to Penn and embracing him. "We'll move somewhere nobody knows us and begin again. I want you to stay alive and fight, Penn, fight to make a life for yourself, and for me, and for the dragonets. Don't give up."

Penn groaned again, hiding his head under Felin's wing. "You are better than I deserve," he said.

"Maybe if it is custom and not doctrine the Church won't mind," Felin said.

"They will call me an Old Believer," Penn said. "There is no doubt they will cast me out."

"I think that's very wrong, casting you out for easing your father's passing," Felin said, settling herself once again firmly beside her husband.

"It was my wrong, not theirs," Penn said, comforted by Felin's unstinting support.

"No, you were doing what you thought right," Felin said. In her mind she was already packing up all the beloved belongings of the parsonage and making ready to start afresh elsewhere, without income or status. She had weathered the blow, although it had been a very hard one, and was ready to go on. "The Exalt will take most of the servants, we can manage with only one."

"What about Selendra?" Penn asked.

Felin remembered uneasily that Penn did not know the full story of Selendra and Sher, nor that they were to meet the next day. "I think we should wait to tell her until after the trial. It may come to nothing, after all, and we may all be safe. Or if not, we may be able to come to some arrangement with Avan, if he wins, for him to take over the care of Selendra."

"She will continue to be excited about it," Penn said, despairingly.

"She is a young maiden, let her be as free of care as she might be for a little while more. Let her enjoy this visit to the capital. There's little enough we can do for her now, let us give her that little time."

"I have ruined everything," Penn said. "I had my life all planned and rolling along like a train, and then suddenly this, derailing everything. Even if they don't ask about it, which I can't believe, maybe I should tell everything to the Holiness, make clean pickings of it."

Felin applied her mind to this ridiculous idea. "Do you really believe you were sinning to hear your father's confession?" she asked.

Penn hesitated. "I just wanted to give him comfort," he said. "I thought it was against the present practice of the Church but I didn't think it was against the will of the gods."

"Then if the gods think it was wrong, it will come out in the trial, and if not, you should not invite penalty to yourself," Felin said, as confidently as she dared.

"You are right," Penn said, and embraced her tightly.

49. THE SOCIAL WORLD

Later that afternoon, Selendra and Felin flew down to the station to deliver to the mails the notes that confirmed that Penn and Selendra would attend the court without fail.

Felin was glad to be out of the parsonage. Her head ached with worry, and with the effort of keeping Selendra and the servants from guessing how much might be wrong. The cold air under her wings did her good, as usual, but did not change the proportions of the problem.

"Have you asked about a hotel, yet?" Selendra asked shyly as they flew back.

"I thought you could ask that tomorrow," Felin said. She had in fact forgotten entirely about the matter.

"It'll be something easy to talk about at least," Selendra said, sobered by the reminder. "Oh Felin. I do like Sher very much, but marrying him would be impossible."

"If it's not possible, it's not," Felin said, wondering if she should tell Selendra after all, so she could refuse or accept Sher knowing what the true choices were. No. Sher was more important to her than Selendra, he had been her brother almost all her life, and Selendra had been her sister only these last few months. Sher should have a wife who loved him, no matter what.

They were flying over the church. Felin looked down and saw that the snow was very thickly piled on the roof. "I should brush some of that off before it does any damage," she said, swooping down.

"I'll help," Selendra said. They glided down, the passage of their wings caused some of the piled snow on the roof to slide gently to the ground below.

They landed neatly in the snow and began to clear the roof, taking one side each and applying themselves to their task in silence. Felin would have liked to have lightened Selendra's mood, but was too deep in her own gloom to do it.

A shadow swept over them as they were finishing. Selendra looked up. "It's the Exalt," she said, surprised. "I've never seen her on the wing before, I'd almost thought she couldn't fly."

"Hush," Felin said, reprovingly.

The Exalt glided down and landed heavily in front of the church. She was wearing a knotted hat in black-and-white fleece that was probably very expensive but which made her look old and slightly pathetic. "I saw you working so hard from up at the ledge," she said, graciously. "I thought I'd come and lend a wing to the glory of the church, but I see that you have done it all."

"The offer is deeply appreciated," Felin said.

"I haven't seen either of you for weeks," the Exalt said. Felin bowed, and Selendra looked down. "How are you? Is there any news?"

Before Felin could stop her, Selendra had begun to explain the story of the lawsuit. Felin knew that the Exalt would have had to know, whatever happened, with Penn needing to be away over a Firstday and find a substitute parson. All the same, she would have preferred to have told her herself, in her own way.

"Most unseemly," the Exalt sniffed. "I can't understand why you and Penn are mixed up in it."

"They didn't want to have anything to do with it, they are summoned to Irieth by Order of the Court," Felin explained, before Selendra could make things worse by saying how right Avan was.

"Not a good time of year for Irieth," the Exalt pronounced, diverted at once, as Felin had known she would be. "And where will you stay in the capital?"

"In a respectable hotel," Selendra answered at once.

"Not with your brother?" the Exalt asked.

"We thought it best not," Felin said, gently.

"Yes, probably best not, in the light of this lawsuit," the Exalt agreed. "There is a good reasonably priced hotel in the Migantine quarter called the Majestic's Head. It is next to the church of Sainted Vouiver. It is not beyond your budget, I should judge, and has small rooms, suitable for a parson and his sister."

Felin had not wanted to ask the Exalt about hotels because she knew Sher would consider comfort and cost and not primarily what was appropriate. However, now it had been suggested it could not be refused. "Oh, thank you, Exalt, how wonderful that you know somewhere," she said, thinking that in some ways it would be a relief to be free of the patronage of the Exalt and live elsewhere, even if they would slip below respectable status in the process. "But it will need to be for three of us," she added.

"You, Felin?" the Exalt asked. "Surely they do not need you?"

"No, but I shall go to keep Penn and Selendra in order," Felin said.

"Oh that's marvellous!" Selendra said, smiling. "Oh it'll be so much more fun with you instead of only Penn."

"I hadn't thought you'd feel able to leave the dragonets, as you didn't when Penn's father was dying," the Exalt said, a reproving frown wrinkling her snout.

"The dragonets are a little older now, and there's Amer to take care of them as well as the nanny." Felin was irritated to find herself sounding defensive. She was not, in fact, choosing to leave her dragonets for a pleasure trip to the capital after having used them as an excuse to avoid her father-in-law's deathbed, but as she could hardly explain the details the appearance was unavoidable.

"Amer's very good with them," Selendra said. "And we'll have such fun in Irieth. I'm sure Avan will take us to a theater even if Penn is too stuffy. I've always wanted to see a play."

Felin frowned at Selendra. Fortunately the Exalt, like Selendra and unlike Felin, had not heard of the disrepute into which out-of-season theater had fallen in Irieth. "I hope you might see many. Penn will need to hurry back, of course, but perhaps the two of you might stay in Irieth for a little while after the case is settled and enjoy the delights of the capital. I am quite tired of them, myself, but I don't believe you've ever been there, have you?"

"No," Selendra said. "Never. I was too young, and then Father was too old."

Felin looked down at the snow to hide any trace of resentment that might be in her eyes. The Exalt had promised her a season in Irieth when she had been a maiden, partly to console her over Sher. The season had been postponed for one reason or another, and then Penn had come and she had married, without ever seeing the capital.

"I do think a time in the capital would be just the thing for you," the Exalt said. "I have been meaning to speak to you for a little while, Selendra. I know you are a sensible maiden, because you declined a foolish offer from my son a little while ago. I'm glad you realized how impossible such a thing would be. In Irieth you might be able to meet someone more appropriate, someone of your own station in life. If you will promise me that you will continue in this sensible path, I will arrange for you and Felin to stay in the Benandi town house in Irieth for the case and for a month or two afterwards."

Felin knew this plan was impossible and so dismissed it at once. "I couldn't leave the dragonets for that long," she said quickly.

She was looking at the Exalt, who was looking her usual confident self, under the inappropriate hat. She watched her expression change, and only after the silence was already too long did she turn to her sister-in-law.

Selendra was almost incandescent with rage. Her violet eyes whirled as if they would come out of her head. "Are you saying," she asked, "as you said that my father was not good enough to be mentioned in polite society, that I am not good enough for your son?"

Felin blinked. It was only a few wing-beats since Selendra had been reaffirming to her that marrying Sher would be impossible.

"I am saying that the world we live in is a social world as well as everything else, and that much as I like you, and your brother and sister-in-law, you must see that a maiden brought up as you have been wouldn't be an appropriate wife for an Exalted Lord like my son," the Exalt said, very evenly. "Who are you, to be Exalt Benandi and manage a great estate?"

"You—" Selendra stopped. "I pity you," she said, with dignity.

"You will not undertake to leave my son alone?" the Exalt asked.

"You have no right to ask that of me, or of him," Selendra said, her teeth showing as she spoke.

"Selendra—" Felin began, conciliatingly, not sure how she was going to go on.

"I'm going home," Selendra said, abruptly, and flew up toward the parsonage, a gold streak across the white snow, leaving the two older dragons standing still staring after her.

"I'm sorry," Felin said, after a moment. "She's very emotional at the moment, losing her father and then her sister so suddenly."

"I'll never have a better daughter-in-law than you would have made, Felin, and I was a fool not to settle for you while I could have had you," the Exalt said, still staring after Selendra.

Felin could have cheerfully bitten the Exalt, but she managed to laugh. "There's no unmelting last winter's snow," she said, taking refuge in the proverbial.

The Exalt just shook her head.

50. A FIFTH PROPOSAL

Selendra retired to her sleeping cave and refused herself to everyone. To Felin, when she came to her on her return, she said she wanted to be left alone for a little while. To Penn, who was not persistent, she said she had a slight female ailment and would be better if left to rest on her gold. To Amer, sent by a concerned Felin with tempting preserves and beer, she said she was not sick but angry, and demanded immediate and thorough burnishing.

In the morning she emerged for breakfast looking her best. Every scale was burnished to a clear and shining gold. Her new hat was settled most becomingly on her head, and the chain she had found in the cave was arranged inside it, the jewels glinting. Her eyes seemed darkened almost to amethyst under the brim of the hat. Penn, sunk in his own anguish, noticed nothing, and Felin, apprehensive, dared say nothing in his presence. She ate nothing but a few wrinkled pippins, not wishing to spot her scales with blood. After breakfast she sat down to wait for Sher to call for her.

In truth, she had never been so angry in her life. Long hours brooding in the dark had done little to calm her. She thought over everything the Exalt had ever said to her, from that first insult to her father onwards. No word of it, she thought, had been truly kind, nor other than selfish. She thought of the things she had heard said to Felin, unthinkingly and unnecessarily cruel. How had the Exalt come to have a son like Sher, kind and considerate and valuing dragons for their own worth? She was too inexperienced to realize, as Felin knew so well, that Sher had shaped himself in opposition to his mother, or that he had his own selfishness. Sher, she thought, was more than the Exalt deserved. She thought of what the Exalt had said. "Who are you to be Exalt Benandi?" It was that she cared about, Selendra knew, not the welfare of her son or her demesne, but her own name and status. Her son's wife would supplant her, so although a wife was required, to continue the line of Benandi, she wanted someone she could control. It would serve the Exalt right if she did marry him and then had no children.

Selendra decided to teach the Exalt a lesson. She could not, however, bear to hurt Sher too much in the process. She spent much of the night thinking it out. However much she wished to punish his mother, she could not marry him if indeed, as seemed likely, the numbers of Amer's potion had been against her. By dawn, she had a plan.

Sher duly arrived. He looked at her with such love and longing that her heart melted.

They flew out of the parsonage into a beautifully clear Deepwinter morning. The sky was a clear pale blue, and seemed a million miles above their heads. The snow reflected the golden sunlight and seemed to caress the curves of the trees with a drift of white. It was bitterly cold, so cold that they both felt sure with the wholehearted faith of a child that it was indeed the sun of ice that had risen that morning and not the sun of fire, and they were glad it was Deepwinter and that the sun's fires would be rekindled that night.

Sher did not ask where she wanted to go. He barely spoke to her, beyond asking her to accompany him.

She followed him up the wind and into the hills. The air was dry and bitterly cold, rasping in the back of her throat like ice needles. He descended at last into a high meadow where muttonwools were pastured in summer. She followed him down and landed carefully, anything could be hidden under the snow. It was deeper here than in the valley, coming almost to her belly.

Sher still showed no inclination to speak, merely looking at her until she could barely keep still. Selendra remembered Amer telling her that words spoken beneath the sun of ice would fall coldly on the ear.

"It's a beautiful day," she said at last.

"You are beautiful," Sher said, his voice a little hoarse. "It is beautiful because it has you in it. O Selendra, everything has been so bleak without you. Felin, who has always been like a sister to me, told me to wait, and I have waited and I have not changed. I asked you to marry me once before, have you changed your answer?"

"There are two things before I can agree," she said, as she had planned. "If you are absolutely sure this is what you want."

"I am beyond doubt," he said. The weeks of waiting had affected him. He seemed older, more sure of himself. He took a wallowing step through the snow towards Selendra, who held up a hand to stop him.

"The first is a vow I made."

"A vow?" He looked at her blankly.

"When I left Agornin, my sister, Haner, my clutch-mate, and I vowed that we would not marry without the other approving the proposed husband."

Sher looked relieved. "I thought you meant—that's actually terribly sweet of both of you. She must stay with us often when we are married. I will happily meet your sister. How soon can she come here?"

"I don't know. There is a court case between my brother Avan and the Illustrious Daverak, who is her guardian, and I need to go to Irieth for the twelfth of Deepwinter. She'll be there as well. After that, possibly."

"And will Penn go to Irieth with you?" Sher frowned.

"Penn and Felin are both going."

"Then let us all go. I'll have Benandi House opened and we can all stay there. I can meet your sister. I'm sure it won't take long to have her approve me."

Selendra sighed inwardly, because her plan called for Haner to refuse her approval once the Exalt had suffered enough. Sher took another step towards her. She retreated. "Not until my sister has approved you. And there is another condition."

"Another? Selendra, you are beautiful gold but I long to see you pink."

"Your mother." Selendra's voice was hard.

"I can deal with her," Sher said.

"I will not marry you unless your mother approves. She must treat me as if I am your equal. She said some very hurtful things to me yesterday. I like you so much. I thought about it after we got out of the cave, how resourceful you were, how brave, and what

lovely funny things you say." She was entirely sincere saying this, she smiled, and Sher's heart turned
over. If he had been a maiden he would have glowed
pink just from her words. "But we would need to live
in Benandi, at least part of the time, and I can't live
with your mother disapproving of me in her way and
forever nagging me and acting as if I am half a dead
venison you dragged in covered in flies. If we are to
be happy together, she must welcome me into the
family."

Sher blinked. "Selendra—we needn't live with my
mother. We can visit her now and then for a day or
two, but we can live anywhere. I have four estates in
addition to this one. If you don't like any of them we
could buy another estate. I usually go to Irieth for the
season, we could do that, or not just as you like. My
mother needn't figure in our lives."

"She will, even if we avoid her. Our children, when
we have them, will need to know Benandi. She will
make my life a misery whenever she can, and theirs,
telling our children that I am not good enough to be
your wife and their mother. You remember what
she said about my father. I can't marry you if you
have doubts about my family, or if she is going to act
like that."

"Then she will welcome you," Sher said, his jaw set
at an angle of determination that would have surprised his friends and his mother very much. "In Irieth. Where your sister will also approve me."

"Oh Sher," Selendra said, loving him, no artifice

in her at all now. He stayed where he was, staring at her, smiling a little. For Selendra, although the day was as cold as ever, it felt as if the Deepwinter fire had been kindled already in her heart and the sun burned warm again. Sher did not take advantage to press her further at that time, although she would no longer have desired to be capable of stopping him.

"I must speak to your brother," Sher said. "Come, dearest Selendra." They rose up to fly home together.

51. A FIFTH CONFESSION

It has been baldly stated in this narrative that Penn and Sher were friends at school and later at the Circle, and being gentle readers and not cruel and hungry readers who would visit a publisher's offices with the intention of rending and eating an author who had displeased them, you have taken this matter on trust. No examples of this friendship have been shown you, such as the two dragons exchanging confidences, or setting out together to enjoy themselves on a day out. The truth is that the very real friendship they had once shared as children had attenuated through time and the nature of their adult lives. Their lives and their enjoyments were now very different, so confidences and shared enjoyment had become matters of memory rather than commonplaces.

This was, of course, as the Exalt would have delighted to point out, largely because of their different stations in life. Sher had the dignity and finances

of his position, and Penn those of a country parson.
Even his living as a parson had been Sher's, or rather
the Exalt's, gift, and it takes a great deal of resilience
in a friendship to be able to endure charity given by
one friend to the other. It is often not the giver who
resents this, who, though they have lost in worldly
ways, have gained the delight of heaven, and also
the joy of gift-giving, but the one who must, having little, accept more than they can hope to offer
in return. If there is a return expected and granted,
as between Penn and the Exalt, where spiritual and
pastoral duties were exchanged for worldly comfort,
then all may be well. But with Sher, Penn felt he had
been given much and was returning nothing at all.
Naturally he resented this, and naturally, he tried
not to resent it, and resented the necessity of effort.
Equally naturally, Sher sensed both resentment and
effort, which put a constraint into the ease of their
relationship. Besides all this, Sher's life remained
very worldly and full of enjoyment while Penn over
time grew more and more devoted to the Church and
to his parish. They had in fact grown apart, and they
both regretted this extremely, for they had at one
time done everything together.

Thus when Sher returned with Selendra, still without the pink that would speak for itself, it was awkward for him to seek out Penn, more awkward than
it would be if they had never been close. Selendra
wished to accompany him, more to avoid being
left alone with Felin than for any other reason, but

he gently discouraged her. "I need to speak to your brother alone. We may need to discuss matters unsuitable for you."

Felin was out when they returned, visiting parishioners. Selendra took up a book, relieved to be alone.

Penn's office had a door, a very plain door that had been put in to replace the old carved door some generations ago. Sher knocked upon it with a careful claw. "Come in," Penn called, dolefully. Sher entered, and stood looking about him awkwardly. The room was Penn's, and held books and writing utensils which Sher recognized as Penn's, yet in some sense it belonged to Sher, as did the whole parsonage. Penn was supposed to be writing his Deepwinter sermon, to be read to the congregation after he had kindled the fire, but he was in fact lying supine staring at the Order commanding his presence in Irieth and considering the sin of suicide.

"Sher!" Penn said, pulling himself up sejant and trying to smile. "Good to see you."

"Good to see you, too," Sher said, fitting himself with some difficulty into the study and closing the door.

"Not in trouble, I hope?" Penn asked, with a heartiness that sounded false in his own ears.

"I hope not," Sher said, smiling awkwardly. "In fact, the opposite. I asked your sister Selendra to marry me, and she has agreed, once we have worked out a few details."

"Oh thanks be to Jurale!" Penn said, and promptly burst into tears.

Sher was extremely puzzled by this reaction. "It's not as bad as that," he said. This had no effect. "I'll take good care of her," he tried. Penn sobbed on. "What's the matter?" he asked at last.

Penn pushed the Order towards him. Sher took it and read it. "Selendra already told me about this," he said. "You're all going to Irieth, she said. I've offered you the use of Benandi House."

"You may not want to," Penn said, getting back a little control. "You may not even want to marry Selendra when you know."

"Know what?" Sher asked. "I find it very hard to think of anything that would stop me wanting to marry Selendra."

"Then that's one burden you've relieved me of," Penn said. "The worst of disgrace is bringing other dragons down with one."

"Disgrace?" Sher asked quickly.

"Ah, yes, it's different marrying the sister of a re-spectable parson and marrying the sister of a dis-graced parson," Penn said.

Here Penn did his old friend an injustice. Sher would never have considered marrying some abstract sister of a disgraced parson, nor indeed any-one who suffered under any great social burden. He would never, for instance, have contemplated falling in love with Sebeth. Yet now he had fallen so firmly in love with Selendra he would not have wavered whatever had happened to her family. "Tell me what the problem is," Sher said, with commendable calmness.

"I heard my father's confession on his deathbed, and it will come out in this trial, and I will be ruined and thrown out of the Church," Penn said, succinctly.

Sher blinked several times. He considered and dismissed several responses. He was not, in fact, shocked that such a thing had been done. He had heard it whispered that the Old Religion was quietly thriving. He was, however, shocked that Penn, who he secretly thought had grown rather stuffy and conventional since he became a parson, had done it. "Can you get your brother to call off the case?"

"Not after the First Hearing," Penn said. "He'd be subject to penalty for bringing it frivolously if he did that now."

"Then can't you get him to agree not to call you?" he asked.

"Avan did agree, it's Daverak who has called me," Penn said.

"Then how about Daverak?"

"He doesn't care a mouldy plum about me." Penn shook his head sadly, shaking tears from his snout.

The old school term made Sher smile in reminiscence. "Daverak's your brother-in-law. Care about you or not, he can't want you disgraced."

"Berend is dead."

"Even so, there are dragonets who are her hatchlings who are Daverak's heirs. You could talk to him and emphasize the social side of this, the effect on him," Sher said.

"I can't bear the thought of his knowing," Penn said.

"He's going to know if you tell the whole world in court," Sher said, a touch of impatience in his voice. "Illustrious, isn't he? Daverak? I've met him, I think. He cares a lot about rank and things like that. I'll come with you to see him if you like, it might help."

"That would be extremely kind of you," Penn said, then laughed through his tears. "Oh Sher, I'm sorry, I don't mean to talk to you like that when you're so good to me."

"Don't forget I have a vested interest in keeping you out of disgrace. I might not care, but my mother would, and Selendra has made it a condition that my mother be enthusiastic."

"The Exalt will never do more than tolerate—" Penn said, staring.

"The Exalt will do a great deal more than that," Sher said, his voice hard. It softened to a teasing tone. "But it will be a great deal easier for me if she sees you as a respectable parson who is almost always here for Firstday and never ever flies even over a ravine or goes hunting."

Penn laughed. When he had just taken up his cords he had slipped them for a day's hunting with Sher and only narrowly avoided being recognized.

"You have my blessing for marrying my sister,"

Penn said. "Her dowry is inadequate enough, but no doubt you have enough for two."

"Her dowry is magnificent," Sher said. "Hasn't she told you?"

Penn stared at him. "Told me what?"

"About the treasure we found?"

"Treasure? The dragonets are always talking nonsense about that treasure but surely it isn't real—"

"Real. Treasure. Gold. Jewels. Very valuable treasure. Your dragonets and Selendra and I found it, and divided into four parts I'd say it would be worth several hundred thousand crowns each, if not more. I haven't been trying to get it out, because of the snows, but come spring your two hatchlings will be receiving a fortune, and so will Selendra. So none of you will have to worry about gold, no matter what else, and no doubt my mother will be pleased to see that I have enlarged the coffers of Benandi as no heir has before me for several thousand years."

It was on his land, and he could have claimed it all, but what good was gold to him compared to the good it could do to his friends? Penn looked stunned. "I had no idea," he said. "I should apologize to Wontas for disbelieving him."

Sher laughed. "I'll come with you to speak to Daverak," he said. "I'll arrange about the treasure in the spring. And I'll marry your sister as soon as it's convenient for us all."

"That's wonderful," murmured Penn.

"And now I know you still break the laws of the Church from time to time, how about a day's hunting when we get back? All of us, Felin and Selendra too?"

Penn opened his mouth, couldn't speak, caught between tears and laughter. After an endless moment, laughter won.

14
COMING TO IRIETH

52. A SIXTH PROPOSAL

The Illustrious Daverak brought his household to Irieth for the hearing. Only the dragonets and the as yet unhatched eggs stayed in Daverak, along with sufficient servants to take care of them. Although it was not the time of year for Irieth, he had Daverak House aired out and completely opened. Haner, clutching her Order, came along meekly. She brought Lamith, less to burnish her scales than to run interference. She had plans of her own for how to spend her time in the capital. With Lamith on hand to say she was unwell or engaged in female pursuits she could be free to go about her own business.

They came up by train and arrived on the seventh day of Deepwinter, a week before the day set for the trial. Haner spent the first day overseeing the servants as they draped the walls with tapestries packed away while the house was empty. Only the sleeping caves were underground, in what amounted to arched cellars. Most of the house stood clear in the air. Some rooms even had windows. Haner had never seen anything like it and didn't like it at all.

Daverak, not without some hesitation, had listened to his attorney's advice and invited Frelt to stay with him. This was a complete surprise to Haner. She only just managed not to recoil when she saw him in the outer corridor of Daverak House. He was his usual dapper self, well burnished and handsome enough in his conventional way.

"Respected Agornin," he said, bowing. "I'm glad to see you well, and offer you my condolences on the loss of your sister. May she be reborn with Camran."

Haner had never liked the slightly proprietary way Frelt spoke about the gods. She bowed. "Greetings, Blessed Frelt, what brings you to Irieth?"

"The same thing that brings you, this sadly mistaken court case your foolish young brother is bringing." Frelt shook his head in mock sadness.

"You are to give evidence?" she asked.

"Yes indeed." Frelt nodded several times. "I shall be one of the most important witnesses I'm afraid, witnessing to what was said and done in the undercave as well as to your father's beliefs and state of mind."

Haner looked down her snout at him. There was no point in saying that he knew nothing about her father's state of mind. "I hope you're not nervous about it," she said.

"No, a parson gets used to standing up and talking," Frelt said. He smiled at Haner, showing his teeth. She was the youngest of the Agornin sisters, and not the prettiest, he thought, but she was more timid than Berend and quieter than Selendra. She might be just what he needed.

"Where are you staying?" she asked, conventionally.

"Why, Illustrious Daverak has been kind enough to offer me the hospitality of his house," Frelt said, with a leer.

"Then we shall no doubt be seeing a lot of you," Haner said, her heart sinking.

"How pleasant that will be," Frelt said. "Do you miss Agornin?" he asked.

"Yes," Haner said, stepping unobtrusively a little away from him.

"I have been considering taking a wife," Frelt said, baldly.

"I hear that many maidens come to Irieth to find husbands," Haner said, backing even farther away.

Frelt laughed. "You included? I wondered if you might like to return to Agornin with me, Haner?" He advanced towards her.

"No, sir," she said, and fled. She could hardly believe his effrontery.

She fled to the dining room, where Daverak was waiting. "Here you are at last, Haner," he said. "Have you seen the Blessed Frelt?"

"He's just coming," she said. In Daverak's presence she felt safe at least from being pressed as Selendra had been pressed. She thought of dear Londaver and felt reassured. A moment later Frelt came in, as composed as if nothing had happened. He ignored her and talked to Daverak. The conversation largely concerned the forthcoming trial. Haner sat quietly saying nothing, and was ignored. Food was brought in, beef that was not very fresh. Haner ate as swiftly as she could, hoping to be able to escape sooner.

"Mustan tells me they may well ask about Bon's intentions in making the will," Daverak said.

"As I said at the time, I'm quite sure they were as you think," Frelt said.

"Haner?" Daverak asked.

"What?" She looked up, surprised to be addressed. "Father's intentions? I knew nothing about them, I told you that and I shall tell the court that."

"Good. I know you won't say anything to harm me. You understand where the meat comes from to sustain you at least." The threat was veiled only by the thinnest smile.

Frelt smiled at Daverak's hard tone. "I'm sure Respected Agornin would do nothing impious," he said.

"I will tell the truth as it says on the Order I was sent," she said in an even tone. "I may not know much, but what I know I will say."

"When I have destroyed your brother you will have your reward, in your dowry, as I told you," Daverak said. Haner shuddered a little, and knew that Frelt saw her shudder.

"I'm not sure the maiden wants to marry," Frelt said, silkily.

"Oh, she has a hanger-on already, Londaver, a neighbor of ours at home," Daverak said casually, but not cruelly.

"That explains it," Frelt said. "She should have said

that when I made her an offer, instead of running away. I don't know what she was expecting."

"You?" Daverak looked up at him, blood from the beef dripping from his jaws. He managed to put more contempt into the single word than Haner could have managed in a week.

Frelt laughed, awkwardly. Haner stood. "I've finished, I think I'll retire," she said.

"No," Daverak said, shortly. "Sit down."

Haner sat obediently.

"Frelt, I don't know if you're ill, or what it is that makes you think you could aspire to marry someone connected with my family, but put it entirely out of your mind," Daverak said. This was much more polite than he would have been had he not known he needed Frelt's evidence. "You should marry someone of your own station, a parson's daughter," he went on. "I'll see if I can find one to put in your way. Now do enjoy the hospitality of my house, but leave my sister-in-law alone."

Frelt spluttered. "I had no intention of making unwelcome advances."

"You can go now, Haner," Daverak said.

For the second time that evening, Haner fled.

53. LEAVING BENANDI

Felin could almost have felt sorry for the Exalt in the whirlwind of preparations that followed Sher and

Selendra's Deepwinter flight. Sher had always before tried to charm and cajole his mother, or else ignored her entirely and taken himself off. Now he was making demands, and being insistent. He demanded that Benandi House in Irieth be opened instantly, that they remove there immediately, that they hold an entertainment while they were there for whatever company might be found in Irieth in midwinter, and that hospitality be offered there to the parsonage family. In the midst of this, he demanded that his mother welcome his intended. Felin might have laughed at the confusion this caused, had she not been able to see the Exalt's genuine distress.

"He's completely set on having his own way," she told Felin, grimly, while at the same time making lists of what must be packed. "I could have been doing this for weeks past except that he refused to consider a move. Now it's all to be done at once. No, you can't help, I know what's to be done." A hot tear trickled down her snout. "I have lost my son now. That it's my own fault doesn't make it any easier to bear."

"You haven't lost him," Felin said. "Selendra will make you a good daughter-in-law if you'd just accept her."

"After this beginning? I think not." The Exalt sniffed, and was all practicality again. "You could tell me how many servants you're bringing, and if you really want to help, perhaps you could arrange to reserve four carriages on the train for us from here to Irieth."

Felin left the Exalt to get on with creating order.

She found Sher sitting in the parsonage talking to Selendra and the children. Sher looked dazed, like any bridegroom. The children looked excited. Wontas was still limping, but only a little, Felin assured herself, as she did every time she saw him. He would heal so that nobody would know the difference. Nobody would think him a weakling in danger of consumption. Selendra sat curled up, with Gerin between her and Sher. She would have looked like a bride, except that she remained the shimmering and pure gold she had been since Felin had first met her. She would not talk to Felin about it, saying only that she had made conditions to Sher and would not go further than she might turn back until those conditions had been met. Felin feared for the conditions, and feared for Sher—except that when, as now, she saw Selendra looking at Sher she was reassured by the love that was plainly visible in her slowly turning eyes. Worse than Selendra's refusal to talk about her conditions was Penn's refusal to discuss Selendra's coloring. He grew embarrassed and changed the subject every time Felin tried to raise it. Selendra was his sister, of course, but he was a parson and not usually squeamish about such matters.

The four of them were making ridiculous plans about what to do with the treasure. Felin still did not quite believe in the treasure, though she had been shown the pieces the dragonets had brought out, and Selendra's chain. She supposed it would be some consolation if they were ruined to be rich and not poor, though riches without position are an empty thing, as Penn said. She could not quite take in either the riches or the ruin. Part of her still believed that life would revert to normal after the trial and that she would always live here.

"How is my mother?" Sher asked, after Felin had greeted him.

"Harried," Felin said.

Selendra smiled. It was not at all a nice smile.

"She will do everything perfectly when it gets to it," Sher said.

"I am so looking forward to Irieth," Selendra said. "The theater. A rout-party."

"We will go there in season and go to balls," Sher said. "You may as well get what pleasure from it you can before it all gets dull."

"We'll have to get you some new hats," Felin said, considering her own meager supply of headgear.

"Not too many," Sher warned.

"Why?" Wontas asked. "We have the treasure, Aunt Sel can afford whatever hats she wants."

"Yes, but have you never noticed how dragons buy hats to match their scales?" Sher asked, addressing Wontas but looking over at Selendra. "Aunt Selendra's scales are a beautiful gold now, but soon they will be an even more beautiful bridal pink, and she'll need a whole new set of hats."

Felin was looking at Selendra and thought she looked distressed rather than flattered at the thought.

"The Exalt wants to know how many servants we are taking," Felin said. "I thought just two?"

"Can we take Amer?" Selendra asked. "I know she'd like to see Haner and Avan."

"I need Amer to stay here and look after the children," Felin said. "I don't like to leave them with just the nanny. Amer's experienced."

"Can't we come?" Gerin asked.

"I've never been to Irieth," Wontas said.

"We might find more treasure," Gerin said, coaxingly.

"No," Felin said, horrified. "The last time was more than enough treasure hunting. You could have all been killed."

"Why not bring them, though, if they promise not to treasure hunt?" Sher asked. "There's room."

Felin had never been in Irieth either. Mixed as were the reasons for this trip, she would have liked to have been able to enjoy what she could of it without the responsibility of the dragonets. She could not say this while they were there, silently hanging on her every word. "They should stay here out of trouble," Felin said. Both dragonets groaned. "The Exalt won't like it," she said, knowing this had a strong effect on the children.

"My mother won't mind," Sher said, as decisively as he had been saying everything recently. The children cheered.

A week later, having packed up everything possible, the seven of them, accompanied by nineteen servants, were on their way to Irieth, in five carriages. Penn looked abstracted, the children looked overexcited, Sher looked blissful, Selendra looked calmly golden, the Exalt looked like a barely contained volcano, and Felin was sure she herself looked as if she needed a week of sleep rather than a week of entertainments in the capital. It gave her some satisfaction to see the dragonets carefully settled with Sher and Selendra, and to seat herself comfortably in another carriage with Penn and the Exalt.

54. HANER TAKES A WALK

Haner left Lamith with strict instructions to say she was unwell and admit nobody. She was dubious as to Lamith's ability to do this if Daverak insisted, but he was unlikely to insist, or even to be awake. It was still early in the morning when she ventured out of the establishment and set off for her appointment.

She had read *The Subjugation of Servants* and had, greatly daring, written to the publisher expressing her appreciation. She had received a letter back from Calien Afelan himself, and since then they had been corresponding. She knew that she should not hold any correspondence without the approval of her guardian. Since Daverak assumed all her mail was from Selendra, he paid no attention to it. She was always careful about taking her letters to the post herself. She did have qualms about the unauthorized nature of her activities, but consoled herself with the thought that Londaver was her proper guardian, and he had given her the book, and would have approved. Whether Londaver would have approved of her going alone through the streets of Irieth to meet a stranger, she did not pause to consider.

She knew better than to arrange to go unaccompanied to the home of a stranger, so she had arranged to meet Calien in a public park by the river. To get there from Daverak House she had to walk for quite some distance. She did not dare fly in the dangerous crossdrafts. She trudged diligently through the dirty city snow, so different from the white folds of country snow she was used to.

Haner had never learned Sebeth's trick of removing her hat, so she attracted quite a few curious glances as she made her way through the slushy streets. Unaccompanied maidens whose hats proclaim them to be Respected are not a common sight in any city. Twice, red-scaled and motherly looking dragons, out for early marketing with a servant at their heels, asked her if she was lost or needed help. Both times she excused herself and walked on. Three times elderly and indigent dragons came up and importuned her for a crown, which she gave at the first application. Afterwards she had nothing to give, having only provided herself with one crown for her expedition, and could only smile apologetically. She was sorry for its loss when she walked through the little market with its enticing smells of freshly killed swine, still warm, and honeyed pears.

After the market, her way led her past the huge slaughterhouses and stockyards. The dragons working in them were all bound servants, rushing to and fro with the animals. The snow was churned up here, and more yellow and brown than the gray it had been. From time to time carts passed her, spraying her with the unpleasant slurry. She was growing chilly, and some snow had balled uncomfortably under one of her feet. Fine fresh snow began to fall.

At last she reached the riverside park where she had arranged to meet Calien. She stood looking around for him. She was carrying a copy of his book, which they had agreed as a sign of identification. The park was deserted. Those who worked in the nearby offices and factories were at their jobs already, and those dragons of the polite world who were in Irieth at that season had hardly yet risen. Haner walked to and fro. Here the snow was hard and slippery, except where the newly falling snow covered it with a thin layer of softness. It was white, at least. Haner walked down to the river and contemplated the great Toris, artery of Tiamath. Ice extended from the banks, but the center of the river was dark and fast flowing.

Calien came up beside her as she stood there. "You are the Respected Haner Agornin?" he asked.

She swung around in surprise, and then was further surprised to see that the black-scaled stranger bore the red cords of a priest and was little more than ten feet long. "Respectable—I mean Blessed Afelan?"

He bowed. "I am Calien Afelan. I thought we might

walk across the river to the Skamble so I might show you how some of my parishioners live," he said.

Haner was already tired of walking in Irieth, but she assented. As they walked they spoke of the different conditions of servants in the country and in cities. "I saw some of them working in the stockyards," Haner said.

"They do not meet the cruelty and abuse they might in a country establishment; the problem here is more neglect." Calien sighed. "There are many accidents in the slaughterhouses. They are necessary, of course, a city the size of Irieth needs to have its meat supply organized or we would all swiftly perish. Yet they could be operated with more thought for the dragons who work in them."

Haner nodded agreement. "I don't know anything about the cities really," she said. As he was telling her about conditions in Irieth, Haner could not help thinking of the mystery of how small he was, for a parson and for a dragon of sufficient birth and education to have written and published a book. She dared not ask. If his parish were among the poor, he would likewise be poor, but surely the poor needed to be culled, and died, like everywhere else, and the parson's share would fall to their parson?

"Blessed Afalen," she began, and he interrupted her gently.

"I am not a parson but a priest of the True Religion, the Old Religion you would say. So the usual form of address would be Blessed Calien." He smiled, and

Haner tried not to recoil. "I see that I have shocked you," he went on. "The True Religion is not illegal. It is merely frowned upon by those who have turned away from our faith. For the last thirty years we have even been allowed to defend ourselves in court if we are attacked, though not to bring an action against another."

"I have never met anyone of your faith," Haner said, entirely flustered.

"I will leave you if I cause you distress," Calien said.

"No," Haner said. "No, stay. Why does it matter, after all. You are trying to make a difference for those who are helpless to improve their own condition. It speaks well of your Church, and badly of mine, that it is you who is doing this. I want to visit the dragons you want to show me. I want to do what I can to help, even if it is very little."

Calien smiled at her in approval, and led her on. "Every voice raised against the subjugation of servants is a help," he said. "A voice such as yours can do inestimable good, especially if you become mistress of a demesne."

"I was thinking about the way they do it at Londaver," Haner said, stepping aside to avoid the plume of slush sent up by another passing cart.

"Ah, Londaver," Calien said, looking at her shrewdly. "Exalt Londaver is one of my strongest supporters."

"Her son lent me your book," Haner admitted, caressing the book she held. "But while what they do there, or my father did at Agornin, is better, and kinder, I wonder if even that goes far enough. If I become mistress of a demesne, I think I would free all the servants."

"And how would you run your demesne then?" the priest asked.

"As you say in your book, free dragons coming together for mutual benefit," Haner quoted.

"I should very much like to see it tried," Calien said, and guided her onwards.

When at last she returned to Daverak House she was cold and exhausted. She was not expecting to find Daverak pacing the hall, waiting for her. "Where have you been?" he demanded.

"For a walk," she said.

"I am not a fool, Haner, and I'll be obliged if you don't treat me like one. You have been to collude with your brother Avan."

"I have not!" Haner was indignant. "Where I have been is my own business, but it had nothing to do with Avan."

"The two of you have doubtless been getting your stories against me straight with each other," Daverak said, flame billowing around the edge of his words and melting snow on Haner's scales.

"If you must know, I have been seeing someone about the rights of servants."

Daverak laughed. "Your servant tried to lie to protect you. There was hardly anything to her, but I won't tolerate insubordination from servants. Nor will I tolerate it in poor relations for that matter."

"You ate Lamith?" Haner asked, appalled.

"Was that her name? Yes. Now, in court. You will tell them you knew nothing of your father's will or his intent."

"It is the truth and I said I would say that," Haner said, backing away a little.

"Go to your room!" Daverak bellowed, and the flame singed her tail as she fled.

"You are insane," Haner said, slamming the door of her sleeping room. "I will tell the truth, and I am telling the truth now when I say I haven't seen Avan."

"You'll not take his side, I'll see to that," Daverak said, and she heard a series of blows against her door. At first she had cowered at the far side of the cave, afraid he was breaking in to eat her. Then she realized that he was piling up something on the outside, to make it impossible for her to get out. She was still clutching the book.

"Londaver," she thought, and the thought was like a prayer. Then she did pray, the most simple of children's prayers, quick to the tongue. "Camran the truthbringer, Jurale the merciful, Veld the just, help me now." The blows to the door continued. When silence fell at last, nothing she could do could open it.

55. BENANDI HOUSE

Since she had accepted Sher's proposal, since the night before that when she had not slept, since the afternoon before that when the Exalt had said she was not good enough for Sher, Selendra had been living on her nerves. Everything had the clarity of midnight. Her greatest joy and her greatest dread both were that she saw Sher every day, for a large part of every day. He did not try to press her physically, though every day he reminded her verbally one way or another that she was not yet fully his. She liked him, indeed, she loved him far too much to want to hurt him, and she was beginning to see that it wasn't possible to carry out her plan without hurting him a great deal. It was also too late to withdraw. She had to go through with it, which meant she had to act, and act well.

It wasn't all bad. She would wake at night with her heart hammering and feelings of terrible love and guilt beating at her. But there was much to enjoy. She could torment the Exalt whenever she had the opportunity. Thus far despite all Sher had tried, the Exalt had not unbent towards Selendra at all. So Selendra took a perverse delight in forcing her to acknowledge her position of Sher's intended, as the future Exalt Benandi. Besides, Sher's intended had access to pleasures, simple and complex, which Selendra had always wanted. She was going to Irieth, and there she would attend a rout-party, with the added joys of forcing the Exalt to arrange it and present her. She would also go to the theater, a treat she had always before been denied. She swore she would enjoy what she could now, and leave later for later. She avoided Felin's eyes as much as she could.

She found the journey tedious, although she rose up above the train with Sher as often as she wanted. The dragonets were soon bored, and required entertaining. It was better than the journey from Agornin, but trains, as she told Sher, were inherently dull. "We'll fly everywhere once we're married," he assured her. They arrived at Irieth late at night, so late that they did nothing but find the rooms assigned to them and fall asleep. It was not until morning that Selendra even noticed how grand her sleeping cave was, or realized that the gold she had slept on was part of the Benandi treasure. Almost every piece bore a crest. This was no guest room, but the great room of the mistress of the demesne. Sher must have insisted that his mother give it up to her. For a little while she imagined that she could truly marry Sher and enter this room by right. If only she could blush! She ground her teeth at the thought of Frelt.

She was disappointed, at breakfast, by the staleness of the meat. "It's impossible to get good beef in Irieth," Penn told her.

"We usually manage better than this," Sher said, chewing hard.

"I usually send the servants down to the slaughterhouses late at night to be able to buy the meat as soon as it is on sale in the morning," the Exalt said. "We arrived too late last night. They went down, but they were too far back in the queue to get anything good. It will be better tomorrow. Now, how do you intend to amuse yourselves today? I will be busy addressing cards to invite our friends to the rout. Selendra, dear, can you write? Would you care to help me?"

Selendra did not in the least want to spend the day addressing boring rout cards, but could not say so now that her maidenly skills had been insulted. "Of course I can write," she said. "I have been writing for father for years."

"That's settled then," the Exalt said, smiling, knowing she had won a battle. "What will the rest of you do?"

"It's snowing so I can hardly see my tail," Sher said. "I don't doubt it'll stop in an hour or so, by which time you'll doubtless have finished with Selendra and I can take her out to see the sights. Would you like to come with us, Felin? I'm sure we can take in a milliner's establishment on the way." Selendra smiled gratefully at Sher. The Exalt looked a little sour.

"I ought to look after the children," Felin said, regretfully.

"I can watch the children, dear," Penn said.

"But they want to see half of Irieth," Felin protested.

"I can take them to the Church of Sainted Vouiver, that provides enough sights for any number of dragonets, and will be good for them," Penn said, in a determinedly cheerful way.

"Take Amer with you," Felin suggested.

"If you think so," Penn said, getting up and wiping his chest. He bowed to Sher and to the Exalt. "Shall I see you at dinner?"

"Yes, and be on time, because I'm planning to take everyone to the theater afterwards," Sher said.

Selendra bounced up as if she were just growing her wings, almost leaving the ground in her excitement. "The theater?"

"Nothing unsuitable for my sister, I hope?" Penn asked, trying to smile and not quite succeeding.

"Nothing unsuitable for anyone. Etanin's *The Defeat of the Yarge*." Sher smiled amiably at the company. "I have taken space enough for all of us including the dragonets."

"It's a classic," Penn said reassuringly to Felin, who had made a motion of protest with her tail. "Etanin is a great poet. It's educational. We acted it in school."

"Historical," Sher said, nodding at Felin. He stood suddenly, brought his tail forward, and raised his arms in a careful pose of horror. "Why then, 'tis treason!" he said, in an appalled tone. He crouched down low, his wings flat on his back and his tail stretched out behind him and spoke in a low confiding voice. "Do you say treason? That I'll not deny. But you mean treason to the Yarge, our lords, while I say every day they are our lords is treason to our own, our dragon-nature. You say we took an oath that we'd be true, but what is truth when keeping oaths makes lies, makes twisted souls, makes claws bent into hands—" he bent his claws alarmingly. "Scales shaken off," he shuddered, "wings bound upon our backs—why, living thus is treason to ourselves."

Selendra clapped her hands enthusiastically. "You're as good as a play yourself!"

"Why thank you, Majesty." Sher bowed like an actor. "Merely re-enacting the history of our glorious nation."

"Not the real history," Penn interjected. "There's more poetry than history in that. The Yarges beat us because they had weapons, and once we had weapons too, we threw them out again. You'd think from Etanin's play that we did it with bare claws and flame, when the Conquest had already proved that claws and flame don't get anywhere against cannon."

"Don't be boring, Penn," Sher said.

"Don't be romantic, Sher," Penn said, in exactly the same tone, and for a moment everyone could see the dragonets they had been, scarcely ten years older than Gerin and Wontas when they met at school. For an instant the three females present were united, smiling fondly at the males.

"I must get the children ready to go out," Felin said, breaking the moment. "I shall look forward to the play, Sher, historical or not it will be an experience. I have never seen one."

"Neither have I, and I have always always wanted to, ever since Penn used to tell me about the theater when I was a hatchling," Selendra said, stepping towards the door. "I shall freshen up and then join you to work on the invitations, Mother."

She left, and Penn and Felin followed her out.

"Mother," the Exalt repeated, bitterly. "She meant that as a blow."

"You shouldn't pick fights with her," Sher said. "I'm sure you'd like each other if you'd stopped waging open warfare."

"She wants to fight with me," the Exalt said. "Can't you see that? Oh, I know it's my fault for provoking her in the first place, but I can see I'm going to pay for it. I sometimes wonder if she wants to fight with me more than she wants to marry you."

Sher paused, considering. He had been trying to reconcile the two of them for more than a week now, with very little success. "I can see how you might think so," he said, rejecting the urge to defend Selendra blindly and giving it consideration. "But no, I know she loves me."

"I don't see it in her scales," his mother said.

"She is waiting until you accept her, I have told you that," Sher said. "I have seen love in her eyes."

"Eyes can lie," the Exalt said. Selendra's pristine gold was the only thing in the situation that gave her any comfort. "I don't think she loves you at all, I think she wants revenge on me because I asked her to leave you alone."

"I am quite sure she loves me," Sher said, thinking steadfastly of what he had read in her eyes in the snowy meadow on Deepwinter morning under the icy sun.

"I'm quite sure you're a fool," the Exalt said. "And which of the wretched maiden's siblings should I invite to the rout-party, since they are at law with each other?"

"Haner, and Daverak," Sher said.

"I see you have some social consciousness after all," his mother said. "If she is bringing anyone to the family who has any rank at all, it is Daverak."

"You're to be polite to her," Sher said, leaning forward and catching his mother's eye. "Whatever you think and whatever you feel, you will be polite, you will stop picking fights and trying to make her unhappy, you will organize this rout for her, and when I tell you to, you will tell her you welcome her into the family."

"Veld will strike me blue for lying."

"I am the head of this family. I am the Exalted Benandi," Sher said.

"Everybody is well aware of that," the Exalt said.

"Then listen to me as head of the family. You'll welcome Selendra when I tell you to, or I'll serve you at our marriage feast."

"You dare?" she said.

Sher just looked at her.

"You wouldn't dare," she said. "To be known as the Exalted Lord who ate his mother when she was strong and well?"

Sher smiled, and turned to go. He paused in the doorway and looked back. His mother had lowered her head to the ground, and he saw that she was weeping.

15
AFFAIRS DRAW TOGETHER

56. A SEVENTH PROPOSAL

There was more polite company to be found in Irieth on the tenth of Deepwinter than the Exalt had imagined, or than would have been usual. She sent cards, as a matter of course, to all those she knew who were present in the city, but also to the great houses. She addressed these "to those of the Household presently in Irieth." Because eccentric old Eminent Telstie was dying, and dying in Irieth, and dying without naming an heir, and dying obsessed with reconciling himself with everyone with whom he had ever quarrelled, more members of the great Households were in Irieth than was usual. Most of them were delighted to have some entertainment other than waiting for the Eminent to die. The rout was a great success. It was not the crush it would have been in the season, where as the saying has it, a maiden would be in danger of returning from a walk across the room unsure who had turned her scales. The great ballroom of Benandi House, five hundred feet long, with a floor inlaid with amethyst and mother of pearl, was scattered with dragons in elegant headgear. Snacks of beautifully arranged fruit and meat were laid out in an adjoining dining room. Servants carried around great steins of beer. Thirty-five dragons graced the reception.

To the disappointment of both Selendra and Sher, Haner was not among them. The Illustrious Daverak came, accompanied by the Blessed Frelt, both burnished to a high gloss and wearing fine dark hats. "Felicitations, Selendra," Daverak said, bowing. "What a fine match you have made for yourself."

"Thank you," Selendra said. She was wearing a new hat, black and gray, as was appropriate for mourning, but decorated with two diamonds on little stalks, which she hoped he would not see as disrespectful to Berend's memory. "Where is my sister Haner?"

"She is a little indisposed," Daverak said. "She went out two mornings ago, for some air she said, and became very chilled. A doctor has seen her, and says she needs rest and warmth. Her maid is looking after her. She sends her good wishes and asks me to pass on her apologies."

"Please send back my good wishes," Selendra said. "Is her maid good at tending the sick? Our old nanny is here in Irieth with me, I could send her over to you if she might be of use."

"Oh, we have plenty of servants of our own at Daverak House," Daverak said, dismissively. He moved on to greet the Exalt, who was already welcoming the Exalt and Exalted Rimalin. This left Selendra, already a little unhappy, confronted with Frelt.

Frelt was angry with Daverak, although he had not

allowed this to show. He felt insulted not by Haner's rejection of him, but by Daverak's way of dealing with it. He now wished to offer his help in the way of the testimony he might give in court, to Avan. He knew Avan would not be present at the rout, as Daverak had been invited, but he knew Penn and Selendra would, and hoped to be able to speak to them about it.

"My dear Respected Agornin," Frelt said, bowing carefully, a stein of beer clutched in one claw. "Betrothed and still gold?"

Half a dozen guests had already asked this question, and been answered politely by Sher or Selendra. It was a natural one in the circumstances. Frelt knew nothing of the color change she had suffered from his proposal at the end of summer. He had almost forgotten he had ever considered her. He had not loved her, as he had flattered himself he loved Berend, he had merely been looking for a wife. He continued to look for one. He smiled.

He was not at all prepared for her reaction. "I never want to see you again," Selendra hissed, through her teeth. "Go away."

Frelt recoiled, backwards, almost tripping over his tail.

Penn, who had seen Frelt approaching and Selendra's tail beginning to twitch, came to interrupt at this point. "Frelt," he said, in a guardedly friendly way.

"Penn," Frelt replied, cautiously, bowing.

"I am glad to see you here," Penn said. "Please do enjoy Exalt Benandi's hospitality, but please, if I might ask as much, keep away from my sister."

Frelt bowed again, shortly, and stalked away. The Agornin family were all as bad as each other, and he resolved to keep away from them in future as they so clearly wanted. He remembered Avan casually insulting him as he came to call. He would do none of them any more good than he had to. In the far corner of the room he caught sight of a beautiful maiden, accompanied by a formidable dowager and a priest. "Who is that?" he asked Sher, who was passing.

Sher glanced over. "Oh, that's Blessed Telstie with his wife and daughter," he said.

"Blessed Telstie, the brother of the Eminent Telstie who is at present dying?" Frelt asked.

"Precisely," Sher said, bowing politely. He had no idea who Frelt was, other than some priest Daverak had brought in place of Haner, but he knew his duties as a host. "Would you like an introduction?"

Sher led Frelt over to the Telstie party. "Blessed Telstie, Blest Telstie, Respected Telstie, may I present Blessed Frelt, a friend of the Illustrious Daverak."

"I am the parson of Undertor, and have known the Agornin family for years," Frelt said.

"Congratulations on your engagement, Exalted Benandi," Gelener said to Sher, her smile so icy he would hardly have been surprised to see frost on her teeth.

"Love takes its own course," Blessed Telstie said,

looking remarkably cheerful for a dragon whose daughter had lost a suitor and whose brother was dying. Perhaps he found the prospect of his elder son's inheriting his brother's title some consolation, Sher thought.

"Thank you," he said. "I must leave you for the moment, I must go and greet my intended's uncle, August Fidrak."

"Perhaps a game of dice later?" Blessed Telstie asked.

"There will be dice in the little room," Sher said, turning back. "Through there," he waved his arm. "I believe there may be dragons in there already."

Blessed Telstie was beaming when he left, Gelener was sitting like a gilded ice-statue of a maiden, and Blest Telstie was beginning to interrogate Frelt about his prospects.

The August Fidrak, whom Selendra had once protested she did not know, was in Irieth to visit the deathbed of his longtime colleague and rival in the Noble Assembly. He was a genial old dragon, happy to acknowledge the connection with the beautiful maiden and the powerful Benandi family. He was too old to seek again for office, though he held on to his seat, but his son might well need friends, even if the blood relationship was distant. He called Selendra "niece" and spoke fondly about her mother. The Exalt came close and listened deferentially.

Some gently born dragons who cling tightly to the rank in which they were born, or have achieved by marriage or accomplishment, do not favor those whom life has placed in rank above them. The Exalt did not suffer from this fault. There were not many who ranked above her own Exalted status, but those there were, Eminents and Eminences, Augusts and Augustas, she courted assiduously. She often regretted the loss of the Majestics and Highnesses and Honorables of old, there was nothing she would have liked so much as the thrill of having a Highness deign to drop in on a party she had arranged. Deprived of this, she made the most of August Fidrak, who endured her fussing graciously.

Sher managed to draw Selendra away. "I told you these things were a terrible bore," he whispered to her.

"They wouldn't be if one could choose the participants," Selendra whispered back.

"But one never can," Sher said, bowing at a dowager. "For parties in the country, one can choose. In Irieth, when everyone returns to their own beds at the end of the evening, it's necessary to go with convention."

"I much preferred the theater," Selendra said.

Sher laughed. "Soon the crush will thin out a bit, as dragons go off to play dice and eat, and we will be able to dance. Do you realize I've never danced with you?"

"Is there room?" Selendra asked. "This is a big cavern, but I have never danced indoors before." She was secretly a little nervous about her dancing, which she had learned from Berend and not practiced for a long time.

"You'll find there's room," Sher said. On the other side of the room, he caught sight of Penn signalling to him. "Excuse me for a moment," he said.

"But what should I do?" Selendra asked, in consternation. She knew almost nobody.

"Talk to Felin," Sher advised, indicating Felin, who was conversing amiably with Exalt Rimalin. He set off across the room. Selendra watched him go, the assurance in his step. He had been crossing rooms like this half his life, she supposed, while she—maybe the Exalt was right about the differences in their station. She drew her head up and stepped out towards Felin. If she lacked experience, she would make it up with confidence and style. If the Exalt expected to intimidate her, she would be surprised.

A handsome young stranger paused beside her. He was perhaps thirty feet long, with fine bronze scales and a well-formed tail. "What a delightful rout. Thank you so much for getting unseasonably betrothed and allowing us an excuse to come here and dance. I love these evening affairs, don't you?" he asked.

"Don't you find that it leaves you tired in the morning?" Selendra asked.

"Well, I generally sleep in the morning, in the season," he replied. "After all, our eyes were not designed to work so much in daylight. They become tired. I'm sorry. You don't know me. I'm Respectable Alwad Telstie."

"I know your sister," Selendra said.

"I know, she told me. She said you were beautiful, but left out half of it. It's hard to melt information out of Gelener."

Selendra was no longer confused by idle compliments. She cast her eyes down mockingly, laughed, and remembered her first meeting with Gelener and the Exalt's hurtful advice. "Did she tell you that my father grew up on the Telstie estate?" she asked, deliberately.

"No. How fascinating. Did he know my uncle? My uncle might want to see him. He appears to want to see everyone he ever knew, to be reconciled, before he dies."

"He's dead himself, this autumn, so it's too late," Selendra said.

"I'm sorry," Alwad said. "It's just been so much on my mind lately. I'm my uncle's heir, but we quarrelled last year."

"Has he reconciled with you?"

"Not yet, there's apparently someone he wants to see first. It's all very mysterious, it's as if he has a script for how he's doing it. He told my father he'd see me two days from now. I'll be on my best behavior the whole time, you can be sure." He laughed and took another stein of beer from a passing servant.

"But doesn't it matter to you?" Selendra asked.

"What? To be reconciled to my uncle? A little. I like the old dragon. Or to inherit his lands and title? Not at all. I would almost prefer not to, to continue in my fine life in the army. As for his wealth, well, that would be useful."

Selendra hesitated. "I had supposed the three to go together," she said.

"I suppose they might, though where else he imagines he'll find a relative to take the demesne is beyond me. He's never cared much for rank, but he really cares about family."

"I think that's better than thinking rank is everything," Selendra said.

"Why yes. Have you seen your future mother-in-law fawning over old August Fidrak, the legislator? Fidrak hasn't two crowns to rub together, his lands are mortgaged to the wingtip. He lives on the charity of his daughters' husbands, and on his stipend in the Assembly. Yet there's the Exalt treating him as if he's of much more worth than she could ever be, when she has Benandi, and half Tiamath besides."

"I don't think wealth or rank are the important things," Selendra said.

"Then how do you consider dragons?" Alwad asked, his head tipped curiously on its side.

"By the worth of themselves," Selendra said. "I love Sher not because he's an Exalted but because he's Sher. If I'd fallen in love with you, for example, without any title but Respectable, I'd think you just as good as he is."

"You're a radical," he said, stepping back, laughing. "A free-thinker! Does Sher know of this? I'm quite sure my mother doesn't, she'd have told me."

"I don't need to be a radical to think that who a dragon is counts more than birth or wealth," Selendra said, with what dignity she could.

"Why, that's the very definition of a radical," he retorted. "We shall have a radical Exalt among us soon, which is indeed a charming notion. What a pity you can't take a seat in the Noble Assembly and delight us all with your notions."

Meanwhile, Frelt was making a good impression on the rest of the Telstie family. He had even made Gelener laugh once, graciously. "You're just the kind of parson the Church needs," Blessed Telstie said, taking a deep draught of his beer and almost forgetting about the lure of the dicebox.

"And if I may say so on so little acquaintance, but in which I have been greatly struck by her beauty and accomplishments, your daughter is just the sort of wife I need," Frelt said.

"Say no more before we visit our respective attorneys and speak to our mutual friends," Blest Telstie said, stepping forward as if to indicate that she was willing to interpose her body between them if necessary.

"If that all proves satisfactory I should have no objection," said Gelener quietly, looking at Frelt unsmilingly. She would not have thought to have settled for as little as a country parson when first she came to Irieth, but now that she was facing a third season still unmarried, she had lowered her sights considerably.

On the other side of the room Daverak was still refusing to listen to Penn and Sher. "Quite impossible," he kept saying. "Consider, it is Firstday tomorrow, and the day after is the case. I need your testimony, Penn, Avan is attacking me, he is being perfectly unreasonable. No, I won't consider, why should I."

Penn would not speak about the real risks in the ballroom where they might be overheard. "Can we visit you tomorrow to talk about it?" Sher asked.

"Not tomorrow, no," Daverak said, and softened it slightly, remembering Sher's rank, which counted with him as August Fidrak's did with the Exalt. "Tomorrow is Firstday."

"I think it is important enough to visit you even on Firstday," Sher said.

"Oh very well," Daverak said. "Come to see me in the evening. Come and dine. But I warn you, I have no intention of changing my mind."

Then the dancing began. The party continued until the sky was beginning to lighten, and everyone agreed as they left that it had been the best entertainment held in Irieth for many months.

57. A THIRD DEATHBED AND A SIXTH CONFESSION

It was Firstday, and in the usual way of things Sebeth would have accompanied Avan to church in the morning. There she would have made her public devotions, and while we know that her private devotions were quite otherwise, the world did not. On this particular Firstday, the eleventh of Deepwinter, the day before the Second Hearing of Avan's case, she prepared herself as she would for church, with a flat formal cap of navy blue trimmed with white fleece.

"Do you know where your book of prayers is?" she asked. "I'm going now."

"I'm nearly ready," Avan grumbled.

"I'm not going with you today," she said, straightening her cap unnecessarily.

"Aren't you coming to church?" Avan asked, surprise whirling in his golden eyes.

"Not today," Sebeth said, in the way she had learned of closing off discussion.

Avan closed his mouth. She had always gone to church with him before, ever since she had come to live with him. They had never talked about religion, but she had indicated amused approval of his choice of the parson famed for his short sermons. She tried not to look nervous. "See you later," she said, and left him gazing after her.

She knew he would not follow. She trusted Avan for that. They had kept to their understanding for a long time now. It was very cold outside. The snow was hard and slippery under her feet. She walked briskly towards the river, breathing shallowly, wishing she had not agreed to Blessed Calien's entreaties. His soul, she thought, his soul could be saved to go on to new life or it could perish utterly, and if she could do something to save it, however bad he had been in this life, however much penance he would bear in his new life, she should. He was dying. This would be his last chance.

Telstie House was on the riverfront, in the Southwest quarter. She was almost surprised that she remembered the way. She had avoided it for years, walking purposefully on other streets if her business had taken her in that direction. She had not been here since she was a maiden barely out of the care of a nanny. It looked a little smaller, a little shabbier, the snow on the lintels looked unfamiliar, she had never been here in winter. She almost walked on past. It was not too late. But Blessed Calien had done so much for her. She owed him this, as he had said. What was an hour or two to her? An attempt to save his soul? She did not forgive, but he was dying, and his soul, think of his soul. It would cost her nothing to try. For Calien's sake, then, not for her own or her father's, she asked admittance.

The servant was a stranger. "Your name?" he asked, politely enough, but coldly. "Eminent Telstie isn't well and the house is in uproar. I don't know if anyone can see you."

"Sebeth," she said. "Eminent Telstie sent word that he wanted to see me." She still did not know by what channels he had sent, that it had come to her by way of her priest.

The servant looked at her differently, as if assessing her. She couldn't tell if he recognized her name or was simply reacting to the lack of a title and family name. She was dressed like the respectable clerk she was. He couldn't tell anything from that. She saw his eyes linger on the marks on her wings where once she had been tightly bound. "Wait, I'll ask," he said, and left her alone above ground in the hallway while he hurried downwards. It was too late to flee, Sebeth told herself sternly. Much too late. She should never have let herself be persuaded to come. Why did she care if he was dying?

The servant came back. "Come this way," he said. As she followed him down, she thought for the first time that she might have to deal with her brothers and sisters and uncle and cousins and not only with the dying dragon she had come to see. If she had left it too late, if he was too bad to see her, she would leave immediately.

"Exalt Sebeth Telstie," the servant announced, the name strange and familiar at once. So he had known her. She swept in past him, as if she were indeed the Exalt she was by right of birth.

It was a sleeping cave, domed, plain stone. He was lying curled uncomfortably on his gold. His scales were beginning to fall already, he could not have much time left. His eyes were faded from the brilliant blue they had been, the blue hers still were. They met hers as she took a step inside. She stood completely still. "Sebeth, my daughter," he said, as the servant retreated.

"No," she said, all the anger she had been trying to fight down pushing its way to the surface. "You lost the right to call me that a long time ago. You have dragonets enough, remember?"

His eyes closed. She thought she would go. Then they opened again and met hers, whirling slowly in the pale blue depths. "I asked you to come so you could forgive me that," he said.

"Forgive you for abandoning me in the caves of kidnappers and rapists?" she asked. "How could anyone, how could any maiden brought up as I had been, ever forgive someone who owed them a father's care for that?"

"I did not mean to abandon you. I refused to pay the ransom because I believed I could rescue you. I thought I knew where they were holding you. I planned to follow them back and free you. But they had fooled me. When I reached the cave it was empty."

She weighed this, considering.

"Don't you believe me?" he asked.

"I don't know," she said, honestly. "It hurt me so much that you had said that, that you had left me there. It almost doesn't matter why."

"I tried to contact them again, but there was no way of finding them," he said. "I thought that you must be dead."

"Not dead," she said. "Death might have been preferable, but I have survived."

"I won't ask how you have lived," he said. "I can't bear to know. I see the marks on your wings, and I won't ask you how you come to be free now. You didn't come to me. I thought you might come to me, if you were alive and free."

"You had dragonets enough," Sebeth repeated, through tears that she had not known she was weeping.

"I thought you might come when your brother Ladon died," he said, ignoring that. Sebeth stared at a gold cup beneath her father's foot. She had seen that cup when she was a hatchling playing with her mother's gold. On the side turned down into the other gold now, she knew it was inscribed with an S, and her big brother Ladon, the oldest, the heir, the special one, who was August Ladon Telstie, when the rest of them were nothing but Exalts and Exalteds, had said it must be an S for Sebeth. It was the first letter she had read.

"I didn't know Ladon was dead," she said, as calmly as she might.

"On the border," her father said. "Ten years ago now. You are the only child I have left. I am dying, Sebeth."

Three brothers and two sisters, all dead, without her knowing? But why would she know? She had sought no knowledge of them, shunned it rather. "I didn't know," she repeated, feeling stupid.

"I was an arrogant fool not to ransom you," Eminent Telstie said. "But will you believe it was folly and not cruelty?"

"I wish I had known that all these years," she said. "Forgive me, Father, for believing that of you."

"I will forgive you if you will forgive me for failing to find you," he said. They were both weeping now.

Sebeth embraced her father and forgave him, and he forgave her, but even as she wept and asked forgiveness, somewhere inside her was a hard shell, and inside the shell was a self who was not sure if she believed the story her father told her. He had not sought for her until he was dying, after all, until all his other children were dead.

"Now I must call the attorney and draw up a will to make you my heir," her father said. "You must marry your cousin Alwad. He will take you, whatever disgrace you have been in, if he knows the title and the demesne goes with you."

"No," Sebeth said. She could remember Alwad as a mischievous hatchling. "I will not be married off like soiled goods. I have been in no disgrace, I have done nothing wrong. I fell into misfortune, and rescued myself. I have been working as a respectable clerk. I have a—" She hesitated, thinking how to describe Avan. "A partner. Not a husband, but more than a lover. He cares about me. I have honest work."

"You have done much, much better than I imagined. I see the marks of binding. Like the Honorable Lords of old, you have risen on your own wings. It makes me proud. Who is your partner? A dragon of Respectable rank you say? Gently born?"

"He is Avan Agornin, son of the Dignified Bon Agornin." Sebeth thought of the way she had come up from the depths, a finger-length at a time, from the servitude of a streetwalker to being Avan's clerk and partner.

Tears sprang to her father's eyes again at the name. "Bon Agornin was a friend of mine when I was a dragonet. I have scarcely seen him since he left my parents' demesne, but I wept when I heard that he had died recently. He was a good and worthy dragon, and like you, he rose by his own merit. You have said his son cares for you, do you care for him?"

It had begun as something for her advantage. She thought of Avan that morning, not asking her the questions that must have burned in his mouth. "I have come to care for him a great deal," she said, precisely, knowing it true only as she said it.

"And is he a strong dragon?"

"He is employed at the Planning Office," she said. "He is rising there. He is thirty feet long, but he will grow."

"Then if he will change his name to yours and become a Telstie, marry him and bring him the demesne as your dowry."

"Do you mean it? You hardly know either of us." Sebeth could hardly believe it. "And the scandal on the name . . ."

"There will be no scandal. You will be *Eminence Telstie*. That is enough to enable you to outstare anyone. There are few enough advantages to rank, but that is one."

"My cousins?"

"I will have my attorneys settle everything so there

can be no dispute. Avan Agornin. Dignified, you say?"

"Respectable," Sebeth corrected. "And if he will not marry me?"

"Then he's a fool," her father said. "If he will not, you should marry your cousin, or whoever you choose. But marry. You cannot hope to hold the demesne without. Telstie is too big to leave to a—" he hesitated. She was not maiden, wife, or widow, there were no words for what she was.

"I will find a husband if Avan will not agree," she said. Then she stopped, her mouth open, remembering as she agreed to her father's wishes what Calien had said about her father's soul being the most important thing. She hesitated. He had not known what her father would offer her. Safety, marriage, rank— dared she risk it now? It was not real enough to her to seem a risk. She swallowed. "Father, one more thing. I survived, I rose in the world as I could, with the help of the True Church. Will you see a priest to confess, Father? For me?"

"You were too young to know the True Church," Eminent Telstie said.

"Too young? How could I be too young? The priests were there in the streets where the most degraded work, teaching me their way. The parsons were not there, they were safe inside their churches, living on their dues, while the priests were helping us. I know what I learned, and I learned that confession and absolution free the soul, when all else is dross, and that

Camran was a Yarge who died to bring the word of the gods to dragons." Sebeth briefly felt like one of the great martyrs of old, like Sacred Gerin, who bore witness to the truth of religion despite the risk of losing all earthly things.

"You misunderstand me. I meant you were too young for me to teach you all of that before you were captured," Eminent Telstie said, dryly. "I have confessed to my own priest, and will confess again if I am given time. The True Church has been a long belief in our family, held very close, very secretly. Your priest might have known, but names of other believers are not spoken, not even whispered."

"It is not illegal, now," she said. "You could embrace it in public. For everyone to know that an Eminent Lord was a True Believer would be a great comfort."

"It is not illegal now because those of us who kept quietly to the true ways have worked to bring that situation about," he said. "Besides, legal or not, dare you flaunt it openly as a clerk?" His eyes seemed brighter. "You are my daughter and my true heir," he said. "If you wish to live openly in the True Faith, do so, but consult the priests first, they have counselled me to silence for many years. Now, tell them to call my attorney. And you should speak to your— partner. To Avan."

"I will," Sebeth said.

"But stay here," he said. "Don't go. I don't know how long I have. I will see the attorney, and the priest. But stay with me for this little time I have. My daughter.

A true Telstie, rising on your own merit and finding the Church on your own. You will grace the rank of Eminence."

She embraced him then, without hesitation. She still did not know whether or not he had betrayed her, but it no longer mattered. "I will stay with you until the end," she said.

58. A THIRD DINNER PARTY AND
A SEVENTH CONFESSION

After three days shut in her room, desperate for food and water, Haner would have admitted to anything and agreed to anything. Her vision was beginning to fade. She was no longer strong enough to shout. She had her gold, and it gave her comfort lying down on it or turning each piece in the dark. Berend died on this gold, and so will I, she thought, and Daverak killed both of us. She prayed, in her heart, for all the gods to help her. She thought of Londaver, and of Selendra. She prayed for Lamith's soul. She wondered if Daverak would let her out for the court case, or whether she would be dead by then. She had no way to tell how long it had been.

As Penn and Sher had been told that her illness was minor, they were surprised not to see her at dinner. "Her maid is looking after her in her room," Daverak said. To Penn's relief, Frelt was not present either. "He has gone to the evening service in the Cupola with Blessed Telstie," Daverak explained. He led them in at once to the dining room, where they were served with indifferently fresh swine.

"Will Haner be well enough to testify?" Sher asked, trying not to gag on the sweetish smell of meat that has been dead for days. Penn, beside him, was too nervous to either eat or speak.

"I'm sure she will," Daverak said. "I'm planning to talk to her later tonight about that."

"The court would accept a doctor's certificate," Sher said. He thought Daverak looked almost ill himself, full of nervous excitement.

"I haven't called a doctor," he said. "It isn't bad enough for that."

"To be ill for four days together isn't like Haner," Penn said, rousing himself. "I'll look in on her myself later."

"There's no need, you'll just disturb her," Daverak said.

"We'll see her tomorrow in any case," Sher said, deciding it was better not to annoy Daverak on this issue now. "We must speak to you about that."

"There's nothing to say." Daverak spread his claws. "I told you yesterday. Avan is attacking me, attacking my perfectly justified behavior. If he didn't think it justified, as you argued with me at the time, Penn, then he should have said then, or said something to me later."

"He seems to have managed to distress you considerably," Sher said, trying to sound sympathetic.

"He has destroyed all my peace, and probably

driven my wife to her death with worry," Daverak said. "Before all this started I was a calm and contented dragon, taking care of my demesne, enjoying Irieth in season, watching my family grow. Now I am a mass of nerves."

"Over such a little thing, really," Sher said, consolingly.

"It's not little," Daverak snapped, blood from the swine dripping down his jaws. "It questions my integrity. I will not have things like that said about me."

"Well, we don't condone saying them," Sher said. "We just want you to agree not to call Penn."

"But Penn's evidence is central," Daverak said, looking at Penn, who had not touched his meat. "Penn was at his father's deathbed. Penn can tell us what his father said then."

"If Penn does that, his career and prospects will be ruined and he will be disgraced," Sher said.

Daverak didn't seem to hear for a moment, there was silence and all three waited. "I'm sorry to hear it," Daverak said after a moment.

"You surely don't want your brother-in-law, the uncle of your dragonets, disgraced and thrown out of the Church?" Sher asked.

Penn cast his eyes down and ground his teeth audibly.

Daverak frowned. "But why would he be?"

"Because I heard my father's confession on his deathbed, and gave him absolution," Penn said, very quietly. "They will call me an Old Believer and cast me out."

"Do you have to tell them that?" Daverak asked.

Sher and Penn looked at each other, eyes wide. "I beg your pardon?" Sher asked.

"Why mention it? Why not just tell them that Avan is wrong, it wasn't what your father meant."

"I cannot lie, Daverak," Penn said. "Even if I could lie outright like that, I will be under oath. They will ask me exactly what my father said. It would be perjury."

"Nobody will know," Daverak said.

The piece of meat that had been in Sher's mouth fell to the ground.

"I think we will see Haner and then go," Penn said, in a very controlled voice.

"You cannot think it better to be disgraced than to lie," Daverak said, cajolingly.

"Any right-thinking dragon would," Sher said. "Now we will leave. But first, take us to Haner," Sher said.

"I can't," Daverak said, his eyes whirling uncomfortably.

"Why not?" Penn asked, frowning.

"You can't come here and insult me and then demand to do what you want in my establishment."

"I wish to see my sister, who is unwell," Penn said.

Sher pushed the dining room door open and caught hold of a passing servant, who trembled in his grasp. "Take me to Respected Haner Agornin," he demanded. The servant looked past him to Daverak, clearly terrified.

"No!" Daverak roared, flame shooting from his mouth.

The servant twisted free and fled down the corridor. Sher and Penn followed him, Daverak on their heels.

Haner's room, with the great pile of stones outside it, was easy to see.

"I can explain," Daverak said, sounding almost apologetic.

Sher looked down his snout at him. "I doubt it. You can, however, help in removing these stones."

It took some time to clear the way to the door. They did not speak as they worked. Sher wondered if Daverak was quite mad, and how long piling the stones must have taken. They were clearly the stones from a number of guest beds. He must have brought them out of spare sleeping caves and piled them here. He feared for how long ago it might have been. He needed Haner to approve of him, what would Selendra do if her sister had starved to death?

At length it was possible to open the door. Penn opened it and went in, calling Haner's name. Sher heard her croak an answer. Penn came out carrying a limp form, so pale a gold as to be almost green.

"Daverak—" he said angrily, breaking a long silence.

Sher interrupted him. "Daverak, I think you are a

disgrace to the order of the Illustrious." He strove to keep each word distinct and clear.

Daverak swung around to face him. "That is an insult," he observed, conversationally.

Sher almost laughed, though it was the correct response to his challenge. He had learned the code long ago, but never used it, never even thought of using it. "It would be an insult if you were a dragon," he said, his next line, if he did not want to back away. He had no intention of it. He would have fought at that moment, had it been possible.

"I will send a friend to you."

"You will find me in my House," Sher said.

Penn struggled forward with Haner. Her eyes were half closed. "We need to take her home right away," he said. His voice was choked with tears.

"She'll recover," Sher said, more confidently than he felt.

They left Daverak speechless.

59. THE SECOND HEARING

Avan was barely intimidated by the court this time. He was too worried that Sebeth had not come home all night. He wondered if he would ever see her again, if she had found some stronger protector, if she thought he would lose everything in this case. He had come to care for her more than he should, he knew, but he had not thought she would go off without a word like that and not return. He missed her.

He hoped she had not come to some misfortune on a solitary adventure, and knew he might never know if she had.

Hathor looked confident, his three wigs on the slab before him. "The jury are half on your side already," he assured Avan as he sat down. The jury, all seven of them, crouched on the steps below the judges' seats. They were all staring at Avan, or at Daverak, who was glowering at him from behind his three attorneys.

Behind them, around the walls, the witnesses stood. "Don't look 'round, but your sisters just came in," Hathor said, looking 'round. "One of them looks awfully pale."

"Which one?"

"How would I know? They're with a priest and a lord."

"The priest must be Penn, but I don't know who the lord is. Can I look?" Avan was worried.

"It doesn't make a good impression on the jury if you twist about. Don't worry, the lord's coming over to us."

Avan looked up to see a bronze dragon, sixty feet long. He recognized him, from Penn's wedding, and from the holidays he had taken at Agornin as a dragonet, just as he was introducing himself. "Good day. I am the Exalted Sher Benandi," he said, pleasantly. "I am betrothed to your sister Selendra."

"Nobody told me," Avan said. "Congratulations." The first thing he thought of, naturally, was Selendra's premature coloring at Agornin. Had everything gone smoothly? He could not possibly ask.

"Congratulations," Hathor put in. "But the judges will be coming out any moment, you should go back to the wall."

"It's quite recent," Sher said, gently ignoring this. "The thing is that yesterday I had reason to challenge Daverak's fitness to belong to the Illustrious Order. He's had time to send to me, but he hasn't seen fit to do so. I'll be making the demand, today, in court, that he fight me. I'd like to do that at a time that doesn't interfere too much with the prosecution of your case."

"You're planning to kill him?" Hathor asked. Avan could only gape.

"Oh yes," Sher said, casually.

"Will they say it's fair?" Hathor jerked a claw towards the steps for the judge and jury.

"Oh, I should think so. He's ten feet shorter than me, but he has fire and I don't. Undoubtedly they'll let us fight if we do it properly here. Judges are supposed to like to see blood spilled, after all. Now, I'd also like to have this case settled against Daverak."

"Wait until afterwards then," Hathor said. "We'll win. Look at the jury."

"No, I need to do it before he calls Blessed Agornin to give evidence," Sher said.

"Ah," Hathor said. "Wait until I've established what the will means and what a bully he is then."

"He has shut up Respected Haner Agornin and starved her in an attempt to bully her into complying with his wishes that she give false evidence," Sher said. At this point Avan just had to risk a rapid glance behind. Selendra looked beautiful, and wore jewels in her hat, but was a clear and shining gold. Gold? Still? How did Sher feel about that? Haner looked pale, as Hathor had said, but resolute.

"Ah. Can you prove it?" Hathor asked, not sounding in the least disconcerted by the alarming news.

"If you can call Daverak's servants, otherwise there is only my testimony, the maiden's, and her brother Penn's."

"The maiden's wouldn't be admissible, but with you and the parson I could prove it to the jury."

"Penn Agornin absolutely must not be put to the question at this trial," Sher said.

Hathor thought for a moment. Avan tried to speak, to ask why not, but Hathor held up a claw to stop him. "Shut her up how?" Hathor asked.

"In her sleeping cave, with stones before the door," Sher said.

The judges were coming. "Be ready to challenge when I get Daverak up and ask about that," Hathor whispered, then made a motion shooing Sher back to the wall.

Avan was bemused. He wondered if he had perhaps not woken up that morning after all, if it could be a dream. He had been looking forward to this case for so long, and now it felt as if it were getting away from him. And Sebeth, where was Sebeth?

Hathor stood to address the judges, pleadingwig on his head. "Honorables, this case concerns three young dragons who were cheated of their inheritance by the bullying of their more powerful brother-in-law. Dignified Bon Agornin left a will, which will be read to you, in which he states that he leaves all he dies possessed, all his wealth, equally between his three younger children; his two older children, being already established in the world by his aid, should take only a token. The eldest son, Blessed Penn Agornin, is a parson with a good living, and the eldest daughter, Illust' Berend Agornin, who was then living but who has since herself died, was married to the Illustrious Daverak. It was understood by myself, as Bon's attorney, and by all the members of his family, that the wealth he spoke of included his body. We are not all lords, Honorables, to eat those dragons of the demesne too weak to survive. But we are all free dragons who may all hope in the fullness of time to eat our parents and thus grow as dragons should grow. Avan, Selendra, and Haner Agornin, dragons of no more than Respectable rank, were robbed of this right, and their father's intention, by the bluster and bullying of one who is a lord, who should have been their protector, their brother-in-law, the Illustrious Daverak. I will show you, Honorables, how Daverak demanded more than the one bite that was his by right, and how he and his wife and dragonets, those who of all the family of Bon Agornin least needed dragonflesh, came to consume the larger share of his body. I will show you what was Bon Agornin's intention, I will show you how the Illustrious Daverak bullied his sisters-in-law, and I will show you how he attempted to threaten and bully his brother-in-law Avan, but how this bullying was unsuccessful."

Dignified Jamaney stood up to answer this for Daverak. "Honorables, Bon Agornin did indeed leave his gold as my colleague has described," he began. "The Illustrious Daverak has never disputed this. But gold is not dragonflesh, as we shall show. Avan Agornin has allowed greed to overcome prudence and demanded more than his share of his father's body. If things are as my colleague says," here he tipped his wig to Hathor, "then why are the two sisters' names not set down beside Avan's, why are they not feeling equally deprived? We see here a young dragon's naked greed. He never wanted this case to come to court, he hoped that the Illustrious Daverak, his brother-in-law, would settle with him by giving him some dragonflesh to satisfy his greed, would share with him the bounty of Daverak. Avan Agornin hoped thus to profit by his sister's good marriage. I will be presenting you with evidence of his character, Honorables. He is an adventurer. He is unmarried, but shared living quarters with his clerk, a dragon who he found in the streets, who is not even of Respectable rank, as if married to her. He works in the Planning Office, where he is regularly offered bribes. You will hear testimony from a colleague of his. You will hear testimony from his brother, Blessed Agornin, about exactly what Bon said on his deathbed and what he attended. You will hear the parson of Undertor, Blessed Frelt, speak further on Bon's intentions and what is usual in that area. You will see, Honorables, the way he has persecuted the Illustrious Daverak, even to destroying his health."

Jamaney sat down again, with a flourish of his wig. Avan craned his neck without turning and saw Kest among Daverak's witnesses. If he had known, he could have brought Liralen here to testify to his hard work and good character, but he had not known. Too late now.

The next part of the case went much as Avan and Hathor had planned. Hathor juggled his wigs admirably. Bon's will was read, worthy dragons, including Hathor himself, momentarily wigless, came forward to the center of the circle to testify as to what he meant by "all his wealth" and to the inclusion of his body. Daverak's attorneys challenged and queried everything. Then Hathor had Daverak's threatening letter to Avan read, despite many queries.

"May I ask your indulgence, Honorables?" Hathor asked, attorneywig on his head. "I had intended next to call Respected Haner and Respected Selendra Agornin, to testify to their father's intentions and to Illustrious Daverak's bullying. But it seems that

Daverak's bullying has made the Respected Haner possibly too ill to speak. She is here in court, but I am reluctant to call her in the circumstances. Instead I would like to call Daverak and reveal his character through his own mouth."

"Query!" called Mustan, Daverak's querier.

Daverak and Jamaney were conferring rapidly.

"I see no reason why he should not be called," the black-scaled judge said, wearily, looking over Avan's head, no doubt at Haner.

Daverak went out into the center of the circle. He looked uneasy. Hathor let him stand there a moment as he changed into his pleadingwig to question him.

"You are the Illustrious Daverak of Daverak?" Hathor asked.

"Yes," Daverak said.

"You were married to the Illust' Berend Agornin?"

"Yes." This came out somewhat impatiently.

"You have three dragonets?"

"No. Two. One died."

"I'm very sorry to hear it. I gather that your wife has also died, subsequent to the death of her father?"

"Yes."

"What a very unfortunate year you are having," Hathor said, sympathetically. One or two of the witnesses laughed. The judges frowned at them. "I can see no need to ask you about the deathbed of Bon Agornin. Nobody disputes the facts of what happened, merely the intentions behind them, is that correct?"

"Yes." Daverak looked sulky.

"After Bon's death, you took one of his daughters under your protection?"

"Yes."

Hathor waited until the court was sure that was all Daverak was going to say. "Haner Agornin?"

"Yes, Haner," Daverak snapped.

Daverak's querier shot to his feet. "Query!" he called. "What is the relevance of this line of questioning?"

Hathor whipped off his pleadingwig, kept it in his claw, put on his querywig, and looked at the judge. "I am trying to establish Daverak's bullying of his relations. I have read out his letter to Avan." Mustan could be seen to be shaking his head at this. "I wish to establish how he treated Haner and Selendra."

"It has nothing to do with the case," the bronze judge said.

"It has everything to do with why his sisters are not joining with Avan in this action, which my colleague tried to show in one interpretation and I wish to prove has another," Hathor replied.

"Very well," the judge said. "Continue. But be brief."

"Yes, Honorable." Hathor changed wigs again, quickly. "Illustrious Daverak, briefly, why is it that Haner Agornin is too unwell to give evidence today?"

"She is unwell," Daverak said. "Maidens become unwell from time to time."

"I put it to you that you shut her up in her sleeping cave and starved her?"

"Nonsense!" There was a murmur in the court. Avan could see dragons craning their necks to see Haner.

"I put it to you that you piled rocks before her door to prevent her from escaping?"

"She is unwell."

Mustan was again on his feet. "Query! Is there any evidence for this?"

Sher rose to his feet and came forward. "Honorables, may I speak?" he asked.

Daverak bared his teeth.

"Who are you?" the bronze judge asked.

"I am the Exalted Sher Benandi, and I am here because I am betrothed to the Respected Selendra Agornin."

"Selendra, not Haner?" the judge asked for clarification, looking at a paper before him.

"Selendra, Honorable. Selendra has been living with her brother the Blessed Agornin, in Benandi, where he is my parson."

"Very well, continue," the judge said.

"Last night I visited the Illustrious Daverak, in Daverak House. There I found Haner Agornin starved and imprisoned, exactly as the attorney has described."

"And did you do nothing about this?" the judge asked.

"I had Haner taken to Benandi House, where she

has been in my mother's care. I also challenged Daverak immediately, but he has sent no friend to me. I challenge him again, here, before you all."

Jamaney sat down and put his head on the ground. Daverak snarled.

"Daverak, you are a disgrace to the order of the Illustrious," Sher said. "This is the third time I have repeated it. Will you fight me or shall I add cowardice to the tally of your infamy?"

Daverak rushed forward, flame jetting from his mouth, knocking Hathor aside. Everyone was shouting. A maiden screamed. Avan ducked as Sher went over his head, bowling Daverak over in the center of the court.

Avan heard the black judge saying something about "Most irregular!" The guards came forward, but the rusty-bronze judge waved them away. Sher and Daverak were rolling on the floor of the court, claws scratching and tails flailing. Hathor ducked down behind the slab with Avan. "Not quite what I was expecting," he said. "They normally wait to be given permission."

Fights rarely last long, even fights to the death. It seemed endless, but it was less than five minutes before the whirling flaming clawing heap of dragon sorted itself out, with Daverak dead underneath and Sher, scorched and bleeding, standing triumphantly above. Selendra rushed forward at once to lick the victor's wounds. Before Avan's eyes as she pressed herself against Sher's side she blushed like a bride, from an even gold to a glorious and shining rose pink.

Hathor came to his feet, querywig firmly on his head, pleadingwig lost somewhere out on the floor amid the gore. "I believe we have heard enough of my case," he said.

"Honorable jury members?" the rusty-bronze judge asked.

"Avan," one of them said. "Avan," the others agreed. "We find for Avan Agornin."

Hathor grinned at Avan.

"Clear the court," the judge said, with perhaps more reason than on most such occasions when those words are spoken.

16
REWARDS AND WEDDINGS

60. THE NARRATOR IS FORCED TO CONFESS TO HAVING LOST COUNT OF BOTH PROPOSALS AND CONFESSIONS

When Avan got home, reeling, from the court, Sebeth was there, in the sleeping cave. She replied to his whistle as he went down. The relief was indescribable. He smiled, trying not to let her know how concerned he had been.

"Hello, Sebeth," he said, as casually as he could, throwing himself down on the rocks where they slept.

"How did it go?" she asked, smiling.

"Very well, but surprisingly." He gave her a brief account of the proceedings, speeding up as he noticed that she did not seem terribly interested. "Then once Daverak was dead and they'd decided in my favor, Sher said I could help myself. So Penn took the eyes and the jury took their share, and then Haner and I divided his body, right there in the court. Sher and Selendra just took token bites. It was as if we'd gone back and were doing it properly after all."

"So you feel vindicated?" Sebeth asked.

"It's very strange," he said. "In a way I don't at all, because we didn't go through with the case and have a proper jury verdict or anything like that. I never meant Daverak to die, though if I'd known how he'd been abusing Haner I would have wanted him to. She's going to live with Selendra and Sher now."

"I'm glad you had a sustaining feast," Sebeth said. "You're going to need it."

"Why?" Avan's eyes whirled in concern. "Do you need me to fight anyone?"

"I may," she said. "But first, listen, there's something I didn't tell you."

"Lots of things, but that's our agreement, you don't have to tell me anything you don't want to," Avan said, gently.

"I do now. You remember what I told you about my Eminent father?"

"How could anyone forget?" Avan shook his head. "It's one of the saddest stories I've ever heard."

"He's dead."

"We can't go and claim your share," Avan said, picturing huge Eminent brothers and cousins. "I know it's unfair, but it just won't be possible."

"Not that. Listen. I want to tell you something. I went to see him yesterday, that's where I was. And most of the other times when you didn't know where I was, I was in church."

"In church?" Avan blinked.

"Not your church." She twisted her fingers nervously. "In a church of the Old Believers. I'm an Old Believer, a True Believer."

Avan could think of absolutely nothing to say to

that. "I never quite believed about your other lovers," he said after a moment. "It didn't seem quite real."

"I haven't had any other lovers since I've been with you," she said. "But how do you feel about the Old Religion?"

"I don't know." He frowned. "My brother would turn blue, but he doesn't know about you anyway, not more than that you exist. I'm not a very religious dragon really, Sebeth. I suppose I ought to mind, but in fact it doesn't bother me much if that's what you want and it makes you happy. I've never tried to interfere in your life, you know that."

"I know." She looked uncharacteristically hesitant. "The thing is, my father was a True Believer too."

"An Eminent True Believer?" Avan's eyes whirled.

"In secret. I'll keep it secret too, at least at first, and probably always, unless things change. Blessed Calien, that's my priest, says I should. But it's important that I bring up any dragonets in the True Church, so I had to ask how you felt."

"Dragonets?" As far as Avan knew, Sebeth was assiduous about avoiding all the foods that could bring her into readiness to produce a clutch. It couldn't be a mistake. "I wish I could marry you and have dragonets, but be sensible, we couldn't possibly afford it. Or has your father left you something?"

"My father, Eminent Telstie, has made me his heir," she said.

"His heir?" Avan couldn't believe it for a moment. "You'll be an Eminence, like Kest was calling you."

"Kest had no idea," she said, and laughed. "He had no idea how much it hurt, when it was almost true."

"That's amazing," Avan said, amazed.

"So," Sebeth said, and her voice held none of its usual teasing quality. "I'll be an Eminence, but I'll need a husband, and I was wondering . . . You'd have to change your name. I can find someone else if you don't want to. There's my awful cousin, or there would probably be lots of dragons willing."

Avan's jaw had dropped open. "I can't quite believe this is real," he said. "Oh well, if it's a dream it's a very good one. Sebeth, when you didn't come home I was thinking how much more I'd come to care for you than I ever intended. I was afraid I'd never see you again. I couldn't marry you when it would reduce our status to nothing, there would have been no point. I was thinking that maybe one day we could manage it, or maybe if your father had left you some gold I might be able to take Agornin back from Daverak's cousin Vrimid and take you there. I'm bigger than I was, and I'll have the reputation of winning this case, and I have friends in Irieth. But now you're offering me wealth and position beyond my wildest dreams, but it's you offering it to me, not me offering it to you. I've never taken care of you as a maiden should be taken care of, or a wife either, you've been my clerk, my lover, I don't know that I can accept a position at your hands like this, even when I care so much for you."

"Was that yes or no?" Sebeth asked, tensed as if to spring.

"I don't know," Avan said. "If I asked you to give up Telstie, to come to Agornin and marry me there?"

She hesitated. "I promised my father," she said. "I never wanted to be protected, not by you. We were partners, that's what I told my father. That's what I'd want now, not to be a wife like a thing, to be owned by you, I want to go on being your partner, to make my own decisions."

"It's almost as if I'd be your wife," Avan said, hesitant.

"Why not? Partnership. Two wives sounds as if it would work better than two husbands. Oh come on, Avan, don't you want to be Eminent Telstie and be rich and have fun?" She smiled at him, her eyes teasing again, and he reached out for her.

"Is that what you're offering?" he asked, and she bit his lip gently. "Then I accept," he said. "It's very strange, but I do accept, the beautiful maiden, half the country, the title—there is no higher title than Eminent anymore."

"What shall we do now?" Sebeth asked, looking up from inside his arms. "Traditionally, this is where I should blush, but I am pink already."

And there we will quietly draw a veil over Avan's next proposal.

61. THE SISTERS REMEMBER THEIR VOW

Exalt Benandi was silent when Selendra returned from the court clutched against Sher's side, pink. Her eyes whirled slowly, and she pressed her lips together. Sher was wounded in several places, but radiant.

Amer and Felin helped Haner to her room. "I want to speak to Selendra," Haner said. "I'm feeling much better than I thought I ever would again." There was certainly more liveliness in her coloring than there had been.

"That's the wonder of dragonflesh," Amer said, knowingly, who had never tasted a bite of it. She helped her mistress settle on the gold. "You'll mend. It's just as well, for I'd never have forgiven myself letting you go off there alone if he'd killed you."

"You couldn't have done anything," Haner said, tears welling in her eyes. "He ate Lamith because she tried to protect me. Just ate her. He'd have done the same with you, faster if anything, because you're older."

"He was a disgrace to his order," Felin put in.

"The position of servants is a disgrace to the order of dragons," Haner said, hotly.

"You should rest," Felin said, kindly.

"I can't rest until I've spoken to Selendra," Haner said.

Amer and Felin exchanged a glance, and Amer gave a tiny nod. "I'll fetch Selendra, and then you really should settle yourself. You've had enough excitement for one day," Felin said.

"You said something about the position of servants in a letter to 'Spec Sel," Amer said, speculatively.

"It's something I've been thinking about a lot. It isn't only Daverak, though it was Daverak's cruelty that made me see it. The whole thing is wrong. Binding wings is wrong."

"It was the Yarges who started binding wings," Amer said, turning her face away.

"And we should have stopped it when we got rid of them," Haner said, forcefully.

Selendra came in, pink. In truth, pink suited her far less well than her maidenly gold. No doubt in time she would change to a red against which her violet eyes would again seem striking. For the present, although it is necessary to describe all brides as beautiful, it is best to say that Sher certainly found her more beautiful than any sight he had ever beheld. She was so pink, and so conscious of her state of blush, that no further description of her is required.

"What is it?" she asked. "Are you all right?"

Haner looked at Amer. "I'll go if you don't want me," Amer said.

"It isn't that at all. You know all our secrets," Haner said, and managed to laugh. "We'll talk later."

"You're looking better," Selendra said, examining her sister anxiously.

"I'm feeling better," Haner said. "My felicitations, Selendra. I just wanted to ask, I suppose you've promised Sher the whole sixteen thousand crowns?"

"You can live with us, Haner, Sher says he'd be glad to have you," Selendra assured her sister.

Haner hesitated. "I'll be glad to live with you, only, we did say we'd not get betrothed without the other's approval, and that you didn't want to marry at all."

"You did," Amer said.

"I hadn't forgotten," Selendra agreed. "It was all part of my plan, when I thought I'd be gold forever. He'd asked me, and I loved him so much, and I didn't change. I thought I'd been unlucky with Amer's numbers. But look! I was wrong. I just turned pink in the court, so easily."

"Why did you betroth yourself to him if you thought you couldn't change?" Haner asked.

"Oh, it was to do with his mother," Selendra said. "I suppose she'll hate me forever now and glower at me every time we meet. But it's too late to change now, even if I could." A terrible thought struck her. "Haner—surely you approve Sher?"

"He seems a very fine dragon," Haner said. "I can see it's too late for you to change your mind now! I wouldn't want to make you think about it, and I'm sure I hope you'll be very happy." A tear rolled down her snout. "It's just that I have half engaged myself to marry Dignified Londaver. You remember? I told him sixteen thousand, but I expect you've promised it all to Sher? Anyway, I thought I'd see how things were with the dowry."

"If it's only the money that concerns you, I am rich now," Selendra said, remembering. "Wontas and Gerin and Sher and I found some treasure in the mountains. Sher insists that a quarter of that is mine outright. How much do you need to marry Londaver? I can dower you, what fun!"

Selendra laughed, and Haner wept a little, because it was such a surprise and because she had been expecting disappointment and had found something so much the opposite. "I will write to Londaver, now, immediately," she said.

"You should rest," Amer said.

"And the dragonets want to see you. The Daverak dragonets, that is. Well, Gerin and Wontas would like to see you as well, but the little Daveraks are frightened without you. Sher and I brought them here, but they don't really know us."

"Put them with our dragonets," Amer advised. "That'll do them more good than anything."

"I must see them and comfort them, even if only for a moment," Haner said, sitting up a little. "I do feel much better. I will see them, then they can play with your dragonets and I shall write to dear Londaver telling him to come to Irieth as fast as his wings will bring him."

62. EMINENT TELSTIE'S BALL

"I think it's complete nonsense and should be done away with," the Exalt said. "Is my emerald straight, Felin?"

They were waiting on the steps of Telstie House, in the Southwest quarter, to be received by the new Eminence and her betrothed, the presumed new Eminent.

"It's straight," Felin said, putting a hand to her own headgear. Wontas had insisted that she wear the golden circlet he had found in the cave, and she had found a milliner who could hastily make up a hat for it to fit onto, with black and white fleece and dark green ribbons. She had been afraid the Exalt would disapprove, until she saw the look in Penn's eyes when she put it on, and then she did not care any longer what the Exalt thought.

"When Sher became Exalted he just went to the Assembly the next time there was a session and took his father's place. I dare say a few dragons congratulated him, and we did have a little party, but there was none of this waiting."

"Eminents are different," Penn said, consolingly. "We will get inside soon. We're next."

"Nobody even knows who she is," the Exalt complained.

"She is the daughter of the late Eminent," Felin said. "What is a mystery is where she has been all this time."

"I don't expect we will ever know," Penn said. "It'll be a shock to Gelener's family."

"A terrible blow," the Exalt agreed.

"Is it true that Gelener is to marry Frelt?" Penn asked, unable to keep a slight distaste out of his voice.

"I believe so," the Exalt said. "I don't know what her parents can be thinking."

"Perhaps she loves him?" Felin suggested.

"That block of ice?" the Exalt snorted. "And speaking of ice, I am turning to ice myself. I wish they'd let us in. I am not accustomed to being kept standing about in the snow."

Sher and Selendra had gone ahead with Haner and Londaver, leaving Penn and Felin to escort the Exalt. They were presumably inside already, Felin thought, enviously. The delay was because each dragon, or pair of dragons, was being separately announced and introduced to the new Eminence.

Just then a team of drafters drew up at the bottom of the steps, a carriage behind them with a strange crest. A murmur ran through the waiting crowd of dragons, followed by an anxious whispering.

"A Yarge!"

"The Yarge ambassador, doubtless," Penn said. "I was saying, with Eminents and Eminences it is different. The Yarges believe that if we were ever to choose a new Majestic it would be from among the Eminents, and thus they meet each new Eminent to give their approval."

"Or otherwise?" Felin asked.

"I don't know that they have ever withheld approval. The whole thing is nonsense, as the Exalt said. For one thing, we'll never choose a new Majestic, the idea is preposterous after so long. For another, if we did, we wouldn't look exclusively among the Eminents, any gently born dragon would be eligible."

Felin looked curiously at the carriage, which was enclosed by wood. "Why do they care if we have a Majestic anyway?"

"Oh, they have Majestics of their own, in all of their little realms, and they think a country without a Majestic cannot make war on them."

"But there have been wars along the borders always. My father was killed in one," Felin protested.

Part of the wood of the carriage moved, and Felin realized it was a door. The Exalt shuddered so hard that Felin felt it and turned to her. "Can I help?"

"I've never liked them," the Exalt said, very quietly. "They killed the Exalted Marshal my husband. They are loathsome."

"The ambassador—" Penn began in a soothing tone when the door at the top of the steps opened.

"Next," the servant said.

"It's you, Exalt," Felin said.

"You go, I shall wait here for a moment. I feel a little faint."

Felin would have argued, but Penn took her arm and drew her forward. Felin gave their names to the servant. They were whirled into a glittering ballroom full of splendid dragons and announced: "Blessed

Penn Agornin and Blest Felin Agornin, of Benandi Parsonage."

"I feel a bit of a fraud keeping my parsonage when I should have lost it. I still don't know if I should have confessed everything anyway," Penn whispered.

"The gods have punished you enough, continuing to punish yourself for it is wrong," Felin replied, making it as strong as she could.

Then they stepped forward and bowed to the new Eminence, who bowed back neatly. She was pink and bridal, very beautiful, Felin thought, with a well-shaped tail. She wore a veil and a little coronet. The dragon at her side, the future Eminent Telstie, stepped forward and embraced Penn. "Avan!" Penn said in a strangled tone. The Eminence whooped with very uneminent laughter.

"We've already been through all this with Haner and Selendra," Avan said. "I did want to tell you, but Sebeth thought it would be more fun not to. Meet my betrothed wife, Sebeth, Eminence Telstie."

Outside, the Exalt had bowed her head a little, to avoid having to look at the Yarge ambassador. It was not just that they had killed her husband and that they were the ancestral enemy. It was some deeper loathing that moved in her, something beneath the skin, maybe some ancestral hatred of dragon for Yarge. She waited, breathing cold air and recovering herself. The shock was great when she looked up because some quality in the silence around her changed. She realized at once that the other dragons on the steps must have made way for him, for the Yarge was beside her before the door.

He was utterly abhorrent to her. He stood scarcely six feet high and had no length at all, barely a foot; he was essentially flat. He wore a decent fleece hat, as anyone might, and he had covered most of his body likewise with cloth and jewels. He had hands like a maiden, but his skin was soft and smooth, entirely without scales. He looked weak and unarmored and defenseless, yet beside him the strongest dragon was as weak as a maiden. At his side hung the tube of a gun, with the like of which his kind had once over-powered dragonkind.

He bowed, almost folding himself in half and the Exalt shuddered again.

"I am M'haarg, the Jh'oarg ambassador," he said, as he straightened.

The vile creature could hardly pronounce the name of his own species, the Exalt noted. "Exalt Zile Benan-di," she managed to gasp in response.

The door opened. "Next," the servant said, sounding bored.

"Shall we?" the Yarge asked. He waited for the Exalt to move. She had to move. She was almost paralyzed with disgust. She managed to take a step and then another. He stayed beside her. He gave both their names to the servant.

Inside there was a whirl of dragons everywhere. The Exalt looked about her desperately for relief, for rescue. She felt as if she were in a nightmare. She could not scream. Everyone was here, every lord of Illustrious rank or above in the whole of Tiamath had been invited, and many of them had come. They would all see if she were to disgrace herself. She walked on, beside the Yarge. They would all see this too, but they would know it was nothing she had wanted. She saw August Fidrak in the crowd. Where was Sher? Probably with that terrible maiden he had chosen to spite her. Where was Felin? Felin was her true daughter, she wished she could find a way to tell her so. Or Penn? Her parson would be the ideal dragon to rescue her. Merciful Jurale, was there no dragon to come to her aid?

Then someone was by her side in a swirl of pink, a pretty chain of jewels wound in ribbons on her head. Selendra. Of course. The last dragon she would have wanted. The Exalt looked at Selendra, and saw the maiden realize how frightened she was. Now she would leave her again, rejoicing in her triumph.

Selendra did consider it. She came up to see how the Exalt would react to discovering that another despised Agornin would be set above her in rank. She found the Yarge exotic and strange, nasty perhaps, but not incapacitatingly terrible. The shadows that had represented the Yarges in the play had been more frightening. Yet she saw by the whirling of the Exalt's eyes that she was far gone in terror, incapable of speech, almost incapable of movement, only a little way from collapse. There was no doubt that she would embarrass herself when they reached Sebeth.

Selendra had never before seen the Exalt shaken from her confident pedestal. She knew her mother-in-law was a selfish arrogant old dragon, with wrongheaded views of the way the world was. She knew they had been skirmishing, and that she could win a battle in their war if she left her alone and speechless. She did not like the Exalt, probably never would like her. Yet she could not see her toppled so utterly in what she most cared about. For Sher's sake, and for her own, and because she deserved the dignity of a dragon if nothing else, Selendra spoke gently to her and drew her a little aside.

The Yarge ambassador stopped. "Go on, please," Selendra said to him. "I need to speak to my mother-in-law for a moment."

"Of course," the Yarge said, in his strange accent, and went on. "Delighted to meet you both."

The Exalt looked into Selendra's violet eyes, expecting to see triumph and finding only concern. "You did not mind my saying mother-in-law when that will not be quite true until the wedding?" Selendra asked, then went on, not waiting for an answer, giving the Exalt time to compose herself. "I have been arranging about bridal lace. It's very expensive, because it takes so long to make, but we are buying so much between us, Haner and I, that they may give us a discount. Maybe I should see if I can persuade the Eminence Telstie to come in on that. Come and meet them now. Did you know that the new Eminent to be is my brother Avan?"

"What a lot of new relations you have brought to us, Selendra," the Exalt managed to say, taking a step towards the new Eminence Telstie. She put her hand on the younger dragon's arm for support. "I know we have had our differences, but you are to marry Sher and become the mother of my grandsons, and I'd like you to know that after all, I am very pleased about that."

It wasn't entirely true, and both dragons knew how and where it was not entirely true, but they nodded to each other. And there, as Sher came to join them, as Avan and Sebeth waited to be greeted, as Penn danced with Felin and Haner with Londaver, as the servants carried heavy trays of refreshments about the room, we shall leave them to take refuge in the comfort of gentle hypocrisy.

ABOUT THE AUTHOR

Jo WALTON won the Hugo and Nebula Awards in 2012 for *Among Others*. Before that, she won the John W. Campbell Award for Best New Writer. Her most recent novel is *Lent*.